T0129206

U. S. BORDER EAGLES

JOHNNY RENO

Order this book online at www.trafford.com
or email orders@trafford.com

Most Trafford titles are also available at major online book retailers.

Printed in the United States of America.

ISBN: 978-1-4669-6439-6 (sc)
ISBN: 978-1-4669-6441-9 (hc)
ISBN: 978-1-4669-6440-2 (e)

Library of Congress Control Number: 2012919447

Trafford rev. 10/24/2012

 www.trafford.com

North America & international
toll-free: 1 888 232 4444 (USA & Canada)
phone: 250 383 6864 ♦ fax: 812 355 4082

Contents

Preface

This book is dedicated to the men and the women of the former United States Customs Service. They were the unsung heroes whose job was to protect our country and who received very little recognition. The US Customs Service was born with the passage of the Tariff Act of 1789. Its mission was to collect and protect the revenue. The Customs Service's mission had grown over the last two hundred years. US Customs was enforcing over four hundred laws for over forty government agencies. It had the broadest of powers, more than any other federal agency. In March of 2003, customs, immigration, and agriculture services were combined under Homeland Security and are now known as Customs and Border Protection (CBP). The investigative parts of Customs and Immigration were combined into the office of Customs and Immigration Enforcement (ICE) of Homeland Security.

This book is meant to entertain the readers and provide them with an insight about the former US Customs special agents (criminal investigators) and the law enforcement job they were doing over the last fifty years. They played hard and worked even harder.

This book as well as the future ones will show the different types of investigative cases customs special agents found themselves involved in and the impact the investigations had on our country's economy and security.

The various investigative cases in this book are based on actual cases and events of John Rennish, custom special agent, badge number 0044.

Cases in other books will be based on cases worked by other agents of the US Customs Service as well as those of John Rennish.

Customs investigations involved narcotics, money laundering, export of munitions, technology and nuclear materials, fraud, organized crime, cargo thefts, child pornography, trafficking of women for prostitution, terrorism, and every other imaginable criminal act involved crossing the borders of the US.

You will also see some of the behind-the-scene supports that the agents received in performing their official duties. You will enjoy the suspense, the intrigue, and many humorous anecdotes. These interactions and actual case activity of special agents form the basis for these books.

This book was written to give you hours of enjoyable reading. This book is based on actual cases and events that took place in the 1960s through 1990s. The names and some of the actual facts were changed to protect the privacy of individuals, and very little fiction was added to make the reading enjoyable. It is left to the reader to determine where the facts leave off and the fiction begins, if any.

Author's Note

Prior to being employed by the US Customs Service, I knew nothing about customs. I, like many others, was under the impression that customs people looked in your bags when you entered the US, that their job was to search your bags of dirty clothing for anything illegal, and that this search took place only when you came back to the United States from a trip abroad. This is not so as you will find out as you read this book.

My first encounter with US Customs was when I was in the US Army, returning from Korea in 1960, aboard a US transport ship. I had spent eighteen months as one of the frozen chosen. The day before we arrived at the port of San Francisco, we were told that our duffel bags (everything we owned was in one duffel bag) would be dumped on the ship's deck and inspected by U S Customs officers. We were also told that we would be searched and our living quarters were to be searched while our duffels were being examined. I remember thinking how funny it was when the sergeant said "Your quarters!" Well, my quarters was a large room with five rows high of hammocks as far as you could see. There must have been at least three hundred of us in that one room.

I remember the duty officer assembling everyone from our assigned quarters on deck. The duty officer told us that if customs found anyone with contraband, they would lock up that individual. At the top of his voice, he bellowed, "Customs is looking for any dope, guns, and dirty pictures." He went on to say that if we had any of those things or anything that was not army issued, we would be in trouble. He went on to say that we should throw anything that was not army issued overboard prior to the customs search.

At age twenty with two years of intense discipline, you come away with the thinking that you must do everything the officer in charge tells you to do or you are in for trouble. Well, the next day, I stood on deck with everyone else. I dumped my duffel bag in front of me and stood there for twenty minutes. We were then told to put everything back. I remember thinking, *Boy, this customs guy must be superman. I did not even see him go by.* That was the first time I almost came in contact with a US Customs officer.

My next contact with US Customs came several months later. I was hired by the US Postal Service as a mail handler after leaving the army. I worked in Lower Manhattan from 8:00 p.m. to 4:00 a.m., unloading heavy mailbags. After a few months, I was transferred to the mail facility at JFK International Airport. My duties were to work with US Customs officers. I was to dump mailbags on conveyer belts so customs officers, who were opener verifiers, could examine the incoming mail and packages. What an eye opener that was!

The two customs officers, Al Denton and Myron Vogel, whom I worked with, convinced me to transfer to the US Customs Service. They told me about many of the things that customs officers did besides checking bags and mails.

The two customs men were able to spot contraband in the arriving mail. This intrigued me. They were proficient and very little got by them. They would grab packages and envelopes for examination. They would stamp the packages and then toss them into the various mail sacks across the room. They divided the incoming packages as free, under $250, and over $250. They could spot pornography, drugs, money, jewelry, food, etc.

I still remember what Myron had told me. He said, "Kid,"—that is what they called me—"customs is like a *giant eagle*. Examiners and inspectors are the *eagle's eyes*. The *large wings* represent the import specialist who goes through all the cargo and paperwork to insure that the revenue is protected. The customs lab is the *beak* that rips through the commodities to make sure they are what they are represented to be. The customs agents are the *sharp claws* that grab the bad guys and bring them to justice."

I immediately knew what I wanted to be. I wanted to be the claws of the eagle that caught the bad guys. I also understood that we were all part of the giant eagle and no part could function alone. Working together, the eagle would protect this country.

Chapter 1

In the Beginning

I will tell you about the interesting things that happened in my life as a customs family member. My career spanned almost thirty years from the early 1960s through 1990. I joined the customs family in 1962. I started at the very bottom. I was hired as a GS-2 clerk with the expectation of rising through the ranks to become a customs agent. I took the customs agents examination three times and received scores of over 80 percent each time. What was holding me back was the lack of a college degree, no job openings, and a government freeze on hiring. I scraped together every last cent I had and enrolled at John J. College of Criminal Justice part time. I worked all day and went to school three nights a week. After one year, I was promoted to GS-4 time and leave clerk.

There were seven of us, wanted to be agents, hired as clerks to participate in a pilot program to become customs port investigator (CPI), a journeyman position to a customs agent. Dominick Ronzio and Dick Castalano worked with the agents on the third floor. Tony Bochi worked with the searchers. Mike Wallace worked in the uniformed captain's office. I worked on the first floor administrative office because I was the last hired. The two other clerks hired were Dudley Washington and Victor Bantson, who also worked in the administrative office. They took off more than they worked. They would not go the extra yard on their time to show they had an interest in getting the agents job.

The pilot training program involved various aspects of the job. One was going out with the searchers and searching ships. I remember the first time I went out with the searchers. Bill Bartski, the captain of the searchers, was a very tall Polish man with viselike grips. He stood six foot three inches and weighed 200 lbs. He was in his fifties with a full head of black hair. He would come into the office at 6:00 a.m. to assign ships to the various searching squads. He would drink a half a fifth of Johnnie Walker Red Scotch while assigning the various ship. At eight o'clock, he would take out a squad of searchers to search a ship of his choice. All the sergeants carried a leather bag (flute bag) to carry their paperwork. Captain Bartski was no exception, except he carried a bottle of Johnnie Walker Red to the ships to be searched.

At 8:00 a.m., I got into the van with a squad of searchers and the captain. Once on the ship, Captain Bartski told me to accompany him to the ship's captain's office. He told me, "Kid, I think you are an agent sent here to catch me drinking."

I told him I wasn't and that I was only a clerk looking to get an agents job. We sat down in the captain's office. The ship's captain took out three eight-ounce water glasses. Bill opened his flute bag and took out his Johnnie Walker Red and poured three water glasses full of scotch.

Bill said, "If you are not an agent, drink up." You did not have to tell me twice. I picked up the glass.

We all said, "Na zdrowie (here is to your health)," and took a big swig. When I stopped coughing and wiped the tears from my eyes, Bill was still laughing.

"I guess you are OK, kid. Drink up." I put the glass to my lips and made believe I took another swig. Bill then said, "OK, kid, go see the sergeant. I left the office and found the sergeant, Ken McGee. He assigned me to another searcher, Ace Scales, for training."

There was nothing scarier than going down a ladder in a cofferdam to search for hidden contraband. It was dark, and you had to use your flashlight to look around. You would feel good when you would find something. I have found drugs, a lot of liquor, and pornography. The most sickening thing I ever found was a decomposing stole-away body. The regular searchers liked to have fun with us newbies. They would send us into the rope lockers. You would have to crawl in some very tight spaces. Crawling around and seeing two or four eyes looking back at you is very unnerving. You back out as fast as you can. Rats like to hide in the rope lockers, and they are as big as cats. If the rats feel trapped, they will attack you. There were some good things that made the ship searching worth it. When you search the big cruise ships, you would eat like a king.

Going out on patrol with the uniformed officers and stopping and searching the longshoreman was another aspect of the training. I felt out of place when I first had to search a group of longshoremen. We pulled up to the pier in a marked car, and Sergeant Fox said, "Go stop that group of longshoremen. Tell them you are customs and ask them to face the wall and then search them." I jumped out of the car and told the longshoreman to get up against the wall. I searched them. I really felt stupid and out of place. I was a twenty-year-old skinny kid with no uniform or authority to stop and search them. They were four big, stocky men who looked like anyone of them could pick me up and break me in two. I was scared, and they could tell. I guess they saw the marked car and the sergeant standing behind me and figured it was easier to just comply.

Working with the plainclothesmen and searching passengers and crew from the cruise ships was an experience. While working the cruise ship, I made my first plainclothes' seizure. The teams of plainclothesmen were working the passengers getting off the ship at Pier 92, North River. I noticed crew members coming out of the pier with their one tax-free bottle of spirits. I went into the diner across from the pier. I had a cup of coffee. I looked out of the window and was watching a post office truck and crew members going to the back of the truck. The crew member knocked on the back door of the truck. The door opened, and the crew member gave the bottle to a man in the truck who in turn gave him money. This went on for about an hour. My training partner came looking for me and wanted to know what I was doing. I told him about the truck. Then the truck started up. We ran out, and I banged on the back of the truck several times, and then the back door went up. I had my badge and gun in hand. I said, "US Customs. Put your hands up. You are under arrest." The two postal employees in the back of the truck were shocked and complied. They tried to talk their way out of the trouble they were in. I wrote a summons for thirty bottles of spirits each. I seized the post office truck and arrested the postal employees for smuggling. I drove the truck and spirits back to headquarters.

This caused a big to do between the captains and the agents about seizing a post office truck. The outcome was the two post office employees were suspended and paid a fine for the sixty bottles of spirits, and the post office truck was returned. I also learned to fingerprint and photograph prisoners whom the agents arrested. I participated in crime scene photography. I took pictures with a speed graphic camera, the one that you slide in a photographic plate in the back of the camera. It had a flash attached to the camera, and you had to put in a bulb before you could take the picture. You also had to set the aperture opening and speed. I got real good with the camera. I took several pictures of big seizures. Judge Richard Scoval of the US Customs Court liked the pictures so much that he had made enlargements of some and had them hung in the customs courthouse. I took the seized items including high-value jewelry to the appraising officer's office and then back to the seizure room. I also took narcotics to the customs laboratory for testing. All this on-the-job-training paid off. The five of us eventually became customs port investigators in September of 1964 and then special agents in April of 1970.

I still remember the cast of characters I worked with when I started with customs. There was Ward Rementing, an eighty-year-old passive, white-hair gentleman, who headed the uniformed enforcement patrol division. He retired a couple of months after I was hired. Captain Jim Marris (Jingles) took over for Ward Remington. He was called Jingles because he shuffled a hand full of quarters in his hands. You could always hear him coming. He was the only African-American officer in the New York customs. After six months, he retired, and Customs Agent Bobby Dee Corenzo took over the enforcement division. Then there were two captains in plainclothes who sat in the office I worked in. Willy Dunbar from Connecticut worked for the uniformed division. To this day, I do not know what his job was. He sat at his desk and walked around with papers and left by three o'clock each day. Then there was my nemesis, Captain Peter Furatolla. He worked with Captain Bill Bartski of the searchers. He picked ships to be searched and assisted with logging in only seizures of pornography. He hated Jingles with a passion. He would always make disparaging remarks behind Captain Marris's back. Captain Furatolla was sneaky, and he almost got me fired, but that is another funny story. Then there was the phantom, Captain Joe (Red) Aldridge of the plainclothes division. He smoked a pipe. You knew he was there or had been there by the distinct aroma that filled the air. Then there were the captains in the captain's office next door. They supervised the uniformed patrol officers during the various shifts. The most memorable was Joe Tombetta. He was a tall, thin, gray-hair gentleman. He was soft spoken and almost never had a harsh word for anyone. I only heard him vent his displeasure once, and that was about Captain Furatolla. No one liked that two-faced snake.

There were many people and things that made an impression on me before I became a customs special agent. There were the twins, Jimmy Duncan and Angelo Capone. They were customs patrol officers (CPO). They were both in their late fifties. Jimmy was about 150 lbs, and Angelo was at least 300 to 350 lbs. They always worked together on the eight-to-four shift. They did all the running around to pick up and deliver things to the customs house in Lower Manhattan. They also took seized items to the import specialist for appraisal. I always remember going out to their patrol car to move it so I could get one of the searchers vehicles out of the bay in the building. Lo and behold, I grabbed the driver-side door handle and yanked it open. The whole door came off in my hand. It was not attached. It shocked the hell out of me. At first, I thought it was something that I had done. After a closer look, I was sure that Angelo had it removed so he could get in and out of the car. The next shock was when I looked inside the car. The car's front bench seat was gone. Oh, there were seats of a sort. Well, one sport seat was resting on the floor. It was a black sport car seat on the floor. Next to the seat was a wooden milk crate that Jimmy sat on. The car springs on the driver side must have been broken because the car sloped on the driver side. I kid you not!

Danny Keaton was the mechanic that kept the customs cars and vans running. He did not have a problem with it, and neither did I.

The most devastating thing that happened to me was on the day that the US commissioner of customs came to our office. I was asked to work in the captain's office to help demonstrate, to the commissioner, the latest in technology to track the patrol cars and uniformed officers assigned to the various piers. We had installed this latest technology several days ago. The US commissioner of customs was coming to see this latest marvel. The captain told me to assist him by illustrating, as he explained the workings of the new technology to the commissioner. On the wall was a ten-foot by ten-foot tin map with all the piers in Brooklyn, the East and North Rivers of Manhattan, the Staten Island piers, and the New Jersey piers. Each pier had a small light bulb that could be put on or off from a small console. If there was a ship at the pier, we would put the light on for that pier. If we had men stationed at the pier, we would put a magnetic man at that pier. We would use a long stick with a little hand to move the pieces around. The stick looked like a very long back scratcher. We had little magnetic cars also, which we moved every time a patrol car called in. In July of 1964, this was the latest in technology.

The US commissioner of customs was in a bad mood that morning. He really did not like the New York regional commissioner of customs, Barry Friman. They had been in a heated discussion, disagreeing with the way the region was being run. When they came down for the presentation, my presents in the captain's office set the commissioner off. *What was I doing in this office?* The commissioner said, "A patrol officer should be doing this, not a clerk."

The regional commissioner of New York tried to explain that I was part of the on-the-job training program for customs investigators. The commissioner was pissed off. He blared out, "There seems to be two customs services, New York and the rest of the country." He wanted my name which the regional commissioner gave him. With his face no more than a foot away from mine, he then, in a raised voice, told me that as long as he was commissioner, I would not get hired. He told the regional commissioner to fire me. *Man, was I all shook up?* The assistant regional commissioner, Jack Mendoza, grabbed me and pulled me out of the office and told me to go home for the day.

He told me, "The commissioner had an argument with Barry before he came down to see the new enforcement board. This is his way to get even with Barry. The commissioner will be going back to Washington tomorrow."

Two months later, in September of 1964, the US commissioner of customs went to Paris for a four-day conference, and the New York regional commissioner went to Washington to be the acting commissioner for the week. Upon his return the following week, the five clerks who passed the treasury enforcement agent test were called to the regional commissioner's office. Regional Commissioner Barry Friman, Assistant Regional Commissioner Jack Mendoza, and several customs agents were in the conference room. He then gave us some papers and shook my hand and said, "You guys are the kind of people we want in the customs family. As the acting commissioner, I signed all your schedule C appointment. You are all now customs port investigator (CPI). Congratulations!" The five of us were now CPIs. We were then given a badge, a gun, and US customs credentials, authorizing us to enforce the US customs laws.

Bad things happen, and they will pass. You have to roll with the punches. Take life as it comes. Like Captain Jim Marris (Jingles) said, "Just play the cards you are dealt." Things really did finally work out for us. After that, when things happened to me, I did not get upset. Like the time I was driving Sergeant Joe Fisizo, in uniform, on the midnight-to-eight shift. Joe was an old-timer. It was a stormy night. About 2:00 a.m., after we called in our location to HQ, the sergeant said, "Kid, back the car up over there." He pointed to the spot where he wanted me to park. Like a good rookie, I did. The car had a long trunk. I backed up until the back wheels hit the pier stop. The rear of the car hung over the edge of the pier. We settled in for a good snooze. There was a passenger ship tied up at the pier in back of us. The wind really began to kick up. It shook the car continually.

Close to 4:00 a.m., we were abruptly awoken. The car was tossed up in the air and came down about five feet from where we were originally parked. The only major damage was the car's trunk. It was split down the middle, and the roof was dented in the middle. What happened was the ship's mooring rope had loosened and the hull of the ship partially left the water, lunging forward, and came down on the extended trunk of our car, propelling the car up, causing the ship's bow to crease the roof of our car, throwing us some five feet forward on the pier. The sergeant said from the back seat of the car, "Are you OK, kid?"

I said, "I think so." The sergeant had been thrown from the front seat to the back seat. The steering wheel held me in place. We got out of the car and quickly assessed the damage. We jumped back into the car. Both of us were drenched from the lashing rain. All the sergeant could say was "Shit, let's go to HQ and fill out the paperwork."

We drove back to HQ silently and slowly because part of the trunk of the car was scraping on the street as we drove. Captain Joe Tombetta was on the desk. We walked in to the office, and to his surprise, Joe said, "What are you guys doing here? You are supposed to be on patrol."

Within a blink of an eye and with a straight face, Sergeant Fisizo said, "We were on patrol when we got hit by the *Q E II*. It smashed the back of our car." The captain's mouth fell open as he began to speak the seriousness, the hilarious situation set in all at once.

The captain said, "How the fuck did you (then the laughable set in) get hit by a fucking ship while on patrol? I have to hear this. How did you guys get hit by the ship?"

The way the sergeant told it, with a straight face was, "You see, Cap., we were following this suspicious car. The car was driving with its lights off. We watched the car checking out the pier. The car stopped in front of the pier. We backed up to observe what was going on. The back of our car was hanging over the edge of the piers. When all of a sudden, this ship jumped out of the water and came down on the trunk, tossing our car in the air. The car roof hit the bow as it came down, and that is how the ship hit us. We were not at fault, Cap. The ship hit us." The captain could not help laughing.

"Are you guys okay?"

Just shaken up a little, I said. The sergeant filled out the accident reports, and that was the last we heard about the accident.

Speaking of accidents, how do you tell your boss that you were hit by a 747 airplane? You don't! I was new at the airport. It was a rainy night. The boss Eddy Mac was working overtime. He called me over and said that a flight arrived at the British terminal. He wanted me to check out the flight. Ed said, "Take Ralph Cippi with you. That no-good Guinea needs to be taught a lesson." Ralph was on Eddy's shit list. Ralph was in plainclothes the week before, and he did something to piss off Eddy. So he found himself in uniform. Ralph was ready to go home. He had changed out of his uniform. Eddy told him he could not go home. He was ordered back into uniform to drive me and work the British flight. So Ralph got back in uniform and got the keys to the car. We went out the ships office to the tarmac where the car was parked. It was dark, drizzling, and foggy. The visibility was about ten feet, if that. The car really needed new windshield wipers. A 747 had been pushed away from the gate and was beginning to taxi from the tarmac to the taxiway. Well, somehow we wound up on the taxiway, turning onto the tarmac as the 747 was leaving the tarmac for the taxiway. Well, Ralph turned in time and missed the plane, but the wing's engine came down on the roof of our car, denting the roof. It really dented the middle of the roof of the car. We had to slouch a little to drive the car. The 747 never stopped. It taxied to the runway and took off.

Ralph was all shook up. He said he would never get out of uniform now. I told Cippi not to worry that we were not going to tell Eddy what had happened. If we had told Eddy Mac what had happened, I know what he would have said. "That stupid Guinea hit the plane on purpose to get even with me for making him work overtime in uniform. I'll put him on the midnight shift with a short swing. I'll fix his Guinea ass and make him pay to fix the car."

When I got to the British terminal, I called Freddy Neilson, the sergeant on duty, and explained to him what happened. He told me that Mac had gone home and that I should park the car in back of the IAB. Freddy met us at the ships office and looked at the damage and said that it was no so bad. It looked like someone had jumped on the roof of the car. He then said, "Don't tell anyone about it. I want to see Mac's face when he sees it." The next morning, Eddy Mac looked out of his office window, and when he saw the car, he blew his top.

He reminded me of Jackie Gleason getting mad at Ed Norton. He turned to Sergeant Neilson and said, "Those fucking baggage handlers must have jumped on the roof of our car." He then ordered the sergeant to take a couple of men and search the baggage handlers and find out who jumped on the roof of the car. We questioned the baggage handlers and never found out who jumped on the roof of the car.

Chapter 2

Prelude to Becoming a Special Agent

G rowing up as a kid in the 1940s and 1950s and with the advent of TV, I had aspired to be a cowboy like Hopalong Cassidy, Tom Mix, Roy Rogers, and Gene Autry. As a five-year-old, I remember getting a cowboy hat, a shirt, and two cap guns with holsters. The caps came in roles and were loaded with the gun. When you squeezed the trigger, the hammer hit the cap and exploded with a loud noise. Well, on September 21, 1969, I found myself thrust into my dreams of the old west. I was a CPI at JFK airport at that time. There were rumors that President Nixon was going to increase the number of federal agents in the government. On Tuesday, September 16, at 2:30 p.m., Eddy Mac, captain of the uniform and plainclothes division at JFK Airport, called a special meeting. We knew something was up, *but what?* Eddy Mac stated, "President Nixon has directed the commissioner of customs to send all available law enforcement to the southern border. This will be known as operation intercept. Any customs enforcement officer (CEO) or customs port investigator (CPI) who does not go will find themselves in uniform and never advance to a higher grade. If you CPIs want to be agents, this is your chance. The sergeant has your assignments. Plan to be there for at least one month. The SACs offices along the border have your flights and arrival times."

I, along with John Grillo, had to report to the special agent in charge (SAC) office in El Paso, Texas. We were to leave on Friday morning on September 19. Ten other CPIs and CEOs from JFK got their assignments to the various other border cities. My brother agreed to take care of my house and bills while I was gone. John Grillo kissed his wife and three kids good-bye and met me at JFK airport on Friday morning.

We arrived in El Paso an hour early and were met by an agent from the SAC office. He said that we were early and the two agents from Chicago were going to be late. He dropped us off at the SAC office. In the parking lot was the infamous motorcycle of the SAC Art Shelter. It was a big Harley-Davidson bike. We had heard many stories about the SAC. So John and I went inside the office. We told the secretary that we were here to report to Art for operation intercept. The secretary said, "Art will be with you in a minute." Just then the SAC came out of the office with a drink in his hand, and he was laughing real hard.

The secretary called out, "Art, the two agents are here for operation intercept." Being an hour early, the secretary and Art thought we were from Chicago.

He said, still laughing, "We were just talking about screwing the two CPIs from JFK. John Grillo and John Reno. We will be sending them to the boon docks in New Mexico. You two agents will stay here at El Paso." Two Agents emerged from Jack's office, laughing, and abruptly became silent. The agents were John Trent and Bob Towers.

Art asked, "What are your names?"

I said, "Our names are screwed. I'm Reno, and this is Grillo!"

"Oh *shit*! You guys can stay here, and we will send the other two to New Mexico."

I said, "No, it's all right. John and I want to see the country. We have never been in New Mexico."

Art said, "OK. Agent Merrill Thomas will get you guys set. Cindy, tell Merrill the guys going to New Mexico are here." Art disappeared in his office with Trent and Towers and closed the door behind them, as Merrill entered the area.

Merrill said, "Come with me." We followed him to his office. Merrill was a fraud agent. He worked on the office's fraud cases and left the surveillance and drug cases to the younger agents. Merrill was due to retire at the end of the year. Merrill filled us in on what we were going to be doing. Merrill told us there were two ports of entry we would have to cover. One was Columbus and the other was Antelope Wells. Inspector Ed Brul would be going to Antelope Wells with one of us, and Merrill would be going to Deming with the other. Merrill said we could switch every two weeks. There was a customs building at the Antelope Wells crossing. The Mexican customs official had a trailer on the other side of the border. At Deming, we would have to rent a room in the motel.

Grillo said that he would go to Antelope Wells first. Merrill told him that Ed would be coming to the office in a little while and then we would leave for New Mexico. Merrill looked at us and said, "Have you guys got any long-sleeve shirts? Do you have hats?"

I looked at John, and we said, "No."

"First thing we have to do is get you guys dressed. Let's go." We followed Merrill out to his car and got in, and Merrill drove us to a clothing store. He told us that we had to wear a brim hat and long-sleeve shirts with denim jeans and boots.

"Why boots?" we asked?

Merrill, in his slow drawl, said, "Rattlesnakes." He helped us pick out shirts, boots, and hats. He said, "Do you have your guns?" We replied yes and showed him our guns within the pants holsters. Merrill shook his head, laughed, and said in a low voice, "No no no no." He then proceeded to pick out holsters for us that tied down to our legs. I felt strange, looking at myself in a mirror.

Merrill said, "Put your badge on." We pined our badges on our shirts and strapped our guns on. We were cowboys. My dream had just come true. I looked like a cowboy *but was this the old west?* The next day, when we got to New Mexico, it was like going through a time portal back to the 1800s.

We then headed back to the office. Ed Brul was waiting for us. Merrill told Ed to go with John Grillo to Antelope Wells and that we would be there on Saturday for lunch. Merrill gave John a set of keys to a G-car, and John got his suitcase and bags of clothing and put them in the car. Ed said, "I'm taking my pickup. I have all my cooking gear in the truck."

I asked Merrill why he was taking cooking gear.

Merrill said, "Ed makes the best pinto beans in all of Texas." Then Ed and John took off. I put my suitcase and bags of new clothes in Merrill's car. In the trunk were a rifle and shotgun and boxes of ammo. On the back seat was a large cooler. It was filled with beer and ice. As Merrill put it, "An agent never goes anywhere without his beer."

I drove to Deming, New Mexico. It was a little over hundred miles and took six bottles of beer to get there. We got a cheap motel room for the month. I felt strange wearing my gun exposed and dressed, well, like everyone else. They all wore jeans and western shirts and hats. After putting our gear away, we went to a local diner. We sat at the counter and had a steak dinners. It was about nine o'clock when we got back to our motel room. Merrill took out a bottle of bourbon and put it on his night stand next to our portable radio in its charger.

He said, "You will be on duty every other night. We will take turns. Tonight, you're on duty, and I will drink." He explained that if we got a call from the state police informing us that they made an arrest and the subject had drugs, we would go to their location and pick up the prisoners and we would then go to lodge the prisoners in the Hidalgo County Jail, Lordsburg. I said okay. I then went to sleep.

The next morning, about 7:00 a.m., Merrill was up and shaking me. "Time to get up and get started." I got up, showered, and got dressed. We stopped at the dinner and got breakfast. I looked around, and everyone was still in western wear. We picked up two cases of beer, some steaks, potatoes, and some vegetables. We then drove to Hachita, about sixty miles from Deming. I did not know what to expect when Merrill said we would stop off at Hachita for gas. We went straight west on USA 10. Nothing but desert on both sides of the road. The road seemed to go straight to a pinpoint. It was a boring drive. We turned left on State Highway 146. We arrived at a rundown gas station with one pump. It was outside a bar with a house attached alongside. I looked around, and there were three other houses, one with a general store. This was Hachita; population, if I had to guess, would be about twelve. The town, from what I could see, looked rundown and empty.

A weathered old man hobbled out of the bar after our car crossed over a hose that rang a bell in the bar. Merrill said, "Fill her up and check the oil." The man began to fill the car with gas. We went into the bar. I looked around and could not believe my eyes. There were four old-timers sitting at the bar. They turned and looked at us as we walked in. When you entered the bar, you could see a long wooden bar that was falling apart. The brass foot rail was not attached to the bar on one end. It was resting on the floor. That end of the bar was lower than the rest of the bar. The floor must have dropped from the weight of the bar. There were four brass spittoons on the floor next to the foot rail. The wooden floor was rickety and unlevelled. The wooden planks squeaked when you walked on them. There were three round wooden tables with four chairs around each. The lighting was nonexistent except a kerosene lamp over the bar. The large windows in the front and sides of the building provided just enough light.

Merrill ordered two glasses of beer. The bartender drew two glasses of beer from the bar tap. The beer was cold. I looked down on the long bar. It must have been twenty feet long. Imbedded in the bar were silver and gold dollars. The whole bar surface was covered with coins. Merrill paid cash for the beers and charged the gas on the government's credit card. We drank up and got back into the car.

About ten minutes outside of Hachita, Merrill pulled over to the side of the road. Merrill said, "What do you see out there?"

I looked and said, "Cactus and desert."

Merrill said, "Look at the little puff of sand."

I looked hard and said, "It's a roadrunner." It was my first real roadrunner. It looked like the bird in the cartoon. It was quick. Then Merrill got out of the car, and I also got out. Merrill opened the trunk and then looked out into the desert.

He said, "Look out there." He took binoculars from the trunk and gave them to me. I looked where Merrill said to look. There was Wile E. Coyote. He looked like a large dog. He was gray; his tail was down. His head was looking at us, and his body was going in a different direction. It seemed as if he was using the cactus as cover. He zigzagged his way away from us. Merrill said, "Those critters are very smart and hard to get." By the time Merrill got the rifle out of the case, the Coyote was gone. Not in a million years did think that I would ever see the cartoon characters Wile E, Coyote and Road Runner come to life in their natural surroundings.

We got back into the car and drove another forty miles on State Highway 81 to Antelope Wells. We pulled up at Antelope Wells in the early afternoon. There was a small two-room building with a wood porch and the sign on top that read US Customs Antelope Wells. John and Ed were outside with the Mexican customs officer, Miguel Dispotta. Separating the two countries was a waist-high, striped yellow pole going across the road, separating Mexico and the U S. Three small Mexican children were running around between the Mexican's trailer and the US Customs house. Carlotta, Miguel Dispotta's wife, came to meet us with a very large basket. Ed said, "The beans are ready. Let's fiesta."

Ed had an outside barbeque pit with wood burning. The grill was hot. We took out the food we brought, and Ed and Carlotta began cooking. We opened the cooler and had cold beer until the food was ready. Carlotta had brought a lot of different kinds of Mexican food, and I enjoyed the new type of food. We had a real good time that afternoon. It was the first time I ever had pinto beans. It was real good. Miguel played the guitar, and we all sang as the children danced. Miguel told us that maybe once a week, there was a truck that would come across the border. He also told us that some of the men from the Bar W Ranch would come by when they were rounding up their steers or checking their fences along the border. We were also told about the $25 bounty the ranchers put on each coyote.

Operation intercept was to start on Sunday at 2:00 p.m. We were to search everything coming across the border. Ed and John were told that if they found any drugs, they should call us on the radio or landline. Merrill and I headed back to Deming and arrived about 11:00 p.m. We turned in for a good night sleep. Sunday morning around 10:00 a.m., we woke up, showered, shaved, and left for the dinner. We had breakfast and headed for the Columbus port of entry. We arrived about noon time at Puerto Palomas crossing. That is when I was convinced that I was living in the old west. There were about fifteen houses, a general store, a gas station, and the US Customs station. The customs house was a one-level wood building with two rooms and a rest room. In front of the building was a long hitching post for tying up your horses while you conducted your customs business. There were two customs inspectors stationed there. We were there to lend any assistance to the inspectors and take any prisoners found with drugs.

I was sitting on the hitching post with Merrill when the Luna County deputy sheriff pulled up at the customs house. Now I knew that I was in a dream world, stepping out of the car was this thirty-year-old man who was about five foot nine inches tall and about 175 lbs. He was clean-shaven and had a square jaw. His side burns were long and black. His face looked leathery. He wore a black Stetson hat with a thin Indian bead band, a long-sleeve black western shirt with white pearl snaps. Pinned on his chest was a large silver star with the words DEPUTY SHERIFF. He had a broad chest and narrow waist. He wore black pants and black boots and had two black holsters with pearl handle guns tied down to his legs. His clothing was not disrupted from the car ride. He looked sharp and well dressed. It was Black Bart or Hopalong Cassidy. The icing on the cake was a man getting out the passenger side of the deputy's car. The man was bigger than the deputy sheriff. He wore a tan Stetson hat, a plaid shirt with an open collar, brown pants, and a tan gun belt with one gun. He was five foot seven inches tall and weighed about 190 lbs. His shirt was bunched up, and his belly hung low over the gun belt. Pinned to his chest was a badge, DEPUTY US MARSHAL. His face was full, and he was jovial. When he spoke, I almost fainted. He talked with a raspy voice, reminding me of Andy Devine who played Jingles in the adventures of Wild Bill Hickok and later on the kid's show "Andy's Gang." It was nostalgia time.

The deputy sheriff owned the gas station, so he gave Merrill the keys to the gas pump and told us to leave the credit card slip in the register whenever we filled up our car. The port of entry was opened every day from 8:00 a.m. to 5:00 p.m. The people who lived in the area would go across the border to shop and eat in Las Palomas. They would return before the port closed. The inspectors searched every car that came across. They knew most people by name and explained what was going on. Almost all those crossing the border were in agreement and cooperated. The inspectors had to search every car as the agents looked on and waited for a seizure to be made.

That Sunday, the first day of operation intercept, we made our first arrest. Ten minutes after operation intercept started, everyone across the border knew that every vehicle crossing the border was being stopped and searched for drugs. About four in the afternoon, a Ford Thunderbird Convertible with New York plates pulled up for examination. The driver was asked to exit his vehicle, which he did. The inspector began his meticulous search. Between the coil springs of the front seat was several plastic bags of refined marijuana. The total weight was six pounds. The inspector seized the drugs and seized the car. I arrested the man who turned out to be a New York City lawyer. I handcuffed him, and Merrill and I took him to Hidalgo County Jail in Lordsburg for processing and arraignment. What an exciting first day!

The next day when we arrived at the port of Columbus, Black Bart, and Jingles were there. We had a great laugh about the dumb New York lawyer. They told us that at night, they would wait at known crossing sites for the illegal aliens to cross the border. When they caught a carload of aliens, they would turn them over to immigration and would receive a bounty of $25. They asked us to come with them at night. Well, several times that we went with them, we caught several illegal aliens. Black Bart and Jingles would get the bounty. Jingles knew the dirt roads in the area. It was dangerous to drive at night. Some of the roads had deep ravines. You would be driving along, and then half of the road would disappear.

When we would hear low-flying aircraft at night, we would try to locate where the drug drop site would be. Most of the time you could not find the drop site. You would have to go back in the day light to locate the drop site by following the tire tracks and foot signs. Once you found a possible site, you would plan where you could ambush the smugglers after they got the drugs. This was more interesting than sitting at the port of entry waiting for the inspector to make a seizure. On Thursday afternoon, Merrill and I accompanied Jingles to a suspected drop site. We found tire tracks leading to a clearing with a lot of foot traffic. We also found bits of marijuana. They could not clean up the site in the dark. Based on Jingles's knowledge of the area and tire tracks, we located an intercept ambush point.

The following Tuesday, we heard the low-flying aircraft flying without lights. We proceeded to the intercept point. We notified our customs air command located at the Deming airport. We then set up in the predesignated spots. About an hour later, a pickup truck with his lights off came down the dirt road. We pulled in front of the oncoming truck. Our headlights were blinding the oncoming truck's driver. I blocked the road in front of the driver. The driver had no choice but to stop or go off the steep side of the road. Black Bart and Jingles pulled in back of the truck. Merrill bellowed over the loudspeaker, "Customs police! Stop your vehicle. You are surrounded. Put your hands out the window and do not move." One of the Mexicans riding on the back of the truck tried to run. Black Bart was quicker than he was. He pounced on him and had him handcuffed in no time at all. Merrill jumped out with shotgun in hand. Jingles got out with his shotgun in hand. I had my revolver in hand. We approached the pickup truck and removed three men from the cab and one from the bed of the truck. Black Bart brought back the one who tried to escape. There were ten bales of marijuana in the truck. We handcuffed the prisoners. We put our cooler in the trunk and three prisoners in the back seat of our car. Jingles placed the two handcuffed men in the back seat of the deputy sheriff's car. Back at the office, we separated the ringleader from the loading crew. We interrogated the prisoners. While we were busy, the customs air command at an air base in Deming sent up two planes. They intercepted the small aircraft and forced it to land at the Deming airport where the airplane was seized. The pilot and one crew member were arrested. We turned over the prisoners, truck, and marijuana to an investigative team at the Deming airport.

On the lighter side, the first Thursday, September 25, Merrill and I were sitting on the hitching post. Merrill was whittling a piece of wood. We were watching the inspectors search the few cars that were coming back across the border. The inspectors knew everyone coming across the border. They apologized to people in each car for the inconvenience for the operation intercept searches. The people all said they heard of operation intercept and understood that he had to do his job.

This big Cadillac pulled up, and the inspector approached the car and explained to the driver about operation intercept and asked her and her passengers to exit the vehicle. The passengers all exited the vehicle without any fuss. The driver, however, began to berate the inspector. The passengers were mortified at the behavior of the driver who appeared to have had one drink too many. She asked the inspector if he thought she was a smuggler. He said, "No, mam, just doing my job."

He asked if she had anything to declare that she acquired in Mexico. She said, "No, we went shopping and did not buy anything. We went to the beauty parlor, had lunch, and returned." She then began. "If you think that I bought something, why don't you look in the hubcaps? Maybe I put marijuana in there."

"Yes, mam." And he now pulled off each hubcap and then replaced them.

She then said, "Maybe I hid the drugs under the hood." He then opened the hood of the car and began to look. She then said, "Why don't you look in the air breather?" He then removed the breather and looked inside and then replaced it. "Maybe the drugs are in the trunk." She was laughing at his expense. He opened the trunk and looked in. Merrill had walked around to the back of the car when the inspector opened the trunk. Just empty plastic bags with car polish and rags. Merrill took a closer look at the bags before closing the trunk. The inspector took the declarations to the office, and Merrill returned to his perch.

The inspector came out of the office and asked the women to get back in their car. Before the driver could get back in the car, Merrill was up and off the hitching post. He put his hand on the car door, preventing the woman from getting in on the drive side. The other women looked in amazement. I was now off the hitching post, and the inspector and I walked to the front of the car and observed Merrill in action.

Merrill then said in a loud Texas drawl, "Mam, I am a US Customs special agent. Have you declared everything to the inspector that you got in Mexico?" She became petrified looking at Merrill. He was six feet tall, big, and loud. He had a gun on his hip and a gold badge on his chest.

She began to stutter, "Err, um, yes." I could not believe what happened next. Merrill reached down, grabbing the woman's hair and pulling it off her head. It was a wig. The woman hair was a mess under the wig. She screamed, grabbing her head.

Merrill said, "Just as I thought. You had purchased this wig in Mexico. I'm seizing this wig." The woman began to cry and scream at Merrill, telling him that her husband was a very important person in Deming and that he would have him fired. She jumped into her car and sped off. Merrill said, "Let her go. We got all the information we need on her declaration. Her husband will come here to pay the fine. We will settle this with a fine of two times the domestic value of the wig."

What the Inspector and I did not know at the time was Merrill looked in the plastic bag that said "Ortiz Wig Company." He had removed a receipt with today's date and cost of the wig. He had the bag and the receipt. The inspector thanked Merrill. He said she always gave him a hard time when she came back from Mexico. She thought she could get away with anything because her husband was some political big shot. He also said, "I know that her husband will be coming down here within an hour."

Merrill said, "Don't worry about a thing. I'll handle it." Merrill proceeded with the paperwork for the seizure.

Forty-five minutes later, the Cadillac pulled up at the customs house. A thin man about five foot eight, in a business suit and cowboy hat exited the car. He entered the office. In a loud, angry voice, he said. "I'm looking for the customs agent who took the wig off my wife's head."

Merrill stood up and said in a slow Texas drawl, "I'm Merrill Thomas, US Customs special agent. I seized the smuggled wig." Hearing the word *smuggled* calmed the man down immediately. Being involved with the law, he realized the severity of the charge.

The man said in a much calmer voice, "Can you tell me what happened?" You could tell the man was agitated by the tone of his voice. Merrill told the man about his wife's behavior and obnoxious attitude and the ridiculing of the inspector who was just doing his job. He also told the man and showed him the bag and the receipt for the wig that was in evidence.

The man stood up and raised his bowed head. In a stern voice, he said, "What are the damages?"

Merrill said "$328."

The man took out his checkbook and asked if he could pay by check, and Merrill said, "Yes, sir."

The man then extended his hand and said, "It is about time someone put her in her place. She thinks that because I'm in politics, she could get away with anything. My wife needed to be put in her place and suffer the consequences of her actions. I guarantee that she will never act like that again. I only regret that I was not there to see it happen."

Merrill said, "I can tell you she was humiliated in front of her friends when the wig was removed from her head. Her friends gasped at what was happening." The man laughed. They then shook hands. He asked Merrill which inspector was mistreated so he could apologize to him personally for his wife. Merrill pointed out the inspector. The man went up to the inspector and apologized and told the inspector that if his wife ever acted like that again, he was to call him. He insured the inspector that he would never have a problem with his wife again.

Two city boys John and I were having a great time in New Mexico. On Tuesday morning, John Grillo was searching an old two-ton truck with wooden boards for sides. It was loaded with elephant grass used to feed cattle. A *Cessna* swooped down low over the truck. The airplane had the customs insignia. Ed and the driver were checking the paperwork while John was on top of the elephant grass, looking around and waving to the aircraft. The airplane circled, and the passenger in the plane got on the customs radio. He asked John what he had in the truck that he was searching. John said, "I am looking through a truck loaded with grass." The aircraft flew off. An hour later, the commissioner went on national television, announcing that we just seized two tons of marijuana crossing the border at Antelope Wells. Well, you can imagine all the red faces when they found out that the truck only had elephant grass. The pilot confirmed that Grillo said he was searching a truck of grass but thought he meant marijuana.

On Saturday, Merrill and I went looking at maze farms. Merrill had seen several advertised in the newspaper. Merrill was getting ready to retire. He wanted to buy a farm or two to raise maize and collect subsidies when he did not grow anything. He really knew the country. He was familiar with the areas in New Mexico that we were in and had decided that this was the area he wanted to retire in. After looking at several farms, we headed to a forest. I could not believe there was a forest in the middle of the desert. Well, Merrill took out the shotgun, and we traipsed through the woods and came upon an old wooden shack that was once a two-room house. We attempted to go inside, but the wood was rotted and too dangerous to enter. Merrill found signs of wild pigs. Merrill said, "These pigs are dangerous. They have razor-sharp teeth and will cut through the leather boots." We heard a lot of noises but did not see anything. We started back to the car when out of the brush came this large pig. I thought it was a small bear. Merrill was quick and fired off the shotgun. At Merrill's feet was a large pig with not much of a head. My heart was racing. Merrill whipped out a large knife from the sheaf on his belt and gutted the pig in no time at all. We each took a hind leg and dragged the pig to our car. There was an old tarp in the trunk, and we put the pig on the tarp in the trunk. We washed the blood from our hands with beer. We then drove back to the motel, and the next morning, we headed to Antelope Wells. Merrill called Ed and told him that he was bringing a wild pig to roast. When we arrived, the fire was going.

John had made friends with several of the cowboys from the Bar W Ranch. They brought John a horse to ride. John went out with them to ride the border fences. We were really living our dream. Three of the cow hands showed up that morning to play cards with John and Ed. Well, we all had a good time with the pig and beer and a nice card game. Everyone loved Ed's pinto beans. He cooked the beans for two days. Ed said his secret was the three different cheeses and the Mexican peppers.

On Wednesday, I got a frantic call from Inspector Ed Brul. John was checking under the hood of an old truck coming across the border. John reached across the radiator when the top blew off, scaling John's arm. John was in pain, and the emergency kit did not have anything for burns. I told Ed to take him to the closest hospital. That was in Lordsburg. I told Ed to give John a bottle of whiskey and drive him to the hospital. Ed put John in the car with a bottle of whiskey and sped off to Lordsburg. Three hours later, Ed called and said they were on their way back. John had second-degree burns but will be alright in a couple of weeks. The doctor gave John some strong pills to take for the pain.

Ed and John returned back to the border. The return was not without incident. When they returned, I got a call from Ed. They had a car accident. They both were okay. Ed was driving John back when Ed hit a steer that was in the road. The front end of the car was smashed in. They were still able to drive the car. About halfway from Hachita to the port of entry, the road was like a small roller coaster. The road went up and down. You could not see anything on the road until you got to the top of the small hills. As Ed explained it, the steer was near the top of the hill on their downward side of the road. Coming over the hill, there was not enough time to stop. They hit the steer square in the rump, sending the steer down the hill on his belly, all four feet apart. The road was wet with urine where they hit the steer. The steer got up and wandered aimlessly across the road back into the desert. The front end of the car was pushed in, and the radiator was leaking.

The next day, we had the car towed back to Deming and had it repaired. It cost over $1,400. Then Merrill got a call from the deputy sheriff, investigating a complaint about one of the Bar W Ranch steers being hit by a car and dying. Merrill told the deputy that it was our car that hit the steer and to have the ranch send us the bill. He then told me to write up a report on the incident and make the recommendation to pay the Bar W Ranch bill as attached. Well, that was what I did.

On one of my trips to Antelope Wells, I tried to shoot a coyote. Before I could get the rifle out of the trunk, the coyote was long gone. But I did manage to get a rattlesnake. I was driving down the road when I saw this snake across the road. I ran it over. I then backed up over it and then ran it over again. I got out of the car to see the snake. It was huge and bunched up into a coil. It was gray and had black diamonds on its back. I took my Beretta, 25 cal. automatic out of my pocket. I fired five shots, which just bounced off the snake's skin. That was useless. I took my Smith & Wesson 357 Magnum and took aim. As the snake came out of the center of the coil, I fired. I knew that I had shot off his head. I advanced toward the snake. Out of the moving, coiled-up snake, a head very much attached to the body lunged out toward me. I felt myself running backward. Good thing, I had run the snake over with the car a couple of times. He could not lunge that far. My heart was pounding very fast. *What did I get into?* I raised my gun again. The snake was again in a coil. This time, I was close enough to see his head coming out of the center of the coil. The snake was getting ready for another strike. I took careful aim, and this time, I fired, and the snake's head flew off. It was still squirming around and would for the rest of the day. I picked up the headless and tailless snake and put it in a paper bag I had in the trunk and continued on to Antelope Wells.

When I got to Antelope Wells, with the help of Ed, I skinned the snake and tacked down the skin to dry. It was about five feet long. We cut up the snake and cooked it up. It did taste like an old chicken. The next day, I made hat bands from the skin. There was enough snake skin to make one hat band for Ed, John, and me.

It was not always fun and games. I remember the incident that scared me to death. Working out of Deming, New Mexico, was a new experience for me. The border crossing at Columbus, New Mexico, was opened from 9:00 a.m. to 5:00 p.m. every day. Most night, after the border crossing closed, we would hang around with the deputy sheriff and deputy marshal and pursue the undocumented that crossed the border illegally. Some nights, we would just drive back to Deming. When we arrived back at Deming, we would eat dinner or, depending the time, hang out at the local bar. When we got back to our motel room, I would put the portable radio in the charger and hit the hay.

On this one occasion, after getting back from the bar, Merrill had a few too many bourbons to drink. But it was his night to drink and my night to be sober in case we got a call from the state police. When we got back to our room, it was about ten o'clock. I helped Merrill into the motel room, where he just fell into his bed. He just lay down and went to sleep. I did not mind it at all. I did not drink. I would nurse an Amaretto and 7-up as long as possible, and then I would drink 7-up the rest of the night. So, by eleven o'clock, Merrill had been asleep for about an hour, when the phone rang. It was the state police. They had a man with 3 lbs. of marijuana at the state checkpoint on Highway 10. It would take us about forty-five minutes to reach the checkpoint. Merrill was sprawled out on his bed. He was snoring something terrible. I shook him several times, and he kept saying to me, half asleep, "Go away. Let me alone."

I said, "Merrill, we have to go. The state police called. We have a prisoner to pick up." I helped Merrill out of bed and out the door and into the front seat of the car. I buckled him in his seat. Merrill was out like a light.

I headed for Highway 10. I opened up the windows and put the radio on. It had taken me about fifteen minutes to get Merrill into the car and ready for the ride. It was about 11:30 p.m. when we started out. I was going down Highway 10. The stars were out, and the moon was full. It was a beautiful night, and it was cold. When I look down Highway 10, the ground was flat, and the road came to a point in front of me. The center line of the two-lane highway got narrower and narrower until it was just a dot in front of me. I was driving a vehicle that had a special high-speed police pursuit engine. The car also had four new high-speed pursuit tires. I had opened up the window to get some air into the car to keep me awake. My foot was heavy on the accelerator. I looked down at the speedometer, and the needle had passed the 120-mile-an-hour mark. I was making good time. The high-speed pursuit engine really made this car move.

About ten minutes into the drive, the fresh air began to revive Merrill. He was not fully awake now. He began to groan and moan. I told him that we were responding to a state police call. Merrill said, "Okay, wake me up when we get there." He closed his eyes for about twenty seconds when there was a loud explosion. I froze my hands, holding the steering wheel as stiffly as humanly possible. My body became ridged as I stiffened up. Instinctively, my foot came off the gas pedal. Merrill's head popped up at the loud sound, his eyes were now wide open. There was a look of horror on the sun-beaten leather skin of his face. He reached straight out with both hands and grabbed the padded dashboard in order to brace himself for a car wreck. We had a blow out! My eyes glanced in the rearview mirror, and all I could see was flames from the back of the car. I was terrified, and Merrill was petrified.

My foot had instinctively came off the accelerator, and the car began to slow down. When the car reached thirty miles an hour, I applied the brakes gently by pumping them. I kept tapping the brake with my food. The jolting tossed Merrill back in his seat. When I looked at Merrill, I could not help breaking out in laughter. Merrill in his raspy voice said, "What the fuck are you laughing at? We almost got killed."

I said, "Look at your hands, and what you have done to your car." Merrill looked down, and he had a large chunk of the padded dashboard in each hand. Well, we had to wait about a half hour before the wheel cooled off. The tire was gone; the rim had no rims left. I took my flashlight and looked behind the car, and I could see two groves cut in the cement highway going back a long way. We were lucky to be alive. We finally got the driver's side rear wheel off and put on the spare. I then traveled at a speed of thirty to forty miles an hour. We took our time and finally got to the checkpoint. Merrill was completely sober when we reached the checkpoint. I was still a little shaken up. We took the prisoner from the state police and traveled to Lordsburg and lodged the prisoner at the Hidalgo County Jail in Lordsburg. We then headed back to our motel and arrived at about 4:30 a.m. We plopped down into our beds and slept till about 10:00 a.m.

With this Texas experience, I was ready to be promoted to customs agent. I was riding high. Several months after operation intercept, in April of 1970, I was sent on another assignment. This time, I was sent to Puerto Rico for a narcotics assessment. That is when I was promoted from a GS-9 customs port investigator to GS-11 customs agent. Two CPOs, five customs agents, and I went to San Juan Puerto Rico to conduct a narcotics assessment. The leader of the group was Irving Watermen; he was a GS-12 customs agent. Two agents were GS-7, and two were GS-9 customs agents. The grades are important to understand what happened the fourth day.

The first day, we arrived and went to the International Airport and observed the inspection operation for about an hour and then returned to the hotel to get settled in. The second and third days, we were to continue observing the inspection operation and the CPO enforcement interface with arriving passengers. After we finished on the third day, Irving delegated the scheduling of the work assignment to Rick Sanchez, a GS-9 customs agent. Rick was lazy, obnoxious, and a spiteful person. He thought he was better than anyone else. Rick would change his ethnicity whenever it would benefit him. One time he was Puerto Rican, the next time, he was African-American, and the next he would be Arabic.

Rick made up a schedule for the CPOs and CPIs from New York and those assigned in Puerto Rico. The way Rick had made the schedule, all the CPOs and CPIs would do all the work and one agent would oversee those working and the rest could go sightseeing or sit on the beach. Word got out about his proposed schedule. The morning of the fourth day, all CPOs, CPIs, and agents met at the CPO office at the airport. Before the meeting started, Irving had given me a letter from the regional commissioner's office, which contained news about my promotion. Five days earlier, I had been promoted to GS-11 customs agent.

Rick began briefing everyone at the meeting about their work assignments. The CPOs from Puerto Rick were all pissed off and let it be known at the meeting that the scheduling was unfair. They began to yell and boo and hiss at Rick. Of course, I also made my feelings known about the unfair schedule. I told Rick, "Rick, this schedule is unfair to the CPOs."

Rick's answer to me was, "I am a grade 9 customs agent, and you, Reno, are only a CPI. You do what I tell you!"

That is when I said, "No, not so, I received a letter from the New York regional commissioner, informing me that five days ago, I was promoted to GS-11 customs agent. Therefore, I am your boss. You and all agents will be in the schedule which I will revise." Everyone cheered, and Rick left the room while he was hissed and booed at. The next day, Rick did not show his face; Irving Watermen sent Rick home.

Our observation of inspectors over the three-day period revealed business as usual. A flight would arrive, and the passengers would take their bags to the inspection tables. The inspectors would shake hands with the passengers and hug them. The passengers would give the inspectors packages, and the inspector would sign off on the declaration, and the passenger would leave. I asked the CPO stationed in Puerto Rico what that was about. He said, "Oh, that was the inspector's cousin." It seemed that everyone was related, and very few people got examined. That fourth day, after an inspector released the passenger, we stopped and searched the passenger and reexamined their bags. We would make seizures of all undeclared merchandise and then seize the gifts the inspectors received from their relatives. CPOs were instructed to select passengers after the inspector finished the examination, and if the inspector accepted things from a passenger, he would be fired. Three inspectors were fired; eight inspectors retired rather than face prosecution as a result of our assessment. We cleaned house.

I was working with CPO Carlos Hermanas, observing arriving passengers. Carlos was eager to learn how to select passengers. A flight had arrived from Santa Domingo. We observed the passengers getting their bags. I told Carlos to observe four young adults. They were in their early twenties. Two guys and two girls. I asked Carlos what looked suspicious to him. Carlos was hyper and very excited. He kept saying "I don't know."

"What do you see?" I asked him if he ever made a seizure on a passenger.

He said, "No, the inspectors would not let us stop anyone to search."

I asked Carlos again, "Which of the four would you take in?" He walked around and looked and looked but could not choose.

I said, "Carlos, do you think that it is strange that one of the kids was carrying a boom box?"

He said, "No."

I said, "Look at him. He keeps looking at the various inspection tables. He looks like he is shopping for an inspector who is not going to do much looking." I told Carlos to keep observing the actions of the guy with the boom box. After the inspector completed the customs examination, they were leaving. I told Carlos, "Let's stop them." We did. We identified ourselves as customs officers and showed them our badges and identification and asked them to accompany us to a search room.

The kid with the boom box seemed to be the leader of the group. It turned out he was the son of a famous home builder from New York. The three other kids were his friends. He had paid for their vacation trips so he would not be alone. I told Carlos to take him and his bags into the room to be searched. Carlos put his three bags and boom box on the cart and rolled it into the search room. The kid started to get into Carlos's face, telling that he was a son of so-and-so and that he should not be subjected to this humility. We shut the door. I told Carlos to ask him the customs questions. Carlos proceeded, "Do you have anything in your bags or on your person that you failed to declare to the inspector?" No was the response. Carlos began to go through the three suitcases. I lifted up the kid's boom box. It felt kind of heavy. I put it down. All the time I was looking at the kid's eyes. I could see he was nervous and began to sweat. The kid kept telling Carlos that his father was going to hear about that and he would have his job. I kept my eyes on the kid's eyes. Carlos finished the first bag with no results. The kid took the finished bag and placed it on the floor near the door. When Carlos finished the second bag, the kid took it and the boom box and put them near the door. Carlos finished the third bag and found nothing.

The kid said, "You see, I told you I had nothing."

I asked Carlos if he had searched the kid. Carlos said, "No." Carlos then proceeded to check every pocket and then felt up and down his legs and around his body.

"Nothing," Carlos said.

I said, "Carlos, you never checked the boom box." Carlos turned on the switch, and the radio began to play.

He said, "Nothing here."

I told Carlos, "Keep checking the boom box. Did you remove the batteries?"

Carlos began to remove the batteries. "There is tape in here," Carlos exclaimed.

"Remove the tape, Carlos," I said. Carlos fumbled with the tape and removed it, and lo and behold, there were plastic bags of a hard brown substance. It was hashish.

Carlos was so happy with his first narcotic seizure that he took the boom box and ran out of the room, shouting, "I made a seizure of hash." I told the kid it was Carlos's first narcotic seizure. The kid knew he met his match and broke down, crying like a baby. He kept saying that his father was going to kill him.

Carlos came back into the room, and I said, "Carlos, what did you forget?" He looked at me with a blank look. I said, "Arrest him and read him his rights." Carlos took out his handcuffs and placed them on the kid's wrists and told the kid he was under arrest. He then read him his rights from a small card. We reexamined the other three kids' bags and came up with a hash pipe in the one girl's bag. Well, we took the prisoner to the local lockup. He was arraigned and made bail of $5,000. The kid had to call his father for help. Daddy to the rescue. He contacted an attorney in Puerto Rico who represented his kid at the arraignment.

It was his first offence, so he eventually received a five-year suspended sentence and a $5,000 fine, which Daddy paid.

Chapter 3

March 31, 1975,
Jamaica, New York

Being a US Customs special agent was a rewarding job. You got to see the end results of your labor after the long hours and hard work. Those results were usually in the form of arresting people involved in drug smuggling, money laundering, cargo theft, export of munitions, import fraud, or inflicting heavy monetary penalties on companies and individuals, who knowingly broke any of the four hundred laws enforced by US Customs. The most exciting cases were those involving narcotics, cargo theft involving organized crime, and neutrality violations like the export of technology and weapons of mass destruction. Being in New York, there were no shortages of organized criminal activity. There were five organized crime (Mafia) families in the New York, New Jersey area: the Genovese crime family, the Gambino crime family, the Lucchese crime family, the Bonanno crime family, and the Colombo crime family. I had worked on many investigations involving members of these various crime families.

In the early 1970s, the major newspaper headlines were about organized crime—how they took over the New York waterfront and airports, how hijackers were stealing millions of dollars of merchandise, and how organized crime was behind it. I supervised a group of customs special agents at JFK Airport, in Queens, New York. One morning, I was summoned to the regional director of investigations (RDI), New

York regional office in New York City. Four agents were ordered to the RDI office: one from Newark, one from New York City, one from the regional office, and I from JFK Airport. The four of us sat in the conference room. A few minutes later, the RDI, John (Footsy) Falcon, entered in his usual stern manner and bellowed the following orders, "I am assigning you four agents, from each of your respective offices to each of you, to form a cargo theft unit. Your cargo theft groups will not report to the fucking SAC. You will report directly to the region. You will clean up the thefts, pilferage, and hijacking. You will get organized crime out of the airports and waterfront. I know you do not have any fucking questions. Now get back to your offices, and I want to see results. If you do not produce results, you will never work in New York again."

That morning had been a bright sunny day. By the time I left the RDI office, I felt I had a black cloud over my head. I had just bought a house, and I did not want to leave anytime soon. Well, in a relativity short time, about three years, our novice unit had made ninety-five arrests and got seventy convictions or pleas with most prosecutions occurring at the Eastern District, New York. We worked with the organized crime strike forces in Brooklyn New York and Newark, New Jersey. In a little over three years, the US Customs cargo theft units had given a serious blow to the five New York mafia crime families' hijacking operation.

The day, March 31, 1975, started out like most day, except today was my turn for being the duty agent at JFK Airport, New York. I awoke and turned on to my side so I could see what time it was. I looked at my silent clock radio; it was 6:00 a.m. *Ah, it's time to get up,* I thought to myself. I hardly, if ever, set the alarm on my clock radio. I was used to getting up at 6:00 a.m. every day, and today was no exception. It was like my body was programed to awake every day at a precise time. Even if I got to bed at 4:00 a.m. in the morning, I would still get up at 6:00 a.m. It's only when I had to appear in court the next morning, after a late-night arrest or surveillance, that I would set the alarm as a backup.

I stared at the silent clock for a couple more seconds. I reluctantly rolled on to my back, and I pulled the gold silk sheet and patterned brown down comforter up to my neck. I felt warm and comfortable, but knew I had to get up. I gazed at the ceiling; it was an old metal ceiling painted a glossy white. The swirling leaf-like pattern of the ceiling began to reflect the beams of the dawn light, glittering in the darkened room. The light was coming through the opened wood grain window blinds beside my bed. As I lay in my full-size bed, I could hear the wind howling outside, and I thought how nice it would be to stay in my nice warm and comfortable bed.

The shadows from the tree outside were dancing on the walls. The shadows quickly reminded me of a haunted house like the one in an old Boris Karloff movie.

I glanced at the window and could see through my half-opened blinds that it was just beginning to get light outside. I rolled over on my side, sat up for a second, and slid my feet into my cold slippers that were by my bed. I stood up and dragged myself out of my bedroom and into the hall.

My first inclination was to turn left and go into the kitchen to put on a pot of coffee, my starter upper, but nature called. So I made a right turn, walking into the bathroom. I sat on the cold toilet seat, which really opened my eyes. I looked down the hall into the kitchen, my bladder feeling the relief of nature's call. Pulling up my pj's, I walked to the sink. I washed my hands and face and looked into the mirror, feeling the stubble growth on my face. I thought to myself, *Hmm, I think I need a shave.* Turning my head side to side, I sensed how much better I would look if I were clean-shaven. I then wondered how I would look in a goatee or a full beard.

Hearing the familiar gurgling sounds of my stomach, I knew it was time for me to get moving and go into the kitchen and put on a pot of coffee.

As I walked into the kitchen, the outside daylight was just beginning to beam into the kitchen. I could see the tree branches outside my kitchen window swaying back and forth in the wind like two old witches. I could feel the chill of the cold wind, even though I was inside my warm house.

Opening the freezer door, I removed a plastic locking bag of coffee. Once I had opened a can of coffee, I dumped the coffee into a plastic freezer locking bag in order to keep it fresh. I kept the bag of coffee in the freezer.

I opened the bag and could instantly smell the aroma of the ground coffee permeating from the bag. *Boy, did that fresh ground coffee smell good?*

I removed the filter containing used grounds from my new Mr. Coffee plastic coffeemaker. I dumped the used grounds into a large metal 3-lb coffee can, which had more used coffee grounds in it. When it was filled, I dumped it in a small compost heap I had in my backyard.

I placed a new brown filter in my coffeemaker. I put three measuring spoons of coffee into the filter. I filled the glass pot with cold water and poured the water up to the eight cup mark in the reservoir. I flipped the switch to on position and anxiously waited for the coffee to begin brewing.

I knew what I had to do next, and I dreaded it. I had to go outside and retrieve my newspaper from the front lawn. Just the thought of going out in the cold sent a chill into my bones. Well, it had to be done. I threw my three-quarter black leather jacket over my pj's, opened the inside metal door and then the outside screen door, and ran down the front brick steps to the cement driveway.

The first light before sunrise cast strange shadows along the driveway as the wind picked up. A piece of newspaper went flying by. It was the March winds that were blowing. I could feel the cold wind slicing into my warm face. I quickly picked up the plastic-wrapped newspaper and darted back into the house. I threw my coat on the back of a kitchen chair. I removed the plastic bag from the newspaper. I placed the paper on the kitchen table and the plastic in the trash can.

I turned on the radio. I always listened to WINS 1010. I paid more attention to the weather and traffic reports than to the news reports. The weather impacted the arrival times of the airplanes. It also dictated what I was going to wear that day. The traffic reports determined the time I had to leave to go to work and what route I would take to avoid the rush-hour congestion. The smell of the fresh brewing coffee filled the air. I could hardly wait to get a sip of coffee. I resisted the urge to pour the coffee before it had finished brewing. I went into the bathroom and took a quick shower, leaving the bathroom door open.

After getting out of the shower, I walked from the bathroom into the kitchen with a towel wrapped around my waist. I poured myself a mug of steaming hot coffee. The aroma was overwhelming. I opened the freezer and removed two ice cubes. I put them in the mug and watched them quickly melt. I never used sugar or milk. I just liked the taste of coffee.

I took a sip of the coffee. As my nostrils sucked in the scent of Columbian coffee, my taste buds awoke to the strong, rich flavor of the coffee. I could taste the richness of the flavor and feel the heat of coffee as it went down my throat. The caffeine always perked me up. I started to feel energized. I returned to the bathroom, wetted down my face, and covered my face with shaving cream. I shaved from right to left, stretching my cheeks with my tongue to get a closer shave. I finished shaving and wetted down my face with cold water and patted it dry with my towel.

Stepping on the scale, I removed the towel. I tossed the towel into the open hamper. I watched the numbers going up and down and finally stopping at 150 lbs. I thought, *That's not so bad, only 2 lbs over my normal weight.* Looking into the large wall mirror over the sink vanity, I flexed my muscles as I admired the shape I was in. This time, thinking aloud, saying to myself, as I twisted sideways on the scale, "Five foot nine, 150 lbs with a twenty-six inch waist, six-pack abs, well-defined muscles, and small, tight, round butts." *Very good,* I thought, *for a thirty-five-year-old.* I got off the scale, feeling good about myself and walked into the bedroom, feeling the definition of the muscles in my arm and forearm.

I opened the top draw on my four-draw maple dresser and removed the blue jockey brief, white T-shirt, and a pair of brown socks. In a flash, I quickly slipped into the brief, T-shirt, and socks. I opened the mirrored sliding door to my closet, scanning my clothes and trying to decide what I was going to wear.

I selected a pair of chocolate-color slacks, a yellow shirt, a matching tie, and a brown and black houndstooth sport jacket. I slipped on the pants and took the yellow shirt off the hanger and put it on. I grabbed a black leather belt off the dresser and threaded the belt through each loop on the pants. I sat on the edge of the bed and put on my socks and brown leather zippered boots.

I reached over to the night table and grabbed my wallet. Before putting my wallet into my pocket, I checked to see how much cash I had. I counted 180 dollars, thinking to myself that was enough to last until payday, which was only two days away.

I picked up my new, shiny black leather case. When opened, imbedded in the inside cover on one side was a gold badge. It was covered with a soft piece of black leather. The other inside cover was a clear plastic pocket, containing my US Customs special agent credentials that authorized me to enforce the customs laws and carry a weapon. I placed the credentials in my shirt pocket. I slipped my wristwatch on and checked the time. I gathered up the loose change and put into my pants pocket.

I pulled open the draw on the night stand. Inside the draw were my two 6 shot speedloader, each with six bullets that were firmly locked in place, my handcuffs, and a .357 Smith & Wesson Magnum. I always kept my gun by my bedside. I picked up the speed loaders and placed them in my jacket pocket. I picked up my gun, removing it from the holster and, as a matter of habit, checked to make sure it was loaded. I replaced the gun into the holster which could be concealed in the waist of my pants. I then shoved the holster into my pants at the waist, clipping the holster onto my belt. I took my handcuffs and placed the one ring into my pants at the small of my back.

I picked up my sport jacket, went into the kitchen, sat down, and began to glance at the newspaper headlines. The radio station was tuned into WINS 1010. That station always gave the traffic report every ten minutes. I had several ways to get to the office. If there was any accident on the Southern State Parkway, I would have to take one of my alternate route. I took another sip of coffee and scanned the headlines of the *Smithtown Messenger*, stopping to read only those local articles that interested me.

Remembering that I had forgot something, I picked up my car keys, threw on the black coat, ran out into the driveway, opened the car door, started the car, and put on the heater. I then ran back into the warmth of my house. I refilled my coffee cup. For the next fifteen minutes, I read the paper, listened to the radio, and sipped my coffee. I looked at my watch; it was almost 7:00 a.m. I downed the last few drop of coffee and placed the cup in the dishwasher. I turned off the coffee pot, poured the remaining coffee into my travel mug, gathered up the newspaper, and placed it into my attaché case. I picked up my black coat to hang up in the closet and exchange it for my new raincoat. I grabbed my raincoat, attaché case, and coffee and left the house.

Seeing my three-quarter black leather coat brought back memories of when I first got the coat. The next day, I got my biggest seizure. It began to come back to me as if it were yesterday.

I had been working for customs for about four years, learning the job as I went along. I made several seizures of merchandise while on patrol in New York and Brooklyn waterfronts. Then in March of 1965, I was transferred to JFK Airport. I dressed in plainclothes (slacks, sport jacket, and tie) and looked like an arriving passenger. We worked in teams of two. It was my job to observe arriving passengers and see if I could spot any bulges on the passengers' body. I enjoyed picking out passengers whom I believed were smuggling something pass the customs inspectors. The plainclothes teams competed among themselves to see who could get the most seizures and the best quality seizures. The most sought-after type of seizure was a narcotic seizure. They were far and few in between and usually were small amounts of pot from passengers off the Icelandic airline flights. I was working less than a year in plainclothes at JFK Airport when I got my big seizure.

It was on a Sunday, January 23, 1966, at approximately 4:30 p.m. A Lufthansa flight from Germany had arrived. I was still a plainclothes CPI. The Captain Eddie Mac had assigned three CPIs to train the newly appointed customs agents this week. Bob Towers was assigned to me. John Trent was assigned to CPI Willy Dean, and Igor Bentovski was assigned to CPI Tom Virgilio. These new agents were going through the training cycle to learn how to stop passages and make seizures. We were working the two-to-ten shift. Sundays were always a busy day. This Sunday was no exception. The east and west wings were in full operation. There were twenty inspectors on east wing and twenty inspectors on the west wing, and the lines to get their bags examined were very long. Rule 21 was in effect. When they announced rule 21 over the teletype machine, the inspectors were to only look in one bag and move the passengers out as quickly as possible. Agent Bob Tower and I were in the east wing, looking at the passengers who had come off the Lufthansa flight from Germany.

In each wing, when the passengers finished their immigration check, they came into the customs area. They would proceed to one of the six baggage carousels in back of the customs examination belts. I was walking around the baggage carousel as the bags from the Lufthansa flight were being dumped on the revolving carousel belt. I was observing the arriving passengers coming into the customs area. I spotted an individual who was alone and later identified as Jean-Paul Girerd. What caught my eye was that he was wearing a three-quarter black leather coat. The day before, I had just bought the same coat. I was admiring my coat's twin when I noticed him walking toward the baggage belt in a funny way. He appeared to be rigid. When he was attempting to get his bag off the revolving baggage conveyor belt, he looked odd. Something was not right. He had kept his coat, buttoned up. It was hot in the building, and most people had their coats open or off.

It was crowded around the baggage carousel. If you did not grab your bag as it came around, you would have to wait until it came around again. The passenger spotted his bag coming around on the belt. His bag was not up right. It was lying down with the handle facing away from him. As the bag came to his position, he attempted to push his way, between two people, in order to retrieve his bag. He attempted to get the bag and only managed to turn the baggage around so the next time the handle would be facing him. I had observed him standing on his toes and leaning over, and yet he could not reach the baggage handle. He was very stiff.

I got my partner's attention. He came over. I explained to him what I had observed. I told him we had to watch him closely, see how he acted at the examination belt, and see if he was traveling with anyone else. I told Bob, "Let's see if he shops for a short line or a short customs examination." As Girerd's bag came around a second time, Girerd again bent over. He stood on his toes again and was very stiff. He looked like someone who was wearing a back brace and could not bend. He managed to retrieve his bag with the help of another passenger. Looking at Girerd, one could say he appeared to be about forty years old. He had short, wavy black hair. His coat was a three quarter black leather coat. His pants were a brownish gray tweed. His shoes were brown. His face looked tired. Water was dripping from his face. He took out a white handkerchief and wiped the water from his face and head. He placed the handkerchief back in his pocket. Girerd then bent at the knees and picked up one bag. He then walked very slowly, looking at each customs examination belt. He passed eight belts in the east wing and walked in back of the staff offices to the west wing. He went to belt number one in the west wing. He got in line. He was third in line.

With rule 21 in effect, Girerd watched the customs inspector examine only one bag, and then he signed the passenger's baggage declaration and handed it back to him. The passenger then took his bag and headed for the door, which was no more than fifteen feet from the examination belt. The examination took no more than three minutes. Now it was Girerd's turn. We watched how Girerd lifted his bag up to put on the examination belt. The belt was three-and-a-half feet high and fifteen feet long. We observed Girerd bending his knees and, with one hand, he was grabbing the handle and with the other, the bottom of the bag; he swung the bag up onto the belt. Unfortunately for him, he purposely turned the bag's handle to face the inspector, thinking that it would make it easy for the inspector to open the bags. He would then be able to clear customs much faster. Wrong, wrong, wrong! Customs inspectors in the United States do not open the bags. The passenger is required to open his own bag and present the contents for examination. The inspector asked Girerd for his baggage declaration. Girerd smiled and handed the inspector his baggage declaration and passport. The inspector asked him if he was bringing any gifts for anyone here in the United States. Girerd replied, "No, I am a tourist."

The inspector asked, "How long will you be staying in the United States?"

Girerd replied, "I will be here for three or four days."

Then the shocker came. The inspector said, "Please open the bag," pointing to the suitcase. Girerd stood on his toes and attempted to bend over as far as he could, finally unlatching his suitcase latches and opening the suitcase top toward him. This convinced me that he was wearing a back brace or had something concealed around his body.

The inspector looked through the bag. He then went to his desk and picked up the passenger declaration, signed it, and handed it and his passport back to Girerd. I could see the perspiration dripping down the side of his face. The exit door was fifteen feet from the first belt. He could see the people in the lobby as he headed for the door. At that point, I stepped in front of him. I showed him my badge and asked him for his passport. He put his bag down and handed me his declaration and passport. It was a French passport in the name of Jean-Paul Girerd. My partner had the baggage cart, and I told him to place the passenger bag on the cart and that we would go up to the search room. I asked Mr. Girerd how long he was going to be in the United States. He replied, "No English."

I asked him if he had any family or friends here in the United States. He replied, "No English, tourist."

I moved to the side of Mr. Girerd in order to allow some passengers to go by. In doing so, I placed my hand on Mr. Girerd's back. I could feel something hard and stiff. I knew I had something. With my hand on his back, we proceeded toward the search room in the west wing.

I said, "What is this?"

He replied, "Car accident. Hurt back."

We entered the search room. I closed the door behind us. Now, Mr. Girerd was really sweating. I asked Mr. Girerd if he was carrying anything on his person that he did not declare to the inspector. Mr. Girerd said, "No, nothing."

I then said, "Mr. Girerd, open your coat." He slowly unbuttoned the three-quarter coat. He was wearing black pants and a white shirt with the top button open and no tie. I now said, "Take off your coat."

Mr. Girard said, "No."

I then said, "Are you wearing a back brace?"

Mr. Girerd said, "Car accident. I have back brace."

I then said, "Open your shirt, and let me see the back brace."

Mr. Girerd then said, "No, only a doctor can check me!"

Agent Towers was standing at the door with the baggage cart. He opened his jacket, revealing a large gun on his hip. There was no way for Mr. Girerd to get out of that room. The sweat was now across his whole forehead. I was standing only two or three feet from Mr. Girerd. I said, "I thought you said you do not speak any English?"

"Only a little," was his reply. In one swift motion, I reached out and grabbed Mr. Girerd's shirt with my two hands. I pulled the shirt open, popping two buttons off his shirt. Under the shirt, a vest with several pockets was revealed. In the pockets were plastic bags containing white powder. The facial expression on Girerd's face told it all. He was caught, and there was no place to go. In a commanding voice, I told him to take the coat off! Mr. Girerd complied and removed his coat. I then told him to take off his shirt, which he did. I told him to sit on the bench. He sat on the bench with the vest on.

I told Bob to go to the staff office and notify the staff officers that we got a body-carry of narcotics off the Lufthansa flight and get the drug-testing kit and scale. I also told Bob to tell the other CPI teams that we got a body-carry of drugs. While I was waiting for the testing kit, I picked up the black coat Girerd was wearing and searched the pockets. As I searched the pockets, I asked, "Who else was on the flight with you?" Girerd did not answer. I asked whom he was bringing this vest to? Girerd again did not answer. I removed everything from the jacket pockets. When I got to the inside of the coat, there was a pocket in the left inside lining. I removed a crumpled-up piece of paper from the pocket. I could now hear the teletype bells ringing. The staff officer was notifying all inspection belts that a 100 percent examination of all Lufthansa passengers was required and for them to be observant for a possible body-carry. I looked at the paper; it was a line of numbers. It appeared to be a telephone number and room number.

Two CPI teams, Willy Dean and his trainee Agent John Trent along with Tom Virgilio and his trainee Agent Igor Bentovski came into the search room to look at the passenger and vest. They then left the search room, which was in the west wing, and scurried to the east wing to observe any remaining Lufthansa passengers. Staff Officer John Horiwitz entered the room with a scale and narcotic test kit. Agent Towers also entered the room. I then told Girerd to stand up. He stood up. I then removed the vest from his body. Girerd then put his shirt back on. I placed the vest on the table. I then placed the handcuff on Girerd's hands in back of him. I sat him down. He was stoned-faced and showed no emotion. There were ten pockets on the vest. I removed the first plastic bag and placed it on the scale that Staff Officer Horiwitz was holding. It read 1.1 pounds or half kilo. I initialed and dated the corner of the bag. I took out my pocket knife and punctured the top of the plastic bag. It was a white talcum-like powder. I asked Bob for the heroin-testing vial. I took my knife and took a tip full of white powder and placed it in the vial opening. I then placed the cap on the vial, making sure that the top was secure. I then squeezed the thin outer glass tube. The more fragile inner glass tube broke, releasing the liquid into the powder. The liquid turned to bright purple as it hit the white powder. It was heroin. I put my initials and date on each remaining nine bag and the vest. There were five kilos of heroin. The lab analysis later showed the heroin to be 99 percent pure.

Looking at Girerd's baggage declaration revealed that he was going to the Diplomat Hotel. Just then, the Duke walked into the search room. "Good job, Reno," the Duke said as he patted me on the back. He then looked at the vest and the bags of heroin. The Duke said, "I told the Staff Officer Lenny Sampton to get all the baggage declarations from the Lufthansa flight." The Duke took Girerd's passport and baggage declaration. I told the Duke that I had found a piece of paper in Girerd's jacket pocket.

As the Duke looked at what was written on the paper, I said, "It looks like a telephone number and possibly a room number."

The Duke said, "It sure does, Reno. I will check it out." The Duke left the room with the baggage declaration, passport, and the paper. He went to his office across from the staff office. He called sector communications center, who patched him into Carl Farone, chief of the region narcotic enforcement unit. Carl lived ten minutes from the airport. He briefed Carl on the seizure and the possibility of more couriers going to the Diplomat Hotel. Carl said he would call Al Healey and bring him up to speed. Al would get his agents over to the Diplomat.

The Duke sat in his office and dialed the number from the piece of paper I had found. A voice on the other end said, "Diplomat Hotel, how can I help you?"

The Duke said, "Can you connect me to Mr. Girerd's room?" There was a pause.

Then the voice on the other end said, "Mr. Girerd has not checked in yet. Is there a message?"

The Duke said, "No, I will call back later." The Duke hung up. The Duke told Carl that the last four numbers must be a room number. It could be the room number of the person he was going to meet or another courier. Duke then called Al Healy directly and gave him the information that was found on the paper and told him that the room number was not Girerd's. It could be another courier's. He told Al of his call to the Diplomat Hotel.

After the Duke had left the search room, I began to fill out a seizure report. After completing the paper, I then meticulously searched Mr. Girerd's bag again. I went through each garment to see if anything was secreted inside the linings. I found nothing. Staff Officer Sampton started bringing customs inspectors into the room, one at a time, to observe the vest of narcotics. Girerd just sat on the end of the bench with his head bowed down. This was the largest amount of heroin ever carried into the United States on a person since World War II. There were larger amounts of heroin that were previously seized in suitcases but never on a person.

Carl Farone arrived at the customs area and met with the Duke. They were excited. This was the largest heroin seizure the NY office was ever involved with. Carl said he sent agents to the Diplomat Hotel. The agents, working with hotel security, found that there had been nine reservations for the day. Agent Bob Tower took the list from Carl and began to check the nine names against the Lufthansa baggage declarations. There were no matches except for Girerd. Supervisor Al Healy called the Duke back and told him that the room number found on Girerd belonged to a Mr. Elie Amouyal, who checked in the hotel the day before. The Duke asked Carl and Bob to stay with the prisoner and drugs and send me to his office. Bob rushed to the search room and told me to go see the Duke. I took Girerd's airline ticket with me to the Duke's office. I entered the office.

The Duke said, "The room number you found on the paper belonged to a Mr. Elie Amouyal who arrived yesterday. Check with your Lufthansa contacts to see if he arrived on any of their flights yesterday." I wrote down the name on a sheet of paper and took Girerd's airline ticket with me. I left the paperwork that I was working on in the office with the Duke and walked down the east wing.

By this time, the Lufthansa flight was finished. I spotted Elsa, the Lufthansa representative, coming from immigration. She was on her way back to her office. I called her. She looked up and saw me. She quickened her pace. "Hi, Johnny, what can I do for you?"

I said, "Right now I really need your help, Elsa." I explained to her that I had just arrested a passenger named Jean-Paul Girerd, from her Lufthansa flight, with narcotics. I told her I needed her to do some checking for me. I gave her Girerd's ticket information and the paper with the name Elie Amouyal. I told her to check all flights that arrived yesterday or the day before for Elie Amouyal. I said, "Also get everything you can on Jean-Paul Girerd." She copied down all the ticket information from Girerd's copy of his ticket onto the paper I had given her. She said she would be back in half an hour. She scurried off into the lobby to her office. I returned back to the Duke's office. I told the Duke that the airline was running a check for us.

Carl received a call from Al Healey, supervisor of the heroin squad. Al told Carl that the US magistrate said that they did not have enough probable cause to get a search or arrest warrant for Elie Amouyal or his room. Ten minutes later, Elsa came looking for me. She found me in the search room with the prisoner. She knocked on the door and then entered. She was out of breath. She must have been running all the way from her office.

Elsa said, "I need to talk to you outside." I could see Elsa looking at Girerd and the vest of narcotics.

Elsa said, "I never saw so much drugs on one person." We left the room and stood outside the door. She said, "I can tie the two, Elie Amouyal and Jean-Paul Girerd together. Look they have consecutive ticket numbers purchased the same day for cash from the same ticket agent." I gave Elsa a big kiss and told her she did great work. This was just what we needed. I told Elsa I would take her out to dinner at the restaurant of her choice.

Elsa replied, "That is a date, and we can go to my place afterward for a drink."

I said, "You're on." CPI Willy Dean and Agent John Trent were outside the search room. I told them to watch the prisoner and drugs while I went to the Duke's office.

I entered the Duke's office, and Carl and the Duke were having a conversation. Carl was telling the Duke that we got to figure a way to see if Elie Amouyal also had a load. I told Carl, "Why don't we get a search warrant for Elie Amouyal room?"

Carl said, "The magistrate said we did not have enough probable cause for a warrant."

Knowing what the outcome was going to be, I told Carl, "Well, I think that we now have enough probable cause, thanks to my beautiful friend Elsa."

I was standing next to Elsa with my arm around her.

Carl said, "What do you mean?"

I said, "Elsa, tell him what we found."

Elsa said, "Well, Johnny told me what to look for so it was easy to get the information he wanted."

Carl interrupted, "What information did you get?" Elsa produced a number of papers from the folder she was carrying.

She said, "Elie Amouyal was not on any of yesterday Lufthansa flights. Girerd's ticket number is the next ticket after a Mr. Michael H. Neybergh. Mr. Neybergh was on yesterday's Lufthansa flight from Paris. He was traveling using a Belgium passport. The tickets are in sequence and were purchased by the same person from the same airline representative in Paris for cash on the same day."

I had pulled the baggage declarations for the Lufthansa flight for yesterday's Lufthansa flight and found Mr. Neybergh's declaration, which indicated that he was going to the Diplomat Hotel. Carl became ecstatic and immediately called Al Healey and gave him the information. The Diplomat Hotel reservation list did not reveal any reservations for a Mr. Neybergh. Well, it turned out that the information was enough for a search warrant.

Carl then said, "Get the seizure, the prisoner, and all the paperwork. We will take them to our office at Varick Street." I then went to the search room and removed the handcuffs from Girerd and had him put his coat on. I again handcuffed him with his hands in back of him. I placed the vest and seizure in Girerd's suitcase. Bob took control of the prisoner with the help of Willy Dean and John Trent. I carried the suitcase with the heroin. We went to the Duke's office. Carl then said, "Reno, you drive the Duke's car. Trent will sit up front with you. The Duke and I will sit in the back seat with the prisoner. Get us to Varick Street as fast as you can." We all proceeded to the ships office and out the back door onto the ramp. Duke got into the back seat, then Girerd sat next to the Duke and Carl sat next to Girerd. Trent took the suitcase with the drugs and placed it in the trunk. He then sat up front with me.

Carl again said, "Reno, get us to Varick Street the most direct way." Well, I took Carl at his word. I drove the car around the tarmac and around the airplanes preparing to taxi off the tarmac. This got Carl a little upset.

Carl said, "What the hell are you doing? You just missed that airplane."

The Duke piped in and said, "Relax, Carl. Reno knows the airport like the back of his hand. He knows what he is doing." I headed out of the tarmac by the South Gate. Then we drove off the airport onto South Conduit Ave and onto Atlantic Avenue. When we got on Atlantic Avenue, Carl and the Duke got very nervous so much so that both of them opened their jackets and kept their hands on their guns. Well, Atlantic Avenue took us through a seedy part of Brooklyn. Carl said, "Why are you going this way?"

I said, "You told me the most direct way. We take Atlantic Avenue to the Brooklyn Bridge and over the bridge to Canal St. and over to Houston Street to the office. I will have you there in no time at all. Besides it is late, and there is hardly anybody out."

Well, there was no traffic, and we made it there in thirty minutes. We pulled in front of the building and took the prisoner and seizure out of the car and into the captain's office. I placed Girerd in a holding cell in the processing room next to the captain's office. Captain Joe Tombetta was the captain on duty. Carl told Joe about the heroin seizure I made. Joe came over to me and patted me on the back and told me, "Congratulations, Reno. I knew that it would not be long before you get the big seizure." When we got settled in, I took the prisoner out of the cell and photographed and fingerprinted him. I was good at this because I had plenty of experience in doing this for the captain's office before becoming a CPI. After I finished the fingerprinting and photographing of Girerd, I placed him back in the holding cell. Meanwhile, execution of the search warrant of Elie Amouyal room took place. Customs agents, with the help of hotel security, used the hotel pass key to enter Amouyal's room. Elie Amouyal was in the room, watching TV when the agents, with guns drawn, entered the room. Elie acted very calmly.

Elie said, "What is the meaning of this?"

Agent Donald O'Donald said, "Customs police! Don't move and keep your hands up where we can see them!" Al Healey and the three agents searched the room and the suitcase of Elie Amouyal. The room search revealed a passport in the name of Michael H. Neybergh and a passport in the name of Elie Amouyal. Also found in his suitcase was a vest identical to the one Girerd was wearing. The vest was empty. There were no plastic bags of heroin. Elie had made his delivery. Mr. Elie Amouyal refused to talk. He refused to answer any questions. He was arrested and taken to Varick Street Office where he was photographed and fingerprinted. Pictures of the empty vest and the vest with the heroin were taken. (See pictures of Agent Johnny Reno and the vest).

Both prisoners refused to talk. They were then taken to the federal lockup at Cadman Plaza in Brooklyn. The next day, they were arraigned and held for trial on $75,000 bond each. Both men pleaded guilty, and Jean-Paul Girerd was sentenced to mandatory five years in a federal penitentiary, and Elie Amouyal was convicted of passport fraud and narcotic smuggling and received a sentence of seven to ten years in a federal penitentiary.

It had been a pleasant memory, but it was not getting me to the airport any sooner. The sun had just risen. I could see the trees bending in the wind. It was a cold, and the wind made it even colder. Jumping into my now warmed car, I settled in for the ride to the office. I could not help thinking about the strong winds. I was wondering if the winds were strong enough to affect the arriving flights today. If there was a tail wind, the flights would be early, and if the flights hit head winds, they would go late. Judging from the bending trees, I could say the wind was coming out of the west. *Just what I needed*, I thought. I had the duty tonight. With strong headwinds, I envisioned myself being stuck at the airport until at least 2:00 a.m. Little did I know what had been unfolding over last couple of days and that it was going to impact me today because I was the duty agent.

I fastened the seat belt in my new 1975 dark blue Chevy Impala. The smell of the new car triggered the thoughts of how great this job was. The government gave me a new car and paid for the gas and maintenance. This was no ordinary car; it had a special high performance engine and tires designed for high-speed chases. I turned on my new Motorola, three frequency customs radio, which also had a public address system and electronic siren. The radio was concealed because I used the cars for surveillance.

I grabbed the hidden microphone from beneath my seat and flipped on the concealed radio switch and called into the twenty-four-hour base station at the airport. "644 to 600, 10-8."

"600 to 644, 10-8 at 0700 over."

"644 to 600, 10-4."

I pulled out my car folder from the attaché case. I recorded the start time and mileage on my car report sheet. I was glad that I was in the habit of recording the mileage and time every time I used the car. It made it very easy to complete the monthly report. It also helped to construct my AUO (overtime) reports.

I turned the car radio on. It was already set to the traffic channel, WINS 1010. The traffic report indicated that there were no problems on the Southern State Parkway today. I pulled out of the driveway and headed to the office. Little did I know what was brewing and that I would be thrust into a lead role in an exciting adventure involving our national security.

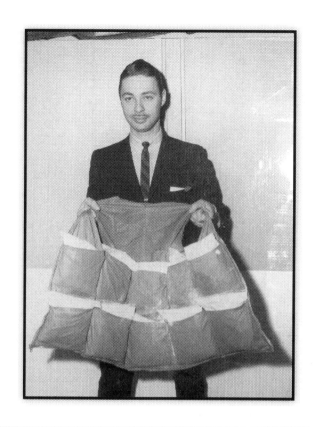

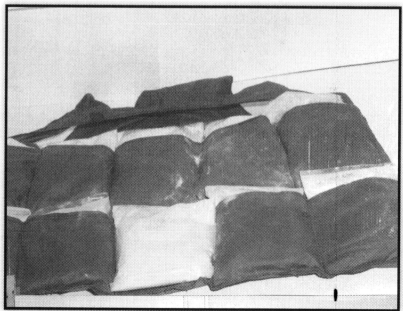

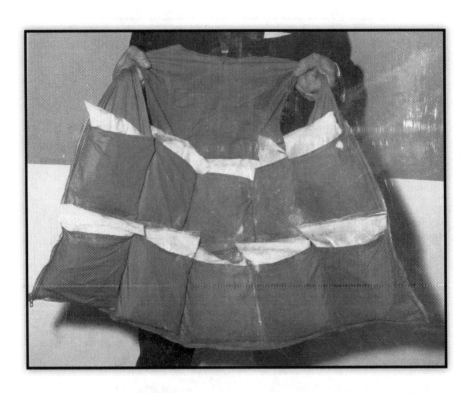

Chapter 4

Office Arrival

The ride to the office, depending on the traffic, usually took me about forty-five minutes to an hour. Today was a good day. There were no accidents, and the traffic was light. I got off the parkway at the Rockaway Boulevard exit and turned onto Rockaway Boulevard.

On the corner was a Latino male selling bouquets of cut flowers. I pulled over, and he came running up to my window. He said, "Flowers, sir, one dollar." There was a rubber band holding the several stems together. I reached into my pocket and pulled out a buck and gave it to him, and I took the flowers.

Now you may be asking yourself, "Why is he buying flowers on his way to work?" Well, my mother always told me that you can catch more flies with honey than with vinegar. She always had these little quips to help mold me into the man I am today. Treat people like you would like to be treated. Be thoughtful, kind, and humble, and the world will be yours.

I had several reports in for typing, and none of them were urgently needed. I had to compete with the other agents in the office to have certain reports typed as expeditiously as possible. The best way to get your reports done quickly was for the secretaries to like you. Do favors for the secretaries, and they will take care of you. So I made it a point to find out what pleased each secretary. I knew that the secretaries always talked about the way the agents treated them and how they became extra friendly when they needed something. So I made it a point to treat the secretaries well, especially when I did not need anything from them. I would bring them things they liked and even take them out to lunch occasionally when I did not need any reports typed.

Amanda loved flowers. For Nadine, it was a couple packs of cigarettes. For Deborah and Lydia, it was cookies or candy. Knowing their likes and dislikes made a difference as to how your work product was handled. Treat the secretaries good, and you always get your work done on time.

I continued down Rockaway Boulevard, and I turned onto cargo road. I could smell the jet exhaust fumes that filled the air. I continued down cargo road until I came to building 179. It was a single-story cement building. At either end, and in the middle of the long building, were steps that led to large brown metal doors. At the far end, above the brown door was a huge sign. The sign read, in thick blue letters, US CUSTOMS. This was the building where the US Customs agents had their offices. I parked the car in one of the several reserved spots. I took the mike from the open ashtray, depressed the top button, and said, "644 to 600, 10-7 Rockaway Boulevard. Over." I released the button. From under the dashboard, where the concealed radio and speaker were located, came a response from the airport base station, "600 to 644, 10-7 Rockaway Boulevard. 0751."

I responded with "644 10-4."

I sat in the car for a few more minutes before turning off the radio. I took another swig of my still warm coffee and took out the car folder from my attaché case. I opened the folder. On the inside left was a pocket where I kept the gas receipts and gas credit cards. On the right side was the mileage sheet forms. I recorded my arrival time, mileage, and destination on my mileage report form. I placed the car keys in the folder pocket and then placed the folder in my attaché case.

I gathered my coat, attaché case, and an almost empty coffee mug. I locked the car and walked to the entrance and proceeded up several steps to the door. I opened the door and went into a vestibule. It was a small carpeted room with three chairs and a small table with some magazines. The door leading from the vestibule to the inner offices had an electrical combination lock. The receptionist sat behind a large, sliding glass window. The receptionist would usually buzz us in. If she was not there, we could put in our four-digit code to open the door. Each week, one of the secretaries would take her turn and serve as receptionist while doing her typing at this front desk.

The receptionist's desk was raised and positioned so she could see who was coming into the office and still remain in her chair. On her desk was the office sign-in-and-out sheets. If someone called, looking for a particular agent, she could easily see if the agent was signed in or out. I walked up to the door, but before I could punch in the code, the door buzzed, and I opened the door and went in. Amanda was playing receptionist this week. She was wearing a floral print blouse with a real low-plunging neckline. I could smell the alluring fragrance of her perfume. I said, "Good morning, Amanda," and she replied in a soft sweet voice, "Good morning, Reno."

I immediately presented her with the bouquet of flowers. Her eyes sparkled as she said, "For me?"

I said, "I know you like flowers." I bent over Amanda's desk and pulled the sign-in sheet a little closer to me. As usual, I was taking my time looking at my wristwatch and then signing in. I could not help looking down Amanda's blouse. As she leaned forward on her elbows, the cleavage and view became greater. I could not keep my eyes from peering at her large milk-white breast. She knew I was admiring her breast as she leaned a little closer, exposing more cleavage. She spoke and said, "Thanks again for the flowers, Johnny."

Amanda was twenty-seven and had been working for us for several years. She made it known to all the agents that she had a boyfriend and was not interested in any office romance. She was always dressed in tight-fitting pants and dresses that accented her busty figure. She was five foot seven 110 lbs with long black hair and brown eyes.

When she first started working at JFK, the guys started a pool in order to guess her measurements. Deborah, one of the other secretaries, then found out that her measurements were 38-26-36 with a C cup. Amanda always wore a low neckline that exposed her cleavage. She made no bones about it. She knew all the guys were always trying to look down her blouse, and she loved it. She was street-smart and could hold her own with any of the guys. She was also a very fast typist who made few, if any, mistakes. The guys knew that they better not do anything to piss her off, or their reports would be at the bottom of the stack. She also knew that she could get away with a lot, and she played the guys in the office like fine fiddles. I was no exception.

As I began to sign in, I could not help seeing her pink bra. Knowing that I was looking, she went into her routine. She tossed long jet-black hair over her shoulder, leaning forward to one side just enough so I could see part of her nipple in her demi cup bra. My face turned red as the pen slipped from my hand. Amanda caught it before it hit the floor.

What a way to start the day! She giggled. I fumbled around a little longer with the sign-in sheet with the excuse I wanted to see who had already signed in. In her flirtatious voice, Amanda said, "I made a fresh pot of coffee, and the Duke brought in some doughnuts today." In a sheepish tone of voice, she said, "Johnny, I took a chocolate cruller and put it on your desk before they are all gone."

Trying to flirt back without being over flirtatious, I said, "What would I do without you, Amanda? Your thoughtfulness is only exceeded by your overwhelming beauty." She laughed and watched me as I walked slowly down the hall to my office, glancing at her over my shoulder. There were supervisors offices on either side of the hall. Mine was the second office on the right.

I entered my office and flicked on the light switch. There, in the middle of my desk, was a chocolate cruller siting on a napkin. I dropped my trench coat on my chair. I carefully placed my attaché case on the desk as I moved the cruller to one side. I took off my sport jacket and placed it on a wooden hanger and put it on the wooden coat tree in the corner of the office. I took my blue trench coat from the chair and placed it on the coat tree hook. I took my holstered gun from my pants, placed it in the desk draw, and locked the draw.

The walls of my office were white. There were no windows. From the doorway, looking in, the first thing you saw was my desk with a high-back black leather chair. I had a credenza against the wall in back of my desk. On the credenza, I had a portable radio in a charger. I also had several picture frames, displaying some of the awards that I received for some of my cases. The wall had a large map of the airport that I got from the airport security council. It took up almost the whole wall. Against the right wall was a four-draw file cabinet, where I locked up my cases that were active. In the left corner was the coat tree. I had large street maps of Brooklyn and Queens on the left wall. The right wall had maps of Nassau and Suffolk Counties of Long Island. The whole office used the maps to check locations and for surveillance briefings.

I grabbed my coffee cup, and I walked down the hall and passed the two restrooms and into the coffee room. I dumped my cold coffee into the sink and rinsed out the cup. The coffee pot was filled with freshly made coffee. The coffee smelled real good. I filled my cup with the coffee. I glanced at the table. I could see two large, almost empty, boxes of doughnuts. There were no chocolate crullers in either box.

I returned to my office. I placed the hot cup of coffee on a coaster on my uncluttered desk. I put my attaché case on the floor. All I had on my desk were my phone, two wooden in-and-out baskets that were empty, and a set of coasters that Cindy had given me. I took a bite of the chocolate cruller. The sweet taste of dark chocolate awakened by taste buds. I took another bite before I took a sip of the coffee. Then I sat back in my swivel high-back chair for a few moments of relaxation.

The first thing that I did each morning was to get my coffee and then go check my interoffice in-and-out box in the secretarial room. So like most mornings, I walked out of my office and down the corridor toward the special agent in charge's (SAC) office. At the end of the corridor, I walked into a large room with twelve desks. Each agent had his own desk and file cabinet in this area.

The area where all the agents had desk was called the bull pen. Frank was at his desk, reading a newspaper and eating a chocolate cruller. DJ was sitting on the edge of Cheech's desk, talking. As I walked through the bull pen, I said good morning and exchanged pleasantries with each agent. I continued on toward the office, in-box. There were an additional four desks where the secretaries were sitting at one end of the room. Deborah and Nadine were sitting at their desk, typing and gossiping. Off to one side was the SAC's office. Lydia, who was the SAC's secretary and supervisor of all the secretaries, had just got up from her desk and was headed for the coffee room with her empty cup in her hand. Against the wall, across from the SAC office, in the secretaries area of the room was a table with a wooden fixture that took up the whole length of the long table. It was the office's in-boxes for each person in the office.

The in-box was made by Special Agent Bobby Nunzzo. The unit was four compartments high with six compartments long. Each compartment had a person's name under it. The only in-box you could have purchased through the government services administration (GSA) was cardboard and would have buckled with all the things we placed in them. I looked at my box, and it was more than half filled. I removed everything and slowly walked back to my office.

I put everything on my desk and began to play solitaire. I took out the two new cases that had been assigned to me. They were fraud cases. I placed them in my in-box. I always looked at the new cases last because once I started to review the case, I just kept on going. I found that I was more productive if I could clear up the other accumulated paperwork first. I took the file copies of the four approved reports and pulled each of the files from my desk and proceeded to file the copies of the completed reports in their case folders. The secretaries had already made the other distribution indicated on the reports. I placed the case folders in the out-box for filing. That left me with the telephone messages and the latest information bulletins, regulation changes, updates on the law, and handbook additions and subtraction sheets. I prioritized the work and dug in.

Chapter 5

Theft at a Customs-Bonded Container Station

A t about 11:30 a.m., I had just finished my second cup of coffee. I had finished going through all the papers in my in-basket, and I was coming up for air when DJ popped his head into my office and said, "Hey, Reno, lunch? We're going to the Diner on Rockaway."

I said, "Okay," and cleared my desk of the few remaining papers. I unlocked my desk draw. I picked up my gun from the draw and stuck it into my pants. I put on my jacket and coat and took the portable radio from the charging unit that I kept on the credenza in my office.

I followed DJ out the door. Frank had already jumped into Cheech's car. DJ got into my car. Cheech and Frank took off. I pressed the button on the portable and said, "644 to 600 10-8."

I released the button and received the reply, "600 to 644 10-8 at eleven thirty-five."

I squeezed off a 644 10-4. Then I pulled out and headed to the Diner.

Dick Castellon, whom all the agent called Cheech, and I started working for US Customs back in 1962. Dick was Italian with a light complexion and jet-black hair. You would never take him for Italian. He looked like he was Irish. He was five-foot eight inches tall and weighed about 160 pounds. Dick tried to be a suave dresser and loved to drive his baby blue Cadillac. There were a number of Italian agents on the third floor in the headquarters office at 201 Varick Street in New York City where Dick worked. That is where both Dick and I started our career with customs. The agents would call out to Dick and say, "Hey, Cheech, get me this. Cheech, go see so-and-so. Cheech do this. Cheech do that." So ever since I knew Dick, he was always being called Cheech by everyone. The name stuck.

Now, Don Jennings started in customs as an inspector in 1970. In 1971, he applied for, and was transferred from an inspection position to, the investigative position in the customs office of investigations at JFK airport. I was his first supervisor. I took the first letter of each name and called Don DJ, and it stuck. DJ was a twenty-five-year-old Irish youngster, fresh out of college who was eager to learn everything he could. He was six feet tall, light complexion, black hair, about 170 lbs and very athletic. DJ was one of the most dependable persons I knew. Ask him to do something, and it got done. It got done right.

Frank Napowski was a different story. He was about thirty-three years old, five feet seven, weighed about 180 lbs, with thinning black hair. Frank was a quiet man. He was a listener and did not talk much. He was not outward or aggressive or inquisitive like DJ. Instead, he was more withdrawn and slow speaking and would try to figure things out by himself instead of asking for help. He took his time at everything he did. Frank was hired in New Hampshire. He came from a small town where everything was slowed down. There was no hustle or bustle like in the big city. If it did not get done today, it would wait until tomorrow. No big deal. So the big city was new to him. Sometimes I think that New York City was overwhelming for Frank. Frank liked to be outdoors and liked to hunt. He did not like city life.

He lived in Nassau County in a quiet residential area. He rented a house on a tree-lined street. It was a bit of country in the city. I had worked on many a surveillance with Frank. We spent a lot of hours together in a car. I got to know Frank pretty well like the rest of the guys who worked for me. Frank felt very comfortable talking with me. It just took Frank a while to get used to working with someone new.

I remember the time, I think it was the only time, that Frank ever got overly excited and very hyper. We were working on a cargo theft case. It involved the New York City mobsters, members of the

Genovese crime family. They were hijacking trucks leaving the New York and Newark airports. Frank went undercover as a security guard at a Newark bonded container station with Jay, another agent from New York City cargo theft unit. One of the regular guards reported to customs that he was approached by some unsavory-looking characters who were feeling him out to see if he would cooperate with a theft of a container. He told them he was only temporarily there until the newly hired guards got their uniforms. He had worked as an informant for customs before, so he contacted his control agent and reported the attempt.

The next day, Frank and Jay went undercover as guards working the midnight-to-eight shift. About two in the morning, a black Caddy with New York tags and tinted windows pulled up to the gate and blew its horn. Jay and Frank exited the gatehouse and stood inside the gate, looking at the car. The door opened. A man dressed in a black overcoat and black hat exited the car's passenger side. He walked to the gate. He was about five foot eight, weighing about 200 lbs. He was about forty-five years old. You could not help noticing the large bulge under his left arm. He was packing a big gun. Frank and Jay kept the gate locked as the man approached them. The man was Italian. His accent was pronounced. He started the conversation by telling Frank and Jay his name was Carmine and he was from the security guard's union. He told them that Veto, the daytime guard, told him that two new guards were just hired and were not part of the union yet. He talked a little about what the union could do for them and that all guards had to belong to the union. He then guided the conversation to their low wages and that they could earn big money if they were smart. Both Jay and Frank said they could use extra money but wanted to know what they had to do to earn it and how much. Carmine told them they could earn two grand each easily and all they had to do was their regular job. "Oh yeah, and leave the rear gate unlocked for an hour," Carmine said. "Stay at the front gate for an hour. Do nothing about a truck coming in the back gate and then leaving with a container. Then you would have to lock the rear gate again. No one would discover the missing container for a couple of weeks." Carmine said, "Think it over. Call me tomorrow." Carmine gave them a union business card with a phone number to call and a time to call. Carmine left as quickly as he had arrived.

A New York City team of special agents were providing a backup for Jay and Frank that night. A discreet surveillance of Carmine's car revealed that the car traveled from the container station to Little Italy in New York City. Carmine parked the car on Mulberry Street. He walked passed a couple of houses and then went across the street into a building next to a restaurant.

The next day at the time indicated, Jay called the number, which turned out to be a public phone. Carmine was waiting in the phone booth. When the phone rang, Carmine picked up the phone. "This is Carmine."

Jay said, "You told me to call you." "Yeah," Carmine interrupted, "the boss wanted to meet the two of you and discuss possible future employment opportunities with our union. The boss set a meeting for 8:00 p.m. this Friday. He wants you to come to Umberto's restaurant on Mulberry Street in New York City and have dinner with him. I checked your work schedules, and both of you are off then." Jay said that they would come to the restaurant. Carmine said, "Just pull up in front. We will save you a parking spot."

The restaurant for the meet was a public place. I had eaten there several times. Even though it was a mob place, the food was good. Jay's car had been registered in Jay's fictitious name and address. DJ and I were Frank's backup, and Vince and Charley were Jay's backup. The restaurant served more as a social club than a restaurant in the morning and early afternoon during the week. Frank and Jay felt very comfortable, knowing that they had backup and the meeting was in a public restaurant. We had discussed them wearing a wire but knew that they would be searched when they attended the meeting. So a listening device was out of the question.

On Friday Jay and Frank drove to Mulberry Street. Carmine was waiting on the street corner with two of his associates. Carmine spotted Frank looking for a parking spot, so he sent one of his associates to park the car for them. As any good mobster would do, he had his boys check out the car and registration in the glove box. Through their contacts with the NY Police Department, they ran a background check on Jay's registration. Our office was meticulous in establishing undercover identities. Jay was given a record for petty theft. Carmine greeted them as they left their car and ushered them into the restaurant. There was quite a bit of traffic on Mulberry Street. We were about ten cars behind Frank and Jay. We could not park in the area, so we parked on Canal Street. We would be able to see their car leaving and could follow them. They did not have to work that night, so Jay was going to drop Frank off at the train station on West Houston Street. We would pick Frank up there and take him home. Things went off as planned, or so we thought, until we picked Frank up at West Houston Street as he got out of Jay's car.

Frank jumped into the back seat of DJ's car. "Get me home! I pissed and shit in my fucking pants. Fucking shit in my pants. I don't need this fucking job. Get me home." Well, Frank never cursed. That was the only time I heard Frank curse. He was really mad. Well, DJ and I were laughing so hard, and it made Frank even more emotional. We finally got to ask Frank what happened. Well, this was what Frank told us:

Frank and Jay were driving down Mulberry Street, looking for a parking spot. They spotted Carmine standing outside of Umberto's Clam House. Carmine was talking with two other men. Carmine spotted Frank in the car and waved to him. He called out to Frank, beckoning him to pull over in front of Umberto's. Jay pulled over and double-parked in front of Umberto's. Frank and Jay got out of the car, and Carmine said, "Hey, Joey, go park the car for my friends."

Joey said, "Sure, boss," and ran over to Jay, took the keys, and pulled away with the car. Carmine walked up to them and put his arms around their shoulders. It was like they were visiting relatives. Carmine told them, as he escorted them into the restaurant, "The boss is going to be a little late, so I hope you guys are hungry." The doors to the restaurant were wide open. The restaurant was crowded. The Italian music flowing from the wall speakers was a Sicilian version of the Tarantella. The music could be heard while walking down Mulberry Street. The atmosphere in the restaurant was jovial. The people were talking loudly and enjoying their food.

Carmine took Jay and Frank to a small private dining room just off the main dining room. Carmine turned to the man, who was his bodyguard, and said, "Hey, Vincenzo, my friends are hungry. Get the antipasto."

"Sure, boss," was Vincenzo's response. The three sat down at a roundtable for six. Immediately, a waiter arrived with a bottle of red wine and several glasses. As the waiter set down the glasses on the red-and-white-checkered tablecloth, another waiter arrived with a basket of hot Italian bread and several small plates. The waiter placed the plates in front of them. Another waiter took a jar of herbs and put a spoonful in each plate and then poured olive oil in each plate. Carmine said, "Hey, munja, eat, eat," as he reached for a piece of Italian bread. He dipped the bread in the plate of oil and herbs and took a bite. The waiters brought a bowl of antipasto salad and placed some in each plate. Then they brought out the stuffed shells and meatballs. Carmine kept talking with them, asking all sort of questions about their background. When they finished eating, Carmine told them to come with him to meet the boss.

They went into a storage room in the back of the private dining room. That was when Frank said he got worried. He said he began to sweat. Both Jay and Frank knew that Carmine wanted to make sure they were not cops. They also believed that Carmine would not hurt them in the restaurant.

Then as they entered the storage room, Carmine told them he thought they were cops. Jay and Frank said they weren't. Carmine said, "Well, see. If you guys are cops, you're dead." Carmine and his two goons, Joey and Vincenzo, pushed Jay and Frank to the back of the storage room. They were big, strong, and mean-looking. They all had guns. Carmine told Joey to search them for a gun or a wire. Carmine had taken out his very large gun and pointed it at them while Joey searched them. After patting them down, Joey told Carmine the two were clean. Carmine said, "Now we will see if you guys are cops or not."

He told them to turn around and face the two mattresses on the back wall. The mattresses were stained with a reddish brown substance. It looked like dry blood. Jay kept telling Carmine that they were not cops. Frank kept saying, "I'm not a cop. Don't shoot me." They kept trying to talk their way out of the bad situation they were in. Frank and

Jay had their backs to Carmine. Carmine had put his gun away and picked up a pool cue. He reached into his jacket pocket and pulled out a couple of firecrackers.

As he lit the firecrackers and dropped them to the floor, he said, "We spotted your backup." The firecrackers started to explode, and Carmine poked Frank and Jay in the back with the pool cue as Frank and Jay fell to the floor. Frank said he knew he was dead. He felt the bullet hit him.

Frank kept saying, "I'm hit. I'm hit." Jay was crying that he was too young to die. Then they heard Carmine yelling for them to stop crying and yelling. He said they were not shot. He said he only did that to see if they were really cops. He said that if they were cops, their backups would be rushing into the restaurant right about now. No one showed up. Frank and Jay lay on the floor for what seemed like a long time. Then Joey told Carmine that no one in the restaurant showed any interest in the noise, and they kept eating. No one came into the restaurant either. Carmine then busted out laughing. He said, "Hey, you guys are not cops. You're okay." He said that he was just having a little fun with them. He said that they passed the test. He took out two envelopes from his pocket. He gave one to Frank and the other to Jay. Each envelope had two thousand dollars in it. Carmine said he would contact them when the container they wanted was in the yard. He told Joey to get their car. Frank and Jay both immediately went to the bathroom, removed their shorts, and cleaned themselves up the best they could. They discarded their soiled shorts in the wastepaper basket.

We laughed and kidded Frank all the way to Frank's house. I told Frank to put in a voucher for reimbursement for a pair of shorts and cleaning bill for his pants. "Under reason, put 'because of threat to undercover operative life, bodily functions were uncontrollable'. In brackets, put 'I was scared shit'." DJ and I both cracked up. We were laughing so hard that DJ almost got us into an accident. Then we laughed about that.

DJ said, "If we got into an accident, we would have to say the reason for the accident was because we were trying to figure a way for Frank to voucher a pair of shorts that he just shit in." It just went on, and

Frank began to see the humor in the situation. Soon Frank began to chime in, and he began laughing about what had just happened to him. Then I knew that Frank was going to be okay. We got Frank home and dropped him off. We offered to have a couple of beers with him. Frank said no. All he wanted to do was take a nice, hot shower and get some rest. He said he would be okay. DJ and I headed back to the office where I picked up my car.

Three days later, we got word from Frank that the theft was probably going to take place that night around 2:00 a.m. Carmine had asked Frank to locate a particular container in the yard. He gave Frank the container markings and numbers. Each container had distinct markings and serial numbers. These were used for tracking the container from manufacturer through customs and to the final destination at the importers' premise. Carmine told Frank to make sure that there was easy access to the container and that no one blocked the container. Once we had the container numbers, I sent a tech team to the container yard. They located the box and placed a tracking device on the container. We were all set. Frank and Jay just had to let them take the container. A check of the container paperwork revealed the forty-foot container had high-value electronics: TVs, cameras, and stereos.

The rest of the undercover sting was standard operating procedure. We would let them take the container. We would stay far away from the container. We let them drive the container around to see if they were being followed. When they were sure that no one was following them, they would go to a warehouse to unload the container. After unloading the container, they would drop off the container in some obscure location. We used the electronic tracking device to tell us where the container was at all times. One of our cars or vans would always be in the vicinity of the container at all times. When the container arrived at a warehouse, we would get a physical description of the premises for our application for a search warrant.

Just before 2:00 a.m., Jay walked through the container yard, shining his flashlight between the parked containers. It was spooky. He arrived at the rear gate. He could hear the engine of diesel truck idling not too far from the gate. Nervously, he put the key into the lock and turned it. Click, the lock sprang open. He turned, shining his flashlight on the ground to see his way. He could hear the truck revving its engine and then shifting into gear. He quickened his pace and headed for the front gate. He went to the guard shack at the front gate where Frank sat waiting for him to return. "How did it go?" Frank asked.

"Okay," Jay replied. "I heard a truck running, and then I heard the truck shift into gear. I could not see anything. It was too dark." Then for a few moments, there was dead silence. Then they heard, faintly, a chain rattle and the squeaking of the old, rusted gate opening. The container yard was a big yard with a lot of containers parked there. Jay and Frank were jumpy and intimidated at the least sound. A cat crying somewhere in the yard made it even more eerie. Jay asked Frank how long they should wait before he closed the gate. Just then, they heard a clank. Metal hitting metal. Then a hiss like air being released from an air compressor.

Jay said, "I think they are hooked up." Then they heard a diesel engine racing in the calm of the night. "Let's give them a few more minutes," Frank said. Jay began a slow walk toward the rear gate. He could hear a clanking noise. He wondered if someone was banging on the gate. He took his time and shone his flashlight at the ground in front of him. He could hear a truck engine getting fainter and fainter as he turned toward the corner of a container. He pointed his flashlight in front of him and could see the rear gate wide open, the chain dangling against the metal gate. He quickened his pace and grabbed the gate and pulled it closer and secured the lock on the chain that had been clanking against the gate. The gate was now locked. Everything had gone as planned. They did not even see the truck pull in and take the container.

A loose surveillance on the container that left through the back gate was initiated. The tracking transmitter kept base station 100 informed where the container was at all times. They drove the container around for about an hour with a spotter car to see if the container was being followed. They then drove to a truck stop off US 1 on Hackensack Ave in Kearny, New Jersey. They parked the container for five hours. An undercover car from our Newark office kept the container under surveillance in case they tried to off-load the goods to another truck. About a quarter to nine in the morning, a black Cadillac sedan pulled up to the truck. A man got out of the passenger side of the black Cadillac and got into the truck. He started up the truck and pulled out with the Cadillac following the truck.

Special Agent Roger Max from the Newark office picked up his microphone and said, "506 to all units. The teddy bear is moving. A black lion is following the bear."

"Base 100 to all surveillance units. Go to Channel 3. Base 100 is now tracking the bear." The tracking transmitter was working properly. The surveillance was on the move. Channel 3 on our radios was a secure channel. Before we had gotten a secure channel, people would monitor our frequencies. Several times, ham operators would call the trucks on their CBs and tell them that the feds were following their truck. Many surveillance were blown because we did not have the secure radio communication. This would piss us off, and we would then track the ham operator down. Because they always gave the truckers their handle, it was easy to find them. We would get them on the CB and thank them for saving us from the Smokey, and to show our appreciation, we would have a small gift for them. They would give us their address to meet them.

What a surprise it would be for them! We would seize their transmitting equipment and arrest them for conspiracy, aiding and abetting, and felony theft. Most of the time, the ham operator turned out to be a kid. Then we would put a big scare in them and their parents. We made them realize that they had put the life of an informant or undercover officer in jeopardy and that they could go to jail for a long time and lose all their equipment. This really was an awakening for them. They always promised to use their radios for good and to help people.

The truck traveled up and down US 1 and 9 several times to see if there was anyone following them. I broke radio silence. "644 to 509."

Max replied, "509 to 644, go ahead."

"644 to 509 proceed to the AUSA's office at Federal Plaza and see AUSA Guillian. Sign the affidavits and get the warrants signed by the magistrate. Call when they are in hand."

"509 to 644 that is 10-4. Over and out."

"100 to all units. The bear is on the sky, heading to the hole in the ground." The truck had gotten on the Polaski Skyway and was heading to the Holland tunnel.

"100 to all units. The bear is out of the hole."

"100 to all units. The Bear is traveling on the Canal."

"100 to all units. The Bear is taking the big leap."

We now knew that the truck was going on the Manhattan Bridge to go to Brooklyn or Queens. "100 to all units. The bear is on BQE to meet the penguin."

The truck was now on the Brooklyn Queens Expressway, heading south for lower Brooklyn. We tracked the truck to a warehouse on Beard St. in lower Brooklyn. I had picked up the surveillance on the BQE. I headed to the area of the warehouse and met up with Special Agent Vince Morano. I pulled into a spot where I could observe the warehouse, and so did Vince. The driver of the truck had been identified as Vincenzo. He pulled the container up to a loading dock. There were three bays; all the bay doors were down. The Caddy had pulled up in front of the building. The driver of the truck had backed the container into bay three. He then walked to the front of the building and met with Carmine, the man from the Caddy. Both men walked to the front door of the building. Carmine removed a key from his pocket and opened the front door. They entered the building. It appeared to be an office. We now had a location. The only car parked in front of the office entrance was Carmine's Caddy. This meant that they had to wait for help to unload the container. We had to stay out of sight, so arriving help to unload the truck would not get suspicious.

A surveillance of the warehouse continued as three cars arrived at the warehouse. We took down their plate numbers. Two men got out of each of the cars. They were dressed in jeans, shirts, and light jackets. Four men wore caps. They all appeared to know each other and walked to the office. They entered the office and went inside. We had enough information. I called the base station and asked them to landline Agent Max at the AUSA's Guillian's office and pass on the information for the warrant.

A federal magistrate had been appraised of the sting by Agent Max and was standing by to sign the search warrants for the warehouse and cars and arrest warrants for Carmine and Vincenzo.

Eight special agents and two New York City police cars arrived several blocks away at a staging area. I briefed the raid teams and gave them their assignments. The NY PD would maintain a perimeter and keep observers out. Ten customs special agents will hit the warehouse and execute the search warrants. There were two ways into the warehouse besides the loading dock—a back door and a front office door. "100 to 644 over"

"644 go ahead 100"

"100. 506 has the warrants in hand and is proceeding to your location. Over."

"644 to 100 that is 10-4."

That was it. We were ready to roll. The loading dock had three bays. Shortly after the six men entered the office, two bay doors opened. The first bay door was down. The second was opened, and the container was backed into the opened third bay. I sent one agent on foot to the back door in case anyone tried to leave through the back door. All units maintained radio contact. When I gave the word, the raid team would enter the warehouse and secure the area. Vince and I would go through the front door and secure the office area.

The problem facing us was that the dock was three-and-a-half feet high. In order to gain the element of surprise, we would have to find a way to get on the dock without being seen. As luck would have it, Vince spotted a UPS truck coming down the street. Vince ran up to the truck in his US Customs police vest on. The truck stopped, and Vince convinced the driver to cooperate with us. Vince took the truck and told the driver to remain across the street until it was safe for him to get his truck. Vince and I got in the front of the truck. Seven agents got into the back of the UPS truck.

Vince pulled up to the warehouse and backed into the open bay. I gave the word, and the teams entered the warehouse. The back door of the UPS truck went up, and seven agents ran into the warehouse with shotguns in hand. Four agents ran toward the men piling the boxes inside the warehouse. Three of the agents went directly into the open container next to the UPS truck where three men were holding boxes to carry out of the container.

"Customs! Police! Put the boxes down and put your hands on your head!" They were startled. They froze and immediately followed directions by dropping the boxes and placing their hands on their heads.

"Come down off the boxes slowly!" The man standing on the second row of boxes complied. Two agents immediately ran up to the three and searched them for weapons. Finding no weapons, the three were handcuffed behind their back and made to sit on the floor. They were secured. At the same time, four agents went directly to the three men who were stacking the boxes already off loaded. They were making piles for TVs, stereos, and cameras. The three turned their attention to the commotion at the container. Coming from the first open bay door, they saw four men dressed in blue with blue ball caps and bright yellow letters *Customs Police* on their vest with shotguns and pistols pointed at them and advancing toward them. What they heard was "Customs! Police! Freeze!" A pause. Then, "Put your hands on your head!" The three complied. They were told to kneel with their hands on their heads, which they did. They were handcuffed and searched for weapons, and none were found. They were made to sit down on the floor.

Vince and I entered the front door and found Carmine and Vincenzo in the office with a new color TV and empty box on the floor. As Vince and I entered the office, we said, "Customs! Police! Don't move. Now put your hands on your head and turn around slowly!" The two complied. Vince started to search Vincenzo and came up with two guns.

Vincenzo said, "Aah, I got a permit for them." A search of his wallet revealed a permit for the two guns. A search of Carmine revealed a gun also. Carmine did not say anything. I asked Carmine if he had a permit for the gun.

Carmine said, "Aah," and shrugged his shoulders. "I want a lawyer." A search of Carmine's wallet did not reveal a permit for the gun. Both were handcuffed behind their back. Carmine and Vincenzo refused to answer any questions. The six men who were unloading the container were taken to our Varick Street office where they were interrogated, and statements were taken. They were then photographed and fingerprinted and lodged with the US marshal's office at West St. in NYC. Vincenzo and Carmine had refused to talk. After being fingerprinted and photographed, they were placed in a holding cell. Carmine made a telephone call to his attorney and waited for their lawyer. Carmine and Vincenzo were then moved to the West Street lockup. Several agents arrived at the warehouse to help inventory the seized merchandise, and Carmine's Caddy was also seized. The container, merchandise, and car were moved to the US Customs seizure facility at 201 Varick St. in Lower Manhattan.

The next day, they all were arraigned in the courthouse at Foley Square. The six loaders were released on a $1,000 surety bond. We had no case against them, so the AUSA dropped the charges against them. Carmine and Vincenzo were released on $100,000 bond. Sixteen months later, after the trial, Carmine got five-year sentence in jail. Vincenzo got five years, with two years suspended and three years' probation. It was a memorable experience. Now it was time to stop reminiscing and get some lunch.

Chapter 6

Stupid Customs Inspectors?

As I arrived at the Rockaway Boulevard Diner, I thought to myself, *not many law enforcement officers can say they put a couple of mob guy away*. I parked my car next to Cheech's car in the diner parking lot, and DJ and I went into the Diner. Cheech and Frank were already sitting in a booth. The waitress, Cindy, was just giving them the menus. As I walked down the aisle, I could not help focusing on Cindy's tight calf muscles. She had the legs of a dancer. She wore a pink uniform dress. The dress came to about two inches above her knees. It had white buttons down the front of the dress. The uniform fitted her like Saran wrap. The uniform emphasized every voluptuous curve on her five-foot-eight body. She was a thirty-six-year-old divorcee with no children. She had shoulder-length auburn hair and fair complexion; her lips were thin and coated with a glossy pink lipstick. She chewed juicy fruit gum and spoke with a strong Brooklyn accent. She flirted with all the men who came to the diner. This insured her of getting bigger tips.

DJ and I walked to the booth. DJ slid in, and I sat on the end. Frank and Cheech had already begun to flirt with Cindy. Cindy had her pad and pencil in hand and bent over and kissed me on the cheek, saying, "How is my favorite agent today?"

I said, "Great" as I winked at her.

Cheech said, "How come he gets a kiss? Where is mine?" She fired right back without batting an eye.

"Johnny is my special . . . special agent. What are you guys going to drink?" Coke, Coke, ice tea, and coffee black were the responses in quick order. Cindy wrote the order down, turned, and walked down the aisle, swaying her hips, just a little, as she turned between the two counters to get the glasses to fill the order.

I was grinning. Little did the guys know, I had been dating Cindy for about two months. We had to keep it a secret, especially where she worked, and she fully understood it. Most of the people who ate at the diner worked at the airport, and some of them knew that I worked at US Customs. I may have been observed showing up when uniformed customs officers stopped and searched cars and trucks on the airport roads. These searches sometimes uncovered stolen cargo or contraband.

People do not like to be stopped and have their cars searched when they are leaving the airport. Because of this, Cindy and I discussed keeping our dating to ourselves. Dating me could affect the tips she would receive from the airport workers. It also caused concern for her safety. A few shady characters ate and hung out at the diner. Her tips could also be affected if the truckers and cargo handlers, working for the airlines, thought that Cindy was dating someone and she was not available. She believed that she got good tips because she was flirtatious and the guys kept trying to date her. It was a male macho thing. Even I left large tips so she would remember me and give me extra attention. So we kept our relationship quiet.

I looked over the menu. The Diner special that day was pot roast, mashed potatoes with gravy, green beans, cup of split pea soup, corn bread and coffee with blueberry pie. All for only $3.75. Cindy returned with the drinks. After giving us our drinks, she took her pad from the pocket of the white lacy apron she wore. She took the pencil from her hair and said, "the special is pot roast. What are you guys going to have?"

Both Frank and I ordered the special. Cheech ordered the chicken parmesan platter with a Italian salad. DJ ordered the triple-decker BLT. I figured that I better make this my main meal for the day just in case I got a duty call and would have no time to eat at all. When you have the duty eating was catch as catch can. *Boy, was I right?*

The four of us talked shop about ongoing investigations from our office and the SAC, New York Office. Cindy returned with our orders. She placed them in front of us, asking if there was anything else we needed. We all said, one by one, "No" as if each one of us wanted to be the focus of her attention. We were all acting like little boys.

Cheech, leaning out of the booth, looking at Cindy as she walked away, said in a low voice, "Boy, I would love to have her wrap her legs around my neck."

Frank said, "She would probably strangle you."

I laughed and thought to myself, *She does have strong legs,* remembering our hour-long sex escapades of the other night. Cindy was reaching the big *O* as she tightly wrapped her legs around my body. She began squeezing her legs so tight that I thought she had broken my ribs. My ribs were saw all the next day, but it was well worth it for the extreme pleasure we both enjoyed.

We ate the food and continued to talk shop. Frank said, "Hey, Reno, I was talking to Inspector Wayne Harrison the other day, and he was telling me that you are his hero. Something about taking out a female passenger? What was that about? All the inspectors really look up to you. What is Harrison talking about?"

The guys were eager to hear about it, so I said, "Oh, it was nothing. It happened some time ago. Back when I was a customs investigator." I then began to tell them about the incident.

I had been observing the arriving passengers from a British flight. Nothing much was happening. My partner for working the arriving flights was Customs Investigator Willy Dean. Willy said he was going to the captain's office to fill out a leave blank. I said, "Okay. I'll be sitting by the search room." Willy left and went to the back stairway leading to the second floor where the captain's office was located. I walked between the inspection belts toward the bathrooms and search room. I sat down on the bench outside the search room next to the ladies' room. There were some bags next to me that someone left while going to the restroom.

I was looking at the passengers who arrived from London on a British flight and were getting their bags examined at the different customs examination belts. There had been strong head winds, and most flights were late. There were long lines, and the arriving passengers were irritable. Many had missed connecting flights. At the belt to my left was a couple with their backs to me. Inspector Wayne Harrison had begun to ask the passengers the normal routine questions, "May I have your customs declaration? How long were you gone? Was this business or pleasure? What countries did you visit? Did you declare all purchases and gifts acquired abroad? Do you have anything else that you may have failed to put on the declaration?"

There were two other flights on the floor, and two more had just landed. It was getting crowded in the arrivals area. People were in long lines at the various inspection belts with their baggage. One of the duties of the staff officer was to keep the people moving through customs as fast as possible. In order to achieve this, a staff officer would send a teletype to each customs inspection belt, notifying the inspector that rule 21 was in effect. Rule 21 meant that the inspector would ask the passenger if they had anything else to declare. If they said no, he would ask to see an item that was on the declaration. He then would check to see if their exemption was correct and figure out if there was any duty owed. Most people declared items that were free of duty and coupled with their exemptions would pay no duty. The inspectors were to look only in one bag and not to fully examine it. He would then sign off on the customs declaration and tell the passenger to hand the stamped and signed customs declaration to the guard at the exit. The passenger usually left happy.

This one couple on Inspector Harrison's belt were just handing him their customs declaration. The woman was about fifty-five years old. She was skinny. She must have weighed about 100 lbs. She was five foot seven inches tall with a light complexion. She had faded blond hair put up in a bun and a silly-looking flower hat. The woman wore a long, plaid olive green skirt with matching suit jacket. She had a light pink blouse under her jacket. She wore clear framed glasses. She had sharp facial features. She reminded me of an old-time school teacher that frightened the kids in her class.

The woman was becoming obnoxious in her answers to the inspector's questions. She was giving Inspector Harrison a hard time. When asked about the jewelry she declared on the declaration, her response was loud and in a demeaning tone. She took some receipts from her hand bag and threw them on the belt saying, "Here add them up. What do you think we are crooks?" She was asked if any of the jewelry she was wearing was purchased on this trip. She said, "I travel a lot. I purchased it several trips ago."

"Did you declare the jewelry then?" Inspector Harrison asked.

"Are you calling me a crook? I want to talk to a supervisor and report you." The woman turned to her red-faced husband and said, "The nerve of this man questioning me like that." Her henpecked husband reminded me of Mr. Peepers. He had hopelessly looked on and appeared to be embarrassed by his wife's actions. Inspector Harrison figured out the duty which came to about $30.

He signed the declaration and gave it to the husband and said, "Hand this to the guard on the way out, and the supervisor's office is right across from the guard."

The husband took their suitcases and put them on the baggage trolley and left the belt. As she turned away from the inspection belt, I could see a big smile on her face. It was like she got away with something. They walked several steps when she spotted the ladies' room. She told her husband to wait while she went to the ladies' room. When she came out, I overheard her tell her husband, "I just talked to a woman who told me that British Airways will send a representative in here to collect our baggage and take them to our connecting flight. You will not have to carry them."

She then told her husband, "Hurry to the lobby and get the airline representative to come get our bags. I will sit here and wait for you. Now hurry back." The woman sat down next to me. She looked very pleased with herself. Then she struck up a conversation with me, which I encouraged. She then asked me what flight I came on. I told her I came in on the *TWA* flight. I immediately asked her how she liked London and what other countries she had visited. Well, it did not take much prompting for her to show how affluent she was or alleged to be. I commented on the great bargains one received in Madrid and London.

I also told her how eager the clerks were to sell the merchandise that they offered to give me receipts showing I paid a lower price. She acknowledged that she got great bargains in jewelry and that the salesman, in order to make the sale, gave her duplicate receipts to give to customs for half the value.

I then said, "Please excuse me for my poor manners. I'm Johnny Reno."

She said, "It's okay. I'm Isabel Stanton from Georgia."

She then began to tell me how stupid customs inspectors were. She started to brag how easy it was to smuggle things through customs especially with the dumb inspectors. *Boy, could she berate someone?* She then told me that the inspector was so stupid that she was able to smuggle in a lot of jewelry and clothing. She went on to tell me that she got duplicate receipts for lower values for her clothing. Then she said, "I hid the actual receipts in my blouse." She was laughing about her accomplishments. All the time, I was agreeing and encouraging her to incriminate herself more. Every time she berated the customs inspector, she would raise her voice, knowing he could hear her.

I could see Inspectors Harrison's face as he glanced in my direction. His face was red because he could hear her calling him stupid. He knew she was mocking him. But he suddenly began to smile as if he knew something was up because he recognized me sitting next to her. After boasting to me about all the things she smuggled through customs and how dumb the inspector was, she said, "Johnny, what did you smuggle in?"

I reached into my pocket, saying to her, "I'll show you Isabel." I bent forward and looked from side to side to make sure that no one else was looking, and she followed suit by actually bending forward and looking in each direction. I took out my credentials case with my shiny gold badge inside. She must have thought it was a jewelry case. She said, "How much is the jewelry worth?"

I opened the case, pushing the badge about six inches from her face. I said "I'm a stupid US Customs agent. Your passport please!"

There was a two-second delay before it struck home. In those two seconds, she realized what she had done. Her eyes rolled back, and as she fell forward, she uttered a strange loud sound, like an animal in pain, "Oh!" She continued falling forward, collapsing onto the floor. I immediately stood up, putting my hands up in the air as if to say that I did not knock her over. I glanced at Inspector Harrison as he turned toward the sound, surmising that I got her and she was going to be searched. He brought his right arm with fist clinched across his body with a loud "Yes" that could be heard several belts away.

I picked Isabel up off the floor as a crowd began to form. I took her and her bags that were sitting on a baggage cart into the search room, which was only ten feet away. I called out to Inspector Harrison, who was still looking at us, "Call a staff officer." Inspector Harrison flipped on the staff officer alert switch. All inspection stations had two switches, one to notify agriculture of an agriculture seizure and the other to call for a customs supervisor for a problem or a seizure at the belt.

Staff Officer Lenny Sampton approached Inspector Harrison's belt. His face was red, and he was mad that he had to come down to the belt. Before he could admonish the inspector, Harrison yelled out, "The agents want you in the search room." So Sampton headed to the open search room door. I came out of the search room and told Sampton of the mocking of the inspector and her admissions of smuggling jewelry and clothing and that she had the true invoices in her blouse. Staff Officer Sampton's expression and attitude immediately changed. No one was going to call his inspectors stupid. The bottom line was I got Inspector Harrison off the inspection line to reexamine the woman's baggage. I seized the jewelry and clothing, and Staff Officer Sampton hit her with two times the domestic value for the jewelry and clothing.

It turned out she was also a bullshit artist. She exaggerated to me the true values of the goods she was smuggling in. The true value was only five thousand dollars. So I did not arrest her. We just hit her in the pocketbook where it hurt. When her husband returned, he almost had a heart attack. This turned out to be a very expensive trip for them. The guys were laughing. Frank almost choked on his drink. Cindy came back to our booth and asked if we needed anything else. We said, "No, just the check." She wrote out separate checks and left them on the table. As she turned, she winked at me and whispered in my ear, "Call me tonight." We finished our drinks and then we each put a buck down as a tip. We took the checks to the register where we each paid our own bill. We left and got into our cars, and DJ and I returned to the office.

We got back to the office at about 1:00 p.m. I picked up my telephone messages from Amanda. I then went back to my office and began returning the telephone calls and completing the paperwork that I had started earlier that morning. It must have been about one-thirty in the afternoon when my phone rang. I picked up the phone, and before I could say my name, the voice on the other end of the phone shrilled in a commanding voice, "Reno, the SAC wants to see you in his office now."

It was Lydia, the SAC's secretary. Lydia was a mature woman in her forties. She had thinning red hair and wore clear thick-framed glasses. She was big busted and was getting her middle-age spread. She had a shrilling voice when she raised it; otherwise, it was a normal voice when she spoke calmly and low. She was in higher pay grade than the other secretaries and supervised them and their work. I told her, "Okay, I'll be right there," and hung up the phone.

Being a special agent meant that you were constantly analyzing people and making decisions about them and their personalities. It could make or break a case and could save your life in dangerous situations. It came like second nature to me. I mention this because Lydia said; ". . . the SAC wants to see you . . . ," Not "the Duke wants to see you." The difference being that if she said Duke, then I would anticipate a casual bullshit session or something of no urgency. So, sensing the urgency, I picked up my coffee cup. The coffee was cold. I thought to myself, *I will warm it up on my way back from the SAC's office.* I picked a pad of paper from my desk. I walked down toward the SAC's office.

Philip Dukonis, also known as the Duke, was a Greek man, about forty-five years old, who stood about five feet, five inches tall and weighed about one hundred lbs. He had black hair with streaks of gray beginning on the sides. His hair was slicked back with short sideburns. He was always clean-shaven and wore expensive colognes. His suits were expensive and well fitted. His ties were also expensive looking.

He always hounded me to stop buying those cheap dollar store ties and to buy a couple of good ties, like his that cost him twenty-five dollars each. That would be the day when I would buy a tie for twenty-five dollars. I hated to wear a tie. I took mine off every chance I could. When you looked at Phil, you saw money. He looked, walked, and talked as if he was from money. I came to find out later that he was fairly well to do. He owned several tenement houses along the Brooklyn waterfront. Duke was a great boss. He knew the laws and regulations, and most of all, he had common sense. He was open-minded and fare. He was a good man to work for and learn about the job. He was not like some of the other supervisors I had worked for. *Boy, did I have some winners.*

Chapter 7

Flashback to Day One
at JFK Airport

Until 1947, LaGuardia airport was the only international airport in New York City. That changed. In 1942, the city of New York took 1,000 acres of land from the Idlewild golf course to build an airport. Construction began in 1943. In 1947, the port authority leased the airport. In July of 1948, the landing permits for international flights landing at LaGuardia airport were canceled, forcing all international flights to use Idlewild airport. December 24, 1963, one month after the assassination of President John F. Kennedy, the airport was renamed John F. Kennedy International Airport (JFK airport).

The international arrivals building (IAB) at JFK airport in Jamaica, New York, was barely handling the daily amount of arriving international passengers. The lines to clear government entry requirements were always long at immigration and in the customs area. The traveling public were usually mad and irritable by the time they got to the customs clearance area. Passengers traveled across the Atlantic from Europe for eight to twelve hours. Then their airplanes would be circling the airport for another hour or more before landing. When their flight finally landed, they would taxi to a holding area and had to wait sometimes an hour or two just to taxi to a gate. Then you had the long lines in immigration. After getting through immigration, you now had to wait for the airlines to deliver the baggage to the customs carrousel. Once you got your baggage, you look for the shortest line.

Plans were underway to expand the existing terminals, and major airlines were all planning and constructing new terminals. *Pan American* airlines opened its terminal in 1960 and *Trans World* airlines opened their terminal in 1962. The IAB terminal was a large, very long rectangular building with perpendicular finger piers, which would allow a greater number of aircraft to park, thus increasing the amount of people bottlenecking at the stretched government facilities. In front of the terminal was a huge parking lot that accommodated several hundred cars. Two-way roadways ran from the entrance of the airport, around the parking lot, in front of the IAB and back around the parking lot to the airport exit. The roadway in front of the IAB was separated by a medium with walkways going from the IAB to the parking lot. In the parking lot in the front of the IAB entrance was a tall building. It was the airport control tower. The port authority maintained offices in this building. It is also where airport employees got their parking passes for a small sum. This allowed them to park in the employees' parking lot that was adjacent to the roadway at the front left of the IAB.

When you entered the IAB through the main doors, you entered a large hall with airline counters around the perimeter of the building. Each airline had or shared a flight arrival board on the wall in back of an airline desk. The arrival board would let visitors know when a particular airline flight was scheduled to arrive and when the flight had actually landed. After you entered the building's front entrance, looking directly in front of you about 800 feet, were eight frosted glass doors. Each door had a blue and gold customs seals. Each door said, "Do not enter. Restricted area." There was a large sign over the doors saying "US CUSTOMS." On the right in about the middle of the lobby was an escalator that took people to and from the second floor. When you got off the escalator, on the second floor, you could walk straight into a restaurant. If you took a left and walked about twenty feet, you came to these huge ceiling-to-floor glass walls. The glass panels must have been at least twelve feet wide and twenty to twenty-five feet high. They must have been at least an inch or two thick. The walls formed a *U*, twenty feet wide and over a hundred feet long. There were brown leather benches with no backs, about ten feet apart all around the glass enclosure. People could sit and watch passengers getting their baggage examined by customs inspectors below. This area was referred to as the fish bowl.

On this upper level, there was an international currency exchange office where people could exchange their foreign currency. The office was halfway down the hall, facing the glass wall. Some airlines had VIP lounges there also. The customs enforcement office, customs inspector swing room, and locker rooms were also located behind one of the unmarked doors. In fact, none of the doors in the U-shaped area were marked. Only an emergency exit door and the currency exchange door were marked.

Customs hated the idea of having the fish bowl. If an inspector found narcotics in a passenger's bag, it could be observed from above by a conspirator who might be watching from above. People could also look down and see the inspectors examining jewelry, diamonds, and large sums of currency. This put the passenger at risk. But politics prevailed. The port authority, which ran the airport, insisted on this feature so the mass crowds that came to meet the arriving passengers each day would have a place to go. An identical east wing was being constructed. This would double the customs and immigration areas as well as the public viewing area. The west wing would accommodate the additional flights and passengers and disburse the increased amount of people coming to meet the arriving passengers. Pan American was building their own airline terminal next to the west wing of the IAB. TWA was building their airline terminal next to the east wing of the IAB. JFK airport was in the midst of a great expansion in the 1960s.

Downstairs, behind the eight double frosted glass doors inside the restricted customs area was where all the action took place. There were usually two armed uniformed customs enforcement officers whose job was to keep the public out, especially at peak arrival times, which were between 1:00 p.m. and 10:00 p.m. each day. Skycaps were going in and out of the glass doors with their baggage carts to serve arriving passengers. People would continually try to sneak in past the guards or would want to talk to the supervisor on duty.

When the international passengers completed their customs examination, the customs officer would stamp their baggage declaration. Those that had to pay customs duties and taxes would then go to the customs cashier. The cashier's office was just before the exit. The cashier would take their declaration and money and give them a receipt, which they would show to the guard at the door. Those passengers who had no customs duties to pay gave their stamped customs declaration to the guards at the door. The skycaps knew the routine, and they made sure that the passenger whose bags they were carrying had the stamped declaration or receipt ready to hand or show to the guards.

When you first walk through the glass doors going into the restricted area, the first thing you would see was a glass structure which contained three offices. These were the customs supervisory staff officers work place. Picture ten-foot clear glass panels mounted on three-foot-high blue metal wall bases. These three offices took up the width of the eight glass entrance double doors. Customs inspectors and clerical staff were in the first office. The middle office was where the supervisory staff officers were located, and the third smaller office was the baggage declaration office with clerical staff who processed the baggage declarations for each flight.

There was a walkway about fifteen feet wide and three hundred feet long from the front of the staff offices to the end of the building. At the end of the building was a passage way leading into the immigration area, where passengers lined up at immigration booths. Along the left wall, just before the staff office was the cashier's office. Then came a diplomatic scale used for diplomatic baggage inspections. Further down the walk was a couple of brown leather benches with no backs against the wall. Then came the male and female restrooms. A few feet further was the customs search room. It was a twelve-by-twelve foot room. Along the right wall of the room was a twelve-foot tan leather bench. A gray metal table stood in front of the bench. There were also two gray metal chairs in the room.

To the right of the walkway was ten double conveyor belts. These belts were where the customs inspectors examined the incoming passengers' baggage. Each double belts contained a teletype machine that alerted inspectors about suspects on the incoming flights. There were a red button and a green button at each belt. The red button was used to call for a customs supervisor, and the green button was used to call for an agriculture inspector when food or plant material was found in the suitcases. If you looked up from any of the belts, except the one next to the staff office, you could see the public looking down at you. People would bang on the glass walls and make a racket just to get the attention of an arriving passenger. About twenty feet back from the inspection belts were several two-by-two-foot pillars that held up the second story of the building. Just beyond the pillars were six carousel conveyer belts. Each carousel was like a long oval protruding from the rear wall of the building. Belly bags would be taken from the airplane's belly and put on baggage carts and pulled to the rear of the arrivals building. There the baggage handlers would place the bags from the cart onto the conveyer belt, bringing the bags into the arrival area. Passengers would then retrieve their bags and put them on a trolley and bring them to an inspection belt for their customs examination.

One of the most vindictive supervisors I had ever worked for was named Eddie Mac. He was my first supervisor at the IAB, JFK airport. Mac was in charge of the uniformed customs enforcement officers (CEO) and plainclothes customs port investigators (CPI) working at JFK. He was a sixty-six-year-old man, who looked like he was fifty-eight. He was six foot, weighed about 300 lbs, and he had a beer barrel belly that hung over his trouser belt. He did have a full thick head of black and gray hair. He was always clean-shaven, which revealed a face riddled with pot marks. His nose was no exception; it was huge, red, and fat, with pot marks. He was second-generation Irish and spoke with a little Irish brogue. He usually wore a plaid, checkered green sport jacket with brown pants. He always wore a white shirt. When he wore a tie, it would always clash with his jacket. In the summer, he usually did not wear a tie. He always kept his collar open whether he wore a tie or not.

Mac had what I now believe was TMJ (Temporomandibular a joint disorder). Whenever Mac would talk to anyone, he would move his left shoulder upward and tilt his head to his left. His mouth would open slightly and went to the right. He would utter a half sentence and then do the motion again and then finish the sentence without the movement. It was strange to watch. He had a strange aura. Talking to Mac one-on-one gave you a strange feeling. You thought you were talking to a mobster, not a law enforcement officer. He reminded me of the gangster roles played by both Edward G. Robinson (repeating himself) and James F. Cagney (saying, "OK, OK, you dirty double-crossing rats").

Mac went out of his way to hurt his employees, and the paybacks he got were funny, and I guess, in some sense, just. I was told that over the last couple of years, Mac received, at his home, a refrigerator, a stove, several heating pads, two tons of sand, a number of small appliances, lots of books, and subscriptions for magazines and even two blue bowling balls, all of which he never ordered. From what I heard, Mac did not get along with his neighbors either. He thrived on trying to screw people whether it was his neighbors or the people who worked for him.

Mac always worked the day shift, 8:00 a.m. to 4:30 p.m., Monday through Friday. He would come in early and try to catch one of his employees coming in late. He would dock you one hour for being five minutes late by his watch, not yours. I overheard him bragging to one of his sergeant that he actually set his watch and the office clock two minutes fast so if by the clock on the wall, you were less than five minutes late, he could give you a lecture and tell you he was giving you a break this time. But if you were on his shit list that week, you got docked the hour leave for being late.

Mac made up the initial work schedule. He made sure that when uniformed CEOs finished their eight-to-four shift, they would be scheduled to return at midnight for the midnight-to-eight shift, thus a short swing. There was really no need for anyone to get a short swing. If CEOs who were assigned to plainclothes duty got on Mac's shit list before the biweekly work schedule was put out, Mac would go out of his way to make sure the sergeant would place him back in uniform and schedule him for a short swing. When he was really pissed off at a CEO, he would schedule the man to work a 3:00 p.m. to 11:00 p.m. shift, with Tuesday and Wednesday as day off. Then on Sunday, he would schedule him to work 12:00 midnight to 8:00 a.m. shift. He would laugh when he put someone on the extra short shift. He would try to jam you up for just coming to work. He would really try to get certain individuals.

Ralph Cippy was Italian. He was thirty-five years old. Ralph was a customs CEO assigned to plainclothes most of the time. He was married and had three kids. Mac found something wrong with everyone. One day, Ralph Cippy and I had just signed in. We were both leaving the office. Mac told me to stay behind. Ralph left the office. Mac called me over to the window. Looking out the window at the *U*-shaped tarmac, we could see several airplane arrival gates on each side. I assumed that Mac was going to instruct me to do some enforcement action on the tarmac. Wrong! Mac told me, out of the corner of his mouth with his head twitching to the left, "You see that Guinea prick that just left." His head came back to a normal position and then twitched back to the left as he continued to speak, "He's got three kids." His head came back to a normal position. Then as he twitched again with his head going to the left and out of the corner of his mouth said, "He thinks he's a rabbit, making all those kids." He would twitch sometimes two or three times before he got the whole sentence out. "I know he has his kids communion next weekend (twitch), and I am going to make him work Sunday. (Twitch) I'm going to change (twitch) his schedule and cool him off." Mac changed the two-week schedules right in front of me. Ralph was on the plainclothes schedule to work from 2:00 p.m. to 10:00 p.m. with Sundays and Saturdays off. Mac changed Ralph's day off to Tuesday and Wednesday and then scheduled him to be on the uniform schedule for the 8:00 a.m. to 4:00 p.m. shift. Now Ralph was scheduled to work on Sunday, the day of his kid's communion. Well, Ralph banged in sick on Saturday and Sunday. Then Ralph found himself in uniform for a month until someone else got on Mac's shit list.

Mac ate his lunch at his desk, in his office, every day. He would leave his office each day after lunch between 1:30 and 2:30. He would go downstairs to the passenger area. He would do this once a day. It became his routine. He would go to the staff office to bitch to them about what a bunch of bums he had to supervise. The staff officers, without exception, hated him with a passion.

After Mac had pissed off the staff officer or his office staff, Mac would try to sneak into the passenger area. He would try to hide in the working area and try to see if you and your assigned partner were too close to each other. The airport had terrazzo floor tiles that were four-by-four foot squares. Mac would try to hide behind a pole or column and peek out to see if you and your partner were standing in the same square. If you were standing in the same square, he would write you up. Mac's analogy was if you were close enough to each other, you would be talking and not looking at the passengers.

We all knew when Mac was on the floor trying to hide behind a pole. He had a huge beer belly that stuck out past the pole. Mac was so caught up in his bitterness that he could not see the obvious. The staff officers had a standing order that when Mac came on the floor or in their office, they would make an announcement on the PA system. You would hear, "Inspector Ed, catch 'um to the staff office." Well, we all knew Mac was there. He was not going to catch anyone today. Mac never caught on.

Everyone hated Mac, and his sergeants were no exception. He was the only supervisor I ever knew who kept on getting things sent to his house. Anything that came with a free home trial was sent to Mac. He even got a truck load of gravel dumped in his driveway. Getting these things shipped to him really infuriated him. He complained to the sergeants about getting these things and that he thought it was one of the staff officers because he thought they were jealous of his authority and position. Mac was mad because he or his wife did not order the things and someone was playing a practical joke on him. Little did he know that one of the sergeants he complained to was one of the guys sending him a lot of things. It was like a contest of who could send Mac an item that would really get him mad.

One day, after I signed in and was on my way out of the office, Mac called me back. We were the only ones in the office. He closed the door and walked over to the window and then called me over to him. Mac always liked to talk at the window. Why, I do not know. With his wispy voice and usual twitching, Mac told me, "Reno, (twitch) you're not like (twitch) those other pricks (twitch). You know, (twitch) yesterday someone sent (twitch) two blue bowling balls to by wife. They think

I don't know (twitch) what it means. I want you to keep (twitch) your ears open (twitch). Find out who the prick is (twitch) that is sending my wife blue balls (twitch). When I find out who the prick is (twitch), I'm going to give him blue balls (twitch) by shoving the balls up his ass."

I instantly knew why his wife got the blue balls and had all to do to keep from laughing. Every inspector and investigator and even the airline ground representatives were laughing for over a week about Mac's blue balls.

When Mac was off, he would leave his wife a list of things he wanted done at the airport while he was down at the local pub. His wife would call the sergeant on duty and have him change the schedule of individuals, for no apparent reason. His standing orders were, if his wife called and said to do something, she was acting on his orders and you would have to do it. I came to find out that the reason Mac could do no wrong was because his brother-in-law was the assistant supervising customs agent in New York City.

Chapter 8

Two Suitcases of Hashish

As I walked from my office into the SAC office, a distinguished-looking man, in a shark skin gray suit, with a red and gray silk tie, sat behind a large wooden desk. He looked like a professor with those funny-looking Ben Franklin glasses sitting on the tip of his nose.

The Duke stared up at me and said, "Reno, I got a call from John Trent, the RAC (resident agent in charge), Nashville. A guy by the name of Darnovski, from Austria, will be arriving in New York at LaGuardia airport around 6:00 p.m. with a military gunsight camera in a green suitcase. Agent Harris is on the flight shadowing Darnovski now. Supervisory Agent Tony Peters from Chicago called and told me that they have Darnovski under surveillance in the airport. His flight is scheduled to leave at 3:45 p.m. A man traveling with Darnovski by the name of Bron took a flight to Canada. The green suitcase containing the camera is being loaded on the flight for New York. Peters will call you when the airplane departs for New York.

"We believe that Darnovski is going to attempt to leave the US with the gunsight camera. We think it may be transshipped to Russia. John Trent in Nashville talked to AUSA Farmer about the case and said he should be arrested as he attempts to leave the US. We don't know if he'll leave the US and go to Canada or directly to Europe. Set up an around-the-clock surveillance on this guy for as long as he stays in the US. That camera must not leave the US. You got it?"

I said, "I got it." The Duke handed me a sheet of paper filled with notes he had taken.

"You are the duty agent today, and I am assigning you this case." The Duke went on to say that he called John Falcon, SAC NYC office, and asked him to have the undercover cab at LaGuardia, American airlines terminal by 5:00 p.m. Falcon would have two guys on standby in the city in case Darnovski went to Manhattan. The Duke then told me to see who was available in the office and take a couple of guys to work the surveillance.

"It is all yours. I know you can do a great job on this case. And, Reno, I want to be briefed on what is going on in this case. Headquarters is aware of the case, and I need to know what is going on so I can keep them off my back." I told the Duke that I would get right on it. I got up and left his office.

I could feel my heart pounding. The adrenalin was pumping. My heart was racing faster. As I walked back to my office, the reality of what just happened was beginning to sink in. I just knew that this was a major investigation now that headquarters in Washington, DC was monitoring the case. I was getting excited. My mind was racing in fast forward. *What are all the things that have to be done? What are they?* I thought to myself, *Relax, this case is just like any other case you worked. Go back to your office, sit down, take a sip of your coffee, and do what comes natural.* Knowing that I have had many other investigations thrust upon me in the spur of the moment like this put me at ease. I went to my office, put the papers on my desk, and sat back in my chair.

My mind was racing. In a moment, instant recall clicked in, and my mind flashed back to the most recent spur-of-the-moment case I had just completed. Several months earlier, I had gone to the international arrival building (IAB) in the late morning. I had parked my government car on the tarmac in back of the IAB. There were several reserved spots. One was for customs inspection. Two were for customs agents, and one was for the port authority police. The morning flights were finished. I was walking to the staff offices when came upon Elsa, a Lufthansa airline representative, who was checking the leftover baggage from the morning flights. There were about fifteen bags, which passengers did not claim. Due to bad weather in Europe, passengers with connecting flights made the flights, but their bags did not. They followed on the next flight. Now the airlines would have to contact the people and have the bags forwarded to them.

I had worked with and partied with many of the ground representatives from the different airlines. I had also been to some wild airline parties that Elsa also attended, and we became more than just friends. Elsa was one of the woman I had not actually taken out on a date.

To me, the airport was like a candy store. It was apparent to me that a number of the female airline employees were mesmerized with the inspectors and the authority they wielded, which led to many office romances. Customs special agent, like me, were always in plainclothes. In almost all our cases involving arrest and seizures, we solicited assistance from these very same ground representatives. They were able to get us manifest passenger list and ticketing information faster than going through their management. They felt like they were part of the ongoing investigation. It was as if they personally knew a secret agent, a man who dealt in deception and intrigue. We were the James Bonds and 007s of customs to many of these women. In fact my badge and credentials had the number 0044, which added to their fantasy. They wanted to feel as if they were part of the intrigue. They wanted to be able to tell their coworkers and friends they were part of what was going on. They were looking for any little morsel of information they could obtain. But that is another story.

I approached Elsa and the leftover baggage. I asked Elsa if all the bags were cleared by customs. She said, "Yes, Tonto cleared them. He is in the ships office." Tonto was short for Inspector Tontochelli. Tonto was always assigned to the ship or crew office, where the airline crews cleared customs. When a passenger carried a commercial shipment, they would have to post enter the shipment in the ship's office. The customs investigators had a search room or office within the ships office.

Elsa was checking the baggage tags and recording the information on her leftover baggage sheet for the fifteen bags on the floor. I was checking her out. She was squatted down with clipboard and pencil in hand. I squatted down a few feet opposite her, pretending to be looking at a large green suitcase. In reality, I was looking where I was not supposed to. Elsa had milk-white thighs, but I had already known that. She knew I was looking at her legs. She smiled and stuck out her tongue and licked her lips. She said in a slow, sexy voice, "Johnny, do you want to help me take these bags to my leftover baggage room?" I immediately knew what she meant. I could read it in her eyes, and I had been to the leftover baggage room with Elsa before. Elsa just loved to perform oral sex, and she was very good at it.

As I gazed upon Elsa's lovely red lips, she placed her finger in her mouth and began to suck on her finger, and she spread her legs open as far as her skirt would allow her.

I abruptly attempted to stand up by leaning on the green suitcase next to me. I grabbed the handle and found it was hard to move the suitcase. I then stood firmly on the ground and attempted to lift the large green suitcase. It was heavy. Instantly, all thoughts of sexual gratification left my head. I thought to myself, *That's odd. This suitcase must weigh about 70 lbs.* I looked at the baggage claim tag. The bag originated in Berlin. Looking at the group of bags, I spotted another identical green suitcase. I looked at the tag, and it was also coming from Berlin. The tags were in sequential order. This intrigued me. I then looked at the tags from the other bags. These were the only two with their numbers in order. The other bags also came from Berlin. I asked Elsa to open the locks on the two bags while I got Tonto.

I then went back into the crew clearance office and asked Tonto if the bags were cleared, and he said yes. I then asked if they were opened and examined. He said, "No, I just opened two of them. I stamped all the tags."

I said, "OK." I left the office and went back to Elsa and the leftover bags. Elsa had a ring of about a hundred keys. She was still trying keys when I returned. Several keys later, Elsa said, "This one works."

She opened the lock. I lifted the suitcase top, and lo and behold, there was a suitcase filled with bars of hashish. Each bar was about four inches wide by nine inches long and one inch thick. Each was wrapped in wax paper and then wrapped in plastic. Elsa opened the second bag, and it too contained nothing but hashish bars. We opened up all the other bags, but none of the others contained hashish.

I told Elsa that I needed to know whose bags these were and where they were going. "I'll go back to my office and see if I have the missing baggage reports on these bags, and I will try to get you the baggage history from Berlin and Munich," Elsa replied.

I said, "Elsa, try to get the names and the history for the five tag numbers before and after the two green bags." I also asked her to get the complete passenger list from both Berlin and Munich. Elsa winked and puckered a kiss to me and said, "Later, Johnny." She turned and then hurried off to get the information from her office. She said she would return with whatever information she had and would start the inquiry in Germany.

I then took the two green suitcases and put them on a baggage cart. I pushed the cart to the investigative office within the ships office. Tonto came into the room and assisted me. We used the scale in the ships office to weigh each bag. Each one weighed 75 lbs. I dated and initialed the baggage tags. We counted all the bricks in each of the bag. On one of the bricks in each bag, I placed my initials and date on the outer wrapper in an inconspicuous place. I also weighed one brick from each bag.

I opened my attaché case and quickly filled out a seizure report with all the information I had, and I filled out a chain of custody form also. Tonto had notified Staff Officer John Horiwitz that I found hashish in the two leftover bags. John then got on the address system and asked all inspectors to immediately come to the ships office. John then brought out a Polaroid camera, and we took several pictures for my file and for him to show the inspectors what to look for. Several of the inspectors that were in the area came to look at the bags and the content. Then I closed the bags, locked them, and put them back on the cart. I pushed the cart to the agents surveillance office.

The office was to the left of the main exit to the lobby and across from the staff office. The glass walls had floor-to-ceiling blinds so no one could see into the office. In the office, we had a closed-circuit TV system that was monitoring several areas at the IAB and tarmac. I had the two suitcases on the cart with me in the small office. I closed the door and sat on the corner of the desk.

I completed some of the necessary paperwork. I picked up the phone and called the SAC office and spoke to Amanda. None of the agents were in, and the Duke was out also. Amanda took down the information about the seizure. I told her to give the information to the Duke when he returned.

In less than half an hour, Elsa was back with papers in hand. Elsa knocked on the door, and I told her to come in. She came in the office and stood next to me with papers in her hand. I could see the excitement in Elsa's face. She was allowed into the agent's inner sanctum. I could see the look in her eyes. I have seen that look before. She was excited, and she felt like she was privileged to be a party to information and what was going on. Even the customs inspectors had to remain outside the agent's office. The television monitor was off, so Elsa did not know that it was a surveillance system.

She provided me with a passenger list for the flight from the day before which the bags were originally supposed to be on. She told me that all the leftover bags were from passengers who boarded in Berlin. The Berlin flight had been delayed, and the passengers just made their connection in Munich. Their bags did not make the flight. The bags were then forwarded on the next flight to JFK. The passengers came in yesterday, and their bags arrived this morning.

She also provided me with the original missing baggage reports and the Berlin passenger list. She highlighted two names with consecutive airline ticket numbers purchased in Berlin. One was Mr. Frederick Campell, who checked one suitcase in Berlin. The other was Mr. Victor Klienman, who also checked one suitcase in Berlin. Mr. Frederick Campell's lost baggage report gave a contact phone number in Pittsburgh with no address. He attached two baggage claim checks. Mr. Klienman did not fill out a lost baggage claim.

I placed a call to my office. Nadine answered the phone this time and said that all the agents were still out of the office. Duke has not checked in yet. I gave her the information about the two suitcases full of hash I seized. I told her to run a background check in treasury enforcement communications system (TECS) on the two names I had. I asked her to call the Philadelphia office and have them run a crisscross directory check on the phone number Campell gave the airline. Pittsburgh was under the Philadelphia office jurisdiction. I told her I would call her later to get any info she had or she could reach me on the radio.

I asked Elsa if she was calm enough to call Mr. Campell's contact number and inform him that his bags were ready for pickup. Elsa put her finger on my lips as if to say to me that I did not have to say another word and that she would handle it. She then said, "This is what I would normally do."

"Ask him where he wants the bags sent," I said. "If Mr. Campell asked, tell him the bags cleared customs with no problems. I am going to put you on the speaker phone." Elsa dialed the number, and a woman answered. She claimed to be Mr. Campell's mother. She said her son wanted the bags sent to Pittsburgh where her son would pick them up. I nodded the OK to Elsa. Elsa said, "Okay."

The woman asked when the bags would be there, and Elsa said, "I will put the two bags on the next available flight to Pittsburgh. You should have them by about four o'clock today." The woman said OK and that she would wait for a call from the airline, and her son would go down and pick them up. She did not want them delivered to her house because they were her son's bags.

Elsa hung up the phone. Elsa said, looking at her watch, "The next flight to Pittsburgh is at 2:15 p.m. today." It was amazing how the ground reps knew the flight schedules. "Delta handles our traffic to Pittsburgh," she said. I asked her if she knew the number of Delta's manager. She pulled out her trusty guide and gave me the manager's name and phone number. It was Tim Brant, and I knew him from attending the airport security managers' monthly meeting.

I picked up the phone and dialed his number. Elsa was standing real close to me. As I waited for the phone to be answered, I could feel Elsa's hand rubbing on my leg. She was frisky. As she moved her hand to the inside of my thigh, I could feel the excitement, and I was getting turned on. I put my hand over the mouthpiece and told her, "Later," as I stood up. She moved toward the door, turned her head and puckered me a kiss, winked, and left the office.

Tim answered the phone, and I told him of the urgency and that I needed to be on that flight with the two bags. I told him I was making a controlled delivery of narcotics, and I had to verify that the baggage were on and sealed in the aircraft and be present when the belly doors were opened again. He said he would set it up and would meet me planeside in half an hour.

I opened my attaché case and took out the book of government transportation requests (GTR). The GTR was a book of blank government tickets good on any airline at any time. I could write my own ticket whenever the situation arose. I made out one set and placed it in my jacket pocket.

I called Nadine back; no one had returned to the office. The background checks were negative. She gave me the address of Mrs. Campell in Pittsburgh. I told her that I was taking two suitcases of hashish and was going to Pittsburgh to make a controlled delivery. I asked her to notify the Philly office, which covered Pittsburgh, and tell them that I was en route to Pittsburgh and would be in contact with them on my arrival in Pittsburgh. I thought to myself. *All bases are covered.* I took my blue trench coat from the coat tree, put my attaché case on the two bags, and pushed the cart out of the office.

I had Tonto take me and the two bags to Delta planeside with the inspector's car. I had my own G-cars parked in back of the IAB on the tarmac. It would stay there until I returned. We arrived at Delta's departure gate, and Tim and a ramp man were planeside waiting for me. Tim said, "We have to hurry. The flight has to leave in three minutes."

I said, "Here are the bags." A ramp man took the two green bags and put them into the belly and locked the belly door. The stewardess was standing in the aircraft door. I gave Tim my GTR. Then Tim said, "Oh, we have a full load. You will have to fly jump seat."

I said, "OK." I then went up the portable stairs to the aircraft door. I said hello to the stewardess. She opened the cockpit door, and I entered the cockpit.

I took out my credentials to show to the captain. He said, "There will be time for that later." The stewardess closed the door as she left the cockpit. The copilot locked the door.

The captain said, "Pull down the folded seat on the rear wall." The captain told the copilot, "Let's take her out." We taxied away from the gate and pulled up in back of another aircraft that was about to take off. The co-pilot said, "We are third." The captain then said, "Let's see the credentials, lad." I gave him the credentials with badge. He handed them back to me and asked me about the case. I told him I had two suitcases of narcotics and I was making a controlled delivery in Pittsburgh.

The co-pilot interrupted, "Captain, we're cleared for takeoff on one-niner east."

The captain said, "Buckle up. Bill, hand me the flight manual." Bill pulled out a large loose-leaf book and handed it to the captain. I sat there looking at all the instruments.

The captain said, "You will have to bear with me, son. This is my first flight solo. But don't worry. Bill here has been flying a long time." I laughed and surmised that they were playing a joke on me.

Then the co-pilot said, "Captain, I have been flying a long time, but this is my first flight in the cockpit of a passenger plane. I flew helicopters only."

The captain then handed the loose-leaf book to the co-pilot and said, "Here, you look up what has to be done, and you tell me which thing makes the plane go up."

The co-pilot took the book and said, "I think you have to pull back on that gear shift in the middle," as the airplane roared down the runway at 180 miles an hour and gaining speed.

Playing along with them, I said, "Oh shit! I hope you guys are kidding me."

They busted out laughing. "Yeah, we are only playing with you, kid." The flight to Pittsburgh was a quick one. It took about thirty-five minutes. We climbed to 20,000 feet, and then we started the decent. It was up and then down. The plane landed and came to a stop at the terminal gate.

I exited the cockpit and was first off the plane. The Delta Manager Bill Hadden met me at the door and took me to the belly of the aircraft. The ramp crew opened the belly and removed the two green bags. The ramp man placed the two bags on a cart, and Bill drove the baggage cart with me and the two bags to his office. We brought the bags into his office.

It was now after three o'clock. Bill placed a call to the telephone contact number. A woman identifying herself as Mr. Campell's mother answered the phone. He told her that her son's suitcases had arrived and that the office would be opened until six o'clock. The woman said that her son called and was still in Newark, New Jersey, and that he wanted the bags sent to him there. Bill, placing his hand over the mouthpiece said, "She wants the bags sent to Newark." I shook my head okay. He told the woman that he would send them to Newark on the next available flight. He asked her for a Newark contact number so the airline could call her when the bags had arrived. She gave him a number and said, if no one answered, to call her for further instructions. He jotted down the information and hung up the phone.

The manager turned to me and said, "If you are going to Newark, the flight you came in on is doing a turnaround and due to go to Newark and then JFK."

I said, "Well, I guess I'm going to Newark." I made out another GTR and then made a call to Newark, SAC office. I briefed Duty Agent Kelmar, and he said he would meet the flight. I gave him my Delta flight number. The manager and I then took the bags and loaded them on the plane as before. They were the last ones placed on the plane. I then boarded the flight and again sat in the jump seat. I had a few laughs with the same crew, and before I knew it, we had landed in Newark.

Agent Kelmar and Delta Manager Joe Berger met me when the plane door opened. We went to the belly of the aircraft and retrieved the two bags. We took them into the Delta office, and Joe called the number the woman had given to me. The number had been disconnected. Joe then called the original number, and Mrs. Campell answered and said that she had another number where we could reach her son. He had just called her with it. Joe repeated the number as he wrote it down. I recognized the number to be a New York area code number. The extension 1462 confirmed my suspicion that the number was a hotel and the extension was a hotel room number.

Joe Berger then called the new number. A man answered the phone.

Joe said, "This is Joe Berger from Delta airlines in Newark, New Jersey. Is Mr. Campell their?" The man on the other end said he was Mr. Campell.

"Mr. Campell, I have two bags here and was given this number to contact you. Our office will be open until 9:00 p.m. You have to pick them up before then."

Mr. Campell said that he wanted the bags delivered to his hotel, the Waldorf Astoria in New York City. Joe told him he was not operating a delivery service and he would have to come to the office to pick up the bags. He further told him that the airline paid for the shipping to Pittsburgh and then to Newark and that Campell would have to come to Newark to pick the bags up. Campell insisted on having the bags sent to his hotel room and said that he would pay the cost to have the bags sent to his hotel and delivered to his room, but he needed the bags tonight because he had a flight out of town early the next morning. Joe told him he could not do that because he had to sign for the bags.

Campell asked, "Could you put the bags in a cab and I will pay the cost of the cab ride to the hotel and when he delivers the bags to me, I will include a $25 tip and sign your papers?"

Joe said, "I will see if I could get a taxicab to make the delivery and would call you back." Joe asked him for his room number and he said 1462.

I called the SAC Office New York and spoke to the duty agent, Vince Morano. I briefed him on the drug case and the information I had on Mr. Campell, including his hotel and room number. Vince said he would notify Eddy Kent, the soft drug squad supervisor. They will set up the surveillance at the hotel. I told him that I would be arriving at the hotel in about two hour with Agent Kelmar. I sat back in a swivel chair and took a deep breath. The manager brought us each a cup of black coffee. I sat there a few moments and sipped the warm coffee.

I relaxed little more; Joe Berger picked up the phone again and called Mr. Campell back and told him that he finally got a cab that agreed to deliver the two bags along with the airline release papers to sign with a return envelope for the cab driver to mail the release papers back. He told him the fare would be $75 plus a twenty-five dollar tip. Campell agreed.

Ed and I took the suitcases and placed them in the trunk of Ed's G-car. I got on the radio and called to the New York base station.

"644 to 100. Over."

"100 to 644."

"100 contact 221 and tell him we are en route to subject's hotel. Over."

"100 to 644, 10-4."

A minute later, the radio blared. "644 this is 221. Go to secure Channel 3. Over."

I switched the radio to secure Channel 3. "644 this is 221. Can you read me? Over."

"Loud and clear. Over."

"644 park on East Forty-Seventh Street and Park Ave in back of a cab with blinking lights. Over."

"644 to 221, 10-4."

It would be our cab with the blinking lights in case the subject or one of his associates was watching the hotel entrances.

The drive from Newark airport to the Waldorf Astoria took about twenty minutes. We pulled up behind the blinking cab two blocks from the Waldorf. I got out of Kelmar's car and approached the cab driver. It was Agent Vince Morano. "Hey, Vince. How are you doing?"

"OK, Reno," he said.

Agent Kelmar transferred the two bags from the car to the cab trunk. Vince gave me the keys of the cab and said, "You are going to make the delivery. We are going to see if anyone is following you. We have a room across the hall from the subject's room. There has been no telephone activity from the room. We want you to make the delivery. Then in ten minutes, you have to go back to get them to open the door for the bust. We have to see if there is any telephone activity once they have the junk."

I said, "OK."

I then took off my suit jacket and placed in the car and put on my blue rain coat, which had now been noticeably wrinkled. I put on a gray tweed cap. As a precaution, I placed my gun and credential in my attaché case and gave it to Agent Kelmar to hold for me, just in case I was searched. If they did search me, they would believe that I was only a cab driver, not a federal agent. Vince told me that the hotel registration indicated that Mr. Campbell and a Mr. Klienman were registered in room 1462. Vince said that two men in their twenties were observed entering the room a few minutes ago.

I took the keys from Vince and drove the cab to the entrance of the Waldorf Astoria. I parked in front of the entrance. Prearranged through security, I was able to take a waiting bellman luggage cart. I put the two bags on the cart and proceeded to the elevator. No one got on the elevator with me. I exited the elevator and was met by Vince who said, "We know there are two others in the room with Campell."

Vince wanted me to attempt to gain entrance into the room to see if I could tell how many others were with Campell and if I could see any firearms in view. As I proceeded to the room, I could hear Vince say, "We got your back." *Comforting words*, I thought. Now I had to go into my act. I did a lot of role playing both officially and unofficially, but those are other stories.

As I walked down the hallway, I could not help noticing the carpeted floor with its dark colors and intricate woven design. The hallway was dimly lit by its ivory color wall sconces. Room 1462 was the number on the wall plaque adjacent to the door. It was halfway down the hall. I took a deep breath, exhaled, and knocked on the door.

I could hear scurrying and some voices and then a moment of silence. A voice from the other side of the door said, "Who is it?" I could feel eyes peeking at me through the peephole.

I replied, "Yellow cab company with two bags for a Mr. Campell." I could hear more footsteps coming to the door.

I could hear a second person with an accent say, "I think he looks okay." I could hear the door click, and then it opened with the safety latch in place so the person in the room could get a better look at me. I was given the once over, and then another face appeared and looked at me.

The door closed, and the safety latch was removed, and the door opened.

I said, "Are you Mr. Campell?"

He said, "Yes." He was about thirty years old, blond, thinning hair, a brown mustache, clear rimmed glasses, about six feet tall, weighing about 180 lbs. I thought to myself, *Boy, it will probably take two or three of us to take him down if he puts up a struggle.*

"I have your two bags," I said. I pushed the cart partially in the room before I was stopped.

Mr. Campell said, "That is far enough. I can take it from here." I could see three other individuals with no weapons in sight. Two of the men came to the door, and each one took a bag off the cart and brought it into the room. One was a young man, about twenty-two years old, five feet ten inches, blond hair, blue eyes, sharp features, and weighed about 140 lbs. He had a German accent. The other young man was in his twenties with light brown hair, weighing about 150 lbs. The third was sitting on the bed. I could see no weapons in plain sight.

"That will be seventy-five dollars," I said.

Mr. Campell counted out seventy-five dollars. He then said, "Thank you very much."

I said, "Hey, where is my tip? You know those bags were heavy. You said there would be a twenty-five-dollar tip."

Mr. Campell then counted out twenty-five dollars more.

I then said, "I need to return the cart to the bellman." I pulled the cart into the hallway.

Mr. Campell closed the door behind me, and I could hear him going back into the room. I could also hear talking in the room after the door was closed. I put my ear against the door and could hear one man saying,. "Open up the bags. Let's see the stuff." Then they began to converse in German. Vince came out of the room across the hall. I told Vince, "They are going to open the bags now. They started to talk in German." Vince put his ear to the door for a few seconds and listened at the door while I pushed the cart into the room across the hall. I went inside with Vince following me.

Five other agents were in the room. We talked for about ten minutes, discussing how we would make our entrance to catch them off guard. It was decided that I would be the one to get them to open the door without the safety latch. Once that was accomplished, I was to step backward, allowing the entry team to enter. The first two agents from the right side were assigned to take the person opening the door and hold him against the wall, while the other agents had to enter the room, taking down the others.

Then the portable radio squawked, and I heard the voice say, "The subject just made three calls and received two calls. There is no more activity. We got all the numbers. Let's make the bust."

Vince said, "OK, let's do it. Reno, get them to open the door."

I took a clipboard that one of the agents had in the room. I took the release forms and went back across the hall. There was no one else in the hall but me. I stood in the middle and stood very close to the door so if someone looked out the peephole, all they could see is my big face up close. I knocked hard on the door. There was some scurrying, and a voice said, "Who is it?"

I said, "Yellow cab. You forgot to sign the release form for the airline."

He said, "Slip it under the door."

I said, "I can't get the paper under the door because of this rug. The airline guy said if I do not get the forms sign, he will have me arrested for stealing the bags. So you have to sign the forms."

The voice from behind the door said, "Stand back away from the door." I felt the eyes peering out at me. Someone was looking out the peephole, trying to see if anyone else was in the hall with me. Now they were convinced that there was no one in sight and I was the cab driver with a clipboard in my hand and nothing else.

I heard the latch being pushed back against the door. I moved forward toward the door. Vince opened the door of his room slightly. I gave Vince the signal that the door was being opened. Campell opened his door part way. Campell held the door with his right arm as he extended the left part of his body into the open door to get the forms. As he reached out for the clipboard, I placed my foot against the open door. Immediately, I felt bodies and arms pushing against me. My body and face were stuck against the door as it was pushed open by my fellow agents. I had no time to get out of their way. From across the hall, they plowed into the room. As those bodies pushed open the door, I could see the stainless steel guns coming pass my face and over my head.

"Customs! Police! Don't move!" was the deafening sounds ringing in my ears.

I felt as if I went through a revolving door at top speed. My body turned 360 degrees, and now I was facing Vince and Charley. They had

Campell pined against the wall and were placing the handcuffs on him. I turned to see if the other three men had been subdued. The rest of our team were all over the three men like flies on shit. They were forcing the three men to the floor and handcuffing them. One of the three was Victor Klienman who was traveling with Campell. The other two were from Pennsylvania and Michigan.

The Head of Waldorf Astoria security department, George Hardy, was standing in the hall ready to assure guest, who heard the commotion, that there was nothing to worry about. I went back across the hall to the CP and retrieved my jacket and opened my attaché case. I filled out the chain of custody form for the two suitcases of drugs. I turned over the original form and all the papers I had gotten from Elsa to Vince. Vince asked Agent Charley Kosko to go the security office and make copies of all the documents. Charley returned and gave me a set of the copied documents for my file. Vince and the soft narcotics squad would take the case from here.

Vince said, "Hey, Reno, DJ is at O'Donald's pub tonight with some of the guys. You can get a ride back to the airport with him." Vince made a phone call to the pub.

A couple of minutes later, Vince said, "DJ was there, and he is swinging by to pick you up." I said thanks Vince. O'Donald's Pub was owned by the brother of Agent Don O'Donald. It was the regular watering hole for the New York City customs agents. We would drink there, and it would not cost anything. I really do not know how the guy stood in business.

As it turned out, Campell cooperated and controlled deliveries were made in Pennsylvania and Michigan. In all, ten people were arrested in the next couple of days. I completed my reports and had to testify at three trials: one in Pennsylvania and one in Michigan, and one in New York City. Victor Klienman was convicted and sentenced to five years in a federal prison. Frederick Campell, who cooperated, was sentenced to five years with two years suspended. The other two men were found guilty and sentenced to two years in prison. Of the ten others, who were arrested in Pennsylvania and Michigan, eight were convicted and sentenced from two to five years in a federal prison.

Chapter 9

The Assignments

My office was only about fifty feet down the hall from the SAC office. Before I knew it, I was sitting at my desk again. Just thinking of the spontaneity of the hash case made me smile. It boosted my confidence, and I could feel the adrenaline pumping me up again. I picked up the sheet of paper the Duke gave me. I looked over the notes that he had taken. I could actually read the Duke's notes. I was thinking to myself that the Duke could have been a teacher. His penmanship was meticulous. When I looked at my scribbles, it was just that, scribbles. I could hardly read my own hand writing.

I read over the notes that the Duke had taken. I picked up my coffee cup and took a sip. The coffee was hot. Then I realized that I had been so embroiled in my thoughts about the hash investigation, I actually had refilled my coffee cup on the way back to my office.

I picked up the phone and dialed DJ's extension. I asked him to get the Cheech and Frank and come into my office. I told him, "We are going to have a surveillance, and I need to brief you." A surveillance breeds the kind of excitement that all agents thrived on. Participating in a surveillance was much more exciting than doing background investigations or fraud case. Both DJ and Cheech had sensed that something was brewing, especially when the SAC closed the door to his office after I went in.

Both Cheech and DJ came into my office. DJ sat in the chair in front of my desk, and Cheech sat on the edge of my desk. Frank came in and stood by the door, munching on a doughnut.

DJ said, "What's up, Reno?"

I began briefing the guys on the information that I had gotten from the Duke. I told them that I was going to call LA, Chicago, and Nashville offices to get the rest of the story.

Now I had to dole out the work assignments. I said, "Cheech, you meet and team up with Agent Harris who will arrive at LaGuardia on the *American Flight* number forty-four. Harris will have this Darnovski guy under surveillance. You will point him out to DJ in the baggage area. Then you take Harris and go to whichever hotel this guy goes to. DJ will contact you on the air and let you know what hotel they are going to." I also told Cheech to check with American airline's security to see if Darnovski has any connecting flights or has made other reservations. For all we knew, he could have booked a flight out of the US that same day.

"DJ, you find out who will be driving the UC (undercover) cab. Set it up with him so that when Darnovski gets in his cab and tells him where to go, we get that information ASAP."

DJ said, "Don't worry, Reno, I will make sure that sector calls for radio silence on Channel 3 at least an hour before Darnovski arrives."

Our newest radios had three channels. One for undercover, one for regular business, and the third for multiagency use.

"DJ, after you find out the destination, don't forget to call Cheech and let him know. The UC (undercover agent) guy will call in to the cab dispatch with the hotel name. Just to be on the safe side, get in touch with the two agents from the city assigned to us and tell them to monitor Channel 3. The city guys should set up a command post with the hotel security. The command post needs to be across the hall from Darnovski's room, and Harris can crash there."

DJ said, "I'll tell the UC driver to take the long way to whichever hotel he wants to go to. This will give the city guys time to set up at the hotel."

"DJ, you're responsible for coordinating the details with the UC cab, the cab dispatcher, and the port authority police. Make sure the dispatcher puts Darnovski in our cab. Cheech will point out Darnovski to you. You make sure that he gets into our cab, and no screw-ups. Sign out portable radios and make sure the batteries are good and take an extra set. DJ, take the hotel wiretap equipment kit also."

As I spoke to DJ, I observed him jotting down notes on his pad. DJ was a guy who made sure he took notes and did not rely only on memory. DJ said, "Got it, Reno."

Swallowing the last bit of his doughnut, Frank asked, "What do you want me to do?"

I said, "Frank, you have to go home and get some rest. I need you to take over the midnight shift at the hotel."

Frank said OK as he wiped the crumbs from his mouth and tucked the brown checkered flannel shirt back into his pants. DJ and Cheech acknowledged what they had to do. We knew we needed to set up a command post and needed to monitor Darnovski's room at all times. We had to be sure that he did not take the camera from the room and give it to someone else. We had to set up a tight surveillance at the hotel and babysit him.

The four of us kicked around the various possible scenarios of what could happen and the actions we would take. Everyone was in agreement. DJ and Cheech left my office and checked out the various equipment that we anticipated we would need for this operation.

All the equipment was locked in the office equipment room. As DJ was leaving the office, he popped into my office and gave me a fresh set of batteries for my portable radio and said, "A spare set of batteries for your radio, Reno."

I said thanks. DJ left with his attaché case and a couple boxes of equipment. Sometimes we would wonder why DJ was bringing so much equipment. We would think that in all probability, we would not use most of it. But, as it usually turned out, DJ was right on the money.

Frank stuck his head in my office and said he was leaving now. I told him I would call him at eleven o'clock to make sure he was up and let him know where he had to go. Frank said OK and left the office. Well, I told myself, *I think I have all the bases covered so far. DJ and Cheech are on their way to LaGuardia airport. Frank will come in on the midnight shift.* It would be a half hour to forty-five minute ride, depending on the traffic. I knew that I could depend on the guys. We had worked many cases together.

I picked up the phone and called Cindy's house. I knew she was not at home. She did not want to get any personal phone calls at the Diner. I respected that, so I left her a message that I would not be able to see her tonight because I had a surveillance, and I knew I would have to work late and possibly all night. I told her I would call the first chance I would get tonight. If it was too late at night, I would call her tomorrow. I knew that Cindy would understand because we talked about the kind of work I did. She understood that I could be away for days at a time, but I would always call.

I looked at the list that I had made of the things I had to do and crossed off "Call Cindy." The next thing on the list was to call the assistant US attorney for the Eastern District and call LA, then Nashville, and then Chicago. I took a sip of my coffee and got out a pad of paper. I found it very distracting to listen to someone talking and take notes at the same time. I prided myself for my memory. I liked to write down all the facts after I had the complete picture. I would jot down only key words I thought important to jog my memory.

I picked up the phone and dialed the US attorney's office, Eastern District of New York. They connected me with the duty attorney for the day. It was AUSA Richard Bremmier. I had worked with Rich on many of my airport cases. He had a 100 percent conviction rate on all my cases. So we were a great team. I briefed him on the case and reiterated the fact that this might well be a transshipment to Russia. I gave him AUSA William Anthony's phone number in Tennessee. I told him, "We may need a wire intercept order if Darnovski stays in New York."

He said it would not be a problem as the duty magistrate was Paul Schifflit.

On his way out of the office, Duke stopped in my office and said, "Don't forget to call me at home with a status report."

I said, "You got it." The Duke was the best boss I had ever worked for. This brought to mind, as I sat back in my chair, the worst customs supervisor I ever had. As I thought about this numnuts boss, I broke out in laughter.

When I first started with customs, I worked for a supervisor who tried to set me up and get me fired. He was a sneaky underhanded scumbag. Just the thought about Pete brought back the funny consequences to one of Pet's many pranks to get me in trouble.

I remembered the incident like it was yesterday. I leaned back in my chair, placed my hands behind my head, and stretched. Looking at the white ceiling, the memories about Pete raced through my head, bringing a large smile on my face.

My first supervisor tried to get me fired early on in my career with customs. His was named Pete Furatolla. A fifty-year-old Italian Mafia wannabe. He had greasy black hair parted down the middle. His face was round and puffy, with a small handlebar black mustache and bushy black eyebrows. He was five foot six inches tall and about 185 lbs. He smoked a large Don Sebastian Churchill cigars most of the time. Sometimes he would light up a Parody, Toscan-style cigar called the Italian rope or more commonly known as a guinea stinker.

He was a uniformed captain assigned to desk duties in plainclothes. He was primarily assigned to support the ship searching squads. He sat in the same room as me in 201 Varick Street in New York City. Pete was politically connected. He had someone very high up in customs who looked out for him. He sat at his desk, read the newspaper, and looked out of the window most of the day. Every once in a while, one of the uniform captains would come in to get his approval on something. Every day, he would drive his car to work. Once the customs searching squads left the building in the government vans, he would have me or another clerk place his car in the building bay where the vans had been parked. The vans usually returned about three in the afternoon, and then Pete would have to move his car to the front of the building and park at a meter. Parking in front of the building at a meter meant putting money in every hour. Every hour, he would have Tony Bochi (a clerk for the searchers) or Mike Wallace (the captain's office clerk) do it for him.

Between twelve noon and one o'clock, most days, the captain's office was inundated with phone calls, and the overflow was directed to the office I shared with Pete, Willy Dunbar (another plainclothes captain), Dudley Washington (a clerk), and Edie Pedie (Ray Heffer, office manager), and Victor Bantson (another clerk). Three days a week, I brought my lunch and ate in the office. Two days a week, I went to the Italian pork store on Carmine Street in Little Italy and got a hard salami Italian sub. It had salami, prosciutto and provolone cheese, mustard, a little oil, vinegar, and lettuce and tomatoes on still warm Italian hard crust bread. I started off in customs as a clerk in 1962. There were no investigative positions open when I was making my inquiry at the customs personnel office. They sent me down to the supervising customs agent's office for an unexpected interview.

During my interview, I was told something about a freeze in hiring and government budget cuts. I was offered a clerical job until the freeze was over. So I took the job as a clerk because I thought that I would stand a better chance in being hired. I figured they would hire someone from inside customs before someone off the street they did not know, and rightly so. So when the long freeze was over and a position opened up, I was hired.

The supervising agent for enforcement was a young thirty-five-year-old Italian named Bobby De Corenzo. The office had been receiving many complaints that the telephones were not being answered between 12:00 p.m. and 1:00 p.m. So someone had to be in the office every day at that time to make sure the phones were being answered. On this particular day, I had brought my lunch. Dudley and Victor banged in sick. It was Dudley's day to answer the phones. So Pete said I would have to answer the phones. I had my lunch, so I did not care. I immediately said, "OK." Pete did not get an argument from me, and this made him mad. It was Pete's nature to argue with someone in order to feel that he had exercised his authority. Getting someone to do something they did not want to do was a big turn-on for Pete. So I was ordered to answer the phones during lunch from 12:00 p.m. to 1:00 p.m.

About 11:45 a.m., Pete asked me to get him a meatball sub sandwich, with plenty of sauce, for lunch. He asked me to go to the pork store to pick up his sandwich, stating that he would answer the phones for me while I was gone. I said okay and went to the Italian pork store on Carmine Street, which was five blocks away from the office to get Pete his meatball sub sandwich.

It was a nice warm day, so I took my time. A lot of the women were leaving their offices to go outside on this warm day. I had plenty of beautiful women to look at. The pork store was crowded. So I had to wait for my order. Two of the customs agents secretaries from the fourth floor, whom I met before, were getting their bosses' sandwiches. So I had flirtatious conversation with them. They got their order and left.

I got my order and started back to the office. I was in no hurry, so I walked slowly, maintaining a view of the two secretaries in front of me. A slight breeze was blowing with an occasional gust, causing their A-line skirts to flare up, exposing their upper legs. I caught up to them when we reached Varick St. We exchanged some words and entered the building. The girls took the elevator up, and I went into my office.

There were four adjoining offices. Three of the offices had doors where you could enter from the outside hall. The last one was a room we used to fingerprint prisoners, and it had a holding cell for prisoners. Then came the captain's office where the shift captains and clerks worked. There was a large twelve-by-six-foot magnetic board on the wall. This board was the latest in innovative technology. It showed the Brooklyn, New York City, and New Jersey waterfronts. There were white lights at each pier. The light would go on if a ship was at the pier. We had little magnet cars. When a patrol car would call in every half hour, we could move the magnet for that car to the given location. Real high tech.

The next office was the clerical office where the four clerks and the two captains sat. Each of the three office had its own door to the hallway. There was a door between the captain's office and the clerical office. There was a door from the clerical office to Bobby De's office. Bobby was in charge of the uniformed division. There was also a door from the clerical office to the plainclothes division office.

While I was out getting Pete's lunch, Supervisory Agent Bobby De had come out of his office and into the clerk's office. The phones were ringing off the hook. Pete sat at his desk, feet up, the newspaper in one hand, and was smoking his Churchill cigar. In an angry tone, Bobby De told Pete, "Who is supposed to be answering the phone?"

Pete, put his cigar in his mouth, took a puff, and said, "I'm out to lunch. Reno is supposed to answer the phones."

Bobby De said, "Where did he go?"

Pete said, "I ordered Reno to answer the phones during the lunch hour." He went on to say, "I told him not to go to lunch, and he said that he was going anyway. He also said it was more important for him to go to lunch than answer the dam phones." Pete again reiterated to Bobby De that he had ordered me not to go to lunch, but I disobeyed him. The phones began to ring, and Pete answered the phone as Bobby De went back into his office, steaming. If there was anything that Bobby hated, it was questioning his authority.

As faith would have it, I walked in the office just after Pete had gone into the captains office and closed the door. At that moment, Bobby De was coming out of his office with some papers in hand. Seeing me with a brown paper bag in my hand, he turned red and beckoned me into his office. I walked in. Bobby De said in an escalating tone, "Close the door." I obeyed and closed the door.

Bobby De began vetting all his stored-up anger directly at me. He was so mad he fired me four times before I could tell him what had happened. I was standing there, dumfounded. I had to think of something before I was fired for the fifth time. So I quickly turned to my left and quickly walked to a chair in front of the window. I bent down and looked under the chair. Bobby stopped yelling, his mouth slightly open, about to say something, but nothing came out. He was dumbfounded at what I was doing while he was admonishing me. I quickly lifted up the wastepaper basket, looked inside, and then placed it back on the floor.

I completely ignored Bobby De and continued in a quick pace all around the room as if I were looking for something. This left Bobby De speechless with his mouth open. He then asked me, in a loud questionable, irritating voice, "What the hell are you doing?"

I replied softly, "I'm looking for the other guy who is hiding in here."

He said in a loud voice, "What the fuck are you talking about? What other guy?"

I said, "The guy you are yelling at. I know you cannot be yelling at me." He actually stood there with his mouth open in apparent dismay that a subordinate would actually stand up to him.

I seized the opportunity and quickly began to tell him how Pete ordered me to go to the pork store and get him his sandwich and to put a dime in the parking meter for his car and that Pete was going to answer the phones while I was gone. I then said, "Here is the proof. Pete's meatball sandwich." I took Pete's hot sandwich, which was wrapped in clear wax paper, out of the bag, placing it on Bobby's desk. "I brown-bagged my lunch today," I said.

He looked down at the sandwich. Then he picked up the sandwich, pondering what he was going to do next. I quickly turned, opened the door, and, in a quick pace, left the office. I went directly to my desk. I left Bobby De's office as Pete walked in from the captain's office. I could see the smile on Pete's face as I rapidly left Bobby's office. Pete was laughing and pointing his finger at me as if to say, "I got you."

Bobby De came out of his office and, with his finger, motioned to Pete to come into his office. Pete looked at me, a big smile across his face as he frolicked into Bobby De's office. He was laughing because he really thought he had gotten me in trouble. Little did he know what was in store for him.

As Pete entered Bobby's office, he did not get a chance to close the door before Bobby laced into him. Bobby's voice was so loud they could hear him in the captain's office. The extreme anger in his voice was evident. Bobby De opened up on Pete, "You lying son-of-a-bitch! You wanted to get Reno in trouble, you Guinea fuck'n scumbag! You sent him to the pork store to get you your sandwich while you were supposed to answer the phones! You lied to me, you guinea cocksucker."

Bobby was so furious that Pete did not wait for Bobby to finish yelling at him. Pete came running out of the Bobby's office, going straight into the captain's office. I never saw a man's belly go up and down so fast as Pete's as he ran through the office with Bobby De in close pursuit. Bobby was following Pete with Pete's sandwich in hand. Bobby said, "Don't you run from me you Guinea Fuck!" As Pete entered the Captain's Office, Pet's meatball sandwich followed and hit Pete in the head unwrapping and dispersing all over the captain's office. I could hear the Captain scream, "what the hell is going on?"

Pete ran out the captain's office through the back door and out of the building and went home. I ran to the door and looked in the captain's office. There was Captain Joe Tombetta, in his once immaculate uniform, now with Pete's meatball sandwich on his head and sauce dripping down his shirt and meatballs all over the desk in front of him. Joe was the sweetest guy; he was seventy years old with snow-white hair. Joe stood there befuddled, trying to determine what had just happened. His white hair was now meat sauce red. Bobby apologized to Joe. He then came into my office space and apologized to me. Pete took the next two days off. He must have gone to his Rabi (political mentor) to smooth things out with Bobby. So getting a boss like the Duke was a real blessing.

Chapter 10

Los Angles Case

Wake up, Reno! I immediately sprung forward in my chair. Standing in the doorway of my office was Amanda. "It must have been a funny dream," she said.

"Yeah," I said, letting out a sigh. She held an almost empty pot of coffee in her hand.

"Nadine is going to make a fresh pot of coffee. I thought your coffee could use warming up. Have a sip. It will wake you up," she said. She bent forward and poured some hot coffee in my cup.

My sights were on the cup with steam coming out. I went for the coffee, took a sip, and then realized I had missed an opportunity for another look at Amanda's cleavage when she bent over, pouring the coffee in my cup.

Amanda then said, "Don't you find me attractive anymore," in an inquisitive sexy voice, letting me know that she had noticed that I had not looked down her blouse at her breast.

"Of course, I do, Amanda; It's just that I'm all wrapped up in this case. I could see Nadine standing in the hall watching us."

Amanda left the office, twisting her body slightly, giving me a side and rear profile of her body as she blew me a kiss. I wondered to myself, as I watched her leave my office, what it would be like to make passionate love to her. I could hear the two women giggling like two school girls with a big secret. Another sip of the strong coffee brought me back to reality. I put the cup down.

I pulled out the customs agent's office directory from my desk. I looked up Agent Gardner's direct number. I picked up the phone and dialed the Los Angeles SAC office. The phone rang three times before a voice came on the line. "Agent Gardner speaking."

"Hey, Dennis, this is Johnny Reno." I had several other cases that I had worked with Dennis over the past few years.

"Reno, how are things going at JFK?"

"OK," I replied. "The reason I am calling is I caught this Darnovski case. He will be landing in New York in a couple of hours, and I need to be brought up to speed with your investigation on this case."

"OK, I'll start in the beginning," Gardner replied.

Agent Gardner began to lay out the case in a chronological order as it had developed. I came to find out that this case actually started in Los Angeles about March 18, thirteen days before I found out about it.

Mr. Herb Tollman, the president of Photo-Sound Inc. (PSI) had contacted Special Agent Dennis Gardner of the SAC Los Angeles office. Mr. Tollman discussed with Agent Gardner the facts that made him suspicious of an upcoming sale of a KB-25A military gunsight camera to a company called Barolite, Inc of Columbia, Tennessee.

Mr. Tollman stated, "The KB-25A, 16 mm camera, was a camera mounted on our new F-4 Jet Fighter aircraft. The camera recorded each round fired and tracked it to the target and recorded the damage to the target."

Mr. Tollman had explained that on March 15, 1974, Barolite of Canada (hereinafter BWCL) made initial contact with Instrument Market Corp. (hereinafter IMC) in an attempt to purchase the following four (4) cameras.

1. 16 mm 1B (FPS) high G basic on car camera
2. 16 mm action master 500 1-PD documentary camera
3. 16 mm 1VN camera
4. 16 mm airborne KB-25A gunsight camera

He was advised that the 16 mm action master 500 1-PD documentary camera required an export permit from the US Department of Commerce and the 16 mm airborne KB-25A gunsight camera system required an export permit from the US Department of State in order for either of these cameras to be exported to any country other than Canada. All future correspondence concerning the KB-25A camera came from Barolite of Tennessee.

Mr. Tollman stated that his secretary, Mrs. Ann Philips, had copies of all correspondence between Adolf Donaldson of BWCL, I MC and PSI and that she could furnish all necessary information with reference to the transactions. All original documents would be available at the time of trial.

This caused Mr. Tollman to review the purchaser file. Copies of correspondence between BWCL and IMC indicated that Adolf Donaldson originally showed he was with a company called Casper Industries Limited (hereinafter CIL), but later correspondence from him indicated that he was with BWCL, same address and telephone number as CIL, in Moose Jaw, Saskatchewan, Canada.

A purchase order, number 1215, was received by IMC from CIL, dated May 23, 1974, on which cameras number one, two, and four were listed, but due to communications between Adolf Donaldson and IMC, camera number three was added to the list. IMC prepared a work order on May 24, 1974 for all four (4) cameras, showing the purchaser as BWCL, and the word CIL crossed out.

Mrs. Philips stated that the cost of all four cameras and accessories was $20,855 and that a letter of credit dated August 9, 1974 was received from BWCL, payable to IMC in the amount of $20,855. The letter of credit showed that the cameras and accessories were to be shipped to Manfred Darnovski Services Limited (hereinafter MDS Austria).

Mrs. Carol Doyle, executive secretary, IMC, was contacted for further information with reference to the transaction and stated that these were communications between Adolf Donaldson of BWCL and IMC because camera number two required an export permit from the US Department of Commerce and camera number four required an export permit from the US Department of State for shipping to countries other than Canada. (It should be mentioned that both IMC and PSI thought that the KB-25A camera could not be exported to any country without required permit.)

Mrs. Carol Doyle stated that since the letter of credit showed the ultimate receiver of the camera as being MDS in Austria, they notified Adolf Donaldson that the export permits would be required. She stated that Adolf Donaldson wanted to know if the camera could be shipped to Canada without the required permits, and he was told that only cameras nos. 1, 2, and 3 could be shipped to Canada without the permit, but that a permit would be required if camera no. 2, the action master 500, were to leave Canada for another country.

On November 22, 1974, BWCL submitted a letter with a new purchase order request to IMC for camera nos. 1, 2, and 3 with the accessories. The purchase order number 1215 remained the same, but it was for $17,255, which was $3,600 less than the letter of credit of August 9, 1974. This $3,600 represented the cost of the KB-25A gunsight camera and one-hundred-foot magazine designed for that camera. IMC was advised to ship the other merchandise to BWCL and that a new letter of credit would follow. Adolf Donaldson specified that Schenkers International Forwarders, Inc. would be used to ship the camera to Canada.

Mrs. Caryla Murphy, sales coordinator, IMC, US, stated that because the original letter of credit listed MDS, Austria, as the ultimate destination, the invoice prepared by IMC showed MDS as destination where the cameras were to be shipped to; however, in accordance with a telephone conversation with Mr. Henry Stern, Schenkers International Forwarders Inc., the cameras were to be shipped by them to BWCL, Canada. When Henry Stern was contacted about the shipment, he was informed that no export permit had been obtained from the US Department of Commerce for the action master 500 camera and therefore that shipment must go to BWCL, Canada. IMC was informed by Henry Stern that he had been in touch with Adolf Donaldson of BWCL, Canada, and that Schenkers International Forwarders, Inc. would obtain the necessary permits for BWCL.

Agent Gardner examined the air waybill contained in the file. It revealed that the three (3) cameras were shipped to Austria without the necessary export permits on the action master 500 camera, and when IMC was questioned about this, they expressed surprise as they had thought all along the shipment had to go to BWCL, Canada. Agent Gardner now had the evidence that US laws had been violated. Agent Gardner obtained all the documentation referencing IMC's sale of cameras to BWCL, Canada. These violations of US law would be incorporated in the ongoing criminal case.

Mrs. Ann Philips, Photo-sound, Inc., stated that Adolf Donaldson of BWCL, Canada, sent PSI a purchase order number 1216, dated November 22, 1974, for the KB-25A gunsight camera, showing a purchase price of $3,600. PSI forwarded to BWCL in Canada, form DSP-8340 export license, and it was returned to PSI dated December 12, 1974 with the ultimate consignee listed as MDS, Austria. PSI then submitted the DSP-83 along with the application for the license to export unclassified arms, munitions, and implements of war and related unclassified technical data to the office of munitions control, Department of State, Washington, DC, on December 16, 1974. The application was returned to PSI on January 2, 1975, without action, as it did not contain all the necessary information required by the office of munitions control in order for them to make a determination on whether or not the application should be approved.

On January 7, 1975, PSI sent a letter to BWCL, informing them that the application for the export permit, file number 88358, had been returned for the additional information and that BWCL must furnish to PSI the necessary information that was required by the office of munitions control.

On January 13, 1975, BWCL sent a letter to PSI, informing them that the ultimate consignee was MDS, Austria, but they had no way of knowing the type of aircraft the camera would be used on nor could they obtain that information.

On January 29, 1975, PSI sent a letter to Mr. Donaldson, BWCL, Canada, advising him that they would like to sell the camera to him but that they could not ship it without the US Department of State export license, which the office of munitions control would not even consider issuing unless the specific information requested by the office of munitions control was provided.

The request for the KB-25A gunsight camera by purchase order number 1216 from BWCL, Canada, was canceled by PSI, and the camera serial number 1806 was returned to stock.

Mrs. Ann Philips further advised that on February 18, 1975, Adolf Donaldson of BWCL called her and wanted to know if he gave PSI a US consignee addressed for the KB-25A gunsight camera, would PSI be required to obtain an export license from the Department of State. He was told no by Mrs. Phillips, and he next asked if PSI would have to inform the US Department of State of the new consignee. He stated that if the PSI informed him that they could ship to the US consignee without being required to notify US Department of State, then he would send a written purchase order change notice.

A telex was sent by PSI to BWCL, attention Adolf Donaldson, on February 18, 1975, informing BWCL of the new instructions with reference to the designated shipping address and letter of credit. Adolf Donaldson responded by telex on February 26, 1975, that a new purchase order was being forwarded but that shipment was required by March 10, 1975.

Adolf Donaldson sent another telex to PSI on March 11, 1975, advising that a new order and check was en route and that it was imperative that the camera be shipped to the designated Tennessee address prior to March 24, 1975.

Adolf Donaldson sent a letter to PSI from BWCL, Canada, dated March 11, 1975, that contained an unnumbered purchase order for the KB-25A gunsight camera and check number 0019 in the amount of $3,600 drawn on the BWCL bank account in Moose Jaw, Saskatchewan, Canada. The purchase order directed that the camera be sent to Barolite, Inc. (hereinafter BI), PO Box 88, Columbia, TN 38401.

PSI prepared a shipping invoice, shipper number 18326, for the camera, serial number 1808, for shipment to BI, Tennessee.

On March 23, 1975, Adolf Donaldson of BWCL called Mrs. Ann Philips and wanted to know if PSI had shipped the KB-25A gunsight camera to Tennessee. He was then told not yet, and then he inquired as to the reason for the delay; he was told that because of the required government testing in order for the camera to qualify as a KB. He wanted to know why it was necessary to test the camera and was informed by her that PSI produced a commercial camera of almost the same specifications, and in order for the KB to receive its military designation, it must be tested. He wanted to know why PSI couldn't ship the KB camera and call it a commercial camera, and he was told then that PSI would be in violation of the government regulations. He stated that the camera was urgently needed in Tennessee by March 28, 1975.

Adolf Donaldson called Mrs. Philips of PSI on March 26, 1975, to find out when the camera was going to be shipped. He was informed by her that it would be shipped the next day or so, and he advised her to ship via air parcel post, insured and addressed to Barolite, Inc., marked to the attention of Mr. Carl R. Krowell.

Mr. Clyde Billings, office of munitions control, US Department of State, was contacted telephonically on March 19, 1973, and again on March 25, 1975, by Special Agent Gardner with reference to the submission of the application for an export permit by PSI for BWCL to MDS. He confirmed that application number 88358 had been returned to PSI without action because it did not contain all the required information. He also confirmed that the KB-25A gunsight camera was on the restricted list and that it was listed under 22 CFR 121.01 as a military camera, category XIII (a). Mr. Billings was informed about the attempt by BWCL to shift the camera to BI, Tennessee, and he agreed that the shipment should be allowed but that the camera should be kept under close surveillance after it was picked up by BI. He emphasized that even though the camera could be legally exported to Canada without the required export permit, in the event it was being sent to Canada by BI, it should still be seized, and under no circumstances, should the camera be allowed to be exported from the United States.

Special Agent Gill Stein, chief intelligence division, Department of Commerce, was contacted on March 25, 1975 and March 27, 1975 and informed of the shipment of the action master 500 camera to Austria. He confirmed that no export permit had been issued and that the camera was a COCOM-controlled item that came on the export control laws. CC L number 86150 (2) (A). He requested the office of investigations to investigate the matter and ascertain why the camera was shipped to Austria instead of Canada as originally intended.

Ann Philips was informed by Agent Gardner on March 21, 1975, not to ship the camera to BI in Tennessee until further advised and that the matter was under investigation, and to stall BWCL but not to let them know that US Customs was investigating the transactions.

On March 26, 1975, Agent Gardner told Herb Tollman to go ahead with the sale to Barolite, but they would initiate a controlled delivery. Mr. Tollman agreed to cooperate with this sting operation. Dennis then told me that he called John Trent, RAC (resident agent in charge) Nashville, to give him a heads-up on the case and to conduct a discreet background on the individuals and company involved in Tennessee.

Gardner then contacted Postal Inspector Tom White, with whom he had worked many controlled deliveries. Gardner asked White to meet him that afternoon at PSI in order to make a controlled delivery to Tennessee.

Later that day, at approximately 2:30 p.m., Special Agent Dennis Gardner and Postal Inspector Tom White arrived at PSI's office and met with Herb Tollman. Together, the three observed the packaging of the KB-25A military gunsight camera. They verified the serial number as 1808 before placing it in a cardboard box that was about 24" × 24" × 24" in size.

The cardboard box was marked with labels, "Fragile handle with care." It had an address label attached to it, showing the shipper to be PSI, Burbank, Canada, and the receiver to be BI, Mr. Carl R. Krowell, Post Office Box 448, Columbia, Tennessee. An invoice, number 17693, with a shipper number 18326, which was dated March 27, 1975, listing the item sold as a camera, serial number 1808, was slipped in a plastic pocket on top of the cardboard box. The words *invoice/packing slip enclosed here* written in red ink, with an arrow directing the receiver to the location of the invoice on the top of the cardboard box. The box was sealed. Postal Inspector White then completed the registered return receipt requested and issued a US postal service registered number 92543, which he previously obtained to make the controlled delivery.

A letter was prepared by PSI dated March 27, 1975 and addressed to BI, Mr. Carl R. Krowell. It advised that the camera was being shipped in accordance with instructions from Adolf Donaldson of Barolite,

Canada. A copy of the invoice, number 17693, shipper number 18326 dated March 27, 1975, was enclosed with the letter.

On the invoice, a copy of which was enclosed on the cardboard box with the letter, were printed the following:

Above items are of USA origin and manufacture. The above photographic equipment is under United States, Department of State, munitions control list category number XIII (a) and as such must be export licensed by the US Department of State, prior to export from the United States.

The letter was given a separate US postal service registered number 92544 and also mailed registered/return receipt requested. Inspector White took custody of the letter and package.

Special Agent Gardner went on to say that both the cardboard box and the letter were accompanied by White and himself from PSI to the U S post service downtown station in Burbank, CA, where they were placed into the US postal system at approximately 3:10 p.m. He went on to say that he returned to his office and called RAC Nashville, John Trent, and spoke to agents Trent and Harris and filled them in on the details of the controlled delivery that had been initiated.

Copies of the invoice and registered mail chain of custody form VI-41and other papers were being faxed to Trent's office as Gardner spoke to Trent.

Agent Gardner and I talked for several minutes more about local working conditions and results on some of the other cases we had worked on. I told Agent Gardner to obtain the complete file from PSI and IMC involving all of Barolite's purchases for further investigations. I knew that once I made the arrest, I would need to investigate all his purchases and obtain the evidence to put Darnovski away for a long time.

Chapter 11

Nadine in the Office

After talking with Agent Gardner, I had a better understanding of the case. Still with the additional information I just received, it still left many questions unanswered. As I sat back in my chair, I digested the conversation I had with Agent Gardner.

I thought to myself; *my biggest concern will be, where will Darnovski try to leave the US from? Will he fly to Europe from JFK airport? Will he fly to Canada from LA Guardia Airport? Will he take the train from Grand Central Station or take a bus from the port authority bus terminal to Canada? Will he rent a car or meet someone who will drive him to Canada? Will he meet someone and give the camera to them to take it out of the US?* I knew I had to clear my mind and get organized and have backup plans for each of the different scenario. I got up from my desk, grabbing my coffee cup. It was not actually a cup; it was a white ceramic mug with gold trim and a blue and gold Treasury Department seal. Under the seal was my name in large black script, and under my name was my title, "SENIOR SPECIAL AGENT."

There was about a half cup of warm coffee in it. I thought to myself that I needed a refill of hot coffee to get me going again.

I also needed to get up and stretch my legs. I did not like to sit for long period of time. I thought to myself that this would be a good time to clear my mind off this case for a few minutes. I decided to check my in-box. I got up stretched, lifting my arms above my head, and rotated my shoulders. I walked out of my office and headed down the hall with my coffee cup in hand. I had decided that I would check my in-box, and then on the way back to my office, I would get a refill of hot coffee, that is, if it was already made.

As I passed the coffee room, I could see that Amanda and Nadine were standing at the coffee table whispering to each other as they were straightening up the mess the agents had made that day. There was a new pot of hot coffee brewing. The coffee room served as the office water cooler.

As I passed the open door, Nadine said, "Reno, give me your cup, and I will fill it for you." I stopped and walked back into the room, handing Nadine my coffee cup. I told her I was going to check my in-box. Nadine took the half-empty cup from my hand. She said, "I'll bring your coffee to your desk."

I watched her walk toward the sink and dumped the leftover cold coffee in the sink. She began rinsing the cup. I knew what that meant. Nadine wanted something. I said, "That's great." I left the room and proceeded to see if anything new was in my in-box. Nothing of importance was there. Just a couple of information bulletin. So I took the bulletins and went back to my office.

I sat down at my desk. Nadine walked in, closing the door behind her. She put the hot cup of coffee on the coaster on the right side of my desk and said, "I need to talk to you."

I said, "Okay, but I only have a few minutes."

I knew she wanted something real bad. Nadine was an attractive, single, thirty-five-year-old African-American woman. She had a slender figure with shiny black hair. Her skin was a soft light brown, almost white complexion. She had a glowing personality and always thought the cup was half-filled, not half-empty.

Today, she had a brown and yellow neckerchief around her neck instead of a jewelry necklace. She was wearing brown slacks and a white shirt. Her voice was raspy from all the cigarettes she smoked. She was a chain-smoker. You always knew that Nadine was in the office because you could always hear her coughing. She had smoker's cough, and it was bad. Still she refused to give up smoking.

I picked up my coffee cup. I could see the white wispy steam rising from the cup. I took a sip. "Hot," I said.

"Easy now," Nadine said. "I wouldn't want you to burn those delicious lips," as she walked around to the side of my desk.

Standing at the side of my desk, Nadine bent forward and took the coffee cup from my hand and placed it back on the coaster. Nadine was a very modest dresser. Usually Nadine would have only one or two top buttons unbuttoned on her shirts. She was not as well-endowed as Amanda, and she did not want anybody looking down her blouse.

Now she had four buttons unbuttoned and was trying to outdo Amanda in being seductive. I figured that she was in all probability coached by Amanda for the task at hand. I said, "Okay, Nadine, what do you need?"

She moved her shoulders side to side and said, "I need twenty dollars. Tomorrow is payday, and I can give you the money tomorrow after I get paid. The girls want to go out after work tonight, and I do not have any money left. Can you lend me the twenty dollars?"

I looked at her and said, "Okay" as I reached into my pants pocket, bringing out my wallet. I removed twenty dollars and placed it on the desk in front of me. She bent forward again to take the money, and I pulled it back and said, "First, button your blouse. You know you don't have to resort to those tactics with me. Just be yourself." I had lent Nadine money once before, and she was punctual in repaying me. I had no doubt that she would have the money on my desk in the morning. I said, "I do not want this to become a habit."

She said, "It won't."

For a long moment, she remained bent over, exposing the full cups of her bra no more than a foot from my face. It was almost as if she was trying to tell me, "You gave me the money with no questions asked, and no one else would. So, just for lending me the money, I am going to let you see my breasts." She slowly began to button the two buttons as she straightened up.

Then she took the money from the desk, turned, walked to the door, opened the door, and left, turning back to blow me a kiss. I laughed to myself. That little interlude took my mind off the case and gave me a break I desperately needed to recoup my train of thought and plan my next move. I looked down on the notepad on my desk. I had crossed off "call Cindy," "send team to LaGuardia," "call Dennis, LA." Next on the list was "call Trent, Nashville," "call Chicago," and "status DJ."

Chapter 12
Cargo Training at JFK

I picked up the agents' telephone directory and looked up John Trent, Nashville, and wrote down his direct number. I remembered John Trent when he was first hired. The memories of the past filled my mind again. John worked out of the special agent in charge (SAC) office in New York City. John was from New York. He was an Irish Catholic boy, who graduated from, where else, Fordham University. Almost all our Irish agents who were hired in the 1970s were graduates from Fordham University.

He was five feet nine inches tall with red hair and a very light complexion. He had broad shoulders and a thin waist. He always reminded me of the Captain Marvel Superhero, the one that had a small head on a *v*-shaped body. I would almost call him muscle-bound.

I remember John from when he worked as a plainclothes customs port investigator (CPI) in the plainclothes division at Varick Street in NYC. When we worked out in the office gym, you could see the well-defined muscles of his body. He was in terrific shape.

A few years later when John became an agent, he, like all new agents from NY, had to go through training at the JFK airport office for two to four weeks. The training involved both cargo thefts and smuggling by passengers.

The bulk of cargo training was designed to detect cargo theft by employees. A group of five new guys would be assigned to a pair of airport investigators for the training. We would have the trainees observe the cargo building exits and parking lots through binoculars.

We would then take down the tag numbers of anyone placing things in their cars. We would then stop those cars and search them when they were leaving the airport. These stops were usually on cargo road and on Rockaway Boulevard. Sometimes, we would make the stop in the Diner parking lot. These cargo stops and vehicle searches were one of the reasons I could not let anyone find out I was dating Cindy from the Diner.

If we found any foreign merchandise during the search, we would seize them and their vehicle. If the merchandise was of little value, we would turn the individual into an informant. This usually led us to bigger things. We usually made these searches as the suspects left the airport.

Once the seizure and/or the arrest was made, then the investigative work begun. We would utilize the assistance of the customs inspector who was assigned to that particular cargo terminal to get the necessary paperwork without alerting the airline employees.

The training for the new guys on how to obtain the documentary evidence from the airlines and to show that the merchandise was being imported into the US was essential in every civil or criminal case. Most of the agents liked working in cargo area. They would see a violation occurring, and then they would jump into action. They would make the customs stop, conduct the search, and check to see if the item put into the vehicle was foreign or not. If it was foreign merchandise, they would seize the merchandise and the car and might or might not arrest the individual. We would always bring any person found with merchandise back to our office for interrogation. Usually if we caught someone with something small, we could get them to give up someone else so they could get off the hook.

Sometimes we would be lucky and get a call from a customs inspector at one of the cargo terminals telling us he had a seizure of narcotics. Some inspectors would go into the cargo warehouse and randomly select a piece of freight for examination.

One day in June, I got a call from Inspector Marty Hendrickson. He was assigned to Pan American cargo terminal. It was 10:30 in the morning when the phone rang.

I picked up the phone and said, "Customs. Reno speaking."

"Hey, Reno, this is Marty Hendrickson over at Pan American cargo terminal. I just opened a fifty-five-gallon drum, invoiced as feed. It came in on the Air Jamaica flight from Kingston. When I took off the lid, it was full of marijuana. The shipment consist of two 55-gallon drums. I opened the other one, and it too was full of marijuana."

"Marty, secure the shipment, and don't draw a big crowd. I will be right over."

I hung up the phone. I grabbed my attaché case and the keys to my car and was heading for the door. I yelled over to Cheech, "Cheech, get DJ on the air and have him met us at Pan Am cargo building. We got a load of marijuana in a shipment."

Cheech was writing a report. He stopped immediately and said, "Frig this report. I will get to it later." He picked up his portable radio and called DJ, "605 to 606."

"605 this is 606. Go ahead."

"606 meet 644 at Pan Am cargo."

"606-10-4."

Cheech took the portable and placed it in his attaché case. He put on his jacket and followed me out the door. Pan Am cargo building was about three minutes away. Cheech and I arrived and parked the cars in front of the customs office. DJ was standing next to his car. He was just passing the Pan Am cargo building when the call came in. DJ asked, "What's up, Reno?"

As I approached DJ, I said, "Hendrickson got two 55-gallon drums of marijuana. I'm assigning you this case."

The three of us went into the customs office. Inspector Hendrickson was seated at his desk. Off to the side I could see two tan cardboard drums with metal rims.

Hendrickson said in a low voice, "Hi, Reno, DJ, Cheech."

He had some papers clipped together.

DJ said, "Fill us in, Marty."

Marty began to tell us how he was just walking in the warehouse, looking for a shipment that required an export license. He was in the warehouse section for exports and cleared freight. He came across these two 55-gallon drums. The drums caught his eye. He walked over to them and looked at the label markings. Something was not right. The markings on the drums indicated that the drums came off an Air Jamaica flight destined for JFK.

Pan American handled the warehousing of freight from the Air Jamaica flights. So he popped the metal rim handle and removed the lid. On lifting the lid, he saw black plastic covering. Moving it to the side revealed thick, clear plastic bag with a vegetable substance, which he immediately recognized as marijuana. He closed the drums immediately. He wrote down the waybill numbers on his pad.

Luckily, there were no airline employees around to see him opening the drums and finding the marijuana. He could not be sure any employees were involved in this smuggling operation.

He went back to the office to pull the paperwork for the shipment. He could not locate the paperwork for the shipment. He checked the ready-for-pickup shipments and found the paperwork.

He then pulled all the papers on the shipment and found that Inspector Barns had cleared this shipment yesterday. This left questions as to why the freight was still here after it was cleared.

Then the Pan Am warehouseman came into Hendrickson office. He told Inspector Hendrickson that someone was here to pick up a shipment of two drums of grain. The consignee who was here told the warehouseman that the shipment was cleared yesterday. The cleared paperwork and releases were not in the pickup file. He wanted to know if Marty had the paperwork still in this office. Marty told him the customs messenger had just left with paperwork for building 80 and that maybe the paperwork got mixed up. "Tell him to come back after lunch. By that time, we can locate the paperwork."

The warehouseman left, and Hendrickson proceeded to make copies of the paperwork for us. The warehouseman returned a minute later with another man and said, "This is Alfred Johnson, the man whom the shipment is consigned to, and he wants to talk to you." Hendrickson looked puzzled. *Why would the warehouseman bring the consignee back to his office?* Hendrickson was soon to find out.

Mr. Johnson started out by saying, "Inspector, I'm Alfred Johnson, the consignee of the shipment. Inspector Barns told me the shipment was cleared and that I could pick it up today. What is the holdup?"

Inspector Hendrickson told him, "The cleared paperwork and the airline release authorization for your shipment were probably placed in the wrong pickup basket and the customs messenger took the papers over to building 80. I called over to them, and they will locate the papers, and we should have it in about two or three hours."

Mr. Johnson then said as he displayed a silver shield, "Look, I'm NYPD. Is there anything you can do to get the shipment released without the paperwork? You know it has been cleared by Inspector Barnes."

Hendrickson then told him, "The best I can do is to tell the warehouseman to locate and pull your shipment now and get it dockside for delivery. It will be almost lunch time, and they will be closing for lunch. I will go to building 80 and pick up your paperwork during the lunch hour, and you can pick up the shipment at one o'clock when they reopen. Okay?"

Mr. Johnson said, "Okay, I will be back at one o'clock," and he left the building. Inspector Hendrickson followed the man out and watched him get into a black Ford pickup truck. Hendrickson also jotted down the license plate number. There was another African-American man with Mr. Johnson. Hendrickson then returned to his office and called us. He then had the two drums moved to the inspection office where he could keep it under surveillance.

DJ asked Hendrickson for a description of the two men. DJ had his pad out and was taking notes.

Hendrickson then began to describe the two men, "Mr. Johnson was light-skin Jamaican. He spoke with a Jamaican accent. He is about thirty years old. He is approximately five feet nine inches tall. He has long, straight black hair and a thin moustache. He weighed about 175 lbs. He was wearing a light blue short-sleeve shirt. The shirt was not tucked into his black pants. I believe he had a gun stuck in his pants on the right side."

DJ said, "That's great, Marty. What about the second guy?"

Hendrickson continued, "The other guy was a darker-skinned African-American. He was in his early twenties. He had short black hair under his NY Yankees ball cap. He wore a blue and green striped T-shirt. Holey denim jeans and black and white sneakers."

DJ asked Cheech to run a plate check on the tag number that Hendrickson had written on a piece of paper. Cheech went out to his car and called to the base station and asked for a plate and name check. Within a few minutes, Cheech was given the information on the truck. The truck was registered to Melvin Jones of 2743, 127th Avenue, Jamaica, New York. That was not far from the airport. It could have been the second man's truck. There was no record on the name checks. Cheech returned with the information.

Normally Inspector Hendrickson would be in his office. He would ask the warehouseman for one or two cartons from a shipment. Or he would go with the warehouseman and mark the boxes he wanted to examine, and the warehouseman would bring them to his office for examination.

Since the paperwork indicated that Inspector Barnes previously cleared this shipment, there was no need for Hendrickson to be involved. It was strictly between the airline and the consignee. Once customs signed off on the shipment, customs was out of the picture. The airline personnel would get the shipment, collect any warehouse fees due, and deliver the freight to the person picking it up.

Hendrickson said he would give the paperwork to the warehouseman after they closed for lunch. He would instruct them to release the shipment to Johnson.

I asked Hendrickson, "Would you like to come with us on the bust?"

"You bet I would."

"Do you think it would be okay."

"Sure," I said. "DJ, pick up Marty at 12:30 p.m."

I told the team that we would all meet back at the office and iron out the plan. We got into our cars and returned to the office.

We all got our cups of coffee, and DJ made his tea. We all then gathered around the conference table. We discussed the type and place of the customs stop. We decided that the team use the three-car surveillance cargo stop with one marked car. The ideal place to make the spot coming from Pan Am cargo would at the Lufthansa cargo building, just before the airport exit.

"Have all units go on channel one," I said. "DJ, you will follow the truck from here with Marty and call the stop. Cheech, you will position your car on the shoulder of the road across from me. When DJ gives the command, everyone hit the lights and sirens. Cheech, pull onto the road forcing the suspect into the other lane. You will be responsible for the passenger. I will come from the right and be responsible for the driver of the vehicle. DJ, you will pull in back of the truck and assist me with the driver."

"Okay, Reno," DJ said.

"The marked unit will pull in front of the truck. This guy Johnson is either a NYPD cop or posing as one. In any event, Hendrickson saw what appeared to be a gun on this guy. Let's be careful and not take any chances. Have the marked unit announce the customs stop on the loudspeaker and for them to put their hands behind their head."

We kicked around a couple of what-ifs. We felt comfortable with the solutions suggested. Everyone knew what they were going to do.

I said, "If anyone wants to grab a sandwich, now is not the time. Everyone should be in position by 12:45 p.m. The stage was now set."

It was now 12:45 p.m.

We were all in position. DJ broke the radio silence, "606 to all units. Are you in position?"

"644 ten four."

"605 ten four."

"651 ten four."

"All units be advised the subject black truck pulled into the pickup bay dock."

"The two subjects are out of the vehicle."

"They are going into the office."

Five minutes later, the silence was broken.

"All units the pickup bay door is opening."

"The subjects are on the loading dock and are placing the drums on the truck."

"The subject is walking to his truck with the papers."

"Both men are now in the truck."

"They're moving."

"They stopped."

"The driver is out of the cab."

"He is climbing on the truck bed."

"The driver is opening the lid."

"The passenger is now on the truck bed looking into the drum."

"They are giving each other the high five."

"They look happy."

"Okay. They are moving again."

"They are now back on cargo road."

"They are coming up on Lufthansa."

"Let's take them down Now! Now!"

We all hit our red lights and sirens. The marked car turned about fifty feet in front of the oncoming truck. The uniformed offices, with guns drawn, exited their vehicle and assumed the protective stop position. Billowing out over the loudspeaker could be heard.

"US Customs. Stop your vehicle."

"Now!"

"Place your hands on the back of your head."

DJ came to a stop in back of the truck. The front of Cheech's car came to a stop partially in front of the truck on the right side, and I came to a stop on the left front side. The subject was boxed in. Cheech and John Trent, with guns drawn, grabbed the passenger and removed him from the truck and had him handcuffed immediately.

As it turned out, the driver exited his vehicle as I came around the back of my vehicle. He was able to utter the words, "NY . . ."

I shouted, "Customs! Freeze," pulling the new shiny stainless steel .357 Magnum, Smith & Wesson revolver from the left side of my pants holster; so I thought. I pointed the gun at Johnson's chest. I was in the two-hand pistol grip stance. My feet were apart, and I was well balanced. It was just like they taught us in firearms training. You pull out your gun, thrust it forward as you grip your hand and wrist for support and have your trigger finger off the trigger.

In a split second, I realized there was something really wrong. Acting intuitively, I said, "Shit!"

With my left gripping hand, I reached up and, quickly, in one swooping motion, removed my black leather, in the pants holster, that was now shrouding the revolver. It fell silently to the floor beside me. Johnson did not realize that the holster was on my gun. It was happening so fast. Everyone's adrenalin was pumping.

"Hands over your head," I yelled.

His hands went up. He said, "I'm a cop! I'm on the job!"

"Keep your hands up!

"Turn around!" I said in a loud, stern voice.

DJ was now next to me with his gun drawn on Johnson. Johnson turned with his hands in the air. He was now facing the truck, and we were in back of him. He was still saying, "I'm a cop!"

The uniformed officer was repeating on the public address system, "This is a US Customs police stop. Keep your hands in plain view. This is a Customs Stop."

I could also hear John Trent yelling, "Freeze!"

"Keep your hands up."

"You're under arrest."

"Slide out of the truck slowly."

"Turn around."

"Hands on the truck."

"Move back, back, back."

"Spread your legs apart."

"More, more. Okay."

I picked up my holster and clipped it back in my pants and placed my gun in the holster. I moved in back of Johnson and said, "Put your right hand down slowly."

As he brought his right arm down, I grabbed his right wrist, placed a handcuff on his wrist, and maintained control by exerting pressure on the handcuffed wrist. I told Johnson, "Put your left hand down slowly."

I grabbed his left wrist and placed a handcuff on that wrist. He was now secured. DJ placed his gun in his holster. He moved Johnson to the front of the truck. He had him stand three feet from the truck. Then he told Johnson to bend forward resting his head on the vehicle. DJ proceeded to search him. He removed a .38 Caliber Smith & Wesson revolver and a NYC Police Department shield and identification card. Mr. Johnson was a New York City cop. Everything was removed from the two prisoners' pockets and placed into large brown evidence envelopes.

DJ placed Johnson under arrest and read him his rights. Johnson was placed in the back seat of DJ's car. DJ sat in the passenger seat, and Hendrickson drove. They returned to the office with the prisoner. Cheech and John Trent secured the other passenger of the truck. Trent placed him under arrest and read him his rights. They placed the prisoner in the back seat of their car and returned to the office. I instructed one uniform officer to drive the seized truck back to the office with the marked unit following.

The uniformed officers searched and secured the truck and took the two drums into the office and placed them in our seizure room. Johnson was put into the holding pen, and Jones was cuffed to a secure interview table. Frank took Marty back to Pan Am cargo room. He then picked up all the paperwork that Johnson had signed in order to pick up the shipment. Frank interviewed the Pan Am employees and took statements from them.

Back at the office, I took out my New York City Police Department directory and placed a call to Captain Fitzgerald, internal affairs. I knew him from an ethics class I took at John Jay College of Criminal Justice. John Fitzgerald had been a guest lecturer.

The phone rang three times before it was answered.

"IA. Captain Fitzgerald Speaking."

"This is Johnny Reno, US Customs supervisory special agent at JFK airport. We met at an ethics class at John Jay in September."

"Oh yeah! I remember you. What's up?"

"We just arrested two men smuggling in a couple hundred pounds of marijuana through Pan American cargo. One guy had a NYPD shield and ID card. He said he is a New York City police officer. He said he is assigned to 103. Can you run a check and see if he is a cop and give us a description. We do not know if he is a cop, using his ID?"

"What is his name and shield number?" Fitzgerald asked. "I will run a personnel check on him and run him through our files. Give me your number, and I will call you back in ten."

"Albert Johnson, shield number 21186," I said.

I gave him my number and hung up. Cheech and John Trent were interrogating Melvin Jones. Cheech had placed everything found on Jones in a brown envelope. They placed everything found in the truck cab in another brown envelope. The envelopes were now on the table with their contents laid out. Melvin Jones was the owner of the truck that customs now owned.

Jones had told Cheech that he was only helping Johnson pick up the shipment because Johnson did not have a truck. Jones claimed he did not know what was in the shipment. After ten minutes of interrogation, Jones spilled his guts.

Jones told us that Johnson had made several trips to Kingston, Jamaica, and had set up the deal to bring the marijuana into the US. Jones went on to say that Johnson would be handling the imports and he would handle the sales and distribution of the pot. Jones told Cheech that Johnson had a connection in customs that would get the shipment in without any problems.

DJ was interrogating Johnson, who claimed that he was working undercover and was going to bust Jones when they got the shipment to Jones's house. When DJ asked him where his backup was, Johnson said he was working alone because he did not know if Jones was lying when he said he had a load of marijuana coming in.

The phone rang. It was Fitzgerald. He verified that Johnson was a NYPD from the 103 Precinct in Queens. He also told us that they had an active investigation on Johnson involving narcotics distribution. Fitzgerald said he would send the case detectives over to interview Johnson and pick up his shield, ID, and gun. Fitzgerald told me that the Assistant District Attorney Ben Cleaver was assigned to the narcotic task force and was aware of the case opened on Johnson. He gave me the telephone number of Cleaver to give to the AUSA. I took the information down and gave him the directions to our office.

Fitzgerald then said, "Ask the AUSA if he would call Assistant District Attorney Ben Cleaver and discuss deferring federal prosecution because we have an active case against Johnson."

I told Fitzgerald, "I will call the AUSA's office and discuss the matter with him and give him Cleaver's telephone number." If the US attorney agreed, then I would turn over the prisoners and the evidence to them. I knew that as soon as I hung up the phone, Fitzgerald would be on the phone to Cleaver.

I called the duty assistant US attorney. It was Tom Swensen. I had worked many cases with Tom as the prosecutor. He was also used to getting calls from me at two in the morning. I briefed Tom on the case. I gave him DA Cleaver's number and explained the NYPD's interest. His first question to me was, "Is the marijuana refined?"

I told him that the contents in the drum contained twigs and stems of the marijuana plants. The waybill had the weight as 75 lbs for each drum. The marijuana was not refined or manicured. Swensen then said, "Okay, if that was refined, it would come to about 20 lbs per drum. Our guidelines to accept federal prosecution are 50 lbs of manicured marijuana. Let me call Cleaver and discuss this case and see if I can make some points. You never know when you may need a favor."

I briefed him on my concerns that a customs inspector might be involved, according to one of the suspects. He said he would let Cleaver know and get him to agree to let customs clean its own laundry.

He said, "In all probability, we will turn the prosecution of the two prisoners over to City, but I will call you back after I speak with Cleaver."

I thanked him and hung up. I then briefed DJ and Cheech. We proceeded with all the paperwork that was needed to be done. John Trent fingerprinted and photographed the prisoners. Melvin Jones gave us a signed statement and a signed waiver of his rights. Johnson refused to talk and kept asking us for his union representative.

Twenty minutes later, the phone rang. It was AUSA Swensen. He told me that he deferred federal prosecution to the City and that Cleaver had agreed to prosecute for possession and intent to distribute and let customs proceed with smuggling charges against any customs personnel involved. He remarked about Cleaver owing him one. I thanked him and hung up the phone.

About an hour later, Ben Cleaver and four NYPD detectives arrived at our office. After the amenities and some coffee, the detectives took the prisoners, paperwork, and seizure of marijuana. We kept the seized truck. I called customs internal affairs and briefed them on the case and the possibilities that Inspector Barnes was involved with the smuggling operation and gave them the contact of the lead NYPD detective.

As it turned out, Assistant District Attorney Ben Cleaver provided evidence and records to customs internal affairs that Barnes was involved in smuggling of several other shipments. Barnes's bank accounts showed sums of money that he could not account for. Johnson's payoff amounts coincided with deposits Inspector Barnes made. Barnes was arrested by customs internal affairs and lost his job. He was ultimately convicted of smuggling and sentenced to five years hard time in federal prison. Johnson was convicted of running a narcotics distribution ring. He received twelve years sentence in a state prison. Melvin Jones pleaded guilty and testified against Johnson and others. He received five-year suspended sentence.

Chapter 13

Fifteen Kilos of Cocaine;
Shots Fired

Training with the passengers arriving from foreign countries was a bit more trying for the new customs special agents. About 90 percent of those trained were not going to be working with or coming in contact with passengers arriving from foreign countries. It was almost impossible, with a few exceptions, to teach the new special agents how to catch someone who was attempting to smuggle something into the US in a two-week training secession. Besides, it was the job of customs inspectors and port investigators. Customs special agents and the customs port investigators (CPI'S) were both GS-1811s. Agents would only respond if there was a major violation of law. CPIs were junior agents or journeymen to the special agent position. So to avoid complications, the new agents would be assigned as the partners of the experienced CPI. The experienced CPI did the selecting of passengers for further examinations.

The word from our political leaders (congressmen and senators are filtered down through the executive branch) was that we could not profile a person to search. It was not politically correct. We were under strict orders not to profile arriving passengers. To me, this was bullshit. Our political leaders did not know their ass from their elbows. To me, it was ludicrous to say that I was searching someone because I noticed a bulge on their person, although sometimes I did search them for that reason. It is just as true today with international terrorism and the Department of Homeland Security searching children and old folks. Our political leaders and those in the executive branch are like ostriches with their heads up each other's butt. They are only interested in money, and money is power. Don't use common sense; use high technology so lucrative contracts could be issued and politicians can get big kickbacks in campaign contributions.

I remember when Israeli security people came to the US to study how certain inspectors and plainclothes teams made so many seizures on arriving passengers. They talked to our customs inspectors, CPI teams, and the immigration officers. What they found was, someone doing something wrong would react to the first contact of a government official. The first stop with arriving passengers was immigration. Immigration officers would talk to every arriving passenger to check their documents. If their entry documents were in order but their actions were suspicious, they would code-mark the baggage declaration. This would indicate that the person seemed very nervous or was suspicious. Aside from the marked baggage declarations, the customs inspectors told the Israeli how they sized up passengers coming to their examination belts. Their body language was a big tip-off—the countries they were coming from and how they answered various questions. The questions were asked to obtain a reaction from the passenger. This was not taught in customs schools; it was a pure self-initiative on the part of the individual customs inspectors and plainclothes men. I told the Israelis, "I look for a person looking at the different customs examination belts to see who is and who is not giving a thorough examination. I try to look at their faces as they belt-shop. I watch their reaction when the customs inspector asks for their baggage declaration and as he questions them. I notice their body language. I watch their facial expression as they finish their examination and leave the examination belt. When I stop someone as they leave the customs examination belt, I show them my badge and tell them I am a customs special agent and ask for their passport. I tell them I want to ask them some questions. I watch the person's facial expressions and body language." While talking to a person, if you get the feeling that something is not right, then you got to follow your instinct and look further into the matter.

It is like the time I stopped two women who arrived on a Lan Chile flight from Santiago Chile. I was working the Lan Chile flight. It was the last flight in the morning. Most of the passengers had gone through customs inspection. I began to watch two women, who appeared to know each, coming from immigration. They walked around the baggage carousel, looking for their bags. Both women looked like they were in their forties. They both had on long black silk coats and loose-fitting muumuus. They wore no makeup. Their faces and hands indicated they had a hard life. The two women separated after getting their bags. Each stood with their bag and kept looking at the various inspection belts. They were shopping for a customs inspection belt where the inspectors would just do a quick examination. They found two different belts to go to.

My partner Ray Franzone was just returning from the rest room. I briefed him on the two women. I told him that I would stop the first woman, and he would stop the second one. We kept watching these two women as they waited their turn in line. The first woman off the belt was wearing a muumuu dress under her long black silk coat. It was July. *Why would anyone wear a long coat on a July day?* When the Inspector asked her to open the bag for examination, I noticed that as she bent over to open the bag, it did not look like a normal bend. She appeared stiff. The inspector finished the baggage examination. As I watched her close her bag, she stood on her toes, not flat-footed as people normally do. She had gone through the customs examination and picked up her small bag and started heading for the exit.

As she left the inspection belt, I walked in front of her. I then abruptly stopped, turned, and could not help bumping into her. I could feel a hard substance under her clothing around her waist. I immediately pulled my badge from my breast pocket. I showed her my badge and asked for her passport. She became very nervous and began to perspire, and her hands shook as she handed me her passport. It was an Chilean passport. I asked her where she lived. She shrugged her shoulders. She said, "No English."

I asked, "How long were you going to stay here in NY?"
She said, "No English."
I said in my broken Spanish, "Quanto dias en Nueva York."

She said, "Cuarto. Familia aquí? No, turista," was her response. She carried one small bag. I immediately thought the airline ticket cost more than she could possibly make in a year in Chile. *No family. Poorly dressed. A tourist?* The questions and answers did not make sense. I took her to a search room.

I told Ray to go to the staff office and tell them I need a female to search a woman who had something under her clothes. Ray quickly proceeded to the staff office which was about forty feet from where he was standing. The woman whom Ray was watching had yet to begin her customs examination. As luck would have it, a female inspector was in the staff office, typing out some papers for Staff Officer Herb Swane. Herb never gave the CPIs a hard time like the other staff officers. Herb told Inspector Dorothy Bellman to perform the search. No other CPI teams were on the floor. Herb accompanied Dorothy and Ray to the search room. I left the room and immediately went with Ray to get the other woman. Herb stood outside the search room as Dorothy closed the door and began the search.

The other woman had left the belt and was heading out the door. I called out to CEO Phil Seanor; who was stationed at the door in order not to let anyone come into the customs area. He would also collect baggage declarations as the people left the customs areas. If they did not have a declaration or cashier's receipt, he would send them back to the customs belt.

I yelled out, "Phil, stop her!" As she gave Phil her declaration, he heard me. He told her she had to go back. At that point, I got to her, showed her my badge, and asked her for her passport. She became very nervous. Perspiration began to pour down her face. So close yet so far. Ray caught up with me. She had placed her suitcase on the floor in front of her while she took her passport from a small purse she was carrying. I knew that we now had two women who might be carrying drugs.

I said, "Do you have family here, familia aquí?"

"No turista," was her response.

I then said, "How many days here?" Seeing she might not understand, I immediately said, "Quanto dias en Nueva York."

She said, "Cuarto." I took her purse from her hand and looked inside. She had only $50 US currency. *How can anyone stay in New*

York for four days on only $50? Too many questions and the facts did not make sense.

We took her back to the ships office where we had another search room. Ray stood with her while I headed to the staff office. Herb was heading back to his office after stopping at each examination belt to tell the inspectors that we had a drug courier off the Lan Chile flight. The inspectors began a more intensive examination of all remaining Lan Chile passengers. Herb spotted me coming toward him, and he called out to me, "She has about three kilos of white powder." Herb said he was getting a narcotics test kit.

I asked Herb if he had anymore female inspectors at the terminal. He said, "No."

I told him I had another female to be searched in the ships office search room. He said he had no one available. Lufthansa airlines handled the arriving flight for Lan Chile airlines. I spotted Elsa, the Lufthansa ground representative for Lan Chile heading for the exit to the lobby.

I called out, "Elsa!"

She turned and looked toward me. "Did you call me?" I waved my hand, signaling her to come to me.

"Yes, I need your help. I have one of your female passengers whom I need you to search for me." Elsa had searched female passengers for us before when a female inspector was not available. She also acted as interpreter for us. Elsa said she would do the search. She knew the routine.

She raised her right hand before I could say anything else. "Not now, in the search room."

"Okay, Johnny, where is she?"

"In the ships office search room," I said. We entered the search room. Elsa spoke Spanish to the woman. She asked her if she had anything concealed on her person. The woman said no and that she was a tourist. I then told Elsa to raise her right hand. She raised her right hand. "Okay, do you solemnly swear to uphold the customs laws and regulations of the United States of America?"

Elsa said, "I do."

"Now you are a customs officer assisting me. Search her and see what she has under the muumuu." Elsa had the woman take off the muumuu and then remove a large girdle, which was holding six large plastic bags of white powder. Elsa placed the girdle and plastic bags on the table. The woman, identified as Esther A. Etchartea, began to sob.

Elsa told me to come into the room. When I entered the room, I saw the girdle and six plastic bags of white powder. Elsa said, "Should I initial each bag and the girdle now?" She knew the routine because she had done this before.

I said yes, and Elsa began initialing each bag and girdle. She placed very small initials at the corner of each bag. I placed my initials after hers. I asked Ray to get a narcotic test kit from Herb and see what the other woman had. I asked Elsa to go with and help Ray question the other woman while I made a thorough search of Mrs. Etchartea's personal effects.

About fifteen minutes later, Elsa came back to me. She asked me to step out of the room. We stood outside the door and talked. Elsa told me that the woman refused to say anything. She would not answer any questions. Elsa said the soft and the hard approach did not work. Elsa had helped translate for me on many occasions and knew what we were looking for. She was good. Elsa said, "These women are mules. They are from the countryside. If they worked, they would only make, maybe $100 a year. It is very easy to get these country people to be mules. Offer them a paid vacation to the US and pay them $300 or $400. They will do anything." Elsa then said the staff officer's test of the white powder was positive for cocaine.

Herb Swane then came into the ships office. He told me that the woman identified as Linda Ruby Gotes was carrying 6.6 lbs of cocaine. He said Ray was reexamining the baggage and personal effects and had placed her under arrest and had read her rights to her. Herb was carrying a test kit and scales. We went into the room, and I performed the narcotic test of the powder. I punctured one bag and removed a few grains of the salt-like powder. I placed it in the vial and broke the liquid portion of the vial. I shook the vial. The liquid was released into the powder and the substance began to turn bright blue. It was cocaine. I then arrested Esther and read her rights. I then had Elsa read her rights in Spanish.

Esther refused to talk. Going through her wallet, I came across a picture of a younger woman with a baby. Elsa asked her who this was, and she said they were her daughter and granddaughter. Elsa looked at me, and I looked at her. I told her that if she did not cooperate with us, she would go to jail and when she got out and went home, her granddaughter would be holding her great granddaughter. If she cooperated with us, I would tell the judge that she had helped. "We could ask the judge to give you a shorter sentence because you helped us get the others. We know there were others on the flight with you. Tell us everything, and you will be able to see your granddaughter grow up." Elsa put her emotions into this translation, and the woman began to cry hysterically. Elsa gave her comfort and a tissue and kept telling that everything would be all right if she cooperated. Esther then said, "Si, ayudame por favor," as she clutched the picture to her breast. Now Elsa went to work on her. She knew what I was looking for.

Herb popped his head into the room and said, "I pulled all the customs declaration from the Lan Chile flight." Gotes declaration indicated that she was going to the Diplomat Hotel in midtown Manhattan. I had three baggage declarations with the Diplomat Hotel. I gave Elsa a pad of paper and asked her to get Esther complete story of her trip.

Elsa said, "If we remove her handcuffs I think we would get a lot more out of her. It would show our good will. Besides I have my nice, big, strong agent with me. You would protect me, wouldn't you?"

Now that Esther had agreed to help us, I removed the handcuffs from her so she would be more at ease. I told Elsa that I had to make a phone call and I would get an inspector to stay with her. She said it would be okay. I asked the ships Inspector Tonto to stay with the prisoner while I made a phone call.

I went to the Duke's office in front of the staff office. I called the NYC office and asked for Ed Boyle, head of the cocaine squad. Ed got on the phone. I briefed Ed on the two seizures of cocaine and that we suspected that at least three other passengers from the flight were going to the Diplomat Hotel. I gave Ed the names from the three declarations. I told Ed I thought that they would not be at the hotel for at least another hour or so. Ed said, "OK I will send some agents to the hotel."

I knew that the city squad was proficient in what they did. They would coordinate with the hotel security and set up a command post. They would not only get the couriers but also get the person who was to receive the drugs. "If you get anything else, let me know," Ed said. I hung up and proceeded to the ships office.

When I got to the search room, it was empty, and Tonto, Elsa, and Esther were gone. They were all gone. *What happened to my prisoner? Where was Tonto?* All sorts of things ran through my mind. I ran out toward the staff office. Everyone I past I asked if they saw Tonto, and the response was always the same. "He is in the ships office." I continued to the staff office when I spotted Tonto, Elsa, and Esther coming from the ladies' room. I waited for them to reach me, and we all went back to the search room. I asked Elsa what happened. Elsa said that Esther had to go to the ladies' room real bad. Tonto and I took her to the ladies' room. I checked that there was no one in the ladies' room, and we went in.

I said, "Tonto too?"

Yes was her response. "I went into the stall with her and checked her draws for any grease like you have told me many times. There was no trace of grease so no internal body-carry. She did her business and we are now back."

We entered the search room again. "She is a mule," Elsa said. Esther sat at the table with Elsa. Elsa looked at her notes and filled me in. Esther lived in a Montevideo, Uruguay. Her granddaughter needed an operation, but they had no money. One of her friends told her how she could get some money. He introduced her to a man named Pedro. Pedro said he would give her $400 if she went with him to New York and took a small gift with her to give to Pedro's friend. She needed the money, so she agreed. It took over a day for her to get to Santiago Chile by bus. She stood in a hotel room with four other women. They were there for two days before the flight to the US. That was where she met Ruby Gotes. Dolores, Florence, and Luisa kept to themselves. Pedro held all their passports so they could not back out. Pedro had bought all their tickets. Well, those three names matched three of the customs declaration showing the Diplomat Hotel. The man Pedro held their passports until they were ready to go to the airport in Santiago. She said they would be paid their $400 in the hotel room in New York. Pedro was on the flight with them. If they got separated, they would take a cab to the Diplomat Hotel. That was what the $50 was for. She did not know Pedro's last name. Esther told Elsa that she would cooperate and deliver the drugs to Pedro at the hotel if it would help her.

Looking through the customs declarations we came across three Pedros with different addresses in Corona Queens. I called Ed Boyle and gave him the information on the three Pedros we came across. I told him that we had one female who was willing to cooperate and make the delivery to Pedro, the man riding shotgun on the flight. Ed said, "Put the drugs back in the girdle and on the mule and bring her here to the Diplomat Hotel."

I placed clear tape over the small puncture on the one bag. I instructed Esther that when she removed the bags from the girdle, she should put the side that was facing her body down so the marks we put on the bags would not be seen. I then had a test run. I instructed her to remove the bags. She remembered and followed the instructions and carefully laid the bags with the marks face down. Elsa and I placed the bags back in the girdle. Esther put on her muumuu and coat.

I told Ray I was going to meet Boyle and make a controlled delivery. He was to complete the process on Gotes and lodge her with the US marshal's office in the Eastern District courthouse. Ray took CPI Tom Virgilio and took the prisoner and drugs to our Varick Street office in NYC, where she was photographed and fingerprinted. The seizure was photographed and then turned over to the seizure clerk on a chain of custody form IV-41.

When we got close to the Diplomat Hotel in midtown Manhattan, I called Boyle on the radio. I was instructed to bring the subject to room 321 and use the cleaning staff entrance and service elevator. I parked the car on the side street, and we walked to the service entrance. We went in the building. There was no one around, and we quickly took the elevator to the third floor. As we approached the room, the door opened, and we rushed in. In the room was Ed Boyle and several other agents and a host of electronic equipment.

I immediately spotted Agent Victor Mendez. English was his second language. I introduced him to Esther. I told him how I instructed her to remove the bags of dope so our initials would not be detected. Victor sat down with Esther, and they conversed in Spanish for about five minutes. Esther was instructed to tell Pedro that she saw Ruby get caught by the customs and taken into a room. She had passed customs when they stopped Ruby and took her to a room. She immediately left and went directly to the taxi line and took a taxi here.

Victor and Esther left the room and went down the service elevator. There was a taxi parked outside the service entrance. It was our undercover cab. Victor got into the driver side of the cab, and Esther got into the passenger side. Victor drove around the corner and pulled in front of the hotel. Esther gave Victor the fifty dollars, and Victor gave her change. He got out and helped Esther out of the cab. She was to go to the desk, give her name, and ask for a key to her room. As she entered the lobby of the hotel, she saw Pedro watching her. He had watched her paying the cab driver and getting change and exiting the cab. He saw the cab pull away. He watched her enter the lobby before he acknowledged her. He walked up to her and asked her what happened. She told Pedro the story she had rehearsed.

They went up the elevator to the third floor. They went to room 322, which was across from the customs agents surveillance room. Pedro knocked three times on the door. There was a scrabbling noise, and a voice said, "Who is it?"

"It's Pedro," was the response. Dolores opened the door slowly. Pedro and Esther entered the room. Sitting on the couch were Florence and Luisa, watching TV. Once in the room, Pedro told Esther to go to the bedroom and take the bags from the girdle and put them in the suitcase with the other bags. Esther went into the bedroom with Dolores. Esther removed her coat. Dolores helped Esther remove her muumuu. Esther removed the girdle and the six plastic bags of white powder.

Dolores opened the suitcase, and Esther removed the bags as she practiced, placing each one in the suitcase.

Pedro got on the room phone and made a call to Corona, Queens, and told the man on the phone that Ruby could not make it to the party. He said he did not feel like having a party without Ruby. The man, later identified as Hector Sanchez, who was on the phone with Pedro said, "In about five minutes, my cousin Felix will be coming to your door. He is bringing you the food for you and the girls. Give him the bag with dirty clothes. After you eat the food I sent to you, you can leave the party."

Pedro said, "I understand." He hung up the phone. Five minutes later, a man knocked on the door, and Pedro asked who it was.

The man said, "It is Felix; I have your food for the party." Pedro opened the door, and Felix entered the room. He gave Pedro the bag he was carrying. Inside the bag were two large bags of potato chips. Under the chip bags was a large envelope. Pedro took the envelope and gave the girls the two bags of chips. Felix then went into the bedroom with Pedro and came out carrying a green suitcase.

Ed Boyle had decided to make the bust when Felix, who was later identified as Felix Cardoza, was leaving the room with the suitcase. He did not want to take a chance in losing over five million dollars of cocaine in a surveillance going to someplace in Queens. It was too risky. Felix opened the room door to go out. Seven customs agents burst into the room with guns drawn.

"Customs police." Two agents took hold of Felix, and two more agents took Pedro down to the floor. They handcuffed Pedro and Felix before they knew what happened to them. The girls screamed and did not know what was happening. Esther was expecting this to happen. She was handcuffed with the others. In the envelope was $3,000 in twenty dollar bills. The drugs and money were seized. My work was just about done. I had to return to the airport. I had a lot of paperwork to complete. I also had to gather the airline documentation as evidence for the trial.

I guess you want to know what happened to Esther. Well, Ed Boyle's squad turned Felix and made a controlled delivery of the suitcase to Hector Sanchez. But the suitcase now only contained one bag of cocaine, and the rest of the bags were replaced with dummy bags of cocaine from our NY office. Hector received fifteen-year sentence in a federal prison. Felix Cardoza received five years in a federal prison. Pedro received five years in a federal prison. Ruby, Dolores, Luisa, and Florence all got five years in a federal prison. Esther received five years with four years suspended. She was out in less than a year and sent back to Uruguay.

Now, the Israeli security officers understood that I profiled the person and the flight that she arrived on. They understood the questioning and the reasoning behind the questions. The US Government does not. Today, the Israeli government has a five-stop system where individuals are observed at each point. Their citizens do not have to go through the cumbersome, humiliating system we now have.

When I first started in plainclothes, I noticed that only certain customs inspectors were making most of the seizures. I befriended them and picked their brains on how they questioned the passengers and how come they made so many seizures. I started to do research on various commodities and the countries they came from.

The plainclothes teams would mingle with the arriving passengers at the baggage carousels. I would observe the passengers behavior and watch their actions while retrieving their bags from the carousel, looking for a customs examination belt and having their bags examined by the customs inspectors. After they completed their examination and were leaving, I would stop them, talk to them, and then decide if I would take them to a private room and conduct a search of the person. Many times after questioning them, I would let them go without further examination.

The profiling of passengers was an unspoken science. Most of the investigators selected passengers on a few obvious criteria.

If passengers had expensive luggage like Louis Vuitton or Gucci, they probably had money. And if they were nervous and/or were belt-shopping and they came from Paris or Rome, they would be a good candidate for a search.

Knowing the high-value tourist commodities and the economy of the various countries aided in the profiling of passengers. A flight from Amsterdam or Antwerp, the commodity to look for was diamonds. The most likely person not to declare the diamonds would be a Jewish person, more likely a Hasidic Jew. Italians on flights from Rome or Milan would have gold jewelry not declared. Hippies coming from Iceland would have Switchblade knives, marijuana, or hash. Heroin from France and Germany. Cocaine from South American countries.

Knowing the trends, reading the society pages and various trade journals aided in making an informed decision of whom to search for particular commodes. When large shipments of drugs were seized in the US, it meant to me an increase in body-carries.

After a while, you get to know the commodity and countries the best buys are in. The appearance, dress, body language of the passengers added to the mix. Then stop and talk to the passenger and check the countries they had visited, observing their reactions. The smuggler acts different from an innocent person. Philly Brickster was a new special agent who wanted to learn. He was a retired New York City police detective. He understood the concept and how it could be applied to all investigations.

On day four of Philly Brickster's training, in the international arrival building, JFK airport, New York, he was observing an arriving passenger going to the baggage carousel. The man was traveling alone. He was having some words with another passenger. The bags were just coming in on the carousel. They then went to get their bags. One man did not let it go. Philly, dressed in a light tan sports jacket with brown pants, had a white shirt with an open collar and no tie. He held an airline ticket jacket in his hand and blended into the surroundings as an arriving passenger, looking for his baggage. He was about three feet to the left of a man who wore a blue sport jacket. The man was in his forties. He had a full head of black hair with gray streaks on the side. His face was dark with a heavy shadow of beard. His jacket and pants were wrinkled, and shirt was almost out of his pants. Philly was doing his job by observing the passengers and looking for people with bulges in their clothing. The man had appeared to have been drinking.

Picture the next thing to happen in slow motion. It actually took less than fifteen seconds. The man in the blue jacket reached inside his open sport jacket. As his right hand exited the open jacket, a big, shiny object was pulled from its concealed rest place. *It's a gun!* Philly is between the gunman and the intended victim. The victim, who was facing the man and exchanging words with him, sees the gun and tries to get him and his wife out of the line of fire. The man was bringing his hand with the gun across his body, attempting to point it at the intended victim whom he was arguing with and who was now a moving target. A woman started to scream at the sight of the gun. As the man brought the gun out and upward across his body, Philly saw the handgun being pointed at him. It was a Smith & Weston .38 Cal revolver.

Philly instinctively lunges at the man, grabbing for the gun. Philly's left hand was pushing the gun upward as he gripped the man's wrist. Boom! A loud defining noise was heard echoing in the baggage area as the gun was fired. Philly's right hand came down on the top of the gun, seizing the cylinder of the gun, stopping it from being fired again. Philly, with his hands firmly on the gun and the man's wrist, knocked the man down with his momentum. They tumbled to the ground and were rolling over, Philly still clutching the gun for his dear life.

Passengers were screaming, scattering, and dropping to the floor. It was becoming chaotic. Philly's partner for the day was Freddy Neilson, a sixty-five-year-old, white hair investigator, who was retiring in less than a year. Freddy also reacted instinctively. He lunged at the man who was now falling with Philly after the gun discharge. Freddy went down with his fist pounding and grabbing at the man's free arm as Philly maintained his grip on the gun and the man's hand. Philly twisted the gun, ripping it from the man's hand, and rolled away from the man.

I was John Trent's partner that day, and we were several feet away, looking at another arriving passenger when the shot was fired. Turning around instinctively, John Trent and I raced toward the two men with the gun. In an instant, John Trent and Fred Neilson collided with the man's body. They were now all over the man, using their law enforcement training to subdue the man and handcuff him. I immediately went to Philly to calm him down and see if he was injured. I asked him if he was hit. He said, "No. I don't think so."

Philly was all shock up and out of breath. He was breathing hard, trying to fill his lungs with air. His white hair was sticking up everywhere. His face was red as a beet and had some blood on it. His wristwatch was smashed. The back of his hand was cut and bleeding. He took out his handkerchief and wrapped it around his hand. I directed the inspectors to see if anyone was injured by the gun shot and to clear the area.

The customs inspectors who were not armed immediately filled the area and cleared all the passengers from the area while supervisors were notified. We moved the prisoner to closest search room. Other plainclothesmen rushed to the scene to assist. Plainclothesmen and inspectors began to seek out witnesses of the event. The witnesses were taken to the staff office, and statements were taken. The shot had gone wild and lodged in the suitcase of a passenger who was two baggage carousels away. The bullet was found lodged in the passenger's alarm clock. Thank the lord that no one was hurt.

During the scuffle, the irate passenger, with his other hand, must have grabbed Philly's jacket and tore one of the arm off the jacket. One pocket on the jacket was ripped open, and there was a footprint on the back of Philly's jacket.

The follow-up investigation and interrogation of the man and witnesses revealed that the man was drinking heavily on the plane and taking pills. He also started an argument with the intended target and his wife on the plane. He was making sexual remarks and advances toward the man's wife so she changed seats with her husband. A steward and stewardess had to prevent the husband from attacking the drunk man.

The plane had started its landing approach. The irate man became calm and closed his eyes as if he went to sleep when threatened by the passenger protecting his wife. The crew thought the man had gone to sleep. The plane then landed, and the couple left the plane without incident before the irate man awoke and got out of his seat. I called the federal prosecutors office, and the prosecution was declined in favor of New York state prosecution. The man was turned over to the port of New York authority police. The man was convicted of a felony and served three years in state prison.

After that incident, John Trent and the other trainees all of a sudden became interested in how we picked out people to be searched. Now then they wanted to take everyone in the room for a search. John stood another three days before going to his next cycle of training. John and I had worked together in the 1960s on a special operation that took us to Puerto Rico and the Virgin Islands. It involved drugs and money laundering. I was also slated to work with him in El Paso, Texas, on a drug smuggling operation, but instead, I went to Columbus, New Mexico. But those were other stories. The point is you have to look at people and read their faces and their body language. Ask questions, be inquisitive, and be ready to act instinctively.

Chapter 14

Two Kilos of Cocaine at JFK

Unlike most of the other investigators, I took this profiling to another level. I not only kept up with the newspapers and magazines, I visited the US Customs commodity specialists in their offices at JFK and was brought up to speed on the latest trends and market value on certain commodities.

I also talked to some of the agents and analysts I knew in the US Customs narcotics intelligence unit in the New York regional office. I picked their brains on routes, trends, and prices worldwide. I wanted to know which foreign cities had drug labs. I especially wanted to know when large shipments of narcotics were seized anywhere in the US. When a large seizure of drugs was made, the street price would go up and/or the purity would go down. This meant that an immediate supply was needed to keep up with the demand. Then we would see an immediate increase in body-carries of drugs into the US.

The JFK investigative teams would have a monthly contest to see who would get the highest merchandise value seizure as well as the most seizures and penalties. Most of the teams had a 60 percent accuracy rate. I had a ninety-seven percent accuracy rate.

I also had what you would call a hunch, a feeling, a premonition, or just extrasensory perception. Don't laugh. The other investigators laughed when I first told them the reason I made so many seizures was because of my ability to know what a person was smuggling in.

I had never told anyone that my mother, God bless her soul, used to get premonition of things before they would happen. I kept it to myself for fear of the kidding I would get from anyone I told.

Whenever there was a sickness or accident or death, I, like my mother, would get this feeling. We were getting the same types of feelings. One day, Mom told me that she used to get bad dreams about things that were going to happen. She did not want to talk about them. She said, "I'm telling you, so if you get these bad dreams, you do not think you are going crazy."

I would be visiting Mom and Dad, and we would be talking. All of a sudden, Mom would get up, and Dad would say, "Where are you going?"

Mom would say, "I'm going to answer the phone. Stella is calling."

Dad would say, "You're hearing things. The phone didn't ring."

Then the phone would ring, and it was my sister Stella, calling to check on Mom and Dad. Mom actually thought she heard the phone ring even before it rang. I was the same way. I could tell whenever Mom, my sister, or brother Joe was going to call.

In my late teens, I used to practice the use of kinetic energy. I used to try to move small objects and to levitate paper. What I was able to achieve was to hone in on thought waves. I used to concentrate on people who were not facing me and ask them to turn around or tell them they dropped something. They would turn around or look down within a few seconds. I was able to know before the kids I hung with said anything about where they wanted to go or what they wanted to do. After the first year of stopping people and searching them, I began to get the sense I knew what they were carrying. I used to mingle among the arriving passengers to see if I would get a feeling about anyone. I would then concentrate on certain passengers. I would follow them, observing them getting cleared by the inspectors and then decide whether to stop them or not.

I, like the other seasoned investigators, tried to explain to the new training partner about our profiling why we selected certain persons for a more intense examination. Most did not want to be bothered with the details. They said, "Just make the seizure, and put my name on it." To them, this was dull work unless we got a body-carry of narcotics.

I remember this particular incident as if it was yesterday. It was Thursday, March 6, 1969, The day began like any other day. I was working the two-to-ten shift. It was a cold blustery day. I left my house about 1:30 p.m. I parked in the employee section of the parking lot. I tried to find a spot up close to the international arrivals building, which was still under renovation. It was a long day, and I had made one agriculture and one jewelry seizure.

The shift was coming to an end. The last flight for the two-to-ten shift was just finishing up. All the passengers from this particular Lufthansa flight had gone through the customs inspection belts. The flight had come from Santiago Chile. We had taken several suspicious, bulky-looking passengers for a secondary personal examination but came up negative. The inspectors did not come up with anything except fruits and prohibited agriculture products.

There were a few stragglers who were held up in immigration because of their entry documents. These few were now coming into the baggage area. The next flight to arrive would be an Olympic flight. It was scheduled to arrive at 9:45 p.m. By the time the people came into the baggage claims area, it would be after 10:00 p.m., and I would be on my way home.

My partner for the night was Harry Vance. Investigators Ralph Cippy and Ray Franzone were partners, and Joe Catalano and Ray Tillis were partners. Fred Neilson was the supervisory investigator on duty. I finished the paperwork for the jewelry seizure I made. I seized $3,500.00 in gold jewelry from a passenger off the Alitalia airlines flight. Alitalia had arrived about ten minutes before the Lufthansa flight. By the time I finished the paperwork, the passengers from the Lufthansa flight, which arrived from Chile, had all cleared customs. The other investigative teams had stopped several bulky persons who arrived on the flight from Chile, with negative results.

We were all tired and could not wait to go home. We were all standing by the diplomatic scales, discussing the day's activities and about some of the airline personnel. It was a common bull session. The guys were talking about the job and about the female airline ground passenger representatives. We were just killing time before we left the floor and went upstairs to the office to sign out.

The conversation drifted toward how I made the most seizures. They all wanted to know. So I said, "I get a feeling of what a person is hiding." They all laughed at me.

Joe said mockingly, "What do you think you have? Extrasensory perception?"

Ray followed up with, "Hey, Reno thinks he's Amazing Kreskin, the mind reader." They all were having a good laugh.

From the last customs belt in the east wing, I observed a man about thirty years old, five feet five inches tall, black hair, wearing a white opened-collar shirt with a black wool suit, and he was carrying his large brown leather suitcase. He was about fifty feet from us. He looked like most immigrants do when they arrive in the US.

I just blurted out, "I'm going to make a seizure of two kilos of cocaine." The laughter really got loud. I turned to my partner Harry and said, "Harry, get a cart. We are going to get two kilos of cocaine. That guy coming this way has the junk." I started to walk toward the man.

I could hear Harry say, "Hey, Reno, it's almost time to go home." But Harry had no choice; he began to follow me.

As I proceeded toward the man, I could hear the other guys making remarks, "Yeah, two kilos of coke!" in a sarcastic way. They were laughing among themselves. Harry was reluctant to make the stop because it was almost time to go home. He followed me and picked up a baggage cart on the way.

As I approached the man, I could see that he was Spanish or South American, probably off the Lufthansa flight from Santiago Chile. He was about thirty years old and clean-shaven. No five o'clock shadow. This bothered me. *Why did he shave before landing?* He was wearing a straight-cut suit, which looked like it did not fit him or it was not his suit. Something was out of place.

I stopped the man just a few feet from one of our search rooms. I showed him my badge.

I said, in my limited Spanish vocabulary, "I am customs. Do you have your passport?" "Yo soy Aduanero . . ."

"Me das su passaporte por favor?"

I knew he understood that I had asked him for his passport.

In an intimidating manner, I displayed my badge in front of his face. When he saw the bright gold badge, the man knew that something was up. Thoughts must have ran through his mind. His hands began to tremble as he brought his hand up to his jacket and took his passport with customs declaration out from the inside jacket pocket. He handed the documents to me. His hands trembled.

I then asked him if he spoke English.

"De habla ingles?"

He said he could speak a little.

"Un poco."

Harry took the man's bag from his hand and put it on the baggage cart. I looked at the passport. It was an Argentine passport. It had exit and entrance visa stamps from several South American countries. The name in the passport was Gabriel Lesenne. His date of birth made him thirty-one years old. I asked him what kind of work he did. He said that he was a seaman, and he lived in Rio De Janeiro. A light went on. Argentine passport and lives in Brazil? Something is not right.

We started for the search room. The man was on my right, and Harry walked slowly behind us, pushing the baggage cart.

I asked the man if this was his passport.

"Este es su passaporte?"

He said, "Yes."

"Si, Si. Señor"

We walked to the search room. I could see the man was nervous and sweat was appearing on his forehead.

I told him. "It's very hot?"

"Hace mucho calor."

We stopped in front of the search room. I opened the door and motioned the man to go in.

"Entra en," I said.

I followed him into the room.

The room was twelve-by-twelve feet with yellow painted walls and a large travel poster on one wall. There were a gray metal table, padded brown leather-covered bench seat, and two gray metal chairs. The man walked in front of the bench seat. He turned around. His eyes scanned the room. He looked directly at me. I could tell he was petrified. He stood rigid. His eyes met mine. He looked like a man who was facing a firing squad, and I just said, "Ready!"

I was now about three feet from him. He was now sweating profusely. The beads of sweat were large and giving in to gravity, one after another until the sweat was pouring down his face. He looked as if I had grabbed him by the hair and submerged his head under water and then yanked his head out.

I just knew that he had narcotics. I began to smile and almost broke out in laughter. This made him even more nervous. I continued tapping his passport on my open hand in front of him. This seemed to make him even more nervous.

After Harry pushed the cart into the room, he closed the door. I turned my head quickly and looked at Harry. Harry was still not believing and not looking at the man. I caught Harry shaking his head from side to side and heard him say in a low voice, "He is an immigrant, and he doesn't have anything."

Harry is now leaning, in a relaxed position, with his both arms resting on the baggage cart handlebar. I turned back to the nervous and frightened passenger, who was now breathing heavily. I moved slowly toward the man. Now I was directly in front of him. I looked deep into his brown eyes blinking rapidly trying to keep out the salty sweat. I said, "Mr. Lesenne, do you have contraband you did not tell the customs about?

"Senior Lesenne tiene en su persona contrabando?"

What I was really trying to ask him was our standard question we ask everyone.

"Do you have anything in your pockets or on your person that you failed to declare to the customs inspector?"

It did not come out that way in the translation.

As I was saying this to him, I was patting my jacket in the front and sides.

It was as if someone stabbed him with a sharp knife. He moved his head and shoulders back slightly, as he drew in a breath through his lips that formed a small circle. He did not answer. He did not know whether to give up or bluff his way out. It was a game of cat and mouse, and he was the mouse about to be eaten by the cat.

The man said, "No, nothing" in broken English with his palms out stretched. I could see the sweat still pouring down his brow. The man's olive complexion began to leave his face. He became pale. I moved my face a little close to his face. I looked at him straight in the eye with a big grin on my face. I slowly shook my head from side to side. I again began tapping the man's passport on my free hand. Using a stern voice and a big smile, I said, in my pigeon Spanish, "Senior Lesenne! Por favor! Quanto kilos tiene usted en sue persona?"

As I spoke those words and looked him in the eye, I could see that what I had said hit him like a sledge hammer. His mouth opened wide as he sucked in air. His eyebrows arched as his eyes opened wide. The sweat was now pouring all over his face, and a puddle of water appeared on the floor at his feet. I also noticed a small but growing tremor in his body as he looked for words.

At that precise moment, he reminded me of Redd Fox in the TV sitcom "Sanford and Sons." When Fred threw his one arm in the air and the other across his chest and said, "I'm having the big one. I'm coming, Louise. I'm having the big one."

Like Sanford, this man blurted out, "Dos! Dos kilos!"

At this point, his legs collapsed under him, and he melted down to the floor. I picked him up off the floor and sat him down on the bench. I had grabbed his arm to pick him up and could feel something soft wrapped around his arm. As I felt it, I knew I had narcotics. The rush was elevating as I began to breathe more rapidly. I knew I had him. But what kind of narcotics did he have two of?

I grabbed the softness around his arm and said, "Dos. Que es esto?"

He said, "Cócaina., dos kilos de Cócaina."

I turned to Harry and said in an excited voice, "I told you we were going to get two kilos of coke."

I could feel the excitement bursting through me as I blurted out the words to Harry. I could feel the adrenalin boiling over. It was almost as good as getting laid. I got a guy with the big load. This was what all the investigative teams strived for. But it was me. I got the big load of narcotics. It never crossed my mind that I would later get recognition in the form of a commissioner's commendation certificates and a thousand-dollar monetary award for the seizure. It was as if I said some magic words. It hit Harry like a ton of bricks. Harry immediately propped himself to attention from a slumped restful position as the man told us he had cocaine. My reinforcement of telling Harry of the coke prompted Harry to open his jacket, exposing a large .357 silver magnum revolver in a holster on his hip. I could see Harry's hand shanking as he immediately placed his hand on the revolver and attempted to remove it. I knew if Harry ever had to take the gun from the holster in a hurry, he would in all probability shoot me instead of the bad guy. That is, if he had any bullets in the gun.

I said, "Harry, calm down! There is no need to pull your gun out. This guy is not going anywhere."

It was common knowledge that until several years ago, when Sergeant Walter Conrad, affectionately known as Bubbles, came to the airport, the uniform and plainclothes men did not put bullets in their guns. Bubbles went ballistic and gave almost everyone at the airport a three-day suspension. Harry did not have the steadiest hand. He did not like guns. He did not want to carry one. He only carried one because he had to. He was getting close to retirement age. Just a couple of year, and he would retire. He needed to carry a gun to qualify for a law enforcement retirement.

I could feel the excitement. I was on a high. I no longer felt tired. I was wide awake. My mind was racing.

I told Harry, "I am going to search him now. Just let him see you have my back."

My mistake. Harry again pulled his jacket open and turned to the side to show the prisoner that he had a gun on his hip. He, now in an excited voice, blurted out, "Federally! Federally!"

I guess that was the only Spanish Harry knew.

Showing the man he had his hand on his gun made the prisoner very nervous and frightened.

I told Harry, "Calm down."

I then told Mr. Lesenne, "Take off your jacket. Senior, quitar sacar sue ropa."

He started to hesitate, so I began to help him. We got the jacket off. He was wearing a white shirt or should I say a wet shirt. I could see that there was something around his arms.

I told him while motioning with my hands to open his shirt, "Take off your shirt."

At this point, he just complied. He removed the shirt, slowly unbuttoning one button and then the next. With his shirt off, I could see there were wraparound medical bands, about eight inches wide, holding plastic bags of white powder around each his arms. The two bands were wet and gray with sweat. He was soaked.

I then told him to drop his pants.

"Sue pantalón."

He complied.

He was wearing a women white girdle with four plastic bags containing a white powdery substance. He also had plastic bags containing white powder wrapped around his calves and thighs.

I sat the man down.

Harry opened the door and took a few steps out of the room and called to the other teams. "Get Neilson. The guy has two kilos of coke." Of course, the other teams came down to get a quick look to see what we had. We all knew what had to be done.

At this time, Elsa, the Lufthansa ground supervisor, was returning from the immigration area with the clearance documents from the flight. She was curious as to what was going on, especially seeing the other investigators running into the search room and hearing Harry yelling something about two kilos of coke.

Joe said, "You got coke? What flight?"

I said, "The Lufthansa flight. Go to the lobby and round up any passengers from the flight. Bring them back for a reexamination."

The teams, after looking at the prisoner, ran out to try to locate other passengers. I could see Elsa looking into the room to see what was going on. I walked to the doorway. Elsa was now in front of me. Elsa said in an excited voice, "Reno what is going on? Did you catch someone with cocaine?"

I told Elsa, "Elsa, I know I can trust you. I need you to get me some information. I need the passenger list for the flight and the ticketing info for the passengers on the flight."

"Ok, I can do that," she said.

"You can come in but stand in the doorway and take a look and then get me the information, okay?"

"OK, Reno," she replied.

We entered the room. I motioned for the man to stand up. He did. Harry stood frozen with his hand on his gun. I took out my handcuffs. I took his right hand and placed it in back of him and put the handcuff on his right wrist, and then I took his left arm, pulling it in back of him, and placed the other handcuff on the left wrist. With his hands cuffed behind his back, I sat him down on the bench.

"Reno," Elsa called out.

"That's Gabriel. I translated for him in immigration. There was a question of why he was coming here. He said that he was a Spanish seaman. He was meeting a ship in Brooklyn."

I took out my laminated card and read him his Miranda warning in English. I then asked Elsa to read the card to him in Spanish. She read the English version and translated it into Spanish. Gabriel said he understood. I had Elsa sit at the table and act as translator for me. Elsa sat in the chair facing Gabriel.

I said, "Elsa, tell him if he lies or does not tell me everything, I will see that he will stay in jail for a long time. Tell him we already arrested one man and he is speaking to us to help himself. If he tells us everything, I will tell the judge he helped us. He would spend a short time in jail and then get sent back to Argentina. If he lies or does not help us, he will be in jail for a long time. Ask him how many others were on the flight with him."

She spoke to him in Spanish. He answered her. There was a brief exchange between them.

Elsa said, "I asked him if he stayed in the hotel the night before the flight, and he said yes. He also said he thinks there were three others on the flight with him. He is not sure."

Elsa, in a commanding voice, started to speak again to Gabriel in Spanish. After a sentence or two, Elsa paused. She raised her voice in a scolding tone and slammed her open hand on the table. It made a loud startling sound. Gabriel turned white as a ghost as the slamming sound caused his body to jolt back. He looked petrified. Elsa started speaking rapidly in Spanish. A two-way conversation took place. Questions and answers came forth, Gabriel would not stop talking. Elsa kept interjecting questions, and he kept answering.

I interrupted and said, "Elsa, what did you say to him and what is he saying?"

Elsa began, "I told him you have police in Santiago and he better tell you everything because you will find out everything. If you do not tell him everything, and he finds out from the others, you will never see daylight for a long time. He then told me there were three men and one woman in the hotel room with him the night before the flight. The man who taped the drugs on him was called Pablo. Pablo gave them their tickets when they arrived at the airport. Pablo also took the same flight. Pablo said he would meet them at the Diplomat Hotel. He gave them a number to call if they got lost. He gave them money for the taxi to take them to the hotel. He said that they would receive their money, two hundred US dollars and return tickets at the hotel after he got the packages from their body."

"Boy, you are good," I told Elsa.

"I know," she said, "but I had a good teacher. I remembered the other times I helped you interpret for people you caught with drugs. See I'm a fast learner. But I'm also a good teacher."

I could feel Elsa's hand rubbing the inside of my leg. I knew she was a good teacher because I had several encounters with her in her leftover baggage room. She gave me the best blow jobs I had ever had. I think it was the ice cubes that made it different.

I told Elsa, "We will talk about that after I am finished with this case. Business first. Lust later."

I turned and walked to the door.

Elsa got up and followed me to the door.

"This is so exciting. I've never seen anyone getting arrested before," Elsa said.

I could see the expression on Elsa's face. She was bubbling over with excitement. She had a big smile on her face.

"Now let's see how quickly you can get me the information I need. OK?"

"Okay. I will be back as soon as I get the information you need. Would you like to get together tonight?" she said.

"I'm afraid I have to take a rain check. By the time I get done processing the prisoner, it will be too late, and I have to get up early to arraign this guy in the morning."

She said, "Maybe tomorrow night we can get together? You could come home with me, and I will give you the best back rub you ever had."

She ran her tongue over her top lip, back and forth. As I watched her run her tongue over her lips, John Jr. began to twitch with anticipated excitement of what was to come. Elsa turned away slowly as I placed my hand on her ass and rubbed it in an arousing way.

I took a deep breath and said, "I will be in tomorrow afternoon. I have no plans for tomorrow night. Let's talk about it when I get in tomorrow."

Elsa turned her head and rotated her hips while my hand was still on her ass. She turned her head over her shoulder and said she would be right back. She hurried toward the exit. I focused on her ass. It was shapely and wiggled as she walked. I thought, *What great love handles they will make.* I wondered if she would let me screw her instead of just having oral sex.

Elsa passed Lenny Sampton on her way out. Lenny was the customs inspector's supervisory staff officer, and he was on his way down to the search room. Although there was a rivalry between the investigators and inspectors, when it came to narcotics, we acted as one unit and everyone was pitching in to help out. It was understood that any investigative actions would be taken by or at the direction of the investigators. The investigator would call the shots until a customs agent arrived on the scene.

Lenny arrived at the room. He looked at the prisoner and said, "Reno, I'll get an inspector to get all the declarations from the flight. I'll bring you a scale to weigh the powder and get you a narcotics test kit."

I said, "Lenny, can you get some inspectors to help the investigators round up any of the flights passengers still in the lobby and bring them back for a baggage reexamination?"

"Already done, Reno."

"Thanks, Lenny."

I then filled Lenny in on what Gabriel had told us.

Lenny ordered several inspectors who were still in the area to assist the investigators. The plainclothes and uniformed inspectors fanned out into the lobby. Several passengers were brought back to the examination area and searched with negative results.

Harry returned with the narcotic testing kit and a camera. I punctured one of the bags and put a few gains of the sugar like crystals into the test tube. I put the cork in, squeezed the plastic-covered test tube, housing a vial of liquid solution. I broke the vial and shook the tube. It turned the most vivid blue aquamarine. It was cocaine all right. Harry also brought back a Polaroid camera, and I took pictures of the suspect with the narcotics wrapped around his body. Lenny Sampton returned with the scale, and we weighed the powder. It was two kilos of cocaine, worth about $1 million dollars. I conducted a thorough search of the man's person and baggage. Sewn into the jacket he was wearing were three other passports in different names, blank pages, and a plastic bags with five paper-wrapped entry and exit visa stamps. Every scrap of paper I could find was placed on the table.

Fred Neilson had contacted Phil Dukonis, the special agent in charge (SAC) of JFK airport, who contacted the New York regional supervisory customs agent. The customs declaration and visa papers indicated that Gabriel was going to the Diplomat Hotel on the upper east side of Manhattan in New York City.

The Diplomat Hotel was no stranger to us. The hotel guest were usually foreign nationals visiting this country from South America and some from Europe. Some airline crews, usually the South American crews, also used this hotel. We had many a surveillance at the hotel that were drug related.

I now knew the hotel the smuggler was supposed to go. I went up to the front office, while Harry stood with the prisoner. I placed a call to the Diplomat Hotel, using a pretext to confirm that our courier was registered there. The hotel clerk verified that he was registered but had not arrived. While I was on the phone, Inspector Mike Dolan came into the office.

Inspector Dolan said, "I got all the dutiable and nondutiable customs declarations for the Lufthansa flight."

I told him to look for all those going to the Diplomat Hotel. We then checked the customs declaration against those passengers being brought back for a reexamination. None of those brought back were going to the Diplomat Hotel. We located four passenger declarations that indicated the passenger was going to stay at the Diplomat Hotel. The office phone rang, and I picked up the phone and said, "Reno speaking."

The voice on the other end said, "Hi, Reno, this is Al Healey. Fill me in."

I said, "Short version is we got a Spanish seaman arriving from Santiago with two kilos of coke. His name is Gabriel Lesenne. He also had three other passports with different names."

Al said, "Did you get anyone else off that flight? Did you get the customs declaration?"

"Hold on, Al," I said. "We pulled the customs declaration and came up with four other passengers going to the Diplomat Hotel. Al, it is hard to read their names the way they wrote them on the customs declaration."

I started to give him the names of three guys and one woman going to the same hotel, who came off the same flight. Just then, Elsa walked into the open office, waving some papers at me. She was all out of breath. Still on the phone with Al, I said, "Hold on, Al."

I reached out, and Elsa advanced into the office. She gave me the papers. I took them, looking down at the papers, trying to determine what I was looking at. Elsa moved slowly behind me. Her head was now over my left shoulder and against my neck. The sweet alluring fragrance of her perfume entered my nostrils. I could feel the soft warmth of her body pressing against my left side and back. She was breathing hard. She must have run all the way from her office. She pointed her long slender finger onto the paper, pointing to the highlighted names. Her left arm was leaning on my left arm now. Her right hand was resting on my right shoulder. I could feel her hand gripping my shoulder and feeling its way along my back. I looked at the telex papers, trying hard to focus on the task on hand and not the desires on my mind. The passengers were from Santiago. She had highlighted six names on the passenger list.

She said, pointing to the highlighted names, "Those six highlighted names have sequential ticket numbers. Look on page two." Elsa had all the ticket numbers for the flight in sequential order with the passengers' names next to their ticket number.

I said, "Great work, Elsa." Elsa was on a high. She was excited. She was doing something to help in an investigation. She was on the inside. She would be the envy of the other airline representatives. She was working with the customs investigators.

She took the four customs declarations from the desk. She matched the name on the four customs declarations with the corresponding name on the passenger list and placed a large D next to those names. Elsa and Inspector Dolan then began looking through all the customs declarations for the sixth name from the ticket list. There was one name that was not going to the Diplomat Hotel.

"Here it is," Elsa said.

"Al, my airline contact just gave me the sequential ticket list for the flight. We have six tickets in sequential order for the flight. Our guy and the four of the other passengers were going to the Diplomat Hotel, and the other listed an address 23rd Avenue in Corona Section of Queens, NY."

"Great work, John. Give me the names."

I gave Al the names of the other passengers from the passenger list going to the Diplomat Hotel. I then gave Al the name and address of the sixth passenger with the sequential ticket number with the Queens address. I knew that within fifteen minutes, agents would be in place at the Diplomat Hotel, and watching the Queens address. It was a matter of a few hours, and we would have all the people involved and seize all the cocaine that came in tonight.

Agents from our New York City office descended on the hotel, and when the four individuals arrived, a surveillance was set up and a telephone and search warrant was obtained. Telephone calls were made from one of the rooms. After the calls were completed and there was no more telephone activity, the search warrants were executed. The four individuals, or mules as we called them, were arrested with two kilos of cocaine each. Pablo, who was riding shotgun over the mules, decided that it was in his best interest to cooperate. The NY City agents made a controlled delivery to his contact in Corona Section of Queens, New York. A cutting lab and twenty-three people were also arrested.

After passing the information to Al, I began the task of filling out all the paperwork and seizure reports. Harry fingerprinted and photographed Gabriel. Harry and Fred then transported the prisoner to the Eastern District Detention Center in Brooklyn, New York. Lenny Sampson locked up the seized narcotics in the customs vault. After an hour of necessary paperwork, I was ready to go home. It was now midnight. I shut the lights in the office and headed for the back door to get my G-car and go home for a hot shower.

My car was parked in the back of the IAB (a horseshoe-shaped building), where the airplanes parked at the various gates. I headed through the ships office in order to get to my car. Guess who was waiting in the ships office? Elsa!

"Johnny, it will take you an hour to go home. Please come home with me. I only live five minutes from here. I am so excited and turned on. I want to be with you tonight. Please!"

It took me about two seconds to think about it. I said, "Let's go." We went out on to the ramp. I opened the passenger side, and she got in. I got in and started up the car. She moved right next to me. She began rubbing my legs and arms.

She said, "I never was in a police car before." I turned on the concealed radio and took out the microphone.

"644 to 600 10-8."

The response was, "600 to 644 12:04. Over."

I could feel Elsa's heavy breathing on my neck. I didn't know if she could wait until we got to her apartment.

I told Elsa, "Where to?"

She replied, "Go up Lefferts Boulevard." Showing off, I took my red light from under my seat and placed it on the dash and turned it on. I also flipped on the switch to the siren and drove to the ramp and on the taxi way to get to the exit gate. At the gate, I turned off the light and siren. I put my key card in the gate. It opened, and off we went.

Elsa's uniform dress was riding high on her thighs. I placed my right hand on the inside of her thighs and began to gently work my hand up and down her thighs. I could feel her breast rubbing against my arm. She then took my hand and pushed it all the way up her skirt. I could feel the heat and wetness of her pussy. She was not wearing her pantie. She giggled as I pulled my hand away in surprise but found my hand again, seeking the warm, wet spot.

I pulled up in front of Elsa's apartment house and was lucky to get a parking spot in front of the building. I shut off the radio and locked up the car. We proceeded to her third floor apartment. There my wish came true. I was not only laid but was relayed and parlayed. John Jr. found every orifice on Elsa's body. By 2:00 a.m., I was fast asleep with Elsa cuddled right up against me.

The next morning, Elsa made me French toast and sunny-side up eggs. I had two cups of coffee. I took a shower with Elsa, with more passionate sex. After that, I took from my attaché case a pair of socks and jockey shorts. I dressed and drove to the airport. I picked up the lodging paperwork that Harry left for me. I then went to the Eastern District courthouse and arraigned the prisoner before the federal magistrate at 11:00 a.m. The other four mules were also being arraigned. It was like old home week for the prisoners. As it turned out, bail was set at $50,000 each. The US resident's bail was set at $100,000. All six pleaded guilty and received five years' jail time and were then deported. Trials for the other twenty-three people resulted in all receiving jail time.

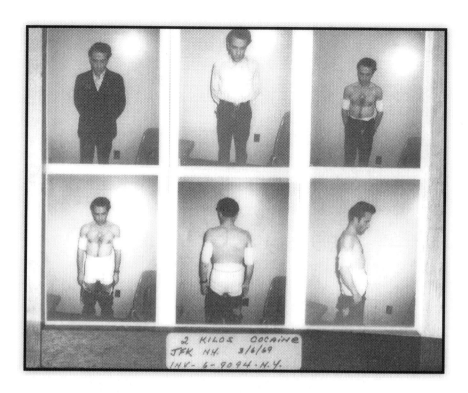

2 KILOS COCAINE
JFK N.Y. 3/6/69
INV-6-9094-N.Y.

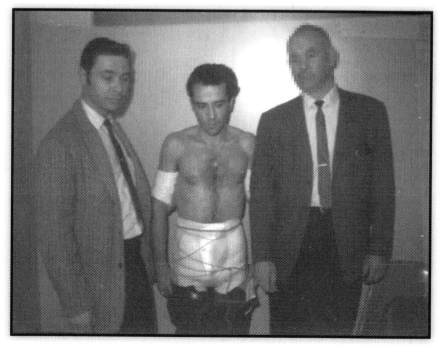

Chapter 15

Nashville
Background Investigation

Coming back to the realization of the present investigation of Darnovski, I picked up the phone and dialed John Trent's number. The phone was answered on the first ring.

"Trent speaking. How can I help you?"

"John, this is Reno."

The voice from the other end bellowed, "Reno, how are you? Haven't talked to you in a while."

"I know," I replied.

"Things are crazy all over the country."

"Hey, I'm calling you about Darnovski."

"I just got off the phone with Gardner and got his input."

The Duke assigned me the case and filled me in on your conversation with him. "I understand that Agent Harris is following Darnovski on the flight from Nashville to Chicago to New York. My guys are due to pick them up at LaGuardia airport when they arrive. Fill me in on what happened with the controlled delivery."

"OK, but how are your guys going to pick up Agent Harris and Darnovski out of a full load of passengers?" Trent asked.

"Don't worry. We got that covered. Cheech will be at the gate with a sign reading, MR. HARRIS NASHVILLE MOTORS."

Trent seemed satisfied and then began to fill me with the details of Harris's investigation.

Trent began by telling me that Agent Gardner had called him from LA and briefed him and Agent Harris, who was in Trent's office on another matter. Trent had put Gardner on the speaker phone and told Gardner that Agent Harris was present and would be assigned this case.

Gardner advised them that a controlled delivery and surveillance to the port of exportation would be needed. A violation of the Export Control Act would not occur until the gunsight camera was presented for export. Gardner told them that the controlled delivery would be initiated through registered mail with the US post office. He said he would notify Harris when the package was put into the system. Gardner faxed Harris the initial paperwork and would send a copy of the file to him overnight. Harris then opened a collateral investigation and initiated the necessary background check.

Trent went on to say that their office did a background investigation on the Tennessee individuals and company involved. The individuals had no criminal records. The company's history and corporate documents were being obtained. He went on to say they initiated an international background on the all companies involved. Barolite had connections around the world. All the inquiries were not back yet.

I asked John to make copies of all the information they had uncovered and include it with the case report. John said he would send me a copy of everything they had. John told me that they had met with the assistant US attorney and would execute search warrants and arrest the individuals from Tennessee who were involved when we took action against Darnovski. I told John that I would call him when we made the arrest of Darnovski in New York.

Agent Trent then began to provide the details of the Nashville investigation conducted by his office.

Chapter 16

Nashville Investigation

After completing the necessary customs paperwork to open the Nashville collateral investigation, Agent Frank Harris initiated a background investigation of the companies and individuals involved. He ordered a Dun & Brad Street check on the domestic and foreign corporations as well as federal, state, and local police checks. He also checked with the Tennessee Department of State, division of business services, corporation, and local county property and tax assessment offices.

After working many years at a job, you become proficient at it. It was like a routine. Harris was no exception. He worked for customs for almost ten years now. Before customs, he was a revenue agent going after stills in the back country. He knew Tennessee like the back of his hand. He was thirty-eight years old. He had black hair and long sideburns. He had piercing steel-gray eyes and sharp facial features. He was a handsome man about five feet ten inches tall and weighed about 180 lbs. He had a strong Tennessee accent. He was a graduate from the University of Tennessee, Chattanooga, Tennessee.

Agent Frank Harris contacted Columbia, Tennessee Postal Inspector Gary Baine, requesting his assistance with the impending control delivery. Harris and Baine had worked together on many controlled deliveries of drugs and pornography throughout the years. It was not uncommon for an agent from one law enforcement agency to call directly to another agent from another agency without going through formal channels. Inspector Gary Baine after being advised of all available facts suggested that they meet at the Columbia post office on Friday morning. At that time, they would go over the preliminary background work that had been done. They would determine what other investigative work needed to be done prior to the controlled delivery.

Agent Harris then contacted Assistant United States Attorney William Anthony, Nashville, Tennessee, to advise him of the investigation underway. AUSA Anthony asked Harris to come to his office at 5:00 p.m. that evening to discuss the case. Harris contacted sector communications to advise them that he would be at the AUSA's office after hours and left the contact number.

At approximately 6:30 p.m., Special Agent Gardner contacted Special Agent Frank Harris at AUSA Anthony's office. Special Agent Gardner was placed on the office speaker phone. AUSA Anthony asked Gardner to go over the facts of the case in detail as they occurred chronologically. Gardner proceeded to explain the events that led up to the controlled delivery. Gardner advised AUSA Anthony on the background of this purchase and previous purchases of cameras by Barolite. Harris, Anthony, and Gardner went over all the facts of the case.

Gardner then briefed Harris and Anthony on the controlled delivery. He stated that he had personally witnessed the packaging of the KB-25A military gunsight camera, serial number 1808 and PSI's shipper number 18326, and invoice number 17693, dated March 27, 1975. He stated further that the parcel containing the KB-25A camera bore registered U S mail number 92543 and the letter addressed to Mr. Krowell bore registered U S mail number 92544, and they were delivered to the US postal service at 2:10 p.m. West Coast time. The shipment was in the US mail and on its way to Nashville.

Anthony asked Gardner why this camera was on the munitions list and what the camera function was. Gardner explained that the camera was developed for use on our latest F-4 fighter jet aircraft. When the pilot squeezed the trigger and fired any of the munitions on board the aircraft, the camera recorded the individual rounds, leaving the ordinances, and tracked it to the target and recorded the hits.

AUSA Anthony, being satisfied with Agent Gardner's explanation, asked Gardner for the specific sections of law that applied to this case. Gardner told the AUSA that 22 United States Code (USC) 1934 and section 22 Code of Federal Regulations (CFR) and 50 USC 2025 were the sections of law pertaining to the export control act and this investigation.

They discussed all aspects of the controlled delivery that was put into motion. USA Anthony thanked Gardner and said he would also entertain charging 18 USC 371, conspiracy, for those involved in Tennessee and said in all probability we would have to conduct a surveillance to a port of export. AUSA Anthony thanked him and ended the call.

Anthony and Harris sat in the conference room, drinking coffee and discussing the surveillance possibilities, search and arrest warrants, and prosecution in Tennessee. It all hinged on when and where the actual violation would take place. The violation will not take place, according to the law, until the camera was presented for export.

Evidence would have to be gathered and a case built. AUSA Anthony told Harris to make sure of the address for application for a search warrant. They did not want to search the wrong place. Harris told Anthony that next day he was going to meet with Inspector Baine and would check out the descriptions for the search and arrest warrants.

On Friday, March 28, 1975, Special Agent Frank Harris traveled to Columbia, which was only half an hour from his home. He arrived at the Columbia, Tennessee main post office. Postal Inspector Gary Baine was already there and met Harris in the parking lot.

Baine was about forty years old with close-cropped gray coarse hair. He had a gray moustache and long sideburns. He wore a gray felt cowboy hat, a white button snap shirt, blue jeans, and a dark blue blazer. His boots were highly shined. He carried a blue raincoat over one arm and carried a brown leather briefcase. After exchanging greetings in the parking lot, the two men walked into the post office employee entrance.

The two went directly to the office of postmaster, Carl H. Philips. Inspector Baine briefed Postmaster Philips about the controlled delivery that was initiated in Los Angeles. Philips picked up the phone and dialed the registered mail section. He asked if they received any registered packages from Los Angeles for Barolite. He hung up the phone and told Harris and Baine that the parcel had not yet arrived. Philips told them that when registered mail arrived from LAX, it would be brought to the registered mail room, which was a secure room with a controlled entry. The registered items would be logged in, and a arrival notification would be placed in the recipient's route boxes or post office box, notifying them that a registered item was being held at the post office. Phillips stated that he would put a hold on the notification of arrival until Baine and Harris were ready.

Harris then asked Baine if he would help him check out the location of the Barolite plant in preparation for the warrant and controlled delivery and surveillance. It was a plan. The Dun & Bradstreet report and the telephone company records listed a physical address in an industrial park in Columbia, Tennessee.

Inspector Baine and Agent Harris then drove in Harris's car to the industrial park in Columbia, Tennessee. Arriving at the industrial park, they observed four rows with two redbrick buildings in each row. The building was a typical two-story high structure about four hundred feet in length. Each building could house up to eight tenants. Some of the tenants had two or more units. Each unit had one to three metal corrugated bay doors that electrically opened, and each had front entry metal door to the unit's office space.

Harris located the address on one of the four buildings. Several different businesses had their bay doors open, and the place was bustling with activity. Trucks and cars were parked in front of many units. As for the address of the Barolite, Inc. plant, the unit did not reflect any corporate name sign, as most of the other businesses did. The Barolite unit appeared to be vacant, compared to the other units. Agent Harris and Inspector Baine left their vehicles and divided up the businesses and began making inquiries concerning the unmarked unit.

Using a pretext of inquiring at neighboring businesses, about renting what appeared to be an empty unit, they found that the unit in question was rented by Barolite, Inc., an import and export business. Further inquiries from some of the businesses established that Barolite, Inc. was either financially associated with or a division of M. Darnovski of Austria. Agent Harris made notations on his pad about the physical appearance and exact location of the unit Barolite, Inc. occupied. The information would be necessary for a future search warrant.

Harris and Baine then drove to the address they had for Carl R. Krowell. The address had been previously verified by Postal Inspector Baine. 1912 Lee Circle, Franklin, Tennessee, was a one-story structure with two dormers in the front. A cement walkway ran from the cement driveway at the garage to the steps leading to the front door. The front of the house was redbrick, and the sides of the house were covered with tan siding. There was a bay window in the front with small shrubs under the window running to the attached two-car garage. From the front red door, there was a stoop with black hand rails and four steps leading down to the cement walkway. The roof was a gray shingle. The house sat on a wooded lot. The closest house was about one thousand feet down the road. The tree-lined driveway ran about two hundred feet from the house to the street. Agent Harris took down all the descriptive attributes of the property for use in a search warrant. Harris and Baine were confident that they had enough information for the search warrant and then returned to the post office.

Returning to the main post office, Inspector Baine and Agent Harris were advised by Postmaster Philips that the parcel had not arrived and the next scheduled delivery from Los Angeles would not be until approximately 2:00 a.m., Saturday, March 29, 1975. Harris then returned to his office.

Later that afternoon, Special Agent Harris met with Assistant US Attorney Anthony in his office and initiated an affidavit in order to obtain a search warrant for documents and files located in the Barolite plant as well as Krowell's house. They carefully drew up an arrest warrant for the Tennessee plant manager Carl R. Krowell. All the preparatory paperwork was in order and in place just waiting for the violation to occur.

Chapter 17

Nashville Surveillance

O n Saturday, March 29, 1975, at 8:00 a.m., Agent Harris received a radio call from Agent John Trent who was already at the office, informing him that Postmaster Philips was trying to reach him to advise that the registered parcel and the letter had arrived and the package retrieval window would not open until 9:00 a.m. Agent Harris requested Trent to contact Postmaster Philips and have him contact Inspector Baine and advise him of the parcel's arrival and to meet him at the post office.

At 8:30 a.m., Agent Harris arrived at Columbia, Tennessee post office. He was met by Postmaster Philips and Inspector Baine. The three proceeded to the registered mail room. Postmaster Philips took possession of the parcel and the letter from the registered mail vault. He brought them to his office, and a positive identification of the parcel and letter were made, utilizing data furnished by Special Agent Gardner. Agent Harris photographed and marked the parcel with his initials and date. Postmaster Philips then returned the parcel and the letter to a registered mail vault. At this time, US Customs form VI-41, chain of custody form, was executed and was updated by postal employees handling the parcel.

Postal Inspector Baine and Agent Harris were then advised by Postmaster Philips that an individual was at the clerk's window asking if the parcel and the letter had arrived. Baine asked Philips to wait about five minutes until they could take up a surveillance position in the lobby of the post office. Inspector Baine and Agent Harris then moved to a location in the main lobby of the post office where they observed a white male, 5' 11" tall, approximately forty years old, 170-180 lbs, full head of black hair, and clean-shaven. He wore a three-quarter-length blue coat, blue pants, and black shoes. The subject (later identified as Carl R. Krowell) signed postal form 3849 (copy two) and 3811 (copy two) required to obtain the registered parcel and the letter.

At 9:45 a.m., the subject placed the registered letter in his jacket pocket and departed the post office, carrying the parcel to a brown 1968 four-door Chrysler bearing Tennessee license 32 HL 172, parked in front of the post office. The vehicle was occupied by one white female and two children. A vehicle tag check revealed that the Chrysler was registered to Mrs. Betty Jo Hillsworth, who turned out to be Carl's girlfriend. The subject placed the parcel in the trunk of the vehicle, entered the driver's side of the vehicle, and proceeded to drive in the northerly direction on Tennessee Highway 31. Inspector Baine followed behind the subject vehicle, and Agent Harris maintained the position behind Inspector Baine's vehicle. The subject proceeded to the outer city limits of Columbia, Tennessee, and pulled into the Quality Inn Motel parking lot.

Inspector Baine pulled into the motel parking lot and observed the subject drive to a parking spot in front of room 134, where two white males were standing on the sidewalk. Inspector Baine observed the subject park his vehicle, get out, and open the trunk. Agent Harris had parked in the rear of a Gulf service station adjacent to Quality Inn Motel. Agent Harris could observe the two males outside the motel doors. Agent Harris observed and photographed Krowell hand the registered parcel to one of the two white males standing in front of the open door to room 134. The subject who took possession of the parcel was later identified as Manfred Darnovski. Darnovski was a white male, approximately thirty-five years old, with blond hair, blue eyes, and sharp facial features. He looked like an actor. He was six feet and weighed about 180 lbs. He wore black slacks and a white shirt with the top two buttons open, exposing his hairy chest. His companion was a white male about sixty-five years old, with blue eyes, white hair, and receding hairline, 5' 7" tall and weighed 185 lbs, wearing dark gray slacks, white shirt, and black vest, and he wore wire rim glasses. He was later identified as Boris Bron, who was an employee of Mr. Darnovski in Vienna.

Darnovski entered room 134 with the parcel and immediately exited, leaving the parcel in his room. As he shut the door, he was putting on a three-quarter black leather coat. Bron exited his room, wearing a long black overcoat. All subjects entered the brown Chrysler and departed the Quality Inn Motel in a northerly direction on Tennessee Highway 31, followed by Inspector Baine. Harris told Baine to follow the subjects while he kept an eye on the room with the package.

After identifying himself to Mrs. Stella Hendricks, desk clerk, and the day manager of the Quality Inn Motel, Columbia Tennessee, Agent Harris was furnished with a guest registration for room 134, reflecting the name of Manfred Darnovski. Mrs. Hendricks also furnished Agent Harris the guest registration for room 136, reflecting the name Boris Bron, stating the two guests arrived together on March 28 in the late afternoon. They were paid up until March 31. Mr. Darnovski charged the rooms on his American Express credit card, and she provided a copy of the charge card slip to Agent Harris. Mrs. Hendricks then accompanied Agent Harris to the Inn Keepers office. The office had a window that had a commanding view of the entire front of the motel where both rooms 134 and 136 were located. Mrs. Hendricks agreed to let the agents use the office to observe the two subjects' rooms and would notify the night clerk that Harris would be using the office.

Approximately one hour later, Inspector Baine returned to the motel and joined Agent Harris in the Inn Keepers office. He told Harris that he followed the subjects to a shoe store in Columbia, Tennessee. The subjects then drove to a home located on Route 7, Red Deer Road, Columbia, Tennessee, where all persons exited the vehicle and entered the home. It was later found that the home was rented by Betty Jo Hillsworth and her two children. Approximately five minutes later, the three male subjects departed the home without the female and children and drove to a nearby shopping center. The subjects were photographed by Inspector Baine entering and leaving Roses departmental store, where the subject, identified as Manfred Darnovski, apparently purchased a green suitcase. The subjects then drove to the Barolite Inc. plant at which time Inspector Baine returned to the shopping center and obtained a copy of the credit card purchase by Darnovski as evidence. He then drove to the motel and met with Harris. They maintained surveillance on the two rooms until 2:50 p.m.

At 2:50 p.m., Darnovski and Bron returned to motel driving a green Chevy. Krowell was not with them. Bron exited the vehicle and entered room 136. Darnovski removed a large green suitcase from the trunk of the vehicle and entered room 134. A check with the Tennessee Motor Vehicle Registration Department for the green Chevy revealed Tennessee license 97 MD 18 registered to Carl R. Krowell, 1912 Lee Circle, Franklin, Tennessee.

At 5:55 p.m., Darnovski and Bron exited their respective rooms, empty-handed, got into Mr. Krowell's Chevy, and departed the motel. Harris and Baine followed the two in their vehicles. They drove about five miles down the road to a Cracketts Down Home Restaurant and Bar. Darnovski and Bron parked the car on the side of the restaurant along the tree line. They walked to the restaurant's front steps and up onto the porch that was lined with wooden rockers. It looked like the front of a Cracker Barrel Restaurant. The two men entered the restaurant.

About fifteen minutes later, Harris and Baine entered the restaurant after parking their cars in positions to observe the Chevy and the entrance of the restaurant. Inside the restaurant, there were two rooms. When you entered the restaurant, you entered into the primary dining area. There was a row of booths along the outer wall: an aisle, a double set of booths and an aisle, and then the sit-down counter facing the kitchen. The larger room had several high tables around the room and in front of the bar. Each table had a red-and-white checkered tablecloths and high-back wooden chairs. The walls were covered with pictures of country western singers, pictures of the old west, horseshoes, bull horns, lassos and guitars, spurs, and a couple of guns in holsters.

The big room had a hardwood dance floor. The ceiling was high. There were two glass balls, about twenty feet apart, which rotated and reflected different colors in all directions. There was a long bar against the inner wall between the two rooms. At the end of the bar between the two rooms was a small stage for a band and the bathrooms that could be accessed from both rooms. There was a wooden sign outside each restroom: one with a pictures of a cowboy and the other of a cowgirl. On the other side of the bar was the kitchen that separated the two rooms. Harris and Baine sat in a booth where they could overhear Darnovski's conversation. They placed their meal order with the waitress. The waitress told them that on Saturday nights, the place got packed with a large crowd. The place started jumping about 8:00 p.m. when the band started playing. Darnovski and Bron only spoke in German to each other, and both Harris and Baine did not understand German, so they just enjoyed their meals when it was served to them.

The waitress brought Darnovski another beer before she brought him his dinner. When the waitress brought the food to Darnovski's table, Harris could see that Darnovski had ordered the largest steak on the menu and a double order of potatoes and a large salad and a beer, while Bron had soup, salad, and a sandwich with a large coke.

At 8:00 p.m., the four-piece country band started to play. Darnovski and Bron then paid their bill and moved to the bar. Harris and Baine paid their tab a few minutes later.

At the bar, Darnovski was observed drinking Jack Daniels and Coke, and Bron was nursed a large coke. The band consisted of three men and a woman. One man played the drums. The other two sang and played both guitars and the fiddle. The woman, in her late twenties, played guitar and sang. All were outfitted in country western clothes. The music was country, and it was loud.

The dance floor was always filled. Darnovski began his pursuit of several women who were at the bar. He began to strike up conversations with several women. He was like a cowboy wrangler, riding the range and herding the cattle and singling out the one that he could put his brand on. He was observed buying drinks for several women at a time. When paying for the drinks, Darnovski flashed a wad of cash that could choke a horse. It was his way to see who showed an interest in him because of his money.

Harris and Baine sat next to Darnovski at the bar. Darnovski would send drinks to small groups of women who were together at the bar. They would take the drinks and walk up to him and thank him. The two or three would stand between him and Bron and hold a conversation. Each time, he would tell the women that he was the owner of several companies in Canada and Austria and he had one in Columbia, Tennessee. He told them that he lived in Vienna, Austria, and was here on business. His accent and his good looks drew the women to him like a moth to a flame. He told them he would be here for a couple of days and was looking for some companionship while he was here. He even got on the dance floor and did attempt to do the Texas two-step. Harris was surprised that Darnovski could dance, almost as good as the regulars, to the country western music.

At about 11:30 p.m., three women showed particular interest in Darnovski. One in particular was very flirtatious with him. She was about twenty-five to thirty years old, 5' 5", and must have weighed only 100 lbs. She was a short blond with a long pony tail. She wore a short tan leather skirt with a country-style white blouse heavily embroidered with shiny white silk and snaps instead of buttons, of which the top three were unsnapped, revealing a light blue bra that was overflowing with her milky-white breasts. She had a blue bandanna around her neck. She wore a tan cowboy hat that matched her tan leather boots. "Mary Sue is my name," she kept telling Darnovski. Baine and Harris could not help laughing when Darnovski kept trying to say Mary Sue with his liquored-up German accent. Darnovski and the blond left the bar and took to the dance floor for a slow dance. Their bodies clung to each other like plastic wrap. They whispered in each other's ears, and then, before the song ended, they left the crowded dance floor.

Bron remained at the bar, drinking coke, talking with the two other women. One woman was named Bobby Jo and the other Darlene. He appeared to be having a good time with the two women, who were laughing and rubbing their young bodies over him.

Bron would put one finger on the Darlene's breast and say, "Darlene," and then on her other breast and say, "Bobby Jo."

Darlene would then take Bron's hand and place it on her breast and say, "No, I am Darlene."

Still holding his hand, she then would place it on Bobby Jo's breast and say, "This is Bobby Jo."

Bron would squeeze their breasts and start over again. They were laughing and giggling and having a good time. They were trying to get Bron to the dance floor, but he was playing hard to get. Finally, the two dragged him to the dance floor. He did OK with the two women. He was laughing and was having a good time.

Darnovski and Mary Sue, the blond, left the bar with Agent Harris following. Darnovski was an observed, taking out his wad of cash and peeling off a couple of bills, probably $100.00 bills, and placing the wad of money back in his pocket. With his arm stretched out, holding the bills, they walked to Darnovski's car. Darnovski and the women got into the back seat of his car.

In about five minutes, the windows began to fog up. Harris could barely see the woman's legs over Darnovski's shoulders with red panties dangling from one of her legs. Darnovski's face was buried between her legs. Now the windows were completely fogged up. Her moans of pleasure could be heard outside the car. The car shook for about three or four minutes, and then there was five minutes of silence. Only the red glow from two cigarettes could be seen through the foggy windows.

Harris thought what a fool Darnovski must be for flashing a large amount of cash at a bar. Some of the locals would not think twice about taking the cash from Darnovski and dumping his dead body far in the woods where it would never be found. *This could have been a setup*, Harris thought. But it wasn't. Darnovski was lucky; he scored a sexual victory using his wealth.

The car door opened, and Darnovski and Mary Sue got out of his car, tossing the cigarette buds on the ground. Harris could see her putting something into her bra and then snap up the lowest button that was open. She straightened out her skirt. Darnovski checked his fly to make sure it was closed. They walked slowly back to the bar. Darnovski had his arm around Mary Sue's waist. She had her two arms wrapped around Darnovski middle. They walked slowly back to the bar. They stopped twice and kissed. The kisses were long. Each time Mary Sue pulled her body close to Darnovski's. She maintained a grinding of her body into his.

They entered the bar. They walked back to Bron and the two other women. Darnovski sat down and picked up his half-filled glass and drank it down. He ordered another round of drinks. The three women then went to power their noses. They returned in about five minutes. Darnovski continued to buy them drinks and go out to the dance floor. He was having a good time.

He returned from the dance floor with the redhead who started to pay a lot more attention to Darnovski. She was all over him like flies on shit. She had been drinking the free drinks, and she was well above her capacity. It was obvious to Harris that after the blond told her friends about the money she got and what she had to do for it, they became very interested in Darnovski in a more sexual way. They leaned against him and Bron, rubbing their breast on them and giggling a lot.

If not for Darnovski, Bron would be, in all probability, sitting alone, and no one would pay any attention to him. He was now getting the chance to cop a free feel or two from the women. This seemed to satisfy him.

Bobby Jo was a redhead. She was about thirty years old and must have weighed 110 lbs. She was about 5' 7", with brown eyes, sharp features, and a large mouth encircled with a luster of pink lipstick. She wore a short black skirt with a red country-style, embroidered blouse with snaps. Her figure was well proportioned. In all probability, her measurements were 38, 26, 36. She really flaunted what she had with the help of the rum she had been drinking. She had a pink bandanna around her neck. Her cleavage ran down into a light pink lacy bra. She wore a black cowboy hat and black leather boots. Bobby Jo was a very good dancer. Her calf muscles were firm and well defined. When she sat on the bar stool, Darnovski could not stop running his hand up and down her calf muscle.

Thirty minutes later, after dancing and socializing, Bobby Jo left the bar with Darnovski, and again he was observed taking out his cash and dangling a few bills in front of Bobby Jo. Harris quickly got into his car and lifted up his binoculars and began to observe Darnovski up close without being seen.

When they got to Darnovski's car, he opened the door and said something to Bobby Jo. She laughed and kissed him. He then tossed a couple of bills into the back seat of the car. Bobby Jo slowly bent over, turning her head and looked back at Darnovski. She licked her lips in a provocative way.

Darnovski moved closer to her bent body. He lifted her skirt onto her back, revealing her pink panties. Darnovski could be observed holding and rubbing her luscious love handles. He began to hump her. He paused, opened his fly, and placed his penis in the crease of her ass. He pressed his groin hard against her rump and grinded her butt for a full minute. The two pushed forward onto the back seat. As Darnovski reached for the car door handle, Harris could see Bobby Jo's head moving into Darnovski's crotch. His penis was disappearing into her mouth as the car door closed.

Harris could see Darnovski on top of Bobby Jo with her legs straight up. Darnovski pounded away. The car rocked. Then there was no movement for a few seconds. Now Bobby Jo was on top and riding the wild horse. Again, the windows began to fog. The escapades went on for half an hour.

After half an hour, Darnovski and Bobby Jo opened the car door. They exited the car. Bobby Jo straightened out her skirt and was observed placing green bills into her bra. Darnovski was brushing his pants legs. They kissed for several minutes. They were in an embrace with his hands holding her love handles, and her arms were around his neck. They returned to the bar.

Shortly after 1:00 a.m., Darnovski, Bron and the three women left the bar. The group stood by Darnovski's car and was laughing and kissing and hugging and getting felt up. Bron could not keep his hands off Darlene's breast. He could be heard saying titty, titty, titty as he groped her breast. Mary Sue kept pushing her breast into Bron's hands and was saying to him, "What about mine?" This went on for about ten minutes. Then Bron and Darnovski got into their car. The women got into their car. Harris and Baine followed Darnovski back to the motel.

At 1:25 a.m., March 30, 1975, Darnovski and Bron returned to the motel, driving Krowell's Chevy. Harris told Baine he would stay until he was sure that the two were in for the night. Harris told Baine that he would take the first shift as long as he was back home at three o'clock in the afternoon for his kid's Easter egg hunt. Baine agreed because he needed the morning to be with his family. Each subject was observed going into their room. In five minutes, Bron's lights went out. However, Darnovski's light remained on.

Harris then proceeded to the motel entrance to observe Darnovski's room. Entering the lobby, Harris saw a woman behind the registration desk. The night clerk was a forty-five-year-old woman named Alice, with graying hair. She was about 5' 5" tall and weighed about 160 lbs. She wore dark pants and a yellow blouse covered with a man's large gray sweater. She was a full-figured woman. Agent Harris approached the woman and identified himself to her. She said she had been told by Stella that some agents would be using the office tonight. The night clerk wanted to know if Harris would be there all night. Harris told the woman he would only be staying until the men went to sleep.

About five minutes later, Darnovski was observed exiting his room and walked to the lobby of the motel. Harris told Alice that Darnovski was drinking and that he would be in the office in case she needed him. "If Darnovski should question you about me, just tell him I'm your husband." She agreed.

Darnovski entered the lobby. Looking around and seeing no one, Darnovski called out, "Is anyone here?" Alice left the office, leaving the office door a little open. Harris listened at the door. Darnovski tried to strike up a conversation with the night clerk. He began asking her about the area stores and restaurants and guided the conversation toward his loneliness and being a stranger in town. Alice cut him off at the knees. She told him she was married and he better go back to his room and sleep it off or she would call her husband, who was in the office looking at TV. Darnovski did a quick turnaround and quickly left the office and returned to his room for the remainder of the night. Agent Harris left ten minutes after Darnovski's lights went out.

Agent Harris arrived back at the motel at about 8:00 a.m. It was Easter morning. Harris wondered to himself what he was doing here so early. He thought he could take his kids to the Easter egg hunt that afternoon when he was relieved by Baine. Baine was taking his family to an Easter Sunday brunch. He went into the motel lobby where Stella was at the registration desk already.

They greeted each other, and Stella told Harris that the two men were still in their rooms. Harris and Stella laughed at Alice's experience last night. Stella provided Harris with the telephone numbers the both men had called and the numbers on the incoming calls. She asked Harris if he wanted a cup of coffee. Harris said he left that morning without having his cup of coffee because he was running late. Stella asked how he liked the coffee and said she would bring it to him in the office. Harris said, "Cream and two sugars."

Stella said, "Got ya."

Harris went into the motel office and called John Trent at home. He gave the telephone numbers to John Trent and asked him to run a check on the local and long distance numbers. Stella came into the office with a large hot cup of coffee and a sweet roll for Harris. He thanked her, and they talked a while.

At about 10:00 a.m., Bron and Darnovski exited their room without any packages. They got into the green Chevy and drove off with Harris following them. They went down the road a couple of miles to a Waffle House for breakfast. The two then drove back to the motel. There were two more incoming calls.

At 1:00 p.m., room 134 received an incoming call. Then both subjects departed the motel, without any packages, driving Krowell's Chevy. Harris followed them to Krowell's house in Franklin. Harris notified Baine of the new surveillance location.

Agent Trent called Harris on the radio and told him that Darnovski contacted Delta airlines and Delta had called him back. Trent told him he then went to Metro Nashville, Tennessee airport.

Agent Trent told Harris that he talked with Delta's airline's manager and established the fact that Darnovski and Bron had made confirmed reservations on a Delta airlines flight, number 760, departing Nashville, Tennessee, on Monday, March 31, at 7:50 a.m. for Chicago, Il. It was further found that Darnovski held reservations for the same date on American Airlines flight number 144, departing Chicago Il. at 4:00 p.m. for New York City. Bron had reservations for an 11:45 a.m. flight to Montreal.

Agent Trent told Harris, "Pack a bag, and be at the airport before Darnovski arrived." Trent said he would meet him there with his tickets. Agent Harris was going to follow the same itinerary as Darnovski ending up in New York City. Trent advised Harris that he had contacted

Chicago's office of investigations and briefed Supervisory Agent Tony Peters who would head the surveillance at Chicago.

At about 2:30 p.m., Harris briefed Baine. Then Harris went home to his kids' Easter egg hunt. At 4:50 p.m., Krowell, Darnovski, and Bron exited the house. They got into a black over green, 1970 Mercury, bearing Tennessee tag 14 CH 20. A check with the Tennessee Motor Vehicle Department revealed that the vehicle was registered to Carl R. Krowell. Darnovski then drove back to the motel with Baine following. Bron went into his room, and Darnovski went into the lobby of the hotel and gathered up a number of newspapers and returned to his room with the papers.

At about 6:30 p.m., Darnovski and Bron left their rooms without any packages. They drove into Columbia and was observed by Baine going to a movie. At 9:00 p.m., they were observed leaving the movie and driving to a local hamburger drive-through, getting their order and driving back to the motel. There was no further activity that night. Both room lights went out at 10:00 p.m.

At 6:00 a.m., the brown Chrysler pulled up to room 134. Carl Krowell exited the passenger side of the car. He waved good-bye to Betty Jo who was driving the car with her two kids in the back seat. Krowell knocked on the door, and Darnovski opened the door, and Krowell was observed going in. At 6:10 a.m., Agent Baine observed Darnovski and Bron exit their rooms with their suitcases. Bron placed one black suitcase in the trunk of the car. Darnovski placed a black and the green suitcases in the trunk of the car. They departed the motel in the green Mercury bearing Tennessee license 14 CH 20, now driven by Carl R. Krowell. The subject vehicle, followed by Inspector Baine, proceeded north bound on Interstate 65 and then to Highway 155 to Metro Nashville airport.

Before Agent Harris left home, he placed his credentials, badge, and gun in his attaché case and locked it. Agent Harris arrived at the airport, and he was met by Agent Trent at the Delta airline ticket counter. Agent Harris had a ticket itinerary identical to that held by Darnovski. Harris carried his attaché case in one hand and a small leather bag in his other. Harris moved to a location from which the Delta airline ticket counter could be viewed.

Approximately five minutes later, Darnovski and Bron entered the airport, followed by Krowell and a skycap with the luggage on a cart. The three men waited on a short line, and then Bron and Darnovski presented their tickets and bags to the airline representative. They were then checked in. Two pieces of luggage, one black and one green, were checked in and tagged through Chicago to New York City. Bron's black bag was checked through Chicago to Montreal.

Agent Trent had arranged with the first-class check-in representative to place two pre-initialed baggage tags on the two bags checked in by Darnovski and one on Bron's bag. Trent had recorded the tag numbers so he could give them to Agent Tony Green. Green would make sure that the green bag was in fact transferred to the New-York-bound flight.

The three men proceeded to the boarding gate with Agent Harris trailing behind. There was no security as we have today. Friends and family could go with passengers right up to the boarding gate to say good-bye. They could also meet arriving passengers when flights arrived at the gate. Darnovski and Bron carried black leather briefcases. Krowell and Darnovski conversed, while Bron followed. They sat in the pre-boarding area, waiting for the boarding call. The first-class passengers were boarded first. Darnovski and Bron boarded with Harris in back of them. Krowell and Trent both waited until the first class was finished boarding. Agent Trent followed Krowell out to his car and watched him leave the airport.

Trent then returned to his office and contacted Group Supervisor Tony Peters in Chicago and advised him of the plane's departure, the descriptions of the three men, and the baggage tag numbers. Green advised that his group was making preparation for the arrival and surveillance at the airport. I thanked Trent for the briefing and asked him to forward a copy of Harris's report after he completed it, with copies of the evidence and photos.

Chapter 18

Chicago Arrival

I took my list of things to do and crossed off "call Nashville." The phone rang, and I picked up the phone. It was Amanda.

"Reno, it's Tony Peters, SAC Chicago office on line 2."

I pushed the button for line two and said, "Hey, Tony, this is Reno. How are you?"

"I'm doing good. We had this Darnovski guy under surveillance at O'Hare. Darnovski and Agent Harris are en route to LaGuardia airport. They are due to arrive NY about 6:45 p.m."

Agent Tony Peters then began to brief me on Chicago's part in this investigation. He told me that Darnovski arrived at about 9:10 a.m. (Central Standard Time) at Chicago's O'Hare airport. Agent Peters then told me what Harris had told him about his flight to Chicago.

Peters said that Harris was surprised that he was flying first class. He was seated in row 3C, and Darnovski and Bron were in 2A and B. He said that he thought that Trent must have had heart failure when he paid for the ticket. He went on to say that as Harris entered the first-class section in the front of the aircraft, he observed Darnovski and Bron getting seated in their seats. Darnovski was observed removing his jacket and asking the stewardess to hang it up for him. Harris placed his attaché case and small bag in the overhead compartment. Harris took off his raincoat and handed it to the stewardess along with his tweed sport jacket. Harris then took his seat and removed a magazine from the seat pocket in front of him.

After takeoff, the stewardess brought Darnovski an alcoholic drink and Bron a soda. Harris had a tomato juice. About ten minutes into the flight, Darnovski rang for the stewardess and asked for a pillow while flirting with her. About half an hour into the flight, Darnovski was up and walking through the aircraft. He returned to his seat after the stewardess showed no interest in him. The rest of the flight was uneventful. Darnovski and Bron remained in their seats and slept until the plane arrived in Chicago.

At 9:10 a.m., March 31, 1975 (Central Standard Time), the airplane arrived at Chicago, IL, O'Hare Field, Gate 6. Darnovski and Bron received their coats from the stewardess. Darnovski and Bron deplaned. Agent Harris opened the overhead and removed his hat, attaché case, and small bag. He exited the plane, not far behind Darnovski and Bron. They exited the aircraft, and they all walked through the waiting area where people were waiting to greet the arriving passengers.

Agent Peters stated that he had been given the description of Agent Harris and the two suspects by John Trent. Agent Peters said, "It wasn't hard to pick Harris out of the crowd or to pick out Darnovski and Bron." First-class passengers always got off the aircraft first. There were only eight first-class passengers on this flight. The guy in the cowboy hat had to be Harris. The good-looking young German traveling with the professor-looking, older German had to be Darnovski and Bron. The other five first-class passengers, three of whom were women, did not fit the description that Trent had given them.

Peters went on to say that he met Agent Harris and other agents from his group and kept Darnovski and Bron under surveillance until Darnovski boarded American Flight number 144, bound for LaGuardia airport in New York at 3:50 p.m. Agent Peters further stated that Bron took an 11:45 a.m. flight to Montreal. Darnovski, after Bron boarded the aircraft, headed for the nearest bar and got a sandwich and beer. He stood in the bar until 3:15 p.m. at which time, he proceeded to his boarding gate.

Agent Peters advised me that the baggage tag information provided by John Trent was given to one of his agents, Dan Clark, who verified the transfer of Darnovski's green suitcase to American Flight number 144, bound for New York's LaGuardia airport.

At 3:50 p.m., Darnovski boarded American Airlines flight number 144 for LaGuardia airport, New York. First-class passengers were seated first. Darnovski was seated in 3A. Agent Harris boarded the flight when the boarding agent announced the last call for first-class passenger boarding. Agent Harris sat in 4C. Harris placed his briefcase and brown felt cowboy hat in the overhead, and the stewardess asked Harris if she could hang up his coat and jacket. Harris gave his coat and jacket to the stewardess, which she promptly hung up in the closet.

I thanked Agent Peters for the briefing and hung up. I took the notepad I was taking notes on and placed the pad in my attaché case along with the case folder. I took a last swig of the coffee left in my cup and headed out of the office for LaGuardia airport.

I got into my car and called DJ on the radio.

"644 to 606." A static sound and then a response.

"606 to 644, go ahead."

"644 to 606, I'm leaving the office en route to your location."

"606 to 644, be advised there was an accident on the Van Wick. Take the service route to Queens Boulevard. When you arrive, park in back of my vehicle. The transport (our undercover taxicab) is here, and the port authority police and the dispatcher were briefed. 216 is the duty agent on call. Over."

I knew that 216 was Agent Vince Morano. Vince had worked at the airport with me for several years before being transferred to the city. It was hard to remember the call signs of all the agents from the New York office, but nine times out of ten, you could tell by the voice who the agent was. For the guys you worked with all the time, you knew their call signs and their voices.

"644 to 606, that is a 10-4. Over and out."

Immediately the radio again blurt out, "216 to 644."

The microphone was still in my hand. I pushed the talk button and responded, "644 to 216, go ahead."

"216 to 644, I have the duty today and will monitor the traffic. I will make a few calls to see if the subject has reservations in any of the uptown hotels. If they are going to a hotel in the city, I will set up a CP before they get there. Do you have an ETA? Over."

"644 to 216. That is a 10-4. The ETA is approximately 6:45 over."

DJ advised that everything was in place. The police were notified so we would not have any problems with parking our vehicles in the arrival area. The dispatcher was alerted to put the suspects in our taxicab. If Vince could not find the hotel Darnovski had reservations for, then, as soon as Darnovski told the cab driver which hotel he was going to, Vince, monitoring the radio call, would go to the hotel, contact security, and set up a command post in a room in close proximity to Darnovski's room.

Setting-up at hotels was never a problem. Most hotels security departments were headed by ex-FBI agents or retired police officers. These guys always went out of their way to help us and looked forward to be part of the action behind the scenes.

The ride between the airports and a city hotel would take about forty minutes. I had worked with Vince at JFK a couple of years after I started at the airport. Hearing Vince's voice on the radio brought back memories.

Chapter 19

Memories with Vince, Rosemarie, and Mary

Hearing Vince's voice over the radio brought back pleasant memories. I was three years older than Vince, but he looked like he was a few years older than me. At the time Vince was about twenty-five years old, I was about twenty-seven. Vince was five feet six and weighed about 170 pounds. The first thing you noticed about Vince was his hair. He had very little. He reminded me and everyone else of Larry of the *Three Stooges*. But that was where the resemblance ended. He was a typical New York Italian with an olive complexion. He spoke fluent Italian. When his sport jacket was unbuttoned, you could readily see that he was carrying a gun.

He was always trying to impress and put the make on some women. When he first got assigned to the airport, I took him around and introduced him to some of the key people he needed to know. The customs supervisory cargo inspectors and import specialist who had offices in cargo building 80. We had to deal with these supervisors on many of our criminal investigations that involved fraud and cargo thefts. All the supervisory offices had secretaries. Most of the secretaries were eighteen to twenty years old. These old customs guys liked young girls for their secretaries. Vince wanted to screw every young woman he met.

Import specialists specialized in certain commodities listed in the tariff schedule like jewelry, watches, cotton clothing, food, etc. When a shipment of shirts came in, the import specialist would determine what section of the tariff schedule applied so the correct amount of customs duty could be collected. There were many women employed as import specialists, import specialist aids, and secretaries in the cargo building 80.

I had set up an appointment to introduce Vince to the US Customs airport director, and fines and penalties supervisor. They were located in building 178, which was at the entrance to the airport. First, we had to go to building 80 to see the deputy director for cargo. These were the key individuals you needed to know to cut the red tape and get things done.

In building 80, Vince could not keep his eyes off the secretary of the deputy director for cargo. The secretary was a nineteen-year-old beauty named Rosemarie Scollari. She was five feet eight, 110 lbs, with long, shiny black hair. Her skin was soft and rosy; she wore little or no makeup. She was wearing a black skirt that came just above the knee. Her legs were smoothed, thin, and muscular. She had an hourglass figure. Her opened white blouse revealed a deep cleavage. We had flirted with each other many times but never had gone out on a date. She was always trying to find out where the agents hung out after work.

I introduced her to Vince, and then we went into Joe Depola's office. Joe was the deputy in charge of cargo. After the meeting, we left Joe's office, and on the way out, Rosemarie asked where we were going to hang tonight.

I said, "I don't know. It depends on what case we are working on. If nothing comes up, we will probably go the Ferruggies."

Vince whispered in my ear as we went out the door, "She is hot for you. She wants to get laid. She is all over you. Call her. It's an easy score."

I told Vince, "Later," and changed the subject.

We went to building 178 to meet the Airport Director Jim Fulton. What we did not know at that time was that Rosemarie called Mary, the airport director's secretary. They conspired to trap us into going on a date. Mary showed an interest in Vince that sent him reeling. All he kept telling me on the way back to our office was that Mary had the hots for him and she wanted to get laid. According to Vince, every girl he saw wanted to go to bed with him. But that's Vince.

About two hours after our meeting with the director, Vince came to my desk and told me that after work he was going to meet Mary at Ferruggies Restaurant for drinks. He then told me I had to go because Mary would not go alone. "Mary wants to bringing Rosemarie, but Rosemarie won't go with her unless I bring you along." So I agree to go with Vince.

We arrived at Ferruggies Restaurant about 5:30 p.m., and the girls were already at the bar. They had their drinks in front of them. Mary was drinking vodka and something, and Rosemarie was drinking rum and Coke. Vince ordered Johnnie Walker Red with water, and I ordered an Amaretto on the rocks. We got our drinks, and we talked for a while.

Ferruggies was one of the best Italian food places in Queens. They kept their prices down at lunchtime. The place was always packed. They got a lot of airport business. There's always some sort of lunch function going on five days a week. Their liquor prices were a little cheaper than the local hotel bar prices. At 6:30 p.m., they brought out the hot hors d'oeuvre and plenty of them. At eight, the band started up.

Most airline and government employees hold their luncheon functions there. At night, it served as a meeting place where groups from the airport would meet. Then some individuals would leave for a more secluded place. At night, Ferruggies was like a watering hole. A lot of people gathered there for a drink but discreetly made arrangements with each other to meet at another location. We were no exception.

We decided to go to a place we called Japan Alley. The Victory Motor Lodge was located on South Conduit Avenue next to the Silver Star Diner. In back of the diner was a ten-car parking lot and a building that was attached to the Victory Motel next door. This building, at one time, was a social club. In back of the diner and motel was a vacant lot with rusted vehicles and twelve-foot high weeds. The property was owned by the New York City Department of Sanitation.

The motel purchased the social club and was renovating it. They were making it into their bar and lounge. They were having some financial problems, so the renovation was taking a very long time. There was an entrance to the bar from the alley in back of the building.

Japan Alley was a dive that was being renovated. There were few lights in the bar. The lit candles on the tables provided the low lighting. The drinks were cheap. There was a jukebox. Next to the jukebox was, what once was, a small dance floor. The floor was wood. There were some small tables to be used for snacks and drinks. You could not eat a meal on them. There were large sheets of plastic covering the entrance to the motel lobby and some of the walls.

The motel kept it open, even though it did not do much business. They utilized the social club's bar and jukebox that was there. We would park in the alley so no one would see our government cars parked in the motel parking lot. That was why Vince named the place Japan Alley.

Mary wanted to leave her car parked at Ferruggies. The girls shared an apartment together and carpooled to work. They also wanted to ride in a law enforcement vehicle. They were cop groupies. It was a turn-on for them. Mary and Rosemarie had on many occasions asked me if I could let them ride in my unmarked police cars. I had always told them they were not allowed to ride in the G-cars. Tonight was no exception. They begged and pleaded with Vince and me. They even resorted to rubbing their hands on our backs and shoulders and rubbed their bodies against ours. That was all Vince needed.

Vince whispered in my ear, "I'm going to take Mary in my car to Japan Alley. She's hot. I know I'm going to score tonight. You take Rosemarie. You can't miss. Rosemarie got the hots for you. You'll score."

I told Vince okay. I then told the girls to meet us around the corner so no one would see them getting into the G-cars. They agreed. They left Ferruggies and went around the corner.

We had the girls leave their car at Ferruggies. Rosemarie got into my car, and Mary rode with Vince. Rosemarie wanted to see the radio and wanted to know where I kept the shotgun. She wanted to know how we put on the siren and flashing lights. I told her to be patient. We arrived in the alley behind the motel. Vince followed me in his car with Mary. Then Vince flipped on the flashing lights and hit the siren for a couple of small whelp. Mary must have had an orgasm. Rosemarie said, "I want to do it too."

I said, "Later."

Vince and Mary got out of the car and went into the bar. Rosemarie moved close to me. She slid along the bench seat. She placed her left hand over my shoulder and begged me to show her how to put on the red lights. She then gave me a big kiss. Then our tongues met. I could feel little Reno waking up. I broke the kiss and told her, "Sit back." I put the car in reverse. I backed into the parking lot. I then proceeded out to the service road and turned down Rockaway Boulevard past the Airport Diner. I stopped on the shoulder of the road. The road in back of the airport was traveled very little at night. There were tall weeds on both sides of the road. I then showed Rosemarie where and how to use the siren. I showed her how to use the loudspeaker on the electric siren. I showed her the switch for the flashing lights.

Rosemarie was sitting so close to me that I could hardly steer the car. I put the car in gear, and we were back on the desolated road. Rosemarie placed her hand on the inside of my thigh, rubbing it up and down, bumping into little Reno. I then told her to hit the flashing light switch. She immediately reached over to the light switch and hit the switch, and the flashing lights were on. I then told her to hit the siren switch. She hit the switch. With the siren blaring and the lights flashing, we headed down Rockaway Boulevard. Rosemarie was very excited; she was holding on to my arm. As we approached the end of the airport property, I told her to kill the siren and lights. She flipped the switches.

I turned the car around and started back. I then told Rosemarie to open the glove box and set the switch to loudspeaker. She turned the radio knob to the speaker, setting without hesitating. I told her to hit the siren and flashing lights. She flipped the switches, and off we went singing into the microphone, "When the moon hits your eyes like a big pizza pie, that's amore." Then I told her to hit the switches and take the radio off speaker. She did it like a pro. She was so excited; her heart was pounding. She was elated. She was so close to me she was almost sitting on my lap. Her hands were all over me.

I pulled into Japan Alley and parked in back of Vince's car. We kissed and swapped spit for about five minutes. I fondled her breasts. I slipped my hand under her breast in its satin cradle under her low-cut blouse. I could feel her cold hand rubbing little Reno who was now big

Reno. This was almost too much to take. She removed her hand from my shorts and said, "Later! Let's go in and get a drink." Her breast was now back in its satin cradle. I zipped up my fly, and we got out of the car.

We walked into the bar. Vince and Mary were sitting next to the jukebox at a small table. There were four drinks on the table. Vince had ordered for us.

Mary asked Rosemarie, "What happened to you guys?" Rosemarie proceeded to tell Mary about our trip down Rockaway Boulevard. She was so excited and, in her bubbly voice, told Mary how she used the flashing lights and siren and the singing over the loudspeaker. Mary turned to Vince and gave him a good punch in the arm and said, "You only let me flip the switch on and then off. He took her for a ride and let her do more."

Vince told Mary, "I will let you do it later."

Mary told Vince, "Give me some quarters to play the jukebox." Vince reached into his pocket and gave her some quarters.

Rosemarie, feeling amorous, put her hand into my pants pocket and removed a hand full of change. She leaned over and whispered in my ear, "I think little Reno is asleep."

I whispered back, "He is resting now." She planted a kiss on my lips, driving her tongue into my mouth and abruptly pulling it back as she got up and went to the jukebox.

A couple of minutes later, the girls returned. Rosemarie said, "What's your favorite song?"

I said, "What's yours?"

She said, "You'll find out. Now tell me your favorite."

I said, "I like a lot of songs, but the one I like the most now is the song by Barbara Streisand. 'The way we were'."

Her eyes lit up, and her face was all a glow. She sipped her drink as I sipped my drink. Our eyes were glued to each other. Vince had also got a bowl of mixed peanuts from the bartender. The first song played was Frank Sinatra's rendition of Volare. The four of us began singing along with Frank. "Voo larrr rea, nell blu dipinto di blu . . ." We popped some peanuts into our mouths, sipped our drinks, and laughed a lot. Volare was another one of my favorites. The next song that followed was by

Barbra Streisand, "The way we were." I grabbed Rosemarie's hand and led her to the dance floor. We stood on the dance floor, our bodies clinging together. Her hands around my neck. My one hand placed lower in the small of her back, firmly exploring the soft well-rounded buttocks. The other rested between her shoulder blades, pulling her toward my body.

She raised her pubis and grinded it into mine. Our hands roamed each other's bodies. Our lips met, and tongues caressed each other. We did not come up for air until the song had ended. Each time, the song started again, we engaged our bodies, and our tongues became entwined again. The heat of our bodies caused us to sweat. The scent of her perfume and my cologne made the encounter a pleasurable experience. She had played the song five times.

After the fourth time the song played, we both agreed that we had to sit down for a while. We were both very thirsty, hot, and aroused. We were the only people, except for the bartender, in the room. When the song ended for the fourth time, we walked to the table. Big Reno was pointing the way back to the table. The lighting was very low. No one could see big Reno except Mary's eagle eye. We sat down, and then Mary told Rosemarie that they both had to go to the ladies' room to powder their noses. They giggled, and both ladies got up and started for the ladies' room, which was inside the lobby of the motel.

Well, wouldn't you know it? Vince was already two steps ahead of me. He had been discussing, with Mary, the sleeping arrangements for the night. He had it all figured out. He had already talked to Mary about the arrangements for that night. There were two options. One was that all four of us would spend the night at the girls' apartment. They shared a two-bedroom apartment. The other option was he would stay at the apartment with Mary, and I would take Rosemarie home with me. I was not crazy about the idea of all four of us in the same apartment. If it was her apartment alone, I would not hesitate; in fact, I preferred it.

The girls were talking about the same thing in the ladies' room. We all had to be on the same page, or it would not work. We were all horny and hot to trot. I told Vince that my sister, from Las Vegas, was staying with me for a couple of days, and I could not bring anyone home with me. Rosemarie was not enthused by the idea of traveling all the way out on Long Island and staying the night. She was more concerned about being in control and liked the home court advantage. When the girls came back from the ladies' room, Rosemarie took my hand and led me to the dance floor. We embraced and began to dance slowly. Our bodies clung to each other. Rosemarie said, "I do not think that the arrangements that Mary and Vince suggested are acceptable. I do not want to have another couple in the next bedroom. I do not want to hear noises coming from their bedroom, and I surely do not want anyone else hearing what is going on in my bedroom. I really do not want to travel all the way to Long Island and get up early to come home to shower and change."

I responded with "Same here."

"But I'm so hot, and I want you to make love to me."

"Me too," I said.

She then whispered in my ear, "I'm so wet. I don't think I can wait. I want to feel your body all over mine."

I said, "I'll tell Vince not to bring Mary home before midnight. That will give us some time together."

"That's good," Rosemarie said. "I won't have to worry about bedroom noises because Mary has her period, so Vince is not getting laid tonight."

"But if you play your cards right, who knows."

We abruptly finished the dance and hurried back to the table. I told Vince and Mary that we were going to leave now and I would see Vince at the office in the morning. Rosemarie whispered the plan to Mary, and they hugged.

Vince said, "Reno, what's the plan?"

I said, "I'm taking Rosemarie home. She's not feeling very well. You can take Mary to get her car later." The player was now being played.

I said, "Let's go." I didn't have to worry about a bar tab because I was in the habit of always paying when served so I could leave on a moment's notice. I opened the back door, and we exited the bar. I took my key and unlocked the car door. I opened the door, and Rosemarie got in. I went around the front of the car, and Rosemarie had slid over and unlocked the driver side. I opened the door and got in. I started the car, and Rosemarie was now sitting next to me with her arms wrapped around my arm. She leaned her head on my shoulder and hugged my arm. I placed my left hand on the steering wheel and turned as if to look out the back window over my right shoulder. She released her grip on my arm, and we found our lips gently touching. I could feel her right hand, fingers apart, going through my hair on the back of my head. My left hand was now gliding up and down the outside of her right leg. Our kiss became more passionate as our tongues met, and now my left hand began to explore the inside of her leg, moving ever slowly up to the inside of her thigh until it found its way to where I wanted to be. My hand and fingers now felt the intense heat from the crevasse between her thighs.

We broke our grip on each other as I threw the car in reverse and made a reverse turn and headed out of the parking lot. I got onto the Van Wyck Express Way. I got off on Queens Boulevard. The building she lived in was only fifteen minutes from the airport. I parked on the street in front of the apartment house. I got out of the car and opened the door for her, and she got out. I locked the car doors, and we entered the building. We walked to the elevator and hit the up button. The door opened, and we got in. The door closed, and we grabbed each other and kissed until the elevator stopped at the eight floor. We got out and walked down the hall to apartment 811. With her key in hand, she opened the door. We went in, and she turned the dead-bolt lock on the door behind us.

I looked around and could see it was clean, and things were in place. It was not messy at all. To the left was a small dining room with a kitchen just beyond the dining room. To the right was a half bathroom and a hall leading to a bedroom. In the front of me was a nice size living room with a door to a second bedroom.

I took off my jacket and hung it on a dining room chair. I turned and faced Rosemarie who was now returning from her bedroom. She looked at me, and her eyes opened wider as she gazed at the gun on my right side. She grew excited. She said, "Could I see your gun?" I carefully removed it from its holster and ejected the rounds, double-checked the cylinder, closed it, and handed it to her. She held it and caressed it like a newborn baby. I showed her how to hold the gun. I stood in back of her with big Reno firmly against the crevice of her butt. My arms around her arms My hands holding her hands which firmly gripped the gun. I whispered in her ear, "One of these days, I will take you to the range to fire the gun. Would you like that?"

She became so excited. I said, "OK, let's put this away." I reloaded and placed the gun in its holster, and we entered her bedroom.

We embraced and kissed our tongues, again reuniting. Our hands were exploring each other's bodies. We began to feverishly undress each other. I gently began kissing her neck while removing her blouse and releasing the hook of her bra. I continued to kiss her shoulders. We practically ripped our clothing off. With each kiss, my tongue would dart out and make a little circle on her warm flesh. I continued this across her shoulders and down between her large soft breast and around her breasts, getting closer and closer to the now erect center of my desire.

Soon I began the journey down her body with simple kisses and tongue circles. My tongue was exploring the rest of her body. Faster. Harder. That's it. That's it. Right there. Ah! Ah! I could feel her fingernails digging deeply into my shoulders as she experienced the explosion of her passion.

It was eleven o'clock when I reluctantly said I had to leave before Mary would be home. I dressed and kissed her good night as we left the bedroom and again as I was going out the door. I took the elevator down and exited the building. I got into my car and began to pull out when Mary pulled up. She took my parking spot. I then headed for home. I would be there in forty-five minutes.

The blaring honking of a horn brought me back to reality and what I was doing. A taxicab was honking his horn at me.

Chapter 20

NY Arrival

While Flight number 44 was circling LaGuardia, waiting for its turn to land, I was still on my way to LaGuardia to join the surveillance. The traffic was bad as usual. Traveling up the Van Wyck Express was no picnic. The traffic was moving once I passed the accident on the Van Wyck Express. I turned onto the Grand Central Parkway, which took me to LaGuardia airport. I went to the arrivals terminal and entered the taxi-only lane.

I was trying to cut through the taxicab line to get to the restricted area where I was supposed to park. That was when the taxi's blaring horn had brought me back to reality. A cab driver was upset that I was cutting him off, and I was not a police car trying to go to a restricted area. He was so mad that he jumped out of his cab and was coming around the front of his cab when I hit the flashers and siren for a small couple of whelp. He stopped dead in his tracks. He threw up his hands. His attitude changed, and he smiled, bowed, and waved me to pass in front of him. I gave him a thank-you wave and drove in front of him and across to a restricted area. I pulled in back of DJ's car. Cheech's car was in front of DJ's. I placed my T-plate (my Government license plate) on the dashboard and hung the microphone over the rearview mirror. As I got out of my car, DJ came over and briefed me on how he had the situation under control.

Agent Don Banning was driving the undercover cab. Don was a twenty-six-year-old Irish lad who could talk to anyone about anything. Don worked in Vince Morano's group in the City. Don and DJ got along very well. Their personalities were opposite. DJ was slow talking and thought before he opened his mouth. Whereas Don was more of a motor mouth and very hyper. He got very excited when he talked. If anyone could get Darnovski to open up in a conversation, it was Don. DJ briefed Don so he could elicit information from Darnovski in a normal conversation. Don was good at that. We needed to know if Darnovski was going to meet someone in New York City. DJ and I walked over to Don's cab and exchanged greetings. Just then, Cheech's voice came over the portable radio.

"Attention all units, the flight has landed and is taxing to the gate."

Don said he would turn on the radio in the cab and call in the location he was taking the fare and then turn off the radio. We said we would be monitoring him. DJ and I then went into the baggage area to await Darnovski's arrival.

At 6:50 p.m. (Eastern Standard Time) American airlines flight number 44 touched down at LaGuardia airport. It was a smooth landing. The plane taxied off the runway to gate 16. Agent Harris sat one row in back of Darnovski. He knew he had to keep Darnovski in sight so he could point him out to the New York agents. Then his job would be done. He could then relax while the other agents took over the surveillance. Sitting one row behind Darnovski, Harris felt confident that he had everything under control. The captain had announced, prior to the landing, that the weather in New York was holding at a nippy 32 degrees with a blustery wind from the northwest.

Once the plane stopped at the gate, everyone began to gather their belongings and stand up in preparation for getting off the plane. Darnovski seemed to be in no rush. He sat in his seat. The man seated next to Darnovski stood up with his coat and briefcase in hand. Row by row, the passengers were gathering their belongings and moving into the aisle, and then they were clumsily moving to the front of the plane. When it was Darnovski's turn, he just sat there. The inpatient man, who was seated in the aisle seat of Darnovski's row, moved into the aisle and followed the passengers in front of him. Agent Harris moved into the aisle with his briefcase and coat in hand. Harris looked at Darnovski as he passed his row. Darnovski was just sitting in his seat, looking at a magazine. Harris continued moving with the flow of passengers toward the exit. Harris thought to himself that he now had time to join up with the agents meeting him and point Darnovski out to them as Darnovski exited the gate.

Harris walked up the jet way ramp. At the door, he looked back and could not see Darnovski. He exited through the boarding gate door. He knew he had a few minutes to locate the agents that were meeting him. Harris could see the people waiting to meet the arriving passengers. Harris spotted a crude sign, being held high, in the back of the crowd. MR. HARRIS, NASHVILLE MOTORS, the sign read. The letters were made in different color crayons. Harris looked over his shoulder and still did not see Darnovski. He moved through the thinning crowd and approached the man with the sign. Cheech, spotting Harris approaching him, lowered the sign and reached out to shake Harris's hand.

"Harris? I'm Cheech. How was the trip?"

Harris said, "It was a smooth flight." Darnovski is still on the plane. "He is wearing or will be carrying a black raincoat and an attaché case."

Harris and Cheech talked for a few minutes while observing the boarding gate. Then Cheech said, "Is that him?"

Harris confirmed that Darnovski just exited the gate wearing his black raincoat. Darnovski passed through the boarding area and turned right down the long corridor of gates leading to the escalator to the baggage area on the lower level. Cheech immediately got on the portable radio and notified all units that the subject arrived and was headed to the baggage area wearing a black raincoat and carrying a briefcase.

They followed Darnovski down the escalator to the baggage area. DJ and I were in the baggage area, and I met up with Cheech and Harris as they came down the escalator. DJ immediately fell in place behind Darnovski. DJ looked like an arriving passenger. He was wearing his tan tweed sport jacket. His white shirt was opened at the color, and he wore no tie. He carried his raincoat over his arm and held an airline ticket folder in his hand. DJ remained in back of, but close to, Darnovski. A skycap approached Darnovski as he was headed for the baggage carousel. I swear that skycaps could smell money. Dressed in his skycap uniform, which was gray with a maroon stripe on each leg and a maroon band on his cap, the skycap had a patch on his right arm, which read in big letters SKYCAP. He asked Darnovski, in his Jamaican accent, "Do you need help with your bags?"

Darnovski said, "Yes, I have two bags, a green and a black suitcase." DJ continued to listen in on their conversation. He heard Darnovski ask the skycap if it would take a long time to get a cab. The skycap told him that there were long lines waiting for the cabs today. Darnovski asked if there was anything he could do to get him a cab more quickly.

The skycap said, "I will see what I can do. They are very strict about working deals with the taxi dispatcher. I'll tell him that you are on your way to the hospital to see your dying parent."

The skycap asked where he was going because there were different lines for taxies to New Jersey or Staten Island and Long Island. Darnovski told the skycap that he was going to the Waldorf Astoria in New York City. DJ smiled with relief upon overhearing the conversation. This was a good break. Now DJ had some work to do. The skycap, who was Jamaican and in his early fifties, left his baggage cart with Darnovski and walked toward the exit. He went outside the building and was walking toward the taxi dispatcher. DJ was right behind him.

DJ called out, "Hey, sky, wait a minute." The skycap turned around, and DJ, with his credentials and badge in hand, identified himself to the skycap as a federal agent.

DJ told him, "I need your help. We are watching the man whom you are helping. We want you to bring him a short way down from the taxi dispatcher." DJ pointed to the spot where he wanted the skycap to bring Darnovski to. "That is our taxicab over there," pointing to the undercover cab parked in the restricted area. "He will be waiting for you with his trunk open. Your job is to bring him to our taxicab. The dispatcher knows we are going to do this and will not give you any trouble."

The skycap then said, "The man wants to go to the Waldorf Astoria."

DJ said, "Great, thanks for the info." DJ had previously discussed with the taxi dispatcher the possibility that Darnovski would try to buy his way ahead of the taxi line. The dispatcher agreed to cooperate and suggested that we park our taxicab a short way down from the lines of people waiting for a taxicab. The dispatcher said that he would let the skycap take our subject to our undercover cab. The skycap understood what he was to do. He then went back into the baggage area to help Darnovski retrieve his bags.

DJ signaled to the undercover cab. The cab moved into position a short distance in front of the taxi pickup points. DJ then told Don Banning that the subject was going to the Waldorf Astoria. Don said that he would only go on the air if there was a change in hotels. DJ agreed.

DJ immediately took out his portable radio and contacted New York City Agent Morano who was on standby. He advised him the subject was going to the Waldorf Astoria. Agent Morano said he would contact the head of security at the Waldorf and make preparations for Darnovski's arrival.

We all watched Darnovski point out two bags to the skycap, who then pulled them from the baggage carrousel and put them on his baggage cart. The skycap, with Darnovski behind him, exited the building. The lines for the taxicabs were long. As the skycap approached the taxi dispatcher, the dispatcher directed the skycap to the undercover taxi. The skycap placed the two bags into the open trunk of the taxi. Darnovski took two twenties from his pocket and gave them to the skycap. The Jamaican man tipped his hat to Darnovski with a "Thank you, man," indicating mission accomplished. Darnovski smiled and gave the skycap a thumbs-up, signaling his satisfaction. The taxi driver asked Darnovski, "Where to?"

Darnovski said, "Waldorf Astoria." The taxi sped off into the night.

DJ notified everyone that the subject was headed for the Waldorf Astoria. DJ got into his car and proceeded to the Waldorf Astoria. Harris had only a hand-carried bag. Cheech and Harris left for the Waldorf. I followed shortly after. Now came the hard part. We had to babysit the man and make sure he did not pass the camera to anyone else.

When Vince Morano got the radio message from DJ that Darnovski was going to the Waldorf Astoria, he immediately contacted the hotel security. Hotel security confirmed that Darnovski had reservations and was scheduled to arrive on March 31 and depart on April 2. Vince made arraignments through security for us to get a room for a command post across the hall from Darnovski. Security would see that we had access to all incoming and outgoing telephone numbers that Darnovski called or received. Vince also contacted the Assistant US Attorney Richard Bremmier and made application for a court-ordered wiretap for Darnovski's calls at the Waldorf Astoria. He sent Agent Bob Lider to the assistant US attorney's office to walk the application to the magistrate's office for him to sign. Hopefully, we would have the order signed by 9:00 p.m. or 10:00 p.m.

Chapter 21

Arrival at the Waldorf Astoria

As the undercover taxicab left the terminal, Don Banning dropped the flag on the fare meter. Don immediately began conversing with Darnovski. Traffic was very heavy on the Grand Central. The traffic was even heaver on the Brooklyn—Queens Express Way (BQE). This gave Don the opportunity to talk to Darnovski. Darnovski was willing to talk; in fact, he could not stop talking. It was like Don was his long-lost friend and they had some catching-up to do. Don turned onto the Long Island Express Way and then onto the Brooklyn—Queens Express Way, heading toward the Midtown Tunnel. From the BQE, Darnovski could see the New York Skyline all lit up in the darkness. It was an impressive sight.

It took taxi just about an hour to go the eighteen miles to the hotel. Don Banning kept Darnovski talking all the way to the hotel. Darnovski bragged about his owning companies in Tennessee, Canada, and Austria. He went on to tell Don he was competing with 3M corporation for contracts involving reflective paint used to paint the lines on the roads and signs. He asked Don where he could get some action with women without getting in trouble with the police. Don told him, "You could usually find high-price hookers at the hotel bar. They will not approach you. They usually check into the hotel as quest. They work deals with the bartenders." Don went on to say that if he struck up a conversation with the bartender and he passed his screening, then the bartender would direct someone to him. Hotel security was always trying to keep the hookers out of the hotel. He also told him that there were escort services he could call that were on the east side, not far from the hotel.

They entered the Queens Midtown Tunnel and exited on E. Thirty-Seventh Street. They turned onto Third Avenue. Darnovski was looking at the large buildings. They turned left onto E. Forty-Seventh Street, right on Park Avenue. The taxicab proceeded to 301 Park Avenue and the impressive entrance to the Waldorf Astoria. The front of the hotel was glittering with its brass overhang canapé. There were three sets of polished brass double doors at the entrance to the hotel. On either side, there were brass flag holders prominently holding waving flags. The small green trees on either side of the entrance in their cement pots were pleasing to the eye in a city of cement.

As they were pulling up in front of the Waldorf Astoria, the doorman, a tall man in a gray uniform with the name Waldorf Astoria prominent on the front left breast of the uniform and embodied on his cap, approached the taxi. The door man opened the cab door and greeted Darnovski.

"Welcome to the Waldorf Astoria," the man said. He held the door open for Darnovski while Darnovski paid the taxicab fare plus a generous tip of ten dollars. The doorman then signaled to the bellman, who then proceeded down to the trunk of the cab. Don opened the trunk, and the bellman removed two bags from the trunk. Darnovski walked up the few steps and entered the hotel lobby. The bellman carried the two bags through the service entrance door. Darnovski walked to the front desk. There were no lines. There were two desk clerks and a well-groomed man in a black pinstriped suit. His name tag indicated that he was the manager. He was talking to a man in a blue suit.

Vince Morano had been standing outside, waiting for the cab to arrive with George Hardy, the head of hotel security. George was a man in his midsixties. He was five feet eight and weighed about 180 lbs. He had short gray hair and gray eyebrows. He was a retired FBI agent. He wore an expensive blue suit. The two men waited patiently for the taxicab to arrive. Vince spotted the undercover cab pull up. They observed Darnovski exit the taxicab. Both men then entered the hotel.

George went behind the registration desk and informed the manager that the man entering was the gentlemen that we were interested in. Darnovski approached the desk. The bellman was in back of him with the two bags. The manager stood at the desk and said, "Welcome to the Waldorf Astoria. May I assist you?"

Darnovski said, "Yes, I have a reservation."

"Your name, sir."

"Darnovski," was his reply. The manager typed in the name. The screen lit up.

The manager then asked, "Will you be keeping the same method of payment on your American Express card, sir?"

Darnovski said, "Yes," and removed an American Express gold card from his wallet.

The manager said, "You are in room 705, sir." He then produced a room key from a rack beneath the desk and gave it to Darnovski. The manager told the bell cap to take the bags to room 705. Darnovski then signed the hotel card and the credit card charge slip. He took the key from the manager and followed the bellman to the bank of elevators on the side of the lobby. Agent Charlie Kosko entered into the elevator with Darnovski. They both got off on the seventh floor. Agent Kosko entered room 704 across from Darnovski.

Agent Morano was sitting in the lobby chair with his newspaper. He told arriving surveillance members that they were going to meet in the Safari Bar. When Harris and Cheech arrived, Vince gave the key of room 704 to Harris so he could get settled in. DJ brought the radio equipment up to room 704. When I arrived, which was shortly after Darnovski's arrival, I was met by Vince. We went into the Safari Bar and sat at the bar.

Vince said, "Hey, Reno, this is like old times. Remember the time we were at Paradise Club on the North Shore?"

"Which time?" I said.

Vince said, "You remember the time you scored with the blond with those great big tits."

"Yes, did I remember."

Vince and I had just finished a surveillance in Centerport on the North Shore of Long Island. Our subject returned to his residence and was in for the night. I assigned an agent to continue the surveillance of his residence until he was sure that the subject was in for the night. Vince suggested that we go to the Paradise Club for a few drinks and to see how the action was. The club was a short distance from where our subject lived. I said OK and that I would follow him to the club. We drove down Route 25A to the club and pulled into the almost filled parking lot. As we walked from the parking lot to the club entrance, Vince said, "Okay, I'm going to be a surgeon, specializing in breast augmentation tonight. You are going to be a racehorse owner." I reluctantly agreed.

We usually played different roles when we went out to keep in practice for our undercover work. We always researched the characters we played. We never entered a roll without being fully knowledgeable of the characters we played. I asked Vince why I should be a racehorse owner.

He said, "Horse owners are rich and have money. The women will eat it up. They will be all over you. Trust me it will work."

"Well we will see," I said. Vince really knew a lot about horse racing, jockeys, betting, training, and raising horses. He really took an interest in it. We used to go to the off-track betting (OTB) at least once a day when we both worked in the city. When Vince did a short stretch at JFK airport, we would go to Aqueduct. I knew a little about owning a racehorse because I had a fraud case involving the temporary importation of a racehorse.

We entered the club and went to the bar. I ordered an Amaretto on the rocks, and Vince ordered Johnnie Walker Red with soda. Vince paid for the drinks with a $100 bill. He left the stack of bills he got as change in front of him on the bar. I took a twenty from my pocket and placed it on the bar in front of me. I intended to buy the next round for me and Vince. I told Vince, "Why are you leaving so much money on the bar?"

Vince said, "Women look to see if you have money in front of you. If you don't have a stack of bills, they will think you are a cheapskate. They will not waste their time trying to flirt with you."

He was right. Out of the corner of my eye, I could see at least two women change their seats at the bar; one closer to Vince and the other across from Vince. The bar was horseshoe in shape. There were patio glass doors on one side of the bar, which led to a veranda with a lawn leading to trees. We sat facing the patio doors. The front of the bar led to a large wood dance floor with a great big mirror globe with multicolor lights sparkling like stars on the dance floor. There was some strobe lights that were uneasy to the eye. The music was loud at the other end of the dance floor where the band was playing. It was not too bad at the bar. At least, you could talk without shouting. There were many women at the bar, looking for pickups. There were more women than men at the bar. Vince sensed victory at hand. He said, "Reno, there are a lot more women than men. We have a good chance to score tonight."

Two nice-looking women returned from the dance floor. They walked to the bar close to Vince. Vince started to talk to me about his profession as a surgeon so the two women could overhear our conversation. In a couple of minutes, the woman next to him started a conversation with him. Vince began to play with the woman and to reel them in. Then Vince put his foot in his mouth. He suggested to one of the women that he would give her a free breast evaluation in his car, not in his office; that was when the woman got up and left. Vince and I talked for a little while. Vince kept looking at all the women around the bar and sizing them up.

Then Vince told me, "Reno, that blond in the black dress, the one across from you, is giving you the eye. She keeps looking at you. She is trying to get your attention." There were two women in black dresses at the bar across from us.

I said, "Which one?"

He said, "The one with the big tits."

Well, he was right. The woman had big tits, and she kept looking at me and smiling. Not to be rude, I looked at her and gave her a smile and an acknowledgment that I saw her looking at me.

Vince said, "She must be at least a 48 triple E." Vince was a pretty good judge of the sizes of women's breasts. He was close this time. She was actually a 48 triple D as I soon found out.

Vince said, "Quick. Buy her a drink. You're bound to score."

I said, "I don't think so. She is not interested in me."

Vince said, "I'll show you." Vince called the bartender over.

The bartender was a young, slender thirty-five-year-old man. He had black hair and could shake a martini. All the women at the bar cheered him on when he took to shaking a drink. It looked like he was doing the samba while shaking the canister and glass. He wore tight black pants. He had a red silk shirt with an open collar that exposed his hairy chest. He wore a black-and-red checkered vest. He was very flirtatious with all the women at the bar. He made a lot of tips from the women.

The bartender came over to us and said, "What will it be, gents?"

Vince said, "My friend here is buying this round, and he wants to buy that lady in the black dress, across from him, a drink."

The bartender looked over his shoulder and said, "Which one?" The blond leaned her head to the left side, looking at me. I raised my glass as if to toast her. She smiled and nodded her head. Vince told the bartender, "The blond with the big tits." The bartender went over to the woman and turned his head toward me, and I acknowledged that he had the right woman. He told the woman that I wanted to buy her a drink and asked her what she was drinking. She told him a vodka sours. He left and then returned with her drink. She held up the glass in a gesture, thanking me for the drink.

That was my cue. As I got up and walked around the bar, I kept thinking, *Vince could be right.* I think I got a good chance to score with this blond bombshell. I sat in the seat next to her.

I said, "I'm Johnny Reno."

She said, "I'm Nicole Swensen."

She said, "Thanks for the drink. I spotted you when you walked in with your friend. I was watching you guys. Your friend thinks he is god's gift to women. I could not help overhearing his line. I guess some dumb broads will fall for his line. I could tell you were not comfortable with what he was doing." At that moment, I knew she knew the bar scene and what was going on.

I said, "You're right on the mark."

"You're not like him," she said. She picked up her drink and said, "I'm going outside for a cigarette. Want to come?" I trailed her with drink in hand. It was a warm night in early May. We had no coats. We strolled on the veranda, without saying much at first. Then it dawned on me I was being picked up.

I could not help noticing her figure as she walked in front of me. She was taller than me. She was every bit of five feet eleven if not more. Her hair was shining in the moon light. She had long platinum blond hair. She had a smooth complexion and a very pretty face. She did have big tits. Her low-cut dress revealed the cleavage between her huge milky-white breasts. Her measurements were 48, 29, 38, and so she later said. Her dress clung to her like saran wrap. There appeared to be no fat on her body, just firm muscle. My first impression was that she was Swedish or Swiss and that she was a skier or a model. Her facial features were sharp and well defined with a square chin and muscular jaws. Her lips were full and inviting with the glittering red lipstick. She had pearly white teeth. Her eyes were big and green, and her eye shadow accented the eyes. From her ears dangled teardrop earrings.

"I could hear your friend saying that he was a surgeon and that you were a racehorse owner. But you were not acknowledging what he was saying. I could tell he was bullshitting, and you were not going along with him. You know that you got the looks, and you do not need to bullshit anyone."

I said, "I know, and I did not feel comfortable picking up women at bars." We talked for about an fifteen minutes, finding out about each other. She told me she was thirty-eight years old and had a sixteen-year-old daughter, whom she could not control. She did as she pleased. She had started to hang out with the wrong crowd. She tried to paint herself as a single mom just out for a night to get a break from raising her daughter. She seemed to be truthful, but I had an uneasy feeling. I don't think I believed her for a minute, but I went along with her to see where this was going.

We returned to the bar. Vince was talking to a pretty young girl, and she was all over him. He signaled me that he was leaving with the girl. He headed for the door. A slow dance came on, and I asked Nicole if she wanted to dance. She said yes. We went to the dance floor, holding hands. On the dance floor, she placed her arms around my neck and pulled me close to her. I placed my hands in the small of her back, pulling her toward me. We did not move our feet, just our bodies. We clung to each other. I could feel the heat from her body. She pressed her breast hard against me and grinded her groin into my groin. I was getting hot. I moved my hands down and held the cheeks of her ass and felt the round softness that I so desperately wanted to hold.

She whispered in my ear, "Do you like what you are feeling?"

Breathing in her ear and kissing it and then gently nibbling on her ear, I said, "You bet I do. You got me so horny."

She said, "I'm even hornier than you. I want you to fuck me."

I could not believe what I had just heard but little Reno did, and he began rising to the call. I found my hands rubbing the cheeks of her ass, gripping them and pulling them close to me so she could feel little Reno rubbing on her heated groin. The dance ended, and we walked back toward our bar seats. Good thing, it was pretty dark on the dance floor. I had a hard-on, which was trying to push its way out of my pants. At this point, my little Reno began to think for me.

I told her, "Get your bag and let's go."

She called the bartender over and asked for her handbag. He removed the bag from a shelf behind the bar and handed the bag to her. I tossed a five spot on the bar and thanked the bartender.

We hurried out of the bar and to my car. I opened the door for her. She sat on the seat and put her legs inside the car. Before I could close her door, she grabbed little Reno. She said, "I want this. I'm so hot."

I said, "You will have to wait. I closed the door and went around to the driver side and got in.

"Are we going to your place?"

She said, "No, my daughter and I sleep in the same room so I cannot have anyone over. We have only one bedroom."

I said, "Okay, we will go to my place." I started the car and pulled out and headed down Route 25A. In fifteen minutes, I would be home.

She unbuckled her lap belt and moved next to me. She was all over me. Her hands explored my body, and she kept little Reno alive. I think that I got more hickeys on the way home than I had ever gotten before. The speed limit was fifty miles an hour, but due to the pleasure I was receiving, I felt myself stiffening up, causing my foot to push harder on the gas pedal. As I glanced at the speedometer, it was reading eighty miles an hour. I eased up on the gas pedal. I did not want to be stopped for speeding. I arrived home in ten minutes. I pulled into and parked in my driveway. I had not told her I had a house.

She said, "Is this your house?"

I told her I was renting. We got out of the car and hurried into the house. We entered the marbled floor hall. We then proceeded to the sunken living room with the fireplace.

She said, "Please put a fire on so we could cuddle by the fire." I threw on an instant fire log, and in five minutes, we had a full fire going.

We cuddled on a rug in front of the fireplace. Our lips met. Her lips were soft and tasty. Then our tongues met, and they explored each other's mouth just as our hands explored each other's body. The heat from the fireplace was no match for our bodies. Our clothes began to peel off. I started to unzip the back of her dress. I reached for the bra hooks and could not find any.

She laughed and said, "The hook is between the cups, silly. I have my bras made special because of my large breasts. And each bra costs over seventy dollars." All I could hear were words that I paid no attention to, as she slowly peeled the dress off one shoulder and then the other, revealing an overflowing black laced bra. We were now kneeling face to face as the dress fell to her waist. Our lips joined once again as my hands roamed through the cleavage of her milky-white breasts. Gripping each side of the bra hooks and clips, I released two of the largest breasts I had ever seen. Instantly, like a little baby that had missed his feeding time, I grasped one breast with both my hands, pulling it toward my open mouth. My tongue was stretching to be first to meet the tan protrusion in the field of milky-white flesh. My tongue and lips were competing for the morsel. I could feel her hands pushing my head hard against her breast. She was saying something about the little baby was hungry. It went in one ear and out the other. All I wanted was to get my hands and mouth on those big breast and to kiss and caress them.

She had managed to get my shirt off, and I could now feel her hands roaming from my head to my shoulders around my back. We got up off the rug as I led her upstairs to my bedroom. She fumbled with my belt and unzipped my pants. They dropped to the floor. Then I pulled her dress from her waist to her knees and let it drop to the floor. We left a trail of clothing, mostly mine, all the way to my bed. After an hour of extreme pleasure, we fell asleep.

It was ten in the morning when I woke up with Nicole's naked body next to mine. I groped her breast. She rotated her hips into my groin and began to moan. Then little Reno rose to the call, and before long, he entered the wet passionate cave of pleasure. We made love for another half hour.

After laying there for a few more minutes, we sat up in the bed. My blinds were up, and sunlight poured in. In the bright light, I scanned her body. Her legs were very long, and her body trunk was long. *Dam, she was well portioned.* She began to talk about the curse of her huge breasts—how they were very heavy and she had to have special bras made with an extra strong support wire, which cost extra, to hold the weight up. I told her they felt nice and soft like a feather pillow. She laughed and told me to sit on the edge of the bed. I slid my legs over the side of the bed. She stood up behind me. She said she was going to drop one of her breast on my head and wanted me to tell her if the tit was light as a feather or not. I said, "You got to be kidding." She wasn't. She took one of her breasts and dropped it on my head. Actually, I think she did not drop her tit on my head. I think she used blunt force and hit my head with her breast. I felt the pain and said ouch. It really hurt. But I had to admit her breasts were very heavy. She said it was a curse to have huge breasts and that there was less surface sensitivity. She explained that the nerve endings were so far apart that she could hardly feel the touching and caressing of her breasts. She went on to say she was saving her money so she could have a breast reduction.

I got out of bed, still naked, holding my head and put on my slippers. She said, "Where are you going?"

I said, "I'm going to take a quick shower, and then I will put on a pot of coffee." She pulled the sheet over her and curled up. I jumped in and out of the shower and quickly brushed my teeth and shaved. I went to my closet and quickly dressed. I came out and pulled the covers down and said, "I'm going to the kitchen to put on the coffee."

She said, "Okay, I'm getting up. I will come to the kitchen after I shower and dress. I promise I will be quick." I went into the kitchen and put on a pot of coffee. I made some toast and bacon and eggs while the coffee was brewing.

She came into the kitchen, towel drying her hair and said, "Make mine easy and over." We sat at the kitchen table and had breakfast. She had no makeup on, and she still looked beautiful. She said that she really had to get home before she caught hell from her daughter. We finished up, and I placed the cups and plates in the dishwasher and turned it on. We then left the house. We got into the car, and she again sat close to me. She used the center lap belt on the bench seat. She held my right arm and snuggled close to me. I took the Sunken Meadow Parkway to the Long Island Express Way (LIE). She had put the car radio on. She tuned in the country music station. She leaned on my shoulder and kept running her hand on the inside of my thighs. *Boy, did she know how to turn a guy on.* She lived in Corona Queens. Following her directions, I was soon in front of a large tenement house. I parked in front and locked the car. We went up several steps to the front entrance. She opened her purse and took out a key and opened the door. We kissed, and then I left her in the doorway. I got into my car and drove off. We went out three times before she introduced me to her daughter.

On the third date, I picked her up at her place. It was a Saturday, and we went to Belmont Park racetrack. After a couple of hours, we left and went to a small Italian restaurant in Smithtown. We had an early dinner. We then returned to my house for an hour of sex. She said she could not spend the night because she was worried about her daughter. We headed to her house. Again, she snuggled close to me and rubbed my inner thigh. We got on to the LIE, and there was light traffic. She kept sticking her tongue in my ear and rubbing little Reno until he tried to escape by growing and trying to push his way out. She then helped little Reno. She unzipped my fly and reached in and pulled little Reno to the safety of her mouth. I could feel my body tighten and stiffen up as her tongue massaged little Reno's head until he blew his top. At that point, I glanced at the odometer, and I was doing well over ninety miles an hour. I immediately pulled my foot from the gas pedal and applied the brakes to slow the car down before we got into an accident or I got stopped for speeding. And the only excuse you had to tell the cop was that you could not help it because you were getting a blow job. I don't think so.

Fifteen minutes later, we arrived at her apartment. There was something about Nicole that just turned me on. We went up three flights of stairs to her apartment door. She opened the door. Her daughter was sitting at the table with some school books. She stood up and faced me as we walked in. I stood there with my mouth open in awe. She was also a knockout. My god! She was beautiful, and she had a sexier figure than her mother. I just could not believe she was only sixteen. She looked like she was a woman of twenty to twenty-five years old. She looked like a model or more like the Swedish pinup girls in men magazines. If I didn't know better, I would have thought that they were sisters, not mother and daughter. She introduced me to her daughter, Andrea. Her daughter was very outspoken and was street-smart. Andrea was not school smart, but she was trying.

I sat at the table with her and looked at the books. They were math books. She told me she did not understand the math problems. She said she needed to study so she could pass her midterms. She asked me to help her study for the test. Nicole was making me a cup of coffee as I talked with Andrea. I tried to explain the concept in language she would understand, using examples that she could relate to. She was quick to grasp what I was teaching her. She said, "Why don't the teachers explain it the way you do?" She took her books and went into the bedroom, saying, "I'm going to study in my bedroom so you two can be alone." She laughed as she left the room and closed the bedroom door behind her.

Several minutes later, she came out of the bedroom in a pale blue see-through top and panties. My mouth dropped and eyes widened, and I was speechless as I soaked in the beauty before me. Her breasts did not sag from the weight but pointed straight out. Nicole yelled and scolded her for leaving the bedroom without putting on a robe. Andrea ignored her mother and went to the sink and got a glass of water before returning to the bedroom. I could not help noticing the beautiful love handles she had as she walked slowly to the sink and bent over while filling her glass. I just wanted to reach out and roam my hands all over the curves of her tight butt. I watched as she disappeared behind the closed door.

The kitchen led to a small living room with a small couch and coffee table and a chair. Off the kitchen was a bathroom and a bedroom. We then went to sit on the couch and make out. After half an hour of making out, she led me to the bathroom, where she unbuckled my pants and pulled them down with my shorts. I sat on the covered toilet seat. Reno stood at attention, and she began giving me a blow job. Before I could come, we heard her daughter knocking on the bathroom door. She said, "Mother, I know you are in there, giving John a blow job. We need to talk."

Nicole said, "John is throwing up, and I am helping him. I'll be right out." We left the bathroom; her daughter was in the bedroom. I began to have second thoughts about seeing her again. *What was I getting myself into?* I thought. This was not normal or a good example to set for her daughter. I told her I was going to leave, and she said, "Call me tomorrow." She went into the bedroom, and I left.

Several days later, I went to Nicole's apartment about 8:00 p.m. Her daughter was out. Nicole said that Andrea was going to be out until 10:00 p.m. I felt a little uncomfortable but could not resist the terrific sex. She put on her see-through pj's and covered them with a cotton robe. We sat on the couch and watched a little TV. Andrea came home at 10:00 p.m. She came into the living room. Her mother and I both stood up. I don't know why we stood up. At first, I thought we were going to go into the kitchen and talk with Andrea. Andrea was wearing a short black miniskirt with a white blouse and short black heels. The top two buttons on her blouse were open. This revealed her cleavage. She kissed her mother on the cheek, and then she stretched her arms out and embraced me. She then gave me a big kiss to which I did not resist. *Wow*, I thought to myself, *where did that come from?* She went into the kitchen and put her bag on the table before going to the bedroom.

I started to get real nervous. For some reason, I again felt very uncomfortable. I really was not ready for what was about to occur. Nicole had told me that Andrea was dating a twenty-four-year-old biker, who was a member of a local gang. She did not like her hanging out with him. The more she tried to stop her, the more she would defy her. I said I would talk to Andrea. When I was helping Andrea with her homework, I managed to give her a morality lecture also about the crowd she hung out with, especially about seeing a gang member. I remember telling her about her going to prison if she kept hanging out with them and that they were only using her for a sex toy.

My mind began to race. *Could this be a setup because I told her why she should not be seeing the bikers?* Then Andrea shouted from the bedroom to her mother. "Mom, you will be glad to know that I am not going to see Daggers anymore." Now I was really concerned. *What if she told Daggers that I told her not to see him? Will Daggers and his crew be waiting for me? Will I have four flat tires?* I calmed down a little because I knew I at least had my gun with me.

Nicole went into the bedroom and talked with Andrea. I yelled to the two of them that I was going to go and let the two of them talk. Nicole said, "Don't go yet." After five minutes or several sips of my coffee, Nicole and Andrea came back into the kitchen where I was sitting. Nicole came over to me and put her arms around me and thanked me for talking to Andrea. Then Andrea came over to me and hugged me and thanked me for showing her the light for not hanging out with a bad crowd. Now I was really concerned. *What is going on?* Then I got the shock of my life, although Vince would have thought that he had died and gone to heaven.

Nicole said, "I want you to spend the night with us." I thought that I was hearing things.

Then Andrea said, "It's like Mom said, 'I want you to spent the night with us'."

Nicole then said, "My daughter and I wanted to have sex with you. We could have a threesome and smoke some pot that I have."

Well, this blew my mind. I stood up and said, "You people are crazy. Nicole, are you out of your mind? You want me to fuck your daughter with you in bed with us? Andrea, you want me to fuck you with your mother there and fuck her with you there and have the two of you both playing with my dick?" I could smell the sweet pungent odor of marijuana smoke coming from the bedroom. They were high on pot.

I said, "I'll call you." I left the apartment, never to come back. I never called her again. I often wonder how things turned out for the two of them.

Chapter 22

The Chameleon

I felt someone was pushing my shoulder. It was Vince. "Hey, Reno, wake up." You haven't heard anything I was saying.

"Sorry, Vince, I was remembering how we met Nicole. You know big tits."

"You were crazy for not jumping on the threesome with her and her daughter. That would be the ultimate to fuck the mother and daughter together."

I said, "I think it was the pot that turned me off. I do not like anyone that uses drugs, especially when I'm sworn to enforce the drug laws. It's an ethics problem for me."

DJ came to the bar and said, "Darnovski had just ordered food service in his room." In all probability, he would be in his room all night. I told DJ I did not think so. Don had said that during the ride to the hotel, Darnovski was asking him about hookers.

"So I really think he will be down in an hour or so. We should all chow down now. DJ, tell the guys to expense it but not to get anything too expensive. I'll approve it in order to maintain the surveillance."

DJ said OK and made all notifications. I could depend on DJ. He was my right-hand man. Most of us ordered from the bar. There were several tables in the bar room. We moved our drinks to the tables and ate our food. About 10:00 p.m., the bar began to get crowded.

DJ came in and said, "Darnovski is on his way down without his coat." Agent Morano left the bar and went into the lobby. Several members of the surveillance team stood in the bar. We were talking for a few minutes when Darnovski entered the bar. He wore black slacks, a blue opened-collar shirt, and blue suit jacket. He was also clean-shaven. He looked as if he was all spiffed up and looking for some honeys. There were several women at the bar; there were a couple groups of women sitting around a few tables. Several of our agents were at tables and at the bar. Most of the people looked like they were staying at the hotel. Several people had coats with them. Most of them were members of the surveillance team.

Darnovski entered the bar and looked around. He then went to the bar and sat down in the middle of the bar with women on his left and right. He beckoned to the bartender. The bartender came over and asked what he was drinking.

Darnovski said, "Jack Daniels and coke." Darnovski remarked to the bartender, "It is not crowed tonight."

The bartender said that it would pick up in a little while. He then left and started to make Darnovski's dink. He brought it to him, and Darnovski took out a wad of hundred-dollar bills. He must have had three or four thousand dollars in the wad. The bartender's eyes lit up, and so did several women's at the bar. The bartender took the hundred-dollar bill that Darnovski was holding out and went to the cash register and rung up the drink and brought back the change. The bartender asked Darnovski if he was staying at the hotel. Darnovski said that he was and would be staying a couple of days. Darnovski and the bartender talked like old friends. The bartender knew right off that Darnovski was a big spender, especially when Darnovski tipped him with a twenty-dollar bill.

The bartender would respond to bar patrons call for drinks but would return to talk with Darnovski. They were like old friends. Darnovski told him about the companies he owned and how he did not know anyone in New York City. He also asked about several of the women at the bar. Darnovski had observed a well-dressed woman sitting at the end of the bar talking to the bartender when he had first entered the bar. During his conversation with the bartender, Darnovski asked if the woman at the far end of the bar was alone. The bartender said, "Yes, she is."

The woman sitting at the end of the bar was about five feet seven inches tall. She had long auburn hair. Her earrings sparkled. She wore a white blouse with the top two buttons open. The blouse was tight. Her breasts bulged in the push-up bra she was wearing. She wore a gray skirt that was an inch above the knee. She sat on the bar stool with her legs crossed. You could not help notice her muscular calves. She was holding her glass with one hand and stirring the drink with a plastic stirrer. She sipped her drink slowly. The bartender, while responding to another patron's call for a drink, looked at the woman at the end of the bar and gave her a signal with his head. It was obvious to us because we were watching everything that was going on. The woman then looked at Darnovski and smiled. She wanted to let Darnovski know that she was willing to accept company.

The bartender returned to Darnovski to talk some more. Darnovski said, "Fill it up again and see if the woman at the end of the bar would let me buy her a drink."

The bartender looked over to the woman at the end of the bar and then back to Darnovski and said, "The woman in the white blouse?"

Darnovski said, "Yes."

"I'll ask her," the bartender said, as he left to make Darnovski another drink. He went to the woman at the far end of the bar and talked with her. He glanced back at Darnovski and nodded yes to Darnovski. He then went to make the drinks. Darnovski smiled because he knew he was being taken care of because he had money. The woman nodded to Darnovski for him to come sit with her. Darnovski picked up his money and put it in his pocket and then picked up his almost empty glass and went to the end of the bar. He sat down next to the woman. She immediately thanked him for the drink. She said her name was Angelica. The bartender brought the two drinks and Darnovski whipped out his money wad in order to impress the hooker.

Vince whispered to me, "Look at that schmuck flashing all that money. He is looking to be robbed." Darnovski ripped off another hundred-dollar bill to pay for the drinks and again gave the bartender a twenty from the change. After ten minutes and another drinks later,

Darnovski and the woman left the bar. They entered the elevator and went to the seventh floor. They both entered room 705.

After forty-five minutes, Angelica left Darnovski's room. She looked just as good coming out as she did going in. She took the elevator down to the bar and talked to the bartender for a few minutes. The bartender put his hand on the woman's hand and then straight into his pocket. She smiled and left the bar and took the elevator to the fifth floor. The hotel surveillance camera revealed that she went into room 518.

It was now obvious to us that Angelica was a high-price hooker, working with the hotel bartender. George Hardy, the head of hotel security, said they had enough evidence on the video surveillance to fire the bartender and ask Angelica to leave the hotel immediately. The hotel registration revealed that Angelica would be checking out in the morning.

Fifteen minutes after Angelica left Darnovski's room, his door opened, and a person resembling Darnovski left and headed for the elevator. Charlie Kosko was on the radio to alert the surveillance that Darnovski was on the move again without any bags. DJ was sitting at the bar between Vince and me. A bellman came into the bar and called out "telephone for Mr. Don Jennings."

DJ got up and said, "He's on the move. I'll go into the lobby and see where he is going." DJ left with two other agents following him. As DJ walked out, Darnovski walked in. Darnovski was now wearing slacks, an open-collared shirt, and a sweater. He combed his hair differently and wore glasses. He looked like a young professor. DJ had to take a double look and still did not know if it was Darnovski or not. DJ went to the elevator bank. There were no elevators on the way down. DJ and the team headed back to the bar. Darnovski entered the bar, which had quite a few people there. He walked to the seat that DJ had vacated.

Darnovski told Vince, "How is the service tonight?"

Vince said, "This bartender is OK, but there are a lot of people for him to take care of."

I chimed in and said, "They should have had more help. It is hard to get a drink here."

Darnovski said, "I'll show you guys how it is done."

Darnovski leaned into the bar with one hand up to get the barkeep's attention.

"Harry," Darnovski said. The bartender immediately dropped what he was doing and came right to Darnovski and said, "Jack Daniels and Coke?"

Darnovski said, "And what my two friends are drinking."

I said, "Amaretto on the rocks," and Vince said, "Johnnie Walker Black with soda."

Darnovski said, "This round is on me."

I said, "Thanks, pal. Do you know the bartender?"

Darnovski took out his wad of $100 bills, which was not as big as it was earlier in the evening and put a $100 bill on the bar. He said, "I was in here earlier in the evening. I think he remembers me."

Vince and I continued the conversation with Darnovski. When the drinks arrived, Darnovski paid for them and gave Harry a $20 tip. Vince told Darnovski that he owned several racehorses, and that had Darnovski intrigued. I took on the part of an importer/exporter. I gave Darnovski one of my undercover business cards. He took it and gave me his business card. He told us he owned several companies overseas and in the US. I nursed my drink, and Darnovski had three more.

All the time Darnovski was talking to us, he kept looking at the women around the bar. His eyes had fixated on a particular blond at the end of the bar. Harry watched Darnovski closely. When Darnovski raised his hand, Harry was there with a drink real fast. Harry could see that Darnovski was interested in the blond woman at the end of the bar. Harry moved close to the blond. He was now standing next to the woman, talking to her. The woman turned to her side to get a better look at Darnovski. Darnovski, sipping his drink, leaned forward to get a better look at the blond. Harry pointed to the woman's drink; it was a Manhattan, and Darnovski nodded his head up and down, saying yes.

Darnovski then, with his drink in hand, got up from his seat and walked over and sat down in the seat next to a beautiful young blond. She must have been in her early thirties. She was about five feet six inches tall. She had a well-proportioned body—36, 25, 35. She wore dark blue evening dress with a plunging neckline. The low-cut revealed a lot of her cleavage. She wore glossed lipstick but very little makeup.

Her skin was clear, and her sharp facial features made her look very sexy with her long blond hair.

The bartender returned and placed a Manhattan in front of the blond and said, "Complements of this gentleman." As she spoke, Darnovski took his wad of bills from his pocket and peeled off a $100 bill, placing it on the bar in front of him. He then placed the rest of the money back in his pocket. The bartender picked up the bill and returned to the cash register and rung up the drinks.

She said, "Thank you for the drink. I'm Victoria."

Darnovski said his name was Manny. "Harry tells me you are from Austria. How long are you going to be here?"

Darnovski told her he lived in Austria and had many businesses around the world. He told her he would be in town for a couple of days. Harry returned with Darnovski's change. Again, Darnovski tipped Harry a with a $20 bill.

"Impressive," Victoria said.

"It just insures that I get the best of service and do not have to wait for service. You get what you pay for." Darnovski then said, "See those two guys over there." He pointed to Vince and me. "They are still waiting to get Harry's attention. They are cheap and do not tip well. They get bad service." They both laughed. She told him she was free for a couple of days and if he wanted, she could show him around the town. She gave him a business card. Darnovski placed it in his pocket. Darnovski told her that he was meeting with some friends and did not know if he would have any free time. They continued to talk for about ten minutes.

Frank entered the bar as Darnovski was leaving his seat. Frank came over and sat next to me. Frank said, "Is he in his room for the night?"

I told him that Darnovski was sitting at the end of the bar and that I thought it would be a long night.

Frank said, "I came a little early so I could give you guys a break."

I said, "Well, take a look at our guy putting his move on the blond down there. He is the guy you will have to watch tonight." I filled Frank in on what had transpired so far tonight. Then Don Banning came in and stood behind us and filled us in about Darnovski's first bar pickup. Frank went with Don to meet George because George was leaving for the night. I told Frank I would meet him in the command post. Don Banning gave Frank his key to the room and told him not to wake up our Nashville friend who was asleep in the room.

At approximately 11:30 p.m., Darnovski and the blond went to his room. Charlie Kosko kept his eye on the TV monitor. He was watching Darnovski's room. Charlie had placed a flexible surveillance camera under the CP door. The camera had a wide-angle lens so he could also see the elevator and the other end of the hall. The camera was hooked to a monitor and printer. We could take pictures and print individual frames at will. Charlie printed several pictures with date and time stamp of Darnovski and Victoria getting off the elevator with Darnovski groping Victoria. Victoria's hands were not idle. She was rubbing the bulge in his pants. Darnovski managed to get his room door open, and the both of them entered the room. Darnovski, with his hands full, kicked the door shut.

Vince and I went to the CP. Charlie showed us the pictures he took. At 12:15 a.m., Darnovski's door opened. Darnovski was wearing a towel around his waist. Victoria placed her purse under her arm and straightened her dress as she left the room. Charlie's camera took several more incriminating pictures of Victoria leaving Darnovski's room. Victoria walked to the elevator and pushed the down button. Victoria was smiling and happy with the big score she made. The elevator door opened, and Victoria got in. Vince notified the surveillance team that she was on her way down and that the undercover cab should pick her up, drive her around the block to the other entrance, and make a stop and bring her to the security office.

She took the elevator down to the lobby. She was observed going to the Safari Room on the security cameras and photographed talking with Harry and Harry placing his hand over hers just like he had done with Angelica. Again, the surveillance cameras caught the money transfer. The undercover taxi was notified that she would be leaving. She then left the bar and headed to the street. Our taxicab pulled up, and she got in.

The cab driver asked, "Where to, mam?"

Victoria said, "East Seventy-Ninth Street and First Avenue." He pulled down the flag and took off down Forty-Ninth Street and then north on Park Avenue. The flashing red light and short burst of the sirens startled Victoria.

The cab driver said, "Let's see what they want," as he pulled over. Three men in suits got out of the car and asked Victoria to get out of the cab. She did, and they took her back into the hotel though the Park Avenue entrance and up to the security office. Victoria kept asking what was going on and why she was being brought back to the hotel. She surmised that it had something to do with her turning a trick in the hotel.

The surveillance team agents took her into the security office and told her to sit down and that someone would be in to explain to her why she was brought back to the hotel. Night hotel security supervisor, Bill Haller, was just as hard as his boss George Hardy. Bill and I both entered the office, and I told the surveillance agents to wait outside. They left the office. Victoria demanded to know why she was being brought into the hotel. Bill said in a stern voice, "Let start off with solicitation, prostitution, and complicity with the hotel employees to commit a crime."

"What?" exclaimed Victoria.

Bill went through a range of questions about Harry and how she operated at the hotel. Victoria was justifiably upset while she denied the allegations of Bill Haller one after another. She kept claiming that she was a patron just stopping off to have a drink before going home. Bill told her that it was late and he did not feel like playing games anymore. He told her she had lied to him. He told her that this time, she would be facing hard jail time. I took her purse, opened it, and dumped the contents on the desk.

Victoria said, "Hey, you cannot do that."

I said, "Well, there is no weapon in the bag. Just 860 dollars, several name cards with your name and telephone number and a Florida driver license." Haller then started to slap down picture after picture. The pictures had the date and time on them. The pictures showed her entering the bar, her conversing with Harry, the introduction of Darnovski, leaving the bar with Darnovski, going to his room, and then leaving and the payoff to Harry. It was overwhelming. It finally sunk in; she was caught. Her mouth began to pucker, her breathing became rapid, and tears began to gush from her blue eyes. She broke down, crying; her mascara was now running down her cheeks. She realized that she was going to go to jail for a long time. She hysterically begged and pleaded for a break. While Bill was showing her the pictures, I photocopied her name card and driver license.

"Please don't call the police! Don't have me arrested. Please!" Haller took a box of tissues from the desk draw and gave it to her. She grabbed the tissues and began wiping the water and mascara trail from her face between sobs.

"Are you going to answer my questions and then sign a statement?" Haller said.

Between sobs, Victoria said, "Yes, I will answer your questions and sign the statement, but please don't have me arrested. I will do anything you ask." At that point I gave her a glass of water. She thanked me and took a few sips.

Haller said, "Here is a pad of paper. Write down why you came to this hotel, your arrangements with Harry, and how much money you gave him. Put down how you made contact in the bar with the guest and about going to his room and the financial arrangement for your services. You do not have to get explicit with the details of the sex."

Victoria took the legal-size pad of white-lined paper and began to write. She kept wiping her eyes and blowing her nose as she wrote down the details. In less than five minutes, she had completed her statement."

Haller said, "Now sign it." She did. Haller took the statement and looked at it. He then said, "Oh, Victoria, this federal agents want to talk to you." Haller then turned and walked to his desk.

I moved to the front of the desk and removed my credentials from my jacket pocket. I opened the case and put them in front of her.

I said, "My name is Johnny Reno. I am a United States customs special agent. You are now involved in a federal investigation involving our national security by turning this trick you put yourself smack in the middle of our investigation. You could be facing federal criminal charges." Her face turned white as a sheet, and a look of horror entered her face. It was overwhelming for her.

She was again sobbing. "Feds, national security? I did not do anything wrong. I was just trying to make a living."

I said, "Victoria, I'm going to ask you some questions. I want you to answer them truthfully."

Victoria said, "Everything I did is in the statement I wrote."

I said, "Have you talked to Mr. Darnovski before tonight?"

Victoria said, "No, I didn't know him before tonight. Harry said the guy was looking for a good time and would pay for it. Our arrangement was purely business."

I told her, "This investigation is a matter of national security, involving your trick from room 705," and I could not go into any details. She shook her head, indicating she understood.

I then took a plastic bag from my jacket and removed a laminated card and placed it on the table in front of her. On the card were rows of three letter followed by equal signs and groups of two, three, and four numbers. I asked her to pick up the card and see if it was hers or if she had seen this before. She picked up the card and held it in both hands and looked at it. She said she did not know what it meant. I took the card from her and returned the card to the plastic bag.

I began to question her about everything Darnovski had talked to her about. "Did he mention how long he would be at the hotel?"

"He said that he was going to be here for a few days," Victoria shot back.

"What else did he talk to you about?"

She then told me that Darnovski was bragging to her about his owning of several businesses. "Manny competes with large US corporations like 3M for painting sign with reflective paint beads. He has an import/export business in Nashville, Tennessee, one in Saskatchewan, Canada, a couple in Vienna, Austria, and a new factory was being built somewhere in Russia." She said that she had told Manny that she was free for the next few days, and if he was lonely, he could call her, and she would show him around or anything else he wanted to do. She gave him her card with her telephone number on it. She went on to say she thought that he was a sex addict. She said he liked role-playing, and all he wanted to do was touch her body and rub his thing all over her. "He wanted me to spank him, and he wanted to play the submissive role while I was the aggressor. When he finally did penetrate me, he could not last. It was over quicker than it started. He was apologetic and very generous with his money. It was the easiest five hundred dollars I ever made. He was very gentle and love-starved. He really was a nice person."

I said, "Victoria, how would you like to help your country and get out of the mess you are in."

"I will do anything to not to go to jail this time."

"So you were arrested before. Did you do any time?"

"No, I paid a fine, and the judge said next time it would be hard time. Please make this mess go away. I do not want to go to jail. I will do anything you want me to."

"Would you be willing to work for me as an informant?"

"Anything, just tell me what you want me to do."

I told her, "We think that Manny will contact you for your services tomorrow. When he does call you, agree to see him. Carry on business as usual. Do not pump him for information. Do not tell him that he is being investigated. If it comes up, we would like to know if anyone is going to meet him before he leaves the country. We would like to know when he is leaving and the airline he will fly out on. If he contacts you at any time after this week, we need to know about it immediately. Here is my card with my telephone number." I then told her that if she did anything to alert Darnovski and jeopardize our investigation, she would be charged as an accomplice and a coconspirator. "If you work with us, we may be able to make this bad situation go away."

Victoria agreed to everything. She then said, "Let me get this straight. If I work for you and I do not alert Manny about the government investigating him, I could get a free pass on this mess."

I said, "I'll see what I can do."

I walked over to Bill's desk and asked Bill if he had everything he needed. Bill said that he had everything he needed. Bill said the hotel did not want the publicity. If she was arrested, it would be bad for the hotel. All he wanted was for Harry to be fired or resign and for the hookers to sign statements so he could get rid of Harry without any publicity. As long as she signed the statement and agreed never to come into the Waldorf Astoria again or any of its other hotels, she was free to go. Bill said that whatever we wanted to do with her was OK with the hotel and him. Bill said that they would hold the money she made as evidence if she was going to be prosecuted. Bill said he got the statements he needed and did not need to hold the money as evidence. He said we could do what we wanted with her and the money.

I returned to the desk where Victoria was sitting. She was sitting on the edge of her chair, her hands clasped in her lap. Her leg was jittery, and her foot was tapping on the floor. She was very nervous.

I said, "Victoria, this is how it is going down. I will use you as an informant. I do believe that Manny will call you as long as he is in New York. I want you to carry on as you normally would. When you see him, do not alert him by asking direct questions. Encourage him by playing to his ego."

Victoria said, "Don't worry. I am good at getting guys to talk and tell me their little dark secrets."

"You will be debriefed by me or another special agent after each encounter. Just let him brag to you about what a big man he is in the business world. Now about this local mess you got into. As long as Manny is not alerted and things go down the right way, we can make this mess disappear on assurance that you will do what we want you to do. We are going to hold as evidence the five hundred dollars that Manny gave you. If things go down without a hitch, you will not be prosecuted, and the five hundred will find its way back to you."

The color in Victoria's face came back with brilliance. It looked as if a huge weight was lifted off her shoulders. She began to cry with happiness. She grabbed a tissue and started to wipe the tears from her eyes. It was a relief to know that she was going home to her own bed and not a cell.

I then escorted her down to the lobby and into our undercover cab and told the driver to take her home. The cab driver asked her what had just happened.

She said, "Nothing, they just thought I was someone else. Everything is all right. Just take me home." Our cab driver could not get anything out of her. I returned to the CP and gave the plastic bag with the laminated card to Frank and told him to run the prints on the laminated card and get her Florida rap sheet and Florida DMV information the next day. Frank took the card in the plastic bag and the copy of her driver's license and said he would start on it the next day.

DJ then filled me in on Darnovski's last move for the night. DJ then told me that at 12:45 a.m., the door to Darnovski room opened. Darnovski exited the room. This time he was wearing a white shirt and tie with brown slacks. He now combed his hair straight back. Frank picked up his radio and announced, "All units, the subject is leaving his room. He is not carrying anything."

Don Banning replied, "This is 218. I will pick him up at the lobby. Does he have a coat?"

Frank replied back with what Darnovski was wearing. Darnovski exited the elevator and proceeded to the bar.

"218 to all units, the subject is in the bar." This time, there were no woman in the bar. Darnovski sat at the bar, and Harry came over. Harry brought Darnovski his drink and said, "This is on the house." They talked for about ten minutes before Darnovski got up and left the bar. He took the elevator up to his room. Several minutes later, the CP advised all units that Darnovski asked for a wake-up call for 11:00 a.m. Frank then observed Darnovski open his door and hung the "DO NOT DISTURB" sign on his door. He was finally in for the night. Frank Napowski had relieved Charlie Kosko in the CP. Frank Harris had turned in for the night, and the rest of the surveillance teams went home. Everyone was told to be back at 10:00 a.m.

Chapter 23

Day Twos in New York

April 1, I awoke early as usual. The weather forecast was for a nice day. The temperature was going to be in the low fifties. No rain in the forecast. I awoke early as usual. I put on a pot of coffee. I showered and shaved. I turned on the radio. It was tuned in to WINS 1010. I was ready for the breaking news reports, weather, and traffic reports. While waiting for the coffee to brew, I went to the front door. I opened the door and sprinted down the steps. I should have put a coat over my pj's, but I did not. It was cold, and there was a mild wind blowing. The air was cool and crisp. I took several deep breath. The cool air filled my lungs. It felt good. I retrieved the newspaper that was clad in its clear plastic bag. It was sitting on my lawn, not far from the steps. I picked up the paper, turned, and sprinted back into the house.

Feeling hungry, I put the newspaper aside. I opened the refrigerator and removed two eggs, the package of bacon, and the butter. I took two slices of bread and popped them into the toaster. I made the bacon and then fried the eggs in the bacon fat. Sunny-side up. It felt good to have a nice hot breakfast to start the day off. I glanced through the paper and enjoyed the breakfast.

Glancing through the newspaper and listening to the radio took my mind off the anticipation of what the day's events would be like. I knew that I could not leave the house before 9:00 a.m. if I were to avoid the rush hour traffic. After I finished reading the paper, I began to wonder what Darnovski was going to do today. *Would this be the day he met up with someone and gave them the camera? Does he know anyone in New York? What was he going to do today?*

I picked up the phone and called Frank at the CP. Frank said that our wiretap order was signed late last night by the US magistrate. The intercept equipment was in place. There was no activity to report as yet. Frank said that Vince was sending a guy over to take the plastic card to the lab for the prints and would run the DMV checks. This put my mind at ease. DJ and Vince Morano would be at the hotel before 10:00 a.m. Vince would have five New York City agents and the undercover taxi at the hotel ready to follow Darnovski if he left the hotel. There was not much else to do. I called the Duke and filled him on what had transpired the night before. As expected, the Duke told me not to let the camera leave the country. If Darnovski rented a car and headed to Canada, I was to follow him and take him down at the border. I told Duke I had everything covered and not to worry. Everything depended on what action Darnovski took.

I filled my travel mug with the remaining coffee. I rinsed out the coffee pot and my coffee mug. I quickly got dressed. I took my 357 Magnum revolver and checked that it was loaded. I put the revolver in my pants holster. I put on my sport jacket. I took my credentials out of the draw and placed them in my jacket pocket. I took a light wind breaker and ball cap with me in case I would need to change my appearance on the surveillance. I packed a small bag with my shave kit, underwear, and clothes for two days. I picked up my keys, coffee mug, and bag, and headed out the door. I left the house, and I placed the change of clothes bag in the trunk of my car. I got in and started it up. I took a sip of my hot coffee. I turned on the customs radio. I grabbed the hidden microphone from beneath my seat and flipped on the concealed radio switch and called into the twenty-four-hour base station at the airport.

"644 to 600, 10-8."

"600 to 644, 10-8 at 0900 over."

"644 to 600, 10-4."

I pulled out my car folder from the attaché case. I recorded the start time and mileage on my car report sheet. I then headed for the Waldorf Astoria.

Frank Harris was up early. He showered and shaved and was dressed when Agents Vince Morano, DJ and Don Banning arrived. The four then went down to the dining room to have breakfast. Frank Napowski stood in the CP and ordered room service. Frank Harris was shocked to see the prices that the hotel charged for breakfast. Frank remarked to Vince that he could have breakfast all week in Nashville for what it cost him for one breakfast here. Vince then told Frank to stop crying that he was getting per diem.

Frank Harris told Vince that he had booked a flight back to Nashville and was scheduled to depart at 3:00 p.m. Vince told Frank Harris that he would have someone pick him up at 1:00 p.m. to take him to the airport. Frank Harris told Vince that he was packed and ready to go and that Frank Napowski had told him that he would drop him off on the way home. Frank and Vince started to talk about the Nashville surveillance of Darnovski and his sexual escapades. That was about the time I arrived at the dining room.

I arrived at the Waldorf at about 9:45 a.m. I went directly to the restaurant. I spotted Vince, Frank Harris, and DJ at a table, went over, and pulled up a chair. I ordered a cup of coffee. I listened to the conversation between Vince and Frank. Frank Harris began telling us about the surveillance of Darnovski in Tennessee and his escapades. We then discussed how we would handle the surveillance of Darnovski. We figured that he would take in some sightseeing and maybe do some shopping. Frank said that he would probably try to pick up a hooker.

DJ said, "Hold on a minute," as he placed hand over his ear and earpiece. DJ started to repeat what Frank was telling him. "Darnovski ordered lunch sent to his room. He received a call from Austria. He then called Pan American airlines and then Lufthansa airline. He booked a flight to Frankfort tomorrow at 7:00 p.m. on Lufthansa"

"Well," I said, "at least, we now know when he is going to leave and the airline." I told DJ to contact Pan American security and see if Darnovski also made any reservations for a flight to Germany. An hour later, DJ contacted me and told me that Darnovski did not have any reservations on Pan American. He did have a reservation on Lufthansa for the 7:00 p.m. flight to Frankfort and then on to Berlin.

Charlie Kosko relieved Frank Napowski in the CP. Frank Napowski and Frank Harris left for the airport. Frank said he would return before midnight to relieve Charlie in the CP.

Just before 1:00 p.m., Charlie notified the surveillance teams that Darnovski was leaving his room without the suitcase. He was wearing a three-quarter black leather coat and black pants. The surveillance teams went into action. Our taxi was waiting at the corner just in case Darnovski would need a taxicab. Two teams were on the street. One team was in the hotel. Darnovski exited the elevator and proceeded to the lobby. There were people at the front desk, checking in. A man was talking to the concierge. There were three people sitting in the lobby.

Darnovski looked around and then sat in a chair and picked up the newspaper off the coffee table in front of him. He looked at the paper for about five minutes. He put the paper down and looked at the people sitting in the area. He then got up and walked out the door on to Park Avenue. Vince and I stood in the command post and monitored the action. We let the surveillance teams do their job. We were saving ourselves for surveillance of the bar that night.

Darnovski walked to the corner of E Forty-Ninth Street and then crossed Park Avenue. He continued along Forty-Ninth Street to Fifth Avenue. He was window-shopping. He walked down Fifth Ave to Forty-Ninth Street and then west along Forty-Second Street. He stopped at many of the stores and looked at the window displays. He looked at cameras, watches, and electronics. He entered several stores and examined some cameras. One store had loads of magazines and X-rated videos. He looked at the videos but did not purchase any. He did purchase several magazines from the store and then headed back to the hotel.

It was 2:18 p.m. when he entered the hotel lobby. He went directly to his room. At five o'clock, Manny ordered dinner in his room. At 9:05 p.m., Manny left his room. Charley notified the surveillance team. He was not carrying anything. He went to the elevator. He exited the elevator and went directly to the front desk. He spoke with the front desk clerk. Darnovski wanted a late departure. The desk clerk said it was not a problem.

He was dressed in gray slacks and a white shirt with open collar. He wore a blue blazer. After talking with the desk clerk, Darnovski went directly into the bar. Harry spotted Darnovski entering the bar. He began to pour a Jack Daniels in coke in anticipation of Darnovski's order. Darnovski sat on a bar stool as Harry laid his drink in front of him. Darnovski peeled off a one hundred-dollar bill and laid it on the bar. Harry took the bill and returned with his change. Darnovski gave Harry a twenty-dollar bill as a tip.

Darnovski and Harry talked for a few minutes before someone was asking Harry for a drink. Sitting at the end of the bar was a gorgeous redhead. She was sipping a Manhattan. She wore a smart tweed suit. The top two buttons on her pastel yellow blouse was open. Her skirt was just below the knee. She wore a gold necklace and a thick gold bracelet. She had dangling gold earnings. She was later identified as Marge Philips. She was a high-price hooker, and she had a record for solicitation and prostitution in Florida, California, Texas, and Puerto Rico. She was banned by several hotel chains.

George Hardy, the hotel security identified the redhead as Marge Philips. She was a guest in room 1156, which was close to the elevator. George was good at his job. He could spot a hooker when she checked in. He would keep the guest under surveillance until she made her move. He also provided our surveillance team with a key to room 1145, which was vacant.

DJ and Vince joined me at the bar. We sat a couple of seats from Darnovski. He acted as if he did not recognize us. He began talking to a middle-aged man who was on the bar stool next to him. Harry came back to Darnovski and leaned forward and whispered something to Darnovski. Darnovski got up and took his drink and walked to the end of the bar and sat down next to the redhead. They talked for about ten minutes. Then the two got up and went to the elevator. They took the elevator to the eleventh floor. Special Agents Vicky Brent and Ed Romano followed Darnovski and Marge into the elevator. Brent and Romano entered room 1145 as Darnovski and Philips went further down the hall to room 1156. Agent Bob Towers monitored the surveillance camera for the eleventh floor. Bob alerted the surveillance teams that the subjects were now in room 1156. At 10:45 p.m., the door to Philip's room opened. Darnovski left the room and took the elevator to the seventh floor and went into his room. Marge exited her room about ten minutes later. She took the elevator to the lobby and went to the bar. Harry approached her and took her outstretched hand. She slipped Harry a fifty-dollar bill. She then left the bar and went to her room. The two were in for the night.

Darnovski called the desk and left a wake-up call for 9:00 a.m. Frank came in for the midnight shift and relieved Charley. The surveillance teams left for the night.

Chapter 24

Trip to the Airport

On April 2, 1975, Darnovski called the front desk and asked for a bellman to take his bags to the lobby. Darnovski left his room at approximately 1:30 p.m. with the bellman and went to the cashier's desk, paying his hotel bill with an American Express card issued to Mr. Darnovski MDS, GESMDS, Austria. Copies of the Darnovski's hotel bill and long-distance telephone charge slips were later obtained from hotel security for evidentiary purposes.

It had been previously established that Darnovski held reservations on a Lufthansa airlines flight to Frankfurt, Germany, departing at JFK airport the evening of April 2, 1975. Our undercover cab was positioned outside the hotel's main entrance as soon as Darnovski left his room. George Hardy, hotel security, stood next to the doorman to alert him to place Darnovski into our undercover cab. Later that afternoon George would fire Harry.

After checking out, Darnovski headed to the main entrance with the bellman pushed the baggage dolly, with Darnovski's two bags. Hardy alerted the doorman as Darnovski approached. The doorman ushered Darnovski to our undercover cab. Darnovski entered the cab. The two bags were placed in the trunk of the cab. The driver got into his cab, and Darnovski told the driver, "JFK airport." The driver threw down the meter flag, and off they went. Our undercover cab's radio was on Channel 3, and radio silence was in effect. The driver asked Darnovski which airline terminal he was going to.

Darnovski said, "Lufthansa."

The driver got on the radio and said, "Dispatch, this is cab 107 en route to Lufthansa airline at JFK airport, over."

"Dispatch to 107 10-4." The driver then proceeded to the airport.

Knowing that Darnovski had reservations on Lufthansa flight to Germany took a lot of the pressure off me. After Darnovski left for the airport, the New York City surveillance group was no longer needed, and they went back to their office.

Agent Howie Winters followed the taxi to the airport. All other airport units went directly to the airport and began to set up a surveillance at Lufthansa airlines. The Duke called me into his office. I told the Duke that Darnovski made a reservation for a first-class seat. He will in all probability go to the first-class lounge until boarding. I told him that after he presented his ticket to the boarding agent, he would stop him, reexamine his baggage, and arrest him.

The Duke said, "Good plan. I'm going with you." We left the Duke's office, and on the way out of the office, I grabbed DJ aside. I told DJ, "I like to cover all my base."

Right now, I felt a little uneasy. *Why did Darnovski call Pan American? Could he possibly switch flights?*

I said, "DJ, go to the Pan American terminal and get with Joe Sullivan just in case he changes plans."

DJ said, "Okay, Reno, I'm on my way." DJ went to Pan American terminal, and the Duke and I went to Lufthansa terminal.

Cheech and Frank met us at the Lufthansa terminal. Agents John Carp and Jerry Nelson were there also. I told Nelson and Carp to go to Pan American and assist DJ just in case Darnovski changed plans. The plan was to pull the checked bags before they were sent down to the baggage loading area without Darnovski seeing. After they left for Pan Am, I felt better. The Duke said, "Did you get another one of your feelings?"

I told the Duke its was better to cover all bases. He just laughed.

The Duke and I arrived at Lufthansa and met with Lufthansa security officer Hanz Dedrick. Hanz said he would pull the bags that

Darnovski checked and he would accompany our agents with the bags through security to the boarding gate.

Well, now all we had to do was to wait, and a good place to wait was in the first-class lounge. We headed for the lounge. Frank and Cheech were waiting for the cab to arrive.

When the taxi arrived at Lufthansa, Darnovski told the driver to take him to Pan American terminal. The taxi then proceeded to the Pan American terminal. The surveillance car, following the taxi, called the airport base station 600.

"Triple duce (222) to 600 over"

"600 to 222, go ahead"

"Triple duce to 600, the subject did not go to Lufthansa. Subject is now pulling in to Pan Am terminal, over."

"600 to 222 that is a 10-4."

"608 to 600 I will pass the info on to 644 over."

"606 to 608 I copied and I am at the Pan Am terminal and will pick up the subject, over."

"608 10-4"

Frank informed me and the Duke that Darnovski was at the Pan Am terminal. It was now 3:20 p.m.

The Duke said, "Good call, Reno." DJ, Carp, and Nelson were with Joe Sullivan, Pan American security, when DJ monitored the transmission. He told Joe that a man named Darnovski would try to make reservations to Germany in a few minutes. He told him that when Darnovski checked his bags, we should intercept them before they went down the baggage shoot for loading. We needed to bring the bags to the boarding gate for export examination after Darnovski presented himself for boarding. We would then search the bags and arrest him. Joe understood what was going to happen. He had worked customs on several other customs export cases.

Joe said, "Pan Am has a flight to Munich at 6:00 p.m." Things were beginning to work out for us.

Darnovski paid the driver the fare on the meter plus a ten-dollar tip. He exited the taxicab. The driver got the two bags from the trunk of the cab and placed them on the curb. Darnovski looked around as the cab left. He signaled to a skycap to take his bags. Darnovski went to the first-class check in counter and obtained a ticket for a flight to Munich, Germany, departing at 6:00 p.m. Pan Am security officer Joe Sullivan arrived at the counter. Realizing that the first-class check-in counter was at the end of the belt and that as soon as the bags were placed on the conveyer, they would immediately begin their journey through the building down to the baggage loading area. There would be no way to pull the bags without Darnovski seeing them being pulled. The next best thing was to have the baggage tag number and description of the bags and meet them down in the loading area. Joe, with his back to Darnovski, copied down the two baggage tag numbers and marked the tags. He then asked the ticketing agent if the bags were ready to go. The agent, knowing that Joe was with security, said they were. So Joe put the two bags on the conveyer belt, and they disappeared down the conveyer highway.

Agents Carp and Nelson then went with Joe to the baggage loading area to retrieve the bags. They were to locate the bags and bring them to the first-class lounge just prior to boarding time. Joe picked up the yellow phone (yellow phones were part of the airport telephone system. You could not get an outside line on them. It was like an intercom system for the airport.) and called the first-class lounge. The receptionist, who was the supervisor of the first-class lounge, picked up the phone. Joe asked her to notify him when it was time to board but not to board anyone until he arrived.

In the Pan American terminal, the first-class VIP lounge was on the second floor, adjacent to the boarding gates. There was a special elevator to take you to the lounge. The elevator door opened into a room, where a receptionist checked people's tickets to insure they were first-class passengers. There was also a place for passengers to place their coats and carry-on baggage. Then they passed into a large open area. There was a big circular bar in the center of the room. There were two hostesses: one was a male and the other a female. They roamed the room, catering to passengers sitting in various parts of the lounge. There was a wall of glass windows where you could look out and see the gates and runway with airplanes landing and taking off. There were leather seats grouped together around small cocktail tables in front of the window wall. Most of the tables had small bowls of pretzels and peanuts. There was a newspaper rack with papers and magazines. On one side were rest rooms. The floor was carpeted with the Pan American logo.

After purchasing his ticket and checking his bags, Darnovski walked to the first-class elevator. He took the elevator to the first-class lounge. When the elevator came back down, DJ, the Duke, and I took it up to the lounge. The doors opened, and we walked to the receptionist's desk. The receptionist looked up at the three of us, with no bags or tickets, and said, "Reno, how are you?"

Standing up from her desk, she came around and embraced me and gave me a big kiss. The Duke and DJ did not look surprised.

"Hi, Anna, I am here on business today. We are interested in the man that just came in before us," I said.

"Oh, Mr. Darnovski, he is going out at 6:00 p.m. on the Munich flight."

"We are waiting for Joe Sullivan to meet us."

"Okay, Joe just called me and asked me to call him when we are ready to board the Munich flight."

"Anna, we are going to watch our guy until the flight is ready to board."

"Okay, if there is anything you need, just let me know." She went back to her desk.

We walked into the large room and sat down where we could observe Darnovski. The hostess brought a drink to Darnovski. He continued to read a newspaper. The hostess came over to us and said, "Reno, DJ, can I get you anything to drink today?"

I said, "Sure, Paula. I will have my usual."

"Amaretto on the rocks, right?"

"That is it."

"7-up with a lemon, DJ?"

"Right."

"What will your friend have?"

The Duke said, "Johnnie Walker Black on the rocks."

"I will be right back," Paula said.

The Duke said, "She knows what drinks you guys drink? What do you do? Hang out here?"

I said, "No, boss, we have to keep our contacts up, and last week we had a lot more VIPs going out for headquarters." When government officials were going overseas and not traveling on first-class tickets, we would take them to the first-class lounge before they boarded their flights. We do the airline favors, and they reciprocate when we need them. This reminded me of the our cooperation with Air Canada and their theft problem.

Chapter 25

Air Canada Theft

C argo thefts at Kennedy airport seemed like an everyday occurrence. Millions of dollars' worth of cargo were being stolen every day from the various airlines. In an effort to curtail thefts at Kennedy airport, the US Customs Service, besides forming a cargo theft squad, required all airlines to fill out and submit a "customs discrepancy in manifested cargo form. This customs form documented if a shipment was manifested and did not arrive or partially arrived, was damaged in transit, or was stolen or arrived un-manifested. Each month, the discrepancy forms were submitted to US Customs by each airline. A copy of the customs discrepancy form was also sent to the airport security council when the form indicated a theft or pilferage. Air Canada had an unusual amount of customs forms being submitted for cargo manifested but not landed and damaged in transit. Each month, my cargo theft squad would collect these customs forms in order to develop targets for investigation.

The airport security council, which met once a month, consisted of each of the airline's head of security, the FBI representative, the port authority police representative, and US Customs representative. The head of Air Canada security was George Noble. George was a retired FBI agent. In fact, most of the airline security heads were retired FBI agents or retired police officials. George was sixty-six years old, with gray hair and piercing eyes. He weighed about 180 lbs. He wore a gray suit all the time. Whenever we had passengers arriving from Canada on the pr-ecleared flights, who were going to be reexamined, we would always ask George to assist us. Things always went like clockwork when George helped us. George always provided a private room for us to conduct the reexamination of the passengers baggage. I asked George why Air Canada did not fire any of the ramp crew when we caught them taking items from passengers baggage. George told us it was the union's fault. They negotiated a contract where employees could not be fired unless convicted of a felony and got sentenced to a year in jail. This was one of the reasons George could not get his former agency, the FBI, to assist him in conducting any investigations of apparent thefts occurring at Air Canada. The pilferage reports amounted to a very small dollar amount. The FBI could not waste their time with such trivial matters.

At a February airport security council meeting, George Noble asked me for assistance, as he suspected that merchandise was being stolen and reported as merchandise manifested but not landed. He explained that he had implemented procedures where, on certain flights, a supervisor, using the manifest, would verify the loading of cargo on the aircraft in Canada. When the flight arrived at JFK, a supervisor would then supervise the unloading of cargo and match it with the manifest to insure that all the cargo arrived. Somehow some of the cargo would disappear while in flight. This led to one conclusion. The loading or unloading crews with aid of the supervisor was involved in stealing the cargo. A majority of Air Canada's customs forms showed "manifested but not landed and damaged" cargo shipments arriving with pilferage of items.

Well, if someone from Air Canada was stealing the shipments of good, they had to get the shipments out of the warehouse and off the airport. For several weeks, we conducted surveillance and stopped every truck that left the warehouse with no results. All the transfer papers and release orders were in order. We had many twenty-four-hour surveillance of the warehouse to see if employees were taking out merchandise and putting it in their cars. We came up empty-handed. We needed a new approach.

The Air Canada warehouse and parking lot were very hard place to conduct a surveillance. We kicked around ideas about the best way to catch the thieves at Air Canada. Agent George McLeavy came up with a brilliant idea to send someone up the light tower with a radio and binoculars. When a cargo employee was observed taking a package and placing it in his car or giving it to someone, then we could stop the vehicle or person receiving the package.

The airport cargo area was lit at night by a high-intensity lighting system on top of 150-foot pole towers strategically placed in the airport.

I said, "Great idea, George. Pick out your pole. You have the first climb."

George said, "I don't want to climb the fuck'n pole. I'm afraid of heights."

I said, "At about 11:30 p.m. tonight, you climb the pole. We will see if any of the midnight shift is stealing the cargo."

Well, George was bitching and moaning as he climbed the pole ladder. His binocular was around his neck. Every few steps, it would hit the pole and clank against the pole. I got on the portable radio and said, "George, stop banging the binoculars on the pole. Stick it in your sweater." George always wore a sweater vest.

His response was, "Stick it in your ass. It is hard enough to climb this fuck'n pole. It keeps swaying." George finally got to the top of the pole and onto the circular platform.

About 2:30 a.m., George called in and reported that an employee carrying a lunch pail went to his car. "He is in the car. He started the car. He is taking something from his lunch pail. He opened the glove box. He closed the glove box. Three minutes later, he shut off the car. He is exiting the car. He is going back to the cargo building."

George then gave us a description of the man and the car with the license plate number. We ran a check of the license plate. The car was registered to Paul Mastone. About 4:00 a.m., two Air Canada cargo employees exited the cargo building and got into one car. George reported they were not carrying anything. DJ and Frank followed the car to the Airport Diner on South Conduit Avenue. The diner was open twenty-four hour. The two employees picked up sandwiches and soup to bring back to the cargo building. They drove back to the cargo building and exited their car. They went into the cargo building with the bags of food. At 6:00 a.m., I told George to come down from his perch. George came down, and I greeted him with a hot cup of coffee. George said that it was cold on the platform.

I said, "I know. That is why I gave you the hot coffee. You and DJ can make the stop on Paul's vehicle as it leaves the airport. If he took any cargo, it will be your seizure." George said that the platform had a commanding view of the front and back of the Air Canada cargo building as well as several other airline cargo buildings.

About 7:45 a.m. that morning, the Air Canada cargo crew began to show up for work. Then the night crew began to leave as more of the morning shift reported for work. There were three cargo handlers and a supervisor on the midnight shift. George Noble, security supervisor, had told us that the night supervisor, Dan Steiger, and one employee, Paul Mastone, would be returning to the 8:00-a.m. to 4:00-p.m. shift on Friday and that the night supervisor and cargo handler were coming back from leave. As the employees left the building, we observed them. The last to leave was Paul Mastone, the employee who George observed placing something in his car. The suspect was driving a blue 1972 Chevrolet. The vehicle proceeded down Cargo Road. DJ, with Frank and George, put on their red lights and sirens and pulled over Paul's car. George conducted a customs search of the vehicle. He found nothing but a half-eaten sandwich in the glove box.

We then decided to look at the various employees who were working when most of the thefts took place and see if they were living beyond their means.

According to Air Canada security, Dan Steiger was the supervisor on duty when most of the midair disappearances took place. George Noble gave us Dan's work schedule and access to his personnel file. Starting on Friday, Dan would be working the eight-to-four shift for the next three months. Dan lived in South Ozone Park on 111th Avenue. He worked for Air Canada for twelve years and had a good record. He was one of the most trusted of all supervisors. Security would always go to him to assist them in searching for documentation for the missing shipments. They would go to him in order not to alert other employees of the security checks. George said his records indicated that Air Canada cargo handler, Paul Mastone, was another employee who was usually on duty when most of the midair disappearances took place. Dan Steiger and Paul Mastone became the targets of our investigation.

Day one of the surveillance was a Friday. Dan was to be off the next two days. Dan was fifty-two years old. He had black hair and a receding hairline. He was five foot ten and 230 pounds. He never wore a hat. He was in good physical shape. He was clean-shaven and very articulate. He was very knowledgeable about the air cargo business. He wore an Air Canada blue shirt and jacket and blue pants—the standard Air Canada uniform. Dan left the Air Canada cargo building at 3:45 p.m. This was about fifteen minutes earlier than his usual time. He carried a black lunch pail. He got into his 1970 black Buick. We had four cars ready for the surveillance, and all units were on secure radio Channel 3. We expected Dan to drive home to South Ozone Park.

Dan surprised us; he drove down cargo road and off the airport, across Rockaway Boulevard to a warehouse building just off Rockaway Boulevard. He parked his car in front of the warehouse and went into the building. The sign on the building read, SUN FREIGHT FORWARDERS. *Why was Dan going to the Freight Forwarders office?* After half an hour, I got on the radio and asked Frank to go in and see what was keeping Dan. Frank said OK and proceeded to go into the building. Frank used the ploy of seeking a job to see why Dan was taking so long. Five minutes later, Frank came out, holding a bunch of papers. Frank got into his car and got on the radio and briefed us. He told us that Dan was the only person in the office. Dan was the night supervisor on duty. Frank went on to say that the company was not hiring now but Dan said he could fill out an application. So Frank took the papers and left the building. Air Canada was never notified that Dan was working at a freight forwarders after his shift with Air Canada. Now we had some idea of how the missing freight was leaving the airport. At midnight, Dan left Sun Freight Forwarders building and got into his car.

"644 to all units, the suspect is leaving."

"608 take the point."

"Ten-four."

"644 to all units, the suspect is making a U-turn, 610, pick him up."

"This is 610 I have the subject in view." Unit 610 followed Dan's car at a distance until the subject was approaching Rockaway Boulevard.

"He is turning onto Rockaway."

Dan traveled along Rockaway Boulevard toward Conduit Avenue. He should go down Rockaway to 116th Street and head home. Well, he was not going home. Whenever we had a cat-and-mouse surveillance, the cat was the car in back of the subject's car (mouse); the cat did not have to use his call sign. He just broadcasted what was happening. Unit 610 was now the cat.

"He is signaling left to go on North Conduit."

"Is now turning left on North Conduit Avenue."

"He is signaling to get on the Van Wyck."

This guy was in a hurry. He was doing 70 mph just getting on the Van Wyck and over eighty on the Van Wyck.

"He is passing 107th Street exit."

"644 it looks like is not going home."

"644 to 608, are you on the service road?"

"608 that is a ten-four. I'm already on it."

"This is 610. I think he just wanted to see how fast his Buick would go. It looks like he's slowing down. I'm going to start dropping back."

"He is signaling to get off at Jamaica Avenue."

"This is 608. I will pick him up as he gets off."

"This is 608. I have the subject in view. He is stopped at the red light. There is one car behind him. He is turning left on Jamaica."

"He is making a quick right on Metropolitan Avenue. I think he was checking me out in his rearview mirror."

"605 to 608, drop back I have him in view."

"605 he is still proceeding west on Metropolitan Avenue."

After following him for five minutes, it was time for a change.

"644 to 605, drop back I have the subject in view."

After several more minutes,

"Subject is turning on 73rd Road. He is parking halfway down the block on the left side."

On 73rd Road., there were three- and four-story apartment houses on one side of the street. The other side of 73rd Road. was a Lutheran Cemetery. The cemetery was enclosed with a black eight-foot wrought iron picket fence. Just inside the fence of the cemetery were a number of old trees. These trees shielded the residence across the street from the grave sites. I told 608 to go past the subject's car and park.

"644 to all units, the subject went into the building with the red Ford in front."

"The lights on the second floor just came on."

"610 take your binoculars, climb over the fence into the cemetery, and climb the tree across from the red Ford."

"Are you kidding me?"

"No, get your ass up the tree and see what he is doing."

I proceeded on foot to the tree and asked George what he could see. George said, "Dan has his arms around a redhead wearing a black negligee. They are leaving the kitchen area and are now out of sight.

Ten minutes later, George said, "The subject and the redhead are now back in the kitchen. I think he's getting ready to leave. He is taking a drink from a cup. Now he's putting it down. I think he's leaving." A minute later, the second floor lights went off. George scrambled down the tree and laid on the floor as Dan left the building. I hid behind a car that was across from the red Ford. Dan walked down the street to his car and got in. He started up the Buick and took off.

"605 to all units, I have the subject in view. He is heading down 107th Avenue. He is signaling left on Crossbay Boulevard."

"This is 608. I'm on Liberty Avenue."

"This is 605. Subject is taking a right on Liberty and now onto Rockaway."

"644 to all units. It appears that the subject is heading home."

"610 to all units. I have the subject's residence under surveillance."

"605 to all units. The subject is turning onto Linden Boulevard."

"610 to all units. The subject has entered 111th Avenue. He is now turning into his driveway. He has entered his house."

"644 to 605 and 608. I will put the subject to bed. Be back at 6:00 a.m., and let's see where he will go tomorrow. 610 and I will be here at eight."

"605 10-4."

"608 10-4."

"610 10-4."

Now things began to make sense. Air Canada did not know that Dan Steiger had a second job. Let alone at a freight forwarding company. Working the night shift at a freight forwarding company gave Dan access to all the necessary papers to forward freight from one airlines to another. Being the supervisor at Air Canada, he would be able to remove the paper trail and any evidence that there was a freight transfer. Still the cargo was going somewhere, and we had to find out where it was going and who else was involved.

Saturday morning, day two of the surveillance. The weather was crisp and clear for the first weekend in April. 605 and 608 took positions on 111th Avenue and waited for the Dan to leave his house. At 6:15 a.m., the front door to Dan's house opened. Dan was wearing denim jeans, a thin black jacket over a T-shirt and a baseball cap and sunglasses. Dan left his house and got into his car and backed out of his driveway and left the Buick running in front of his neighbor's house. He then ran to his garage. He opened the garage doors and backed out a black Dodge 4×4, leaving the Dodge in front of his house still running. He walked back to his Buick, got in, and drove the Buick into his garage. He closed the garage door, walked toward his 4×4, got in, and drove off to his left.

"He is turning on 116th Street"

"Right on Linden Boulevard."

"Right on Rockaway Boulevard."

"He's taking a left on Liberty Avenue."

"608 to 605. I'll take him on N. Conduit Avenue."

"605 10-4."

"He's on Atlantic Avenue. He is slowing down."

"He's backing up to a garage just past Essex Street. I'm going to pass him and come around on Atlantic Avenue in case he makes a U-turn."

"OK I'll hang back and watch him from here."

"605 to 608. He is opening the lock. He has opened both sides of the garage doors. It looks like that two-car garage is full of boxes. He is loading some of the boxes onto the 4×4. I got some good pictures of the boxes in the garage and of Dan loading the truck. I count twelve boxes loaded into the back of the 4×4. He's closing the doors and padlocking it."

"He's in the truck and is turning right onto Atlantic. He's going slow."

"He's still moving slowly. He is now backing into another two-car garage just past Linwood Street. He's unlocking the doors. It's another garage full of boxes. It looks like he's filling up the 4×4." I got pictures of the garage, boxes, and Dan loading the truck.

"I count fifteen boxes loaded. He is locking the doors."

"He's in the truck. He is slowly going to his right on Atlantic. He's now making a U-turn. He's heading back toward the airport."

"He's heading back on Atlantic Avenue."

"This is 605. I'll take him on South Conduit Avenue. He's getting off on Crossbay Boulevard. He's taking a left. He's coming to Rockaway Boulevard. He is hanging a right on Rockaway Boulevard."

"This is 608. I have him." He is now approaching Aqueduct. He's turning into Aqueduct racetrack.

Now on Saturdays and Sundays, the Aqueduct racetrack parking lot turns into a huge flea market. Vendors come from all over to sell their wares. Most vendors arrive between 6:00 a.m. and 8:00 a.m. The flea market is open to the general public starting at 9:00 a.m. in the morning. Most vendors rent their spot on a quarterly basis. This ensures that they get the same spot so people can locate them in the huge flea market.

"He's going through the vendor's gate."

"This is 644 to all units. The flea market opens at nine o'clock. We still have about two hours before they open the gates to the public. We will meet in the parking lot after the gates open. Does anyone have a miniature camera?"

"605 negative."

"608 negative."

"610 negative."

"606 to 644. I have a miniature camera and will be there in about five minutes."

"644 to 606. That's a 10-4."

"605 follow Dan into the vendor's lot. See if he's going to set up or start selling the stuff to other vendors."

"605. That's a ten-four."

"608 to all units. Let's meet at the Crossbay Boulevard diner off Rockaway and get some breakfast."

"644 to all units. That's a ten-four."

"605 to 644. The subject is talking to a vendor. They are looking in some of the boxes. They are now talking. The vendor gave Dan some money. Five boxes came off the truck. I have pictures of the transactions. It looks like he's selling to the vendors."

"644 to 610. Go to the vendor's lot and meet up with 605. 608, 606, and I will go to the diner and get some coffee and doughnuts."

"Ten-four. Ten-four. Ten-four."

Frank and I met at the diner with DJ. We placed our order to go. Frank got his coffee and two chocolate crueler. DJ got his tea with an egg on a muffin with cheese, and I got an egg on an English muffin and coffee black. We got Cheech an egg sandwich on white toast and coffee with cream. We got George an egg on an English muffin and coffee with milk. We then proceeded to vendor's lot with the food. A police car was at the vendor gate, checking the vendor's passes to make sure that only vendors were entering. We showed the officer our ID and were allowed to proceed to the parking area. We met up with George and Cheech and gave them their food. All members of the surveillance unit had 35 mm cameras. 605 and 608 had taken pictures of the garages filled with the boxes that were now being sold to the various vendors at the flea market. Dick and George had managed to get a number of very good pictures of Dan selling the merchandise from the boxes to three of the vendors.

Dan parked his truck in back of the fifth vendor's tent. He then sat down with the vendor and his wife. The wife poured coffee into Dan's cup from a large thermos. The couple were in the early forties. They both wore jeans and sweatshirts. She had black hair, which she wore in a ponytail. The man was five feet eight and weighed about 180 pounds. The wares that they were selling from their tent were mainly women's clothes, men's clothes, and children's clothes. DJ worked his way to the side of the tent. DJ could overhear the couple talking with Dan and discussing the prices of the various items. Dan was telling the vendor, whose name was Billy, that he had several boxes of women's clothes, sweatshirts, and some men's suits. He said he had more in his warehouse. They began discussing the price for the various items that Dan had on the truck. Billy's wife appeared to be very knowledgeable about the price of women's clothing. She was also able to negotiate with Dan a real low price for the women's clothing. In fact, she was more of a businessman than Billy. With a pocket calculator in hand, she input the numbers and told Dan what she was willing to pay the various things. Billy began to give Dan a list of things that he thought he could move very quickly. These were things that people were buying. He wanted name brands for raincoats, outerwear, summer shirts, and pants.

I told Frank to take over while I went to my car to contact the US attorney's office in Brooklyn. I returned to my car.

"644 to 100."

"100 to 644 to go ahead."

"644 to 100. Contact the US attorney's office Southern District and patch me in to the duty attorney"

"100 to 644 standby."

"100 to 644 I have assistant US Atty. John Caden on the landline. Go ahead."

I briefed John on the history of the Air Canada case. The fact that there were over $30 million in thefts at Air Canada intrigued John. I also briefed John on the surveillance of the two garage warehouses that contained the stolen cargo. I told John I needed search and seizure warrants for the two garages on Atlantic Avenue. I also told him that Dan Steiger was selling cases of the stolen merchandise to five of the vendors at the Aqueduct racetrack flea market. John said that the vendors fell in the plain view doctrine and that I could arrest the vendors and search their vehicles and booths. Any merchandise that they bought from Dan and believed to be stolen that was found in the vehicles or premises should be seized. John said he had enough information, and due to the exigent circumstances, he was convinced the magistrate would issue telephone warrants. He told me he would call me when he had the telephone warrants. I told John that I would also need search and seizure warrants for the residents of Dan Steiger and the residents of Paul Mastone, who was an Air Canada employee and was the only one employee to have made repeated trips to Newark, New Jersey. I also needed arrest warrants for the two of them. John said to send an agent to his office to sign the affidavit for the search and arrest warrants. I told him that DJ and Frank were to drop off the prisoners at the US marshal's office and then see him for the warrants. John said he would begin drafting the warrants after he contacted the US magistrate and got the telephone warrants. DJ and Frank could sign all the affidavits when they arrived. We then discussed the possibility of declining federal prosecution in favor of state prosecution on some of the vendors.

John said, "I'll leave that to your discretion. Just let me know whom we are cutting loose to the state for prosecution." I said OK and thanked John.

"644 to 100."

"100 to 644. go ahead."

"644 to 100. Contact 601 and patch him into me."

A minute later, "100 to 644 I have 601 on the landline."

"Go ahead."

"Hey, Duke, it's Reno."

"Reno, do you know what time it is?"

"Yeah, it's time to get up." You could always kid around with the Duke. He was the best boss I ever had. I then briefed the Duke on what was going on. I told him that I needed eight more agents to assist with the searches and arrests. I gave him the names of the agents I already had with me. The Duke said that he would have eight agents meet me at Aqueduct racetrack. When the Duke said I would have eight agents meet me at the track, I knew I would have the bodies there. He also told me that I needed to contact the local PD and notified them of the impending arrests and searches at Aqueduct racetrack. I told the Duke that I would keep him advised.

I then contacted base station 600 and asked them to contact the NY PD's 103rd precinct in Queens and patch me in to the desk sergeant. I explained to the desk sergeant what was going down and requested that he provide two mark units to assist us. The desk sergeant said he would send two marked units to assist us.

I then had base station 600 contact, Harvey Minto of the port authority police. I gave 600 the home phone number of Harvey and Paul. Harvey and his partner, Paul Duro, worked very closely with the customs cargo theft squad. Being a plainclothes detective for the port authority police, if you did not make any arrest, you found yourself back in uniform. So Harvey and Paul were always there for us when we need them.

I remember the time when Air France was having a problem with cargo being stolen. The head of Air France security, Paul Allen, believed that the thefts were occurring on the midnight shift. I contacted port authority detective, Paul Duro. I briefed Duro and his partner Harvey Minto on the situation. Paul said they would do a surveillance of the Air France cargo area that night. About two o'clock in the morning, I received a call from Harvey. They had observed an Air France cargo employee placing a package in the trunk of his car. Now, the port authority police did not have the authority to stop and search anyone at the airport. So Harvey Minto called me and told me that the Air France employee had just left the bonded customs area. I told Harvey and Paul to raise their right hands. I then swore them in as customs offices and asked them to conduct a customs search of the employee's car and to notify me of the results. About half an hour later, Minto called me and informed me that the customs search revealed a case of imported perfume valued at about $2,000. I told Harvey to arrest the man and bring him and the seizure to his office and that I would meet him there in about thirty minutes.

I arrived at the port authority police station in about 20 minutes. The police station was in a white cement building. The police had part of the first floor. The rest of the big building was occupied by the various entities that ran the airport. I entered the building and went to the police desk officer and identified myself to him. I asked him where detectives Minto and Duro were. He directed me down the hall, past the bullpen to the interrogation rooms. I found Harvey and Paul in one of the interrogation rooms with the prisoner. The prisoner was a white male, about thirty-five years old. He was five feet seven and weighed about 150 pounds. He was wearing his blue Air France cargo uniform. Embroidered on the left front breast of the jacket was the name Tommy DeLuca. Harvey informed me that he and Paul played good cop/bad cop and had obtained a signed confession from the prisoner. Of course, Harvey was the good compassionate cop, and Paul was the mean, bad cop.

Harvey told me that he felt that Tommy had more information about what was going on at the airport involving cargo thefts. He felt he could turn Tommy over as an informant and have him work for us. Tommy just needed a little incentive. Harvey felt that if Tommy thought that he was getting a break, he would cooperate. I told Harvey that if we could get at least six arrests and find out what was going on at the other airlines, then it would be worth it to give Tommy a break. So it was settled; we would try to make Tommy an informant.

Harvey told Tommy that I was the supervising customs agent in charge of this investigation. Harvey told Tommy that Paul and he were port authority police officers and that they were deputized as customs special agents. Harvey went on to tell Tommy that he was the subject of a US Customs search, seizure, and arrest. These were federal charges. I then told Tommy what he was facing in federal charges. One charge was 18 USC 549, the illegal removal of goods from customs custody; the other 18 USC 545 smuggling and 18 USC 2315 possession of stolen property. I told him he was looking at seven to ten years in prison. Tommy collapsed and began crying hysterically.

Tommy began to plea with Harvey. He perceived Harvey as the good cop that Harvey was on his side and Harvey might be able to help them. He pleaded with Harvey to help him. He said he would do anything. Harvey, in a nice way, began to put pressure on Tommy. Harvey began to play with Tommy's emotions.

Harvey said, "I know you have a family, and it'll be hard for them if you have to do hard time. I don't know how they will be able to pay the mortgage or put food on the table. You really got yourself in a jam."

Those soft-spoken words of Harvey began to resonate with Tommy. "I really want to help you, but I have a problem myself." Harvey said that he needed to make arrest; otherwise, he would find himself back in uniform and that would mean a pay cut. Harvey explained to Tommy that he needed information. He needed to know who else was stealing cargo at the airport. If Tommy could help them, then he might be able to work out a deal with the special agent. Tommy said that he would do anything that Harvey wanted him to do. Harvey then looked at me. He made a facial gesture to me as if to ask me what I thought about giving Tommy a break. We had played these games before when we tried to get someone to cooperate with us. It was part of our training to make informants.

I then told Tommy he could help himself if he helped us. I wanted to know who else from Air France, or any other airline, was stealing cargo. The man, still sobbing, said he would do anything to get out of this mess that he was in. I again emphasized that if we went with federal charges, he was sure to do hard time. The other option, if he cooperated was, I could get the United States attorney to drop federal charges in favor of state prosecution. He would then be turned over to the port authority police. They would work him as an informant. If he did not produce any seizures or arrest, then he would then be prosecuted by the state for this theft.

I then told Tommy that I wanted a list of people that were stealing cargo. I gave him a sheet of paper and told him to begin writing. He wrote down several names and dates and types of merchandise that were stolen. Paul looked at the list and began questioning Tommy again. Tommy began to tell Paul how they removed the cargo from the various airlines. They would not only steal from Air France but would go to other airlines and steel the cargo that was left out on the tarmac. Paul and Harvey began to get some real intelligence on how thefts were occurring at the airlines and where they would sell the goods.

I picked up the phone and called the assistant US attorney who was on duty. The assistant on duty was Richard Bremmier. I explained to Rich that we had arrested an Air France employee stealing in bond cargo. The value of the case of perfume was about $2,000. I told him I believed that we could turn the prisoner into an informant. I told Rich that he had given us several names and dates and types of merchandise that had been stolen. I told him we might be able to make several good cases based on the information that was being provided. I suggested that we turn the prisoner over to port authority police and let them work him. Richard agreed and said he would decline federal prosecution in favor of state prosecution. I briefed Harvey and told him to be the good cop and convince Tommy that he was getting a good break if he cooperated.

Then Harvey went into his routine again. He began to ask me to give Tommy a break to explain how it would hurt his wife and two small kids and how she would pay the mortgage and put food on the table. Harvey pleaded with me loud enough so Tommy could hear. I could see the expression on Tommy's face as Harvey went through his routine. I told Harvey that I needed assurance that Tommy would provide information leading to arrest.

In front of Tommy, I told Harvey and Paul that I was withdrawing the customs authority that I had given them. I told them that federal prosecution was being declined in favor of local prosecution. You could see a sign of relief on Tommy's face. I told Tommy that he had better thank Harvey because I had to come here at two o'clock in the morning and not get an arrest out of it. He began thanking Harvey for convincing me to give him a break. Harvey was still laying it on when he told Tommy, "I'm going to bat for you and put my reputation with the Fed's on the line. If you do not produce, then the feds will not trust me anymore. You better produce some results."

I told Harvey that they should now proceed and arrest the man for state violations, which they did. This should make their commanding officer very happy. They not only had an arrest, but they had a seizure of merchandise and the vehicle. This made a very good symbiotic relationship. By turning this one arrest into ten arrest would go a long way with their commanding officer.

Over a three-month period, we had made eight arrests and seized over $50,000 in stolen merchandise. Tommy had earned his keep. As it turned out, Tommy received a suspended sentence for his cooperation. He retained his job at Air France at JFK airport because he did not have a felony conviction. He became a loyal informant and reported to Harvey whenever he suspected that an employee was stealing cargo. Now was the time for Harvey and Paul to get more credit for these impending arrest at Aqueduct.

When I got Paul Duro on the landline, I explained to him what was going down. He said that he would contact Harvey, and they would be at Aqueduct racetrack in about fifteen minutes. He said his lieutenant was on their back about making more arrests. Harvey and he did not have an arrest in over a month. They told their lieutenant that they were working on some major thefts and it took time to get the evidence, and they needed customs assistance since it was international cargo. Now

I had two more loyal bodies to assist us. I told DJ to coordinate the arrest and arraignments of all prisoners taken to the Southern District courthouse.

I told DJ that when they got to the US marshal's detention center, they should photograph and fingerprint the prisoners. If possible, they should get statements about Dan's involvement from the five prisoners and then contact AUSA John Caden and sign the affidavits for the two arrest warrants and search warrants for the garages on Atlantic Ave, Dan's house, and Paul's house. The magistrate would, in all probability, sign the warrants at the arraignment. I told DJ to page me when the warrants were signed. This would tie up DJ for most of the day. It was all part of the job. The search teams would be standing by to search the garages. After the garages, we would hit the houses. Well, that was the plan. Now I had to deal with the search and arrest of the vendors and any changes that had to be made to the original plan.

The gates will be opening in fifteen minutes—just enough time to brief those that had arrived. The vendors were open and ready for business. I set up the command post where we parked vehicles. After the vendors were arrested, they would be brought back to the command post. The New York City PD uniformed officers were to be used to control the crowd at the booths that we were searching. Customs Agent Cheech Castelano and Port Authority Police Detective Harvey Minto took one vendor. Customs Agent George McLeavy and Port Authority Police Detective Paul Duro took another vendor. The third vendors' booths would be searched by Agents Bill Seal and Vicky Brent. The fourth booth was assigned to Agents Grillo and Benton. The fifth booth was assigned to Agents Nelson and Malone. Everyone now had their assignments. Frank was watching Dan. Dan had got into his truck, which was now empty, and began to leave. Frank was right behind him. Agents Vance and Shoefall joined Frank.

The teams began to search the five booths. Customs Agent Dick Castalano (Cheech), Port Authority Detective Harvey Minto, and the uniformed NYPD officer entered the first vendor stall as a man was opening one of the boxes that Dan had just sold him. The SUN FREIGHT FORWARDERS labels were on all three of the boxes. This made our job of identifying the stolen merchandise mush easier.

The man looked up and, seeing the uniformed police officer and two plainclothesmen, drove terror through his mind. All he could say was "What's going on?" Cheech approached the man and flashed his credentials, United States Customs. "You are under arrest for receiving stolen merchandise, conspiracy to smuggle goods into the United States, and smuggling."

The man, later identified as Paul Duchane, for a brief minute, just stood motionless, holding an open box. The box had the SUN FREIGHT FORWARDERS labels on it. He dropped the box as fear set in. In his mind, he knew he was caught. Thoughts ran through his mind. *Was the guy who sold him the goods a cop? Was he set up?* The sweat ran down his face. His clothing became wet from perspiration. The man was about five feet seven and weighed about 150 pounds. He was about sixty to sixty-five years old. He wore a tan baseball cap with his white hair protruding around the sides. He was wearing clear-framed glasses. He wore blue denim jeans and a red flannel shirt. He had a tan wind breaker on, and it was open. He stood motionless as Cheech's words sunk in, and Cheech handcuffed the old man's hands behind his back. Cheech read him his rights. When asked if he understood those rights, Paul Duchane said, "Yes."

Cheech told him that he was observed and photographed buying three boxes of merchandise off the black 4×4 pickup a short while ago.

Cheech eased the man into his lawn chair as the man was now breathing very heavily. The blood had drained from the man's face. He was white as a sheet. Cheech feared that the man might go into cardiac arrest. Sitting on the table was a plastic glass with a clear liquid. Cheech asked the man if the glass contained water. Paul said it did and he would like a drink. Cheech removed the handcuffs and told the man to just sit there and drink some water. The uniformed officer stood with the man while Cheech assisted Harvey in gathering up the three boxes that the man had purchased from Dan. There was one box of perfumes and one of colognes. The third box contained assorted cosmetic. Agent Nunzzo had pulled his truck up in back of the tent, and Harvey Minto loaded the seized merchandise into the truck. Agent Nunzzo marked each box, filled out the seizure tags, and placed a tag on each box. As Agent Nunzzo was completing his task, a young man about thirty-five years old, later identified as Joe Duchane, entered the booth with two cups of coffee. Seeing his father sitting down and a police office next to him shocked the man.

"Dad, are you okay?"

"He is okay," responded the uniform police officer.

"What is going on?"

The police officer told the man to calm down. "Your father's health is okay. He has a bigger problem. I will let the customs agent tell you." Cheech explained to the son what had happened.

The son started yelling at his father, saying, "I told you not to buy any merchandise from that crook." The man tried to make excuses for his father to no avail. Joe Duchane then asked Cheech if he could speak to the man in charge. Harvey Minto then handcuffed Paul, and Cheech and Harvey Minto brought Paul and his son to the command post. The uniformed officer stayed behind.

At the command post, Harvey Minto told me that the son of the man who was just arrested would like to talk to me. I spoke with Joe Duchane, and he pleaded his case for leniency. He said he would do anything to help his father. Joe told me that Dan had been coming around for several weeks, trying to sell them goods. Each time, he told Dan that he was not interested in the merchandise he was selling. His prices were a little cheaper than those from the wholesaler he purchased the goods from. I asked him if he was willing to give me a sworn statement about the various conversations he had with Dan Steiger. Joe Duchane said he was willing to give a statement and testify in a court of law against Dan Steiger.

Joe said he had a file box in his car to show that all his merchandise was legit. He and Cheech returned to Joe's car and went through the files. Joe had receipts from wholesalers who sold him the merchandise he was selling at his booth. He said he had receipts to show the police that the merchandise was not stolen. He went on to say that investigators from the various manufactures usually checked flea markets to see if anyone was selling knockoffs. He could prove that he was selling legit goods. Dan Steiger had told Joe Duchane that he would send him an invoice the next day. Joe knew that the price Dan was selling the goods for was cheaper that the legit distributers and therefore was a knockoff or stolen. He said that he warned his father not to do business with that scumbag. Cheech questioned several items of foreign origin, and Joe provided the paperwork to show that he made a legitimate purchase from a reputable dealer. Cheech and Joe returned to the command post where Harvey Minto took a statement from Joe Duchane. I then contacted AUSA John Caden. I filled him in about the Duchane's and what we had so far. He agreed that Joe Duchane should be prosecuted by the state.

After reading the statements, I told Joe that we could defer federal prosecution in favor of state prosecution if he was willing to continue to cooperate. If he continued to cooperate, there would be one charge, receiving stolen goods. Joe said he and his father would both cooperate. I told Port Authority Detective Harvey Minto to take statements from Joe and his father. I told Harvey Minto that we would defer federal prosecution in favor of state charges. Well, as it turned out, Paul Duchane pleaded guilty in state court and received a two-year suspended sentence and a $1,000 fine. Later, both testified against Dan Steiger.

Vendor number two turned out to be another story. Customs Agent George McLeavy and Port Authority Detective Paul Duro entered vendor number two's booth. Behind them was a uniformed officer of the New York City Police Department. An oriental man looked up as the officers entered the booth. The man was in his thirties. He had black hair and a light complexion. He was wearing a light blue shirt and black pants. Approximately five feet seven and weighed 150 pounds. The man was later identified as Mr. Kuan Lee. Mr. Lee lived in Flushing Queens. Mr. Lee was standing at a table with a box on top of it. The box had one of Sun Freight Forwarders' label on the outside. The box had been opened, and some of the merchandise removed.

Customs Agent George McLeavy with his credentials and badge in hand identified himself to Mr. Lee.

"My name is George McLeavy. I am a United States Customs special agent. I would like to ask you some questions." Mr. Lee looked at agent McLeavy's credentials. Mr. Lee became very nervous. Agent McLeavy asked Mr. Lee for some identification. Mr. Lee nervously questioned Agent McLeavy as to what was going on as he pulled his wallet from his pocket. Fumbling with the wallet, Mr. Lee's hands began to shake, as he pulled out his New York State driver's license. Agent McLeavy took the license and looked at it and gave it to Port Authority Detective Paul Duro. Detective Duro began to copy down the information. Lee began to get agitated.

"Mr. Lee, we have reason to believe you have been buying stolen goods and are selling them from this boot." The words of Agent McLeavy struck a chord, and panic set in as the words sunk in.

"I'm not selling any stolen goods! I purchased these goods from reputable wholesalers. I have receipts to prove this."

Agent McLeavy took a handbag from an open box that had the Sun Freight Forwarders label.

"Okay, Mr. Lee, show me the receipts for these handbags."

Lee stuttered and said, "I have my receipt in the trunk of my car."

"Open the trunk and show me the receipts," said Detective Duro. Duro and Lee walked to Lee's van parked in back of the booth as agent McLeavy looked around the booth. There were racks of Gucci, Fendi, Christian Dior, Prada and Louis Vuitton bags. The bags were knockoffs, and some were not even good. Lee took a big cardboard box from his van and brought it into the booth. He placed it on the table and was skimming through the files."

He said, "I know I have the receipts somewhere in here." Agent McLeavy had found twelve boxes with the Sun Freight Forwarders label on them. Lee was stalling for time.

"Mr. Lee, show me the receipts for the twelve boxes I have here," said Agent McLeavy. Now Mr. Lee knew he was in trouble as he frantically looked through the box of files, sweat pouring down his brow.

Agent McLeavy began in a dictatorial tone, "Mr. Lee, you do not have any receipts for these twelve boxes? You were observed and photographed accepting them from Dan Steiger less than an hour ago. You paid him with some cash and a check. He had told you it was hot merchandise. You also told Dan to lower the price because the merchandise was stolen and you had to take all the risk when selling them." Mr. Lee stood petrified as Agent McLeavy placed the handcuffs on him. "You are under arrest for receiving stolen merchandise, conspiracy to smuggled goods into the United States, and smuggling."

Mr. Lee was then read his rights. Mr. Lee's legs buckled as he went down to the ground on his knees. Detective Duro grabbed one arm, and Agent McLeavy grabbed the other. They lifted Mr. Lee off the ground and sat him in a lawn chair.

Detective Duro watched Mr. Lee as Agent McLeavy left the booth for the CP. At the CP, Agent McLeavy explained to me that the booth of Lee was filled with knockoffs. In all probability, Lee had one or more storage facilities. The question then was "Do we seize just the stolen stuff in the booths and let him take the counterfeit goods to his storage facility?" It was very likely that he had more than one storage facility. A search of his file box and checkbook might reveal the addresses of the various storage facilities. I decided that we should make a separate case against Mr. Lee for the knockoffs. I told agent McLeavy to just seize the twelve boxes that Mr. Lee purchased from Dan and his file box of papers. Have Mr. Lee contact somebody to close up his booth. We would then conduct a surveillance of those who picked up the goods from Mr. Lee's booth. We would follow them to a storage facility or Mr. Lee's home. I was hopeful that they would take them to an existing storage facility. This could be a twenty-four-hour surveillance of the goods being picked up.

Agent McLeavy went back to the booth and told Mr. Lee that he would be taken to the federal courthouse in Brooklyn where he would be arraigned. Agent McLeavy then told Mr. Lee that he was seizing the twelve boxes that he had purchased from Dan and his file box. He also asked Mr. Lee if there was somebody that he could call to pack all the merchandise from his booth. Mr. Lee said yes and asked if he could make a phone call to have somebody come to the flea market to pack up his booth and call his lawyer. Agent McLeavy said okay. Mr. Lee was taken to a pay phone, where he placed two telephone calls. He spoke in Korean. Agent McLeavy did not understand what Mr. Lee was saying. Mr. Lee then told agent McLeavy that a Mr. Ahn would come to pack up his booth. Agent McLeavy told Mr. Lee that the police officer would allow Mr. Ahn to pack up the booth and remove the goods from the premises.

Agent McLeavy brought Mr. Lee to the CP for transport. A search of Mr. Lee's file box by Agent McLeavy revealed several receipts for two different storage sites. Mr. Lee's checkbook register revealed that he made monthly payments, the whole year, to two separate storage facilities. We now had the address of both storage facilities. The surveillance team that was to follow Mr. Ahn when he left the flea market was apprised of the two locations plus Mr. Lee's address. Agent McLeavy was instructed to see AUSA John Caden and swear out an affidavit for search warrants for the two storage facilities plus the residence of Mr. Lee and for the vehicle Mr. Ahn used to pick up Mr. Lee's merchandise. Additional documents found in Mr. Lee's file box were his import documents for merchandise being imported from China, India, and Korea. Mr. Lee was the importer of record. Mr. Lee was not the registered representative or distributor for any of the trademarked items being sold. Mr. Lee was importing gray market and counterfeit goods. This changed things.

Taking all this new information and evidence into consideration, I then evaluated the different options I had opened to myself. We had the import documents. From the import documents, I knew Mr. Lee was the importer of record. Agent McLeavy went back to Lee's booth and checked the marks and numbers from several of the different style bags and matched them against the import document invoices. Most of the merchandise found in Lee's booth was merchandise that was listed on the various invoices. We now had a strong case against Lee for 19 USC 1592—false declaration;19 USC 1526—trademark violations; and 18 USC 1001—false statements or entry. We could have just arrested Lee for possession of stolen goods. Now we had the option to tack on the other charges.

We also had the addressees of Lee's two storage facilities, which I believed would contain additional merchandise. Like any good customs agent, I told Agent McLeavy to seize all the merchandise in the booth and the vehicle Lee brought the merchandise to the flea market in. I then contacted AUSA John Caden. I filled him in about Lee and the invoices we had found. I told him about the evidence we found in his file, and the location of the two warehouses believed to contain the shipments of counterfeit goods. He then said he would draw up the affidavits for search warrants for the two warehouses and Lee's house. I told John that the charges will be 19 USC 1592—making a false declaration; 19 USC 1526—trademark violations; 18 USC 1001—false statement or entry; an 18 USC 2315—receipt and/or sale of stolen property. I told John that we had three more booths that had bought merchandise from Steiger. I told John that I would call him back when I had the results of those searches.

As it turned out, we executed the search warrants for the two storage facilities. We seized close to $200,000 in imported merchandise for trademark violations. A search of Lee's home revealed files of paperwork related to his import business. When it was all over, Lee pleaded guilty and received a five-year prison term with two years suspended sentence. His van became property of the US Customs, and he also received a fine of $75,000. All the trademark merchandise was forfeited to customs who destroyed the merchandise, and the merchandise stolen from Air Canada was returned to the consignees.

Agents Bill Seal and Vicky Brent were assigned to booth number three. Agents Bill Seal was in his late twenties, five feet ten and weighed about 160 lbs, with black wavy hair and brown eyes. He was dressed in blue jeans and wore a green St. John's sweatshirt. Agent Vicky Brent was also in her late twenties. She had brown hair put up in a ponytail. She wore tight-fitting Fendi jeans and boots and a New York Giant sweatshirt. The two looked like they were a couple out, shopping for a bargain. They entered the third stall. Standing at the open back of the stall was a young man in his thirties. He was clean-shaven, had black hair, and wore a baseball cap. He had on a red-and-white rugby shirt and blue jeans. He has a box cutter in his hand and was opening one of eight boxes that had the Sun Freight Forwarders label on it.

The man said, "I will be with you in a minute."

Agent Brent said, in a tone that implied that she had shopped there before, "It looks like you finally got in some new merchandise today."

The man replied, "Yeah, I just got this delivery this morning. I am opening the boxes now," as he looked over his shoulder. He immediately spotted her Fendi boots and jeans and knew that he had a customer who had money.

"I just got my shipment of designer clothes, which may interest you."

Vicky answered, "Well, if the price is right, I may buy a few things, right, Bill?"

Bill said, "Whatever your little heart desires, love."

Vicky and Bill browsed through the merchandise, while the man opened several boxes as if he was looking for something.

"Ah, here it is. Just what I was looking for. This is a bomber jacket that is your size. It normally goes for $500. But I will let you have it for half price."

He held the jacket open and said, "Try it on, go ahead, put it on."

Vicky said, "Let me see it," as she took it from the man's hands. She looked closely at the label. It was a Fendi jacket all right.

"Look, I have other Fendi stuff here also," the man said.

Vicky said, "It's too much."

The man then said, "Look, you are my first customer today. If I do not make a sale, then the rest of the day will be bad for business. I will let you have it for $200. That is as low as I can go."

Vicky put the jacket on the table and went into her purse. A big smile came across the man's face. He was happy. He was going to make his first sale of the day. He thought to himself that if he made a couple more sales like this one, he would have the merchandise he got from Dan Steiger paid for, and the rest would be profit. Vicky took her black leather case from her hand bag as Bill also took his out. She opened it in front of the man and displayed a gold badge.

"Customs police. You are under arrest for receiving stolen merchandise and for trademark violations." As Bill moved next to Vicky, his black leather case with gold badge appeared next to Vicky's badge.

The man's face went from happy to shock and petrified. He broke out in a sweat. The water began to appear on his brow. He was speechless. He did not know what to do or say. He then said, "This is not stolen."

Bill said, "Where is your bill of sale for the stuff you received today?"

The man said, "My distributer is sending them to me."

"What is his name and telephone number?" Bill said. The man could not answer Bill. Vicky told the man to turn around and place his hands behind his back. He reluctantly complied. Bill frisked the man and found no weapons. He removed the man's wallet from his pants pocket. His New York driver license was in the name of David Cohen.

David kept saying that he purchased the goods from a distributer and he could get the invoices to prove it.

Agent Bill Seal then told the man that he was observed and photographed buying the merchandise from Dan Steiger. He was told that the eight boxes he unloaded from Dan's truck had the Sun Freight Forwarders label and were stolen from Air Canada, before being cleared by US Customs. Therefore, he was going to be charged with 18 USC 545—smuggling; 18 USC 549—illegal removal from customs custody; and 18 USC 2315—receiving stolen property. Well, this overwhelmed David. It was starting to hit home. His knees buckled, and he went down to the ground. Bill picked him up and leaned him on the table. He was now sobbing. Bill asked him if there was anyone who could take care of the merchandise in his stall. He said his wife had gone for breakfast and was going to bring him back coffee.

Bill told Vicky that he was going to take David to the CP and would send Agent Nunzzo back with the truck to pick up the seizure. The eight boxes were marked and dated by Agent Brent while she waited. She had a plastic bag with David's personal effects also. Agent Seal had placed David's checkbook in the plastic bag. Agent Nunzzo arrived with the truck and began to load the truck. That was when David's wife walked into the stall. Before Agent Brent could do or say anything, David's wife, later identified as Mildred Cohen, began to scream.

"Stop, thief. Put that box down! David, where are you?" In her haste, she dropped the coffee she was carrying. Agent Brent whipped out her badge and identified herself as customs police! She told the woman to calm down. She told Mildred that her husband David was arrested for buying stolen merchandise and customs were seizing the stolen merchandise he had bought.

Mildred frantically kept saying, "I want to see my husband. Where is he?"

Agent Brent told Mildred that her husband was being taken to the Eastern District courthouse at 225 Cadman Plaza in Brooklyn for arraignment later that afternoon. She could see him there. Vicky told Mildred that if they had a lawyer she should call him. Agent Nunzzo finished loading the last of the eight cartons on the truck. Agent Brent looked through the personal effects of David. Of interest to her was his checkbook. The last entry was to Dan Steiger for $1,500. Glancing through the check register, Bent came across another entry for Dan Steiger for $900. A couple of months earlier, a check entry for $1,200. Brent asked Mildred if she and her husband had receipts for the merchandise that they were selling in the stall. Mildred said she had the receipts in a file at home for all the merchandise they had in the stall.

Agent Brent said, "I need the paperwork in order to see what merchandise can be released to you. We are going to seize everything for now. The quicker you provide me with the bills of sale and invoices, the quicker you will get back your merchandise." Agent Brent said, "In fact, Mildred, I have a consent form for you to sign, allowing me to go with you to your house and get the files so I can see what merchandise you can have back today." Mildred agreed.

Agent Nunzzo looked at Agent Brent in an odd way. She went over to Nunzzo and, in a low voice told Nunzzo, "We are going to seize his truck for transporting the stolen goods. We will pack all this stuff into his truck and take it back to the office."

She then handed Nunzzo the keys from the personal effects bag.

He said, "Good my truck is not big enough to load all this stuff."

Brent said, "Like Reno always said, 'Don't leave any stone unturned'. You never know what you will find unless you look." Vicky estimated that the merchandise in the stall was valued at about $20,000. Agent Seal was returning from the CP, where he left the prisoner. Brent filled Seal in on what had transpired. Seal said he would go to Mildred's house with them.

He said, "I will brief Reno and send Agent Roger Max to stay and help Nunzzo." This was a big and complicated case. I could use all the help I could get. We all worked as a team. Everyone knew what was expected of them. We all had the experience of running our own cases, so it was easy for an agent to recognize a lead and follow up on it and take independent action.

I contacted AUSA Caden and filled him in on the third seizure, and he concurred with the actions we were taking. He said we were on solid ground, but at any time the wife wanted to stop the consent search, we would have to stop and call him. In the meantime, he would brief the magistrate and obtain a telephone search warrant for the files at the house. I gave him the Cohen's address for the telephone warrant. He said as soon as he had the warrant, he would call us. I told him we were in the process of hitting stalls four and five. I then briefed agent Seal about the telephone warrant.

About twenty minutes later, Agents Seal and Brent arrived at Mildred's house in Valley Stream. They got out of the car and walked to the front door. The house was one-story, brick, three-bedroom cape cod house. The small front yard was well kept. The house was in very good condition. The inside of the house was clean and clutter-free. The Cohen's had no children. There was an office at the rear of the house. As they entered the house, Mildred had second thoughts about consenting to a search of the office for the files.

Brent said, "You already signed the consent. Let me call the US attorney's office."

Brent asked Mildred if she could use her phone. Mildred said yes. Brent picked up the phone and called the customs office at Varick St. Captain Joe Fox answered the phone.

Joe said, "Vicky, I was trying to get you on the air. The magistrate approved the warrant for the house. A patrol car is en route from the court house to deliver the warrant to you at the warrant address." Brent then informed Mildred that the US magistrate had approved a search warrant for her house. She told Mildred that they were going to get the files and list all the things they were going to seize and leave a copy with her with a copy of the warrant.

Mildred saw that it was futile, so she showed Agent Brent the office and the file cabinet with all the documents. David kept good records and a separate log for the stolen merchandise that he purchased from Dan Steiger. He did not report, as income, to the IRS any of the proceeds from the sale of the stolen merchandise. That showed knowledge and intent. Yes, David was in deep shit.

Well, as it turned out, the value of the stolen merchandise was $147,000. David plea-bargained a deal where they combined all charges against him, and he was sentenced to eight years in a federal penitentiary with five years suspended. He received a $50,000 fine. He also had to pay back taxes and penalties for the undeclared income.

The search of booths four and five resulted in seizures of two case of merchandise at each booth. The two vendors were arrested and taken to the CP. They were transported to the Eastern District courthouse with the other arrested vendors. They had no prior criminal records. They were arraigned before the US magistrate and released on their own recognizance. They pleaded guilty of receiving stolen goods and received suspended sentences.

Agent Vance jumped into the suburban with Frank and followed Dan out of the flea market and on to Rockaway Boulevard Close behind was Agents Shoefall and Benton. Dan headed down Rockaway and turned onto Atlantic Avenue. Frank got on the radio.

"608 to 603. The cat is going to the garage, over."

"603 to 608. We are behind you, over."

"608 to 603. When the cat stops at the first location, I will go by and make a u-ee and watch from across the street. You stay back one block. After he is loaded, we will move in, over."

"603 to 608 10-4." As soon as Dan got to South Conduit Ave, Frank got on the radio.

"608 to 603. The first location is a couple blocks from here, over."

"603 to 608. We will hang back, over."

Dan stopped at the first location between Hale Avenue and Highland Pl. Frank passed him and made a U-turn further down the street. Agent Vance stopped his car a short block away. Frank began to take pictures of Dan when he started to load his truck. Dan pulled in front of the garage. He jumped out and opened the lock on the two wooden garage doors and opened them up. He then got into his truck and backed the truck to the open garage. He shut of the engine and entered the garage. He began to load the truck with boxes. The garage was loaded with boxes. Dan loaded up his truck with twenty-two boxes.

While Dan was loading the boxes onto his truck and Frank was taking pictures, the radio blared out, "100 to 608, over."

"608 to 100. Go ahead."

"608 the magistrate had signed warrants for the garages and houses and arrest warrants for the two subjects, over."

"608 to 100, 10-4."

Frank and the team waited until the truck was loaded and Dan got into his truck. Frank then got on the radio and said, "603 to 608. Let's hit him."

With red lights and sirens blaring, Frank came across Atlantic Avenue and blocked the front left side of the truck. Agent Vance stopped at the right front of the truck, effectively blocking the truck in. Agent Dick Shoefall exited the car with his service revolver drawn and pointed at Dan. Frank and Vance jumped out of the cars with guns drawn. Dick ran to the truck's door. Dan had opened the door and was starting to get out. Frank pulled Dan's door open.

"United States customs," Dick yelled out. Dan looked surprised. As Frank reached the open door, with a gun in one hand and his badge in the other, he told Dan to get out of the truck and keep his hands where he could see them.

Dan got out slowly, saying, "What is going on? What did I do? What's this all about?"

As Frank holstered his gun and put his badge back in his pocket, he said, "You're under arrest for theft of goods from customs custody for a start. We have a warrant for your arrest and a search warrant for the two garages and your house." Instinctively, Dan had put his hands up in the air.

Frank removed the handcuffs from his belt and turned Dan around and told him to place his hands behind him. Dan obeyed. Frank slapped on the cuffs and turned Dan around. Frank searched Dan and removed everything from Dan's pockets—one wallet with five checks, six hundred dollars in cash, driver license, other identification cards from Air Canada, and one box cutter and pocket change. Frank placed everything in a plastic evidence bag.

Frank then read Dan his rights.

"Before we ask you any questions, it is my duty to advise you of your rights. You have the right to remain silent. Anything you say can be used against you in court or other proceedings. You have the right to consult an attorney before making any statement or answering any question, and you may have him present with you during questioning. You may have an attorney appointed by the US magistrate or the court to represent you if you cannot afford or otherwise obtain one. If you decide to answer questions now, with or without a lawyer, you still have the right to stop the questioning at any time or to stop the questioning for the purpose of consulting a lawyer. However, you may waive the right to counsel and your right to remain silent and answer questions or make a statement without consulting a lawyer if you so desire. Do you understand your rights?" Dan was silent. "Do you waive your rights?" Again Dan was silent.

Frank placed Dan in the back seat of his car. Frank contacted me on the radio and informed me of what took place. He told me that the warrants were signed. He said he needed a large truck to haul away the seized merchandise from both garages. I told Frank that I was going to have Agents May and Darski get a large rental truck and help him with the seizures. I told him they should be there in about twenty minutes. I then got Agent May and Darski and told them to go to the truck rental on Crossbay Boulevard and use their government credit card to rent the largest truck available. Agents Darski and May then left for the truck rental place.

Agents Darski and May arrived at the garage with a twenty-six-foot truck. Frank took pictures of the full garage. The five agents began the process of marking and loading all the boxes from the garage. Frank kept track on the amount of boxes being loaded. After garage one was loaded on the truck, Frank locked the empty garage.

At garage two, Frank took the set of keys from the evidence bag and opened the garage. He then took pictures of the full garage. They then began the task of marking and loading all the boxes on the truck. They were halfway finished loading the second garage when I showed up at the garage with a six pack of cold beer. The guys were all sweated up from working in a hot garage with no ventilation except the open front doors. The cold beer really hit the spot. The brief break was well deserved. The guys finished up loading the truck.

Frank and Vance took the prisoner and proceeded to the Eastern District courthouse to lodge the prisoner and arraign him. Agent May drove the truck back to the office. It was late in the day, and we still had two search warrants and one arrest warrant to serve. We still had to inventory the seized merchandise. We grouped back at the office. Frank had recorded every Air Canada waybill number from each box in the both garages. This made things easy for us. I contacted George Noble, Air Canada security. I gave him a copy of the Air Canada waybill numbers. George was then able to pull all the manifest showing for the missing cargo and what the cargo was and its values. We had seized radios, typewriters, clothing, shoes, perfume, TVs, sunglasses, jewelry, etc. The value of all the merchandise was over two million dollars.

A uniformed patrol car arrived at our JFK office with the search warrants and arrest warrants. Well, we were off again. Time to hit the houses. We were looking for any paperwork that tied into the thefts. We did not expect to find much of any stolen merchandise.

A uniformed officer in a marked patrol car accompanied us to Dan's house. Three plainclothes' cars parked on the street in front of Dan's house on 111th Avenue in South Ozone Park. Dan's house was white, one family, two-level cape cod with three dormers. It had black roof shingles. The front door was bright red with a gold door knock. It had a white large single garage door. There were two windows to the left of the red door and one large bay window on the right of the front door. The grass in front of the house was a lush green, and the lawn had underground water sprinklers.

It was about 4:00 p.m. when the uniformed officer rang the doorbell. The bell chimed. A woman with black hair opened the door. She was shocked to see a uniformed officer at her door. He asked her to step outside for a minute. She complied saying, "What is this all about?"

The officer then said, "I am with the United States Custom Service. This is Special Agent Reno. We have a search warrant for your house." He handed her a copy of the warrant. I then told her we had arrested her husband for theft of merchandise from customs custody. She was shocked. She was about fifty to fifty-five years old with black hair. She was five feet five about 130 lbs. She wore a summer printed dress and brown sandals.

I told her to step into her house, and we entered the living room. She was told to sit on the couch while we conducted a search of the house. She wanted to know what we were looking for. I told her the warrant was seeking any stolen merchandise and all financial documents. The first floor had a living room, kitchen, utility room, a full bathroom, and a den. The second level had the master bedroom with a full bath that was shared with another bedroom.

The search of Dan's master bedroom revealed new women's designer clothing (twelve dresses and six fur coats) hanging in his closet in shippers plastic wrap. They were seized. Each article had the manufactures RN number in the label. These numbers would pinpoint the exact shipment they were stolen from. In the second bedroom, there were thirty articles of women's designer clothing still in plastic wrap. There were also twelve men's designer suits. The search of the downstairs office revealed a file cabinet with work files, copies of invoices and shipping documents, and files on the sales of stolen merchandise. We also seized all his banking records.

We found six TVs—three in the house and three of them were still in the original boxes in the garage. We then recorded everything we had seized and gave her a copy with a copy of the warrant. We would file a copy along with the search warrant with the court.

Dan's wife said nothing at first. Then she kept muttering to herself, "That no-good fuck'n crook. I'll cut his nuts off when I get my hands on him." She then said that she had no part in what her husband was doing. She said, "Look at all my clothes. None are designer clothes. Dan told me he was holding the wrapped-up clothing for a friend who was going for a divorce." None of the clothing was her size. The designer clothing would only fit a much slimmer woman like Dan's girlfriend. She said, "I told Dan if he was doing anything wrong, I would divorce him. Our marriage is not what it used to be. I will let that bum rot in jail if he did anything wrong." She asked what her husband was arrested for. I told her for stealing over a million dollars of good from Air Canada.

"What?" was her response. "That no-good bastard! I hope he stays in jail."

I said, "He will go to the jail for a long time, and we may prosecute his girlfriend also." I could not help letting her know about Dan's girlfriend. *Boy did she explode, cursing and swearing and throwing things.*

She said, "I knew it!" She wanted to know who the bitch was. She said, "I will testify in court against that bastard. Tell me her name."

I said, "Your attorney can get that information to use in your divorce. It will come out at trial." Well, we left the house with all the seized items.

Dan stood in jail because his wife would not bail him out. He stood in jail for eight months before his trial. Dan had pleaded not guilty against his lawyer recommendation. Dan stood trial. Several of the flea market vendors testified against Dan. Paul Mastone was one of our witnesses. Paul's testimony was about how Dan formulated the ongoing theft at Air Canada, how he carried out all of Dan's plans, and how he had received payment in cash from Dan. In the end, Dan was convicted 150 counts of theft from customs custody, smuggling, and sale of stolen property. Dan was convicted and was sentenced to fifteen years in a federal prison.

Now it was time to go to Paul's house and execute the arrest warrant and search warrant. Paul lived in Valley Stream on Long Island. It was a short distance from JFK airport. We did not know what to expect to find at Paul's house. It was 6:30 p.m. when we arrived at Union Street, a quiet residential area. Paul lived in a three-bedroom brick ranch with a front load garage. The lawn and shrubs were well taken care of. The uniform car pulled up in front of Paul's house and proceeded to the front door. I pulled into the driveway with Agents Shoefall and May behind me. We proceeded to the front door behind the uniformed officer.

I rang the doorbell and waited for the door to open. The door opened. It was Paul. His mouth opened wide, but no words came out. You could hear Paul's wife saying, "Who is it, Paul?"

I told Paul, "I am Special Agent Johnny Reno, United States Customs. Are you Paul Mastone?"

Yes was his answer. I then said, "Paul Mastone, I have a warrant for your arrest and a search warrant for your house. Step inside please." We all entered the house.

I told Paul to place his hands behind his back, and I placed the handcuffs on him. I then searched him and removed his wallet from his pants pocket and placed it in an evidence bag. Paul's wife came into the room, and seeing the three men and two uniformed officers, she began to yell, "What the hell is going on here?"

The uniformed officer stood in front of her and informed her that we had a warrant for her husband's arrest for theft of merchandise from the Air Canada and a search warrant for the house. He informed her, "If you have any questions, please ask the special agent in charge," pointing to me. I told her to sit on the couch next to her husband. She did. I then read Paul his rights. He said he understood. The search of Paul's house revealed a dozen wigs, two typewriters, a case of perfume in the box with a Sun Freight Forwarders label, forty dresses, two mink coats, and a dozen men suits. We seized 253 items, which we listed and gave Paul's wife a copy of with a copy of the warrant.

We took Paul outs of his house in handcuffs and placed him in Agent Shoefall's car. Agents May and Shoefall took Paul to the Eastern District courthouse and lodged Paul in the US marshal's detention center, where he was photographed and fingerprinted. Paul cooperated and testified against Dan. He pleaded guilty and received five years with three years suspended.

Chapter 26

The Arrest

At approximately 5:30 p.m., Anna came to me and said she was going to announce the first-class boarding of the Pan Am flight 072 to Munich. I thanked her, and the Duke and I headed for the elevator and went down. DJ stayed and got into the elevator with Darnovski. Darnovski followed by DJ headed for the pre-boarding security checkpoint. Darnovski got in line and placed his briefcase on the examination table. The security officer checked his bag and ticket and told Darnovski that he was cleared for boarding.

I observed Mr. Darnovski open his carry-on baggage for security examination. Mr. Darnovski closed his carry-on bag and proceeded to the departure lounge. At that time, Mr. Darnovski tendered his immigration and naturalization form, I-94, and airline ticket to the Pan American representative and then entered the departure lounge to await instructions for boarding the aircraft. The Duke picked up Darnovski's departure documents from the Pan Am representative. Special Agent Jennings and I approached Mr. Darnovski in the pre-departure lounge. After identifying myself as US customs officer, I asked Mr. Darnovski for his ticket and passport and to speak with him privately. Mr. Darnovski was accompanied by Special Agents Jennings, Dukonis, and me to a more private area, where I asked Mr. Darnovski the following questions to which he replied:

"Are you carrying or exporting any merchandise valued at over $250?"

"No."

"Do you have anything that you are taking out of the United States that requires a shippers export declaration?"

"No."

"Do you have any merchandise that you are taking out of the United States that requires a Department of State license?"

"No."

Darnovski appeared a little nervous when I questioned him. He did not give an immediate response to each question. It seemed that he had to think about what his answer would be.

At that time, I asked Mr. Darnovski how many pieces of luggage he had checked with Pan American to be put in the baggage compartment of the aircraft on departing Pan Am flight 072. Mr. Darnovski immediately replied that he had checked two pieces of luggage. Darnovski was asked for his baggage checks. He handed me the airline ticket jacket with two baggage stubs stapled on it. These baggage checks were then turned over to SAC, Dukonis. At this point, Joe Sullivan and Agents Carp and Nelson arrived with two bags on a baggage trolley. I asked Darnovski if the two bags on the trolley were his bags. He looked at them and said that the two bags were his. Agent Dukonis then verified the baggage tags with the baggage stubs Darnovski had. They matched. I placed the two bags on a table and asked Darnovski to open his bags. He opened the bags. At that time, as he opened the bags, Darnovski stated that he had a camera in his bag. He was asked what the value of the camera was, and he replied, "I don't know."

Examination of the suitcase on the baggage tag number 139-666 revealed a camera, serial number 1808 that was on export munitions control list and various invoices and documentation pertaining to the KB-25A camera. Darnovski was asked if he had a State Department License to export this camera.

Darnovski replied, "No." The subject was asked what his citizenship was, to which he stated, "Austrian."

At this point, I placed Mr. Darnovski under arrest. I advised Darnovski of his rights in English to which he replied that he understood. Darnovski was given a card with his rights printed in German language and asked to read them. Upon completion of reading the card, Darnovski was asked if he understood these rights. He replied that he fully understood his rights. I then placed handcuffs on Darnovski's wrist in front of his body. I put his raincoat over the handcuffs. I told him he was going to our office for processing.

Darnovski then asked, "Do you mean that I cannot leave the US today?"

I replied "Yes, that is correct."

I placed my hand around his arm and led him out of the terminal to our car. Agent Jennings walked on the other side of Darnovski, and Agent Dukonis walked in back of us. Agent Carp pushed the trolley with the two bags. We put Darnovski in the car with the two suitcases and took him to the office of the special agent in charge, on Rockaway Boulevard, Jamaica, NY, to be processed. In the office, Darnovski was again questioned by Special Agent Jennings and me.

In the office, I removed his handcuffs to which Darnovski was appreciative of. He was asked if he would like a cup of coffee to which he said yes. I fingerprinted and photographed him. He was allowed to wash his hands after being fingerprinted. He sat down and began to drink his coffee. Darnovski was again advised of his rights in both English and German languages after reading, and being read his rights, according to Miranda, Darnovski stated that he understood these rights. Darnovski was asked the following questions by Special Agents Jennings and Reno.

I asked Darnovski where he obtained the camera, which had been found wrapped as two units inside a green suitcase previously identified by Darnovski as being his personal property. Darnovski stated that he purchased it from the Photo Sound company for $3,000. He was asked where Photo Sound was located, to which he replied, "In California."

He was asked if he went to California to purchase the camera.

Darnovski said, "No, I had it sent to my company in Tennessee."

He was then asked, "Who in the company gave you the camera in Tennessee?"

He answered, "Mr. Krowell gave me the camera."

He was asked, "Did you receive the camera in its present state or was it in a container?" Darnovski stated that it was in a box and that he had taken the camera out of the box in his hotel room in Columbia, Tennessee.

He was asked, "What hotel?"

He answered, "The Quality Inn."

He was asked, "How he got the camera to the hotel."

He stated, "Mr. Krowell brought it to me."

At this point, I questioned him about the airline ticket jacket that Mr. Darnovski had in his possession with writing indicating something concerning Russia. Mr. Darnovski was asked about this writing on the airline jacket. Darnovski stated that it pertained to his bead factory in Russia and that it cost him twelve million Australian shillings to build the glass bead factory in Russia.

He was asked if he would own the factories. He said no. The Russians would own it. He was asked who would build the factory, and he stated the Russians would build the factory and operate it. He was asked if he owned or operated any properties in Russia, to which he said, "No."

I then called John Trent in the Nashville office and filled him in on the arrest of Darnovski and the seizure of the gunsight camera. Trent and Harris went to Krowell's house in Columbia, Tennessee, and executed the arrest and seizure warrants.

After talking to Trent, we continued to ask Mr. Darnovski ninety-seven questions. Most of the questions were asked in such a way as to solicit a response to which we already knew the answer. This way, we could judge if he was lying or not. The question and answer would be used to discredit any testimony that Mr. Darnovski would give at time of trial. It would also be used to show intent to violate the law by Krowell, Donaldson, and himself. Other questions were designed to seek new information about other possible violations. In any event, the questions and answers would be very useful for our follow-up investigation. We told Darnovski that we had watched him in Tennessee and followed him to the Crocketts grill. We also had drinks with him at the Waldorf Astoria. He did not remember having drinks with us. That was until I told him that we were the cheap guys at the bar.

"Oh, now I remember you. The racehorse owner and the exporter."

"That was me," I said. "Oh and Harry is no longer a bartender at the hotel." This gave him a lot to think about.

After the questioning, Darnovski was taken into the Federal Detention Headquarters, West Street, New York, NY at 9:00 p.m., April 2, 1975. James Krowell had been arrested in Columbia, Tennessee, and charged with violations of 22 CFR Sections 121.01 and 123.01, in which he aided and abetted in the exportation of the military gunsight camera without having the necessary export license. He was also charged with violation of title 22 Section 1934. and US code title 18 Section 2. Krowell was arraigned at 11:00 p.m. and released a $5,000 dollar bond. Krowell pleaded guilty and later was sentenced to one-year suspended sentence and fined $10,000.

Darnovski bail was set at $500,000, and he was released. His high-price attorney refused to talk to the Assistant US Attorney Richard Bremmier when he called. His secretary said he was too busy for such frivolous charges and he was going to make a motion to drop all charges and that he would call him later that day. Bremmier was outraged by Darnovski's attorney's attitude. He called back and left a message for the attorney.

The message was, "Your client Darnovski is being charged with espionage." Two minutes later, the attorney called back, now wanting to talk with the assistant US attorney. The secretary told the lawyer to be in the Assistant US Attorney Bremmier's office at 10:00 a.m. the next morning. At ten o'clock, the attorney was sitting in the assistant US attorney's office. They had got off to a bad start. Bremmier said he was going to continue to pursue the espionage charges in addition to the export violations.

Well, that led to the pretrial hearing where his lawyers discovered all the evidence and other violation. The pretrial was just like a regular trial. It was used so the defense could discover how strong a case we had. I remember sitting in the court with the assistant US attorney. I was his second and got the exhibits and evidence ready for presentation.

Chapter 27

Judge with Diamonds

S itting through the pretrial hearings gave me plenty of time to think about other cases I worked on. Looking at the presiding pretrial Judge, Anthony Romero, sitting on the elevated bench, reminded me of a year earlier when I was working an El Al flight from Israel.

I was walking in the baggage area, observing arriving passengers. I noticed this short, stocky gentleman, getting his bags. He was nicely dressed in a black suit and white shirt. He wore no tie. He was clean-shaven with a full head of black hair. He was in his early fifties. He appeared to be very nervous. He picked up one bag from the baggage carousel. He then put on a pair of black rim glasses. He looked at the lines of people waiting to have their baggage examined. He began paying attention to the customs inspectors who were examining bags. He slowly walked from belt to belt with his bag in right hand. He held a black passport in his left hand. Sticking out of the passport was his customs baggage declaration form. After looking at several inspection belts, he walked back three belts and got in a line. He stood in line behind three other passengers. I then observed him placing his bag on the belt that he selected.

It was now his turn. The inspector greeted him and asked him for his declaration. I detected perspiration on his brow, and his hand was shaking a little as he began to hand the inspector his documents. The man gave the inspector his passport with declaration. His shaking hand was slight. I had noticed it only because I had been watching him before he came to the inspection belt. The inspector took one look at the passport and signed the baggage declaration and handed it back to the man and said he could go. No examination. The man took his bag from the belt. He was not shaking now. He walked about three feet from the belt. He stopped. He put his bag down. He wiped his brow with a handkerchief he took from his jacket pocket. He now placed the handkerchief back in his jacket pocket. He picked up his bag and headed for the door. He had a big grin on his face. *He made it*, and so he thought.

At that point, I was wondering why the inspector did not even talk to the man and just handed him back his passport and signed off on the declaration.

I stopped the man. "Sir, I am a Customs Officer and I would like to talk to you. May I have your passport and customs declaration?" As I spoke, I showed him my shiny gold badge. The man's hands began to shake as he handed me the documents. I had a strong feeling that this man had something he was hiding. I asked him how long he was going to be here in the United States.

He said, "Three or four days." I asked him if he had family here, and he said, "No, I am a tourist." I asked him if he was here on business, and he said no.

At this point, I looked at his black passport. It was a Peruvian diplomatic passport. Now I know, you just do not search diplomats: if you want trouble mess with a diplomat. I had this strong feeling about him. He was coming from Israel. I quickly looked at the stamps in the passport as we continued to walk toward the search room. My partner Harry Vance took the bag from the man and placed it on a trolley and followed behind us. Looking at the stamps in his passport, I determined that he had gone from Peru to Israel to the US and was to return to Peru. *Why would he go from Peru to Israel to the US and then back to Peru?* My mind began to process that information. *What could you get in Israel that you cannot get in Peru?* Diamonds came to mind. The pieces began to fit. *If he had diamonds, why come to New York?* It hit me. The Gemmological Institute Association (GIA) was located in New York. They had an office at 580 Fifth Avenue, New York City.

They determined the grade and quality of the stones. It made it very easy to sell the stones if you had a certificate from the GIA. *Where would you go to sell diamonds?* The diamond district in New York City. I had been there many times to get seizures appraised. The thoughts were swirling around my head.

I took my Peruvian diplomat into the search room. As we entered the small room, it must have hit him. He was going to be searched. He could not back out of the room. Harry had the baggage trolley, blocking the door entrance. As Harry pushed the trolley further into the room, he closed the door behind him. Harry now stood at the door. That was when the passenger said, "I am a diplomat. Look at my passport! I am Felix Portocarrero Olave, judge on the supreme court of Peru."

Thanks buddy, I told myself. "You are a judge in Peru. That means you are not accredited to the US. Therefore, you have no diplomatic immunity in the US. You are fair game."

I asked him; "Sir, do you have anything in your pockets or on your person that you failed to declare to the customs inspector?"

He said, "I have nothing to declare. I am a diplomat. I want to see your supervisors."

I then told him, "Sir, you are a supreme court judge in Peru. That is what you told me! As a judge in Peru, you are not accredited in the United States. Therefore, you have no diplomatic immunity and are subject to United States laws and customs searches." I then told him, "What is that in your pocket?" pointing to the slight bulge in his front trouser pocket.

Seeing that he was getting nowhere by arguing with me he then said, "I have nothing."

I said, "Take everything out of your pocket and place it on the table!"

He then said, "I have some diamonds that are gifts for my friends in Peru." He removed a bundle from his pocket. I took it from him. I opened the bundle of tissue paper and removed six small clear paper envelopes. In one of the envelopes were seventeen big sparkling white diamonds. Each envelope contained from five to twenty diamonds. I asked him if he had anymore diamonds on his person.

He said, "No!" I then patted the other trouser pocket. I felt something in the pocket.

I said, "What is this? Remove it from your pocket." He took out another tissue packet. I took it from his hand and opened this packet. I opened the tissues and found six more clear envelopes with five to twenty diamonds each. I opened one of the envelopes and found twenty light blue, light yellow and white, Diamonds. I again asked Felix if he had any additional diamonds on his person. He said, "No." I patted him down again and found two more packets in one back pocket and two more packets in the other back pocket. That was four more packets of five and six envelopes of diamonds in each packet. He again said they were gifts for friends in Peru.

I emptied everything from his pockets. I then stripped and searched him. I checked his underwear, his socks, and everything he was wearing. I then told him to get dressed. He then got dressed. I then told him to sit down on the bench when he finished putting on his clothing. As he was getting dressed, I went through everything he had in his suitcase. I found a paper with the GIA name and the address. There were several other papers that had names and addresses of gem dealers, in the diamond district, in New York City. I then told Felix to stand up. He stood up, and I turned him around.

I said, "You're under arrest for smuggling diamonds into the United Stated."

I took his right hand and placed a handcuff on it and brought it to his back. I took his left hand and brought it back to meet right hand and closed the other handcuff on his wrist. He was now secure. I read him his rights in English and Spanish, and he said he understood. He then refused to answer any more questions.

I then asked my partner Harry to go to the staff office and notified the Staff Officer John Horiwitz that I had just arrested a Peruvian diplomat with five packets of diamonds. Mention the word *diplomat* to a staff officer, and they go nuts. "Why is he stopping a diplomat in the first place?" was the Staff Officer Horiwitz's first response.

Harry said, "Reno checked. This guy is a judge in Peru. He is not accredited in the US." The Staff Officer got out the book with the list of various consulates. He asked Harry for the diplomat's name. Harry gave the passport to John who checked the name against the consulate list for Peru. He was not accredited to the United States. Harry asked John for a cashier's money bag so the diamond seizure can be secured. John got a money bag from the cashier, and then they came back to the search room. I informed John that I had arrested the judge and seized the diamonds. John took out his jeweler's loupe. He began examining some of the diamonds. He remarked that these were very good quality diamonds. It turned out that Felix Portocarrero Olave, judge on the supreme court of Peru, had five packs of Diamonds weighing in at 679 carats and were later appraised at $106,795. Staff Office John Horiwitz then notified the Peruvian consulate of the arrest as required by protocol.

I carefully repacked the diamonds in their respective envelopes. I placed the five packets in the money bag and secured it with a customs seal. We took the prisoner from the search room with his suitcase and diamonds to our office. Once in our office, I fingerprinted and photographed Mr. Olave. I then spread out the diamonds and their individual envelopes and photographed the seized diamonds. I then put the diamonds back in the money bag with the broken seal and placed another customs seal on the bag. I recorded the seals and secured the diamonds in the seizure safe. Harry and I then took the prisoner and placed him in back seat of our car. The car was parked in back of the ships office on the tarmac. I drove while Harry sat next to the prisoner. I drove off the airport and down Atlantic Avenue to the Eastern District Detention Center, 225 Cadman Plaza in Brooklyn, New York. We lodged him with the US marshal's service. The next day, I arraigned him before the US Magistrate Paul Schifflet. He was released to the custody of the Peruvian counsel general. He was later indicted by a federal grand jury. He entered a pleaded of guilty was fined $10,000 and was sentenced to five years' suspended sentence. He lost his diamonds to US Customs and was sent back to Peru on the next airplane. On his return to Peru, he was then forced to resign his position on the supreme court in Peru.

Then for some reason, I remembered Maura McCabe and started to laugh. The judge banged his gavel and said, "I want quiet in the court room."

"Sorry, Your Honor," was my response. Good thing, he did not ask me what was so funny. I was remembered of this:

I was working the 1:00 p.m. shift at the IAB. It was about 7:00 p.m., and the flights had thinned out. An Air Lingus flight was finishing up. I was standing by the diplomatic scale and talking to an Alitalia ground representative. She hurried off as the last of her passengers were going through customs. The pickings were slim. My partner Harry Vance was just coming back from a break. I had chosen to stay on the floor and talk with the ground representatives. We looked over the passengers on the Irish flight and decided there was no one that looked suspicious. There were one or two Italian immigrants coming into the customs area from the last Alitalia flight. I was looking at some of the passengers going through customs.

"Johnny," the Air Lingus representative Maura McCabe was calling to me. As she approached me, she seemed excited.

I said, "What is up, Maura?" Now Maura was about twenty-nine years old with red hair. She had a milk-white complexion. She wore very little makeup. She was five foot seven inches tall. She weighed about 120 pounds. Her uniform gave her an hourglass figure. I had been trying to get a date with her for a long time. She was not interested in me. She told me that I had too many women chasing after me. She said, "I am not going to be another notch on your belt." That made me try even harder to get to her.

She was out of breath from hurrying from immigration.

I told her, "You didn't have to hurry to tell me you will go out with me tonight."

"Fat chance of that happening," was her quick response. She then said, "I want you to look at that man coming off the last belt. Tell me what you see." I knew that I was good at spotting things but I saw nothing.

I said, "He is early sixties and probably an immigrant off the Alitalia flight. If he is immigrating here, he can bring all his worldly possessions. He is carrying an X-ray, so he is an immigrant."

As the man got closer, Maura said, "Can't you see it?" She had me stomped. She then told me, "Look closer. Look at the inside of his legs. Look at the right leg." As I was looking, she blurt out, "I never have seen a man with a dick that long in all my life, and I have seen a lot of dicks in my life."

I do not know if I was taken aback by the fact that the man had a cylindrical shape on the inside of his right leg or the fact that Maura had seen a lot of dicks in her short life.

I then approached the man, who was carrying his one green bag and had an X-ray tucked under his other arm. I showed him my badge and told him I was with customs.

He said, "No, I no buy anything;" as he kept walking. I signaled to Ralph Cippi, who was in uniform. Ralph came over and talked to the man in Italian and told him I was with customs and that he should go with me. I just knew I was going to have a hard time with this passenger. I told Ralph to come into the room with me. I told Ralph that Maura said that this man had a dick that was three feet long. I wanted to see if it was three feet long.

Ralph was confused. He said, "What are you talking about?"

I told Ralph to look at the inside of his right leg. Ralph could not believe his eyes. In the heat of the moment, Ralph lost his Italian language.

He said, "Goombah tu pischa pischa," pointing to the man's crotch and then extending his two hands apart to indicate about three feet. He broke out laughing, and so did the man.

The man kept saying, "Pischa pischa" and laughing.

I then said, "Senior," as I reached down and grabbed the hard cylindrical item on the inside of his right pants leg, and said, "Este." I gestured to him to take down his pants. Ralph regained his composure and told the man in Italian to drop his pants. The man dropped his pants. His dick was a shriveled up one inch. He did have a three-foot hard salami taped to his leg.

I stuck my head out the door of the search room. Maura was outside the door. I told Maura, "Do you want to see the three-foot dick the man has?" Maura pocked her head in the room and observed the man buckling his belt, and on the table was his three-foot salami. Well, we all had a good laugh. We notified Plant Quarantine (PQ) who came and tried to take the man's *pischa pischa*. He did not want to give it up. He kept taking bites out of the salami before PQ was able to get away from him. Meat and plants are prohibited importations. The man followed the PQ inspector to the back where he watched it being ground up and sent down the drain. He then left the arrivals building only to be greeted by his waiting family.

I testified first in the pretrial hearing. I gave an account of the arrest of Darnovski at the airport and the ensuing interrogation and then my follow-up investigation as to previous exporting of specialized glass shields used in atomic, nuclear reactors. I showed evidence of his diversion of items that were not to leave the United States without a license. After my testimony, began a parade of witnesses testifying to their part in getting the gunsight and other exported items to Darnovski. Between motions and side bars, I had a lot of time to think about other incidents that had occurred.

I remember there was the time I was working the two-to-ten shift. Customs Port Investigator (CPI) Ralph Cippi was my partner for the day. Ralph was easygoing and really did not stop many people. He felt more comfortable stopping older people in their sixties. He found that the younger people tended to question his stopping them more. Then his partner would have to jump in and take over from there. He felt more comfortable in uniform. Ralph was Italian and spoke Italian. He felt very comfortable stopping people off the Alitalia flights and flights coming from Milan or Rome. Now I was a young, aggressive person. I realized the authority I had and knew how to use it.

We were mingling with passengers that had just got off an Alitalia flight. There were a number of good targets to choose from. There were also three other teams playing this flight. Ralph spotted a guy whom he wanted to stop and search. CPI Joe Catalano walked up to Ralph and told him that he had already selected the guy Ralph was looking at. Easygoing Ralph said OK and moved on. CPI Ray Franzone then pointed out to Ralph the guy his team was interested in. If there was more than one team on the floor, we would point out to the other teams the person we selected. This avoided any confusion when it came time to stop the passenger.

I told Ralph that we would stop the man that was just coming in from immigration. Ralph notified the other teams that we were going to stop the passenger I pointed out to Ralph. The man was about thirty-five years old. He had a full head of black hair, olive complexion, and a five o'clock shadow. He wore a brownish green suit with a white shirt. His shirt and pants were wrinkled, but his jacket was not. He had a white handkerchief protruding from the jacket breast pocket. He was five feet seven and weighed about 170 pounds. I observed him walking toward the baggage carousel. He looked at the information board that was above each carousel. The board indicated the airline name and flight number. Passengers off that flight could look for their bags at that carousel. He held in his hand an Alitalia ticket jacket and his passport. Hanging from his shoulder was an Alitalia carry-on bag.

He kept pulling on the waist of his pants as if to pull them up. He did this several times. This was something that I looked for. Something out of the ordinary. It was a reflex action on his part. Well, it gave me cause to stop and question the man. He got his one bag. It was green with two brown leather straps around the bag. It was heavy. He picked up his bag and headed for the nearest examination belt. He got on line and awaited his turn. Ralph got the baggage trolley and waited on the other side of the examination belts. We never stood in front of the belt where a passenger we selected was having his baggage examination. If the inspectors had seen us looking at a certain passenger, they would give that passenger a thorough examination, fearing that we would make a seizure from their passenger.

The inspector must have seen Ralph a couple of belts away. He searched the bag very thoroughly. He asked to see the items the man had listed. The man took from his pocket a ladies' watch and ring. The inspector looked very closely at it. He asked the man if he had anything in his pockets. The man said no. The inspector then patted the man's pockets. They were empty. The inspector then signed the baggage declaration, and the man was free to go. He headed for the door. I stopped him before he got to the door. I showed the man my badge and said, "Customs. May I have your baggage declaration and passport please?"

The man handed me the passport and baggage declaration. I looked at the declaration. He had listed several items—a table cloth, children's clothing, two bottles of wine, one watch, and one ring.

I then asked the man, whose name in his passport was Giovanni Pasqual Favarra, "Mr. Favarra, what countries did you visit?"

He said he went to Italy to see his ageing mother and father. I then said, "Put your bag on the trolley and come with me. I need to ask you several more questions." Ralph held the trolley as the man put his bag on the trolley.

I said, "Mr. Favarra, how long did you stay in Italy?"

He said, "Two weeks." We were almost at the search room.

I said, "Do you have a large family in Italy?"

He said, "Yes, I have three sisters and two brothers there. But what is this all about?"

I said, "Please step into the room."

I followed him into the room, and Ralph was behind me with the man's bag.

I said, "Mr. Favarra, did you declare everything to the inspector?"

He said, "Yes, I've written everything down."

I asked him if he received any gifts from the family in Italy to bring back to the US. He said no and he declared everything to the inspector. He said he received the watch from his mother for his wife and the ring was for his little girl. I again asked him if he had anything in his pockets or on his person that he did not declare to the inspector. He again said no. I asked him to remove everything from his pockets and place them on the table. He removed everything from all his pocket and turned it inside out to show me he had nothing. I looked at the things on the table. He had money in US currency and Italian lira, coins from both countries, paper clips and a rubber band, candy wrappers, tissues, and some cheap key chains purchased at the airport in Rome. There was nothing that I was looking for. I then began to pat him down. If there was one thing that I did good, it was to search a person thoroughly. The fact that I observed him pulling his pants up several times weighted on my mind. I told him to pull his pants down. He did. He was wearing jockey shorts. I then felt the waist band and could feel something in the band. I told him to remove his shorts. He grudgingly complied. Stitched in the shorts' front waist band were three wide, heavy gold bracelets. On each sides were several gold rings. In the back waist band were gold necklaces with gold crosses, rings, and bracelets. The shorts were actually two shorts, one sewn into the other, forming a pocket where the jewelry was placed.

I told Mr. Favarra, "You lied to me. Look at all this jewelry."

His response was, and I will never forget it, with his open hand, he hit his forehead and said, "My mother must have sewed them into my shorts while I was asleep." Well, Ralph and I broke out laughing.

Ralph went to get the staff officer. He came back with Lenny Sampton. Lenny took out his jeweler's loupe and appraised the jewelry at $2,900. He was assessed a penalty of two times the domestic value. He could not pay the penalty then, so I seized the jewelry.

I knew that justice will prevail in the end. The pretrial was now over, and I did not have to be concerned about the Darnovski's case anymore. Darnovski pleaded guilty and later was sentenced to five years in a federal prison with three years suspended. They appealed on the grounds that customs did not have the authority to conduct the export search. The appeal went all the way to the supreme court, which ultimately upheld the customs authority to conduct export searches.

Before Darnovski was taken out of the court at the time of sentencing, he came over to me and extended his hand. We shook hands, and he said thank you for not bringing up my indiscretions at the pretrial. I did not want my family to know about my behavior. I told him it was not a federal offense to screw all those women. I was not the morals police. To this day, I am still persona non grata in Austria.

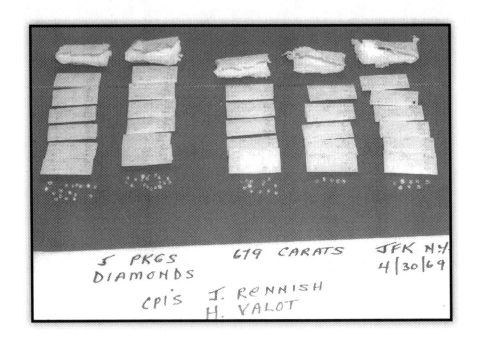